i

Love In A Dying World

Stargazer Press
Charlestown, Rhode Island

Published by Stargazer Press
Charlestown, Rhode Island
http://garypaulcorcoran.com/

Printed in the United States of America
ISBN 978-0997126556

Visit us and blog with the author at
http://garypaulcorcoran.com/

For Jun,
Your friendship and generosity
completely changed my life.
Thank you…with all my heart…

Acknowledgements

A great big thanks once again to Michael for the cover and help with countless other things, and to Mr. Staggs for loaning this series his character and mirth. Ditto the city of Laguna Beach for providing such a lovely and irreplaceable backdrop, and the many haunts and establishments around Southern California, both named and unnamed, without which this story would lack its character, enchantment and color. But most of all, my boundless thanks to Carol I., who started out as my copy editor and ended up being one hell of a content editor, offering countless developmental suggestions, without which, this story would not have been quite the same. Your help was a blessing.

Love In A Dying World

A Michael Devlin Novel

Gary Paul Corcoran

Love In A Dying World

One

By that Monday in late October, the dry, desert winds had been gusting down through the canyons for over a week. Dry, furious, dust choked winds that toppled trees, rattled rooftops and scoured the land of everything not fastened down by tether or latch. Fierce, unrelenting winds that raged and howled through the nights and cast debris up into the sky as high as the sun. Dry, restless winds that sapped the energy out of my every waking minute and left all that was inanimate snapping with electrical charge.

And with the winds came the inevitable wild fires, first one down in Julian last Tuesday, then another one up in Sylmar the following day, then a third one out in Beaumont, the incessant winds wasting no time in turning every errant spark into another conflagration. All it took was a cigarette butt tossed from a passing car, a downed powerline along a remote ravine, or just some fool thinking it would be a brilliant idea to set off fireworks at a family wedding. It had come to the point where, with so many fires, the new ones were now merging with the old ones and the entire Southland seemed to have gone up in flames, from Ventura all the way down to the Mexican border, whole towns razed, neighborhoods burned to the ground, caravans of refugees pouring out of the inferno and wild animals left to wander dazed amidst the smoke and rubble.

I had witnessed one of the fires myself last Thursday, while driving home from my weekly dinner with old Jack Oliver, the flames lit starkly against the dark hills at twilight, the lines of orange and red crawling across the land like molten lava, the feeling of it as if a portal to hell had been opened up and no one could figure out how to get it closed back down.

Awakened late last night from my dreams, I had lain there in the darkness, listening to the wild wind howl and claw at my home and it had seemed in that hour as if the distant mountains were calling to me, calling me to ride the high winds up and off to faraway places, haunting my heart with hopes of escape, but I had awakened at dawn with the wind still rattling my rooftop and flurries of ash now swirling outside my windows like falling snow.

My Monday had begun with a call to testify at the preliminary hearing of a child abuse case, in which a man named Frank Pritchett was a principal defendant. Frank was known to be a lot of things — a thug, a crook and ne'er do well among them — but to say as much was to understate the facts by a long shot.

The truth was, the Pritchetts as a whole were nothing but a bunch of backwoods heathens and two-bit ruffians, the kind of folks who married their own kin, who turned their properties into junkyards. Guns appeared whenever it was time to settle their differences. God help anyone who blew a tire down their back road and went looking for help. One brief encounter with the Pritchetts and any thought of our species evolving died right there in the dust.

I could thank my attorney Jim Harrison for dragging me into the Pritchetts' sordid affairs and Jim could thank a Mrs. Wethersfield for having dragged him in before me. As Jim had explained the situation to me over the phone a few weeks back, Mrs. Wethersfield was just then leaving his office after an initial consult, the woman overwrought with fears that her estranged half-sister Barbara was abusing her own two daughters in some horrific fashion. Fifteen year old twins, the girls had turned out to be, and ripe with pubescent beauty.

Jim's call to me had been along the usual lines. Please look into this and see what you can make of it. Mrs. Wethersfield was determined to gain custody of her nieces, by whatever means legally possible.

Accordingly, I had staked out Barbara's rented townhome and promptly learned two things. Barbara was operating a massage business of some sort out of the house and Frank Pritchett had somehow come to be shacking up with her. In true Pritchett fashion, we had observed Frank going off to work with a roofer one morning but otherwise had not done much of anything besides wander around the house in his socks.

Meanwhile, a steady stream of men kept darkening Barbara's front door; rough looking men, at all hours of the day and night, and not at all the sort you'd expect to be looking for an essential oil treatment and Swedish massage.

About a week or so into the investigation, I was forced into an unthinkable conclusion. Frank and Barbara were pimping the two daughters. There seemed to be no other explanation for all the strange men coming and going.

With this investigation now well above my pay grade, I had turned things back over to Jim and the police and before the sun came up the next morning, both Frank and Barbara were behind bars on felony child abuse charges. The DA had added assorted drugs and weapons violations to the pimping beef and child welfare had taken the twins into custody.

It was at this point that a central element of Frank and Barbara's scheme came to light. Both girls were doped up on Oxycontin, and had been so for some time. The easier to sell them a line, it was presumed. Taking the twins at their word, Frank and Barbara had convinced them that if they didn't do their part, the whole family would soon end up out on the streets.

Hard to say who had been the ringleader in that depraved enterprise. Hard for most civilized human beings to imagine

3

such a thing happening, but there it was, two young girls scarred for life and who knew if anyone could ever sort it all back out.

While waiting for the judge to appear at the hearing that morning, Jim and I had been whispering back and forth when I noticed Frank's younger brother Cole squeezing into a seat directly behind us. Cole had already threatened me once for putting his brother Frank behind bars and I sensed no newfound contrition on Cole's part as he sat down. I was left to hope that the man had not slipped a gun past security.

Some minutes later, with court now in session, I was called up to testify as the prosecution's first witness. I then had Frank and Barbara's defense attorney in my face, doing what any good defense attorney will do under the circumstances, try to punch holes in my testimony.

Asked at one point, "Isn't it true, Mr. Devlin, that you and your operatives never actually saw anyone sexually abusing the two girls?" I had to admit, "No, we were never in the same room, if that's what you're asking."

"Then isn't it also true, Mr. Devlin, that for all you know, the men you witnessed entering Barbara Donner's residence could have stopped by for an innocent game of cards?"

"It would have been an awfully strange game of cards."

That had led to a round of chuckles from the packed courtroom and a reprimand from Judge Forester.

"You will refrain from that sort of theatrics in my courtroom, Mr. Devlin."

"I'm sorry, your honor, but I don't know how you can conduct a game of cards with the participants coming and going every fifteen minutes. Never mind all the...let's just say curious noises emanating from the back bedroom windows."

That led to a number of snickers around the courtroom and another warning from Forester.

Then the defense attorney was back in my face, attempting to parse the matter of two fifteen year old girls being sexually abused for the past six months. As a general rule, I was not one

4

to disparage the lawyerly profession, but I sure would have hated to be defending Frank Pritchett and Barbara Donner.

Allowed to return to my seat a short time later, one of Barbara's neighbors was called up to testify next. Several more witnesses followed, each of them offering their particular knowledge of the case.

Eventually, the judge was alone up there at his bench, shuffling through various briefs and whispering back and forth with his bailiff. The rest of us were left to squirm and wait in our seats. Cole had remained seated directly behind me this whole time, staring at the back of my head.

Finally, Judge Forester rapped his gavel and issued his ruling. Probable cause on all charges. That had elicited a howl of protests from the Pritchetts and several more vigorous raps from Forester's gavel. Another outburst like that and the entire clan would be on its way up to county jail for contempt.

Once order had been restored, Forester set bail at a million dollars each and issued warrants for a number of Frank Pritchett's cronies. He also granted custody of the twins to Mrs. Wethersfield, pursuant to all necessary paperwork and protocols.

You had to figure that none of this would sit well with the Pritchetts and sure enough, as Jim and I were drifting out of the courtroom, Cole came charging at me. Fortunately, two marshals were standing nearby and quickly restrained him. Jim and I exited the courthouse with Cole face down on the commercial carpet, shouting threats at me while being handcuffed.

Out on the courthouse steps, several more members of the clan filed out past us with menacing looks my way. No doubt about it. Those Pritchett boys were just dying to get me in a locked room somewhere. Have a few kicks with snipping off body parts and such before putting a bullet in my head.

Jim and I continued out to his car in the parking lot with the Pritchetts dispersing in the other direction. I kept a wary eye on them and did not relax until they had driven off. Jim paused with his car door open.

"Like me to get a restraining order?"

I looked back at him.

"Naw, that's okay. Last time I checked, I still knew how to shoot back."

"Your call. If you change your mind, just give me a shout."

"You'll be the first to know if I run out of bullets."

Jim smiled and climbed into his front seat.

I waited until he had driven off before crossing over to my own car. Looking east, I noticed the sky was a smoky shade of pink in that direction. Why pink, I had no idea, but assumed that to be the sort of thing you could expect with the world on fire. I climbed in and headed for the coast with those Pritchett boys still doing laps in my head.

Back in Laurel Lagoon, I stopped for gas and found a family fueling up directly across from me. I couldn't help but steal glances at them. It naturally got your attention when someone had a mattress and some furniture strapped to the roof of their SUV. The three kids in the backseat were staring forward, looking catatonic. The entire family appeared to have been traumatized. It was as if I had stumbled upon a carful of fleeing war refugees.

The wife crossed over timidly from their pump to mine and asked if I knew where they could find a vacancy. Their home had burned to the ground down in Anza and every hotel and motel they had tried along the coast was booked. They'd pay any price.

Taking pity on their plight, I called my friend Mikolas and helped them secure a week down at the south end of town. I knew Mikolas always held back at least one room in case the unexpected friend or family member showed up in town.

The couple thanked me to the point of embarrassment before heading down the road, the mattress and furniture strapped to the roof of their car and ashes swirling all about in their wake. It felt apocalyptic.

I headed back to my office downtown and settled in at my desk, feeling under siege. The heat and wildfires did that to me. So did people like the Pritchetts and child abuse. Get me on one of those jags and all I could see was the worst of everything in this world. More and more souls being crammed onto the face of the earth by the minute, wars and famine and wretchedness everywhere I looked, the entire planet being turned into a dystopian wasteland. A disaster of our own making, spiraling evermore out of control, and yet our species seemed powerless to do anything about it.

I spun around in my chair and looked out to sea. Catalina Island was as clear as a bell out there on the horizon. The dry desert winds had buffeted the Pacific into a palette of gay blue colors and dancing white caps. If you were only looking in that direction — and could ignore the swirling ashes — it was a perfectly lovely looking day.

I had been busy there for a good spell longer, daydreaming of faraway places and plotting various means of escape, when my mind came back to the moment. Face it, Devlin. There's no place left to hide in this world. No deserted isle or distant atoll, no white sand beach with coconut palms where the madness of this world won't come to find you.

Life's nothing but a dream, anyway, so what do you care?

But I did care. I had to care…It was that or truly go mad.

I spun back around to my desk and resumed searching online for flights to New England. My Aunt Helen had called from Connecticut the previous evening with news of my cousin Bert's passing. Talk about the breaks. Bert had been one of the world's truly decent human beings but fell victim to liver failure. Complications from hepatitis. He had delayed getting onto a transplant list until he was no longer a viable candidate.

It was Catch-22. Unless healthy enough, you did not qualify for the thing that was killing you. And that was to say, if a liver actually did become available, someone else had bought the farm.

The grief never ended.

Before ringing off from our call, my aunt had given me the day and time of the memorial service. 3:00 o'clock, Saturday after next. The advanced date was to afford everyone an opportunity to make travel arrangements.

Well, Bert had always been one of my favorite people so I planned to attend. The two of us had run together a bit back in the '90s, only to lose touch over the years. How, I honestly couldn't say, but I sat there now, a prisoner of fond memories, fond memory after fond memory passing through my heart.

Then, amidst the many recollections, a long-forgotten summer evening popped into my thoughts, Bert and I out in the woods behind Trinity College, smoking hashish and talking away the world. Bert had been studying drama at the time and was doing some impersonations. His De Niro stuff had me in stitches.

"You talking to *me*?…You talking to *me*?…"

With Bert, it was very camp, more like DeVito does De Niro. But now he was gone. In his early fifties. Barely a year older than me. Jesus.

Two

I was about to book a flight when the street door opened down in front and the unmistakable sound of high heels started up the wooden stairs. I leaned back in my chair. God help me but I loved that clip-clop sound. It conjured visions of feminine beauty and was enough to make my heart skip a beat.

Whoever this lady was, she soon reached the second story landing and started down the hallway, only to stop. I figured I knew why. The hundred year old floral carpets and flaking plaster walls had been known to give people pause. Not that I really cared what anyone thought of the place, this woman included, but the hallway was admittedly a bit seedy.

You could chalk that up to our landlord, Lars, the inveterate cheapskate. About the only way he'd drop a dime to improve things was with a gun to his head.

In his defense, there was a decided lack of demand for second story office space in downtown Laurel Lagoon. Street level space went for a million bucks a square foot. But upstairs? Without the foot traffic? And with the one hour metered parking out in front? You could hardly give it away.

My attention returned to the mystery woman. She was still paused somewhere down the hallway. There was a thought to whip out my Prince Charming routine and intervene, but she resumed her trek before I could push out of my chair.

I settled back and listened to her high heel strut drawing step by step seductively closer, until the woman's silhouette appeared in my frosted glass door. No doubt about it. She was a perfumed doll of some sort. Funny how a man can tell that from a mile away.

I was halfway around my desk when the door opened and the world seemed to stop in its tracks. Dear lord, so much beauty. Too much of it, really, from this woman's enchanting eyes, to the piles of silky dark hair, tumbling down and all around her shoulders, to the heart shaped lips, glistening with red lipstick. A man couldn't be blamed for wanting to drop to his knees and surrender.

I pegged this lady to be in her late 30s, maybe early 40s, and noted her crisp, clean style; Levi's with a white blouse, black pumps and no stockings. I also made note of the St. Laurent leather purse hanging over her shoulder. It suggested money, and money had never hurt in my business.

Well…almost never.

"Michael Devlin," I said with an outstretched hand.

"Oh, yes. Lila Evergreen."

Lila Evergreen. There you have it.

"Please, Ms. Evergreen, do come in." I opened the door the rest of the way. "I assume you were looking for a private detective?"

"Yes. I found you online, but I…um…"

I had reached for one of the chairs at my desk, preparing to get Ms. Evergreen settled, but her progress stalled a few steps into my office. I watched her eyes dart this way and that, unsure what was giving the woman more pause, the clutter of client files stacked atop my desk, the bookshelves overflowing with a jumbled compendium of case law and statutes, or the black antique fan whirling away in one corner.

One message seemed perfectly clear. Ms. Evergreen did not approve of Michael J. Devlin & Associates one little bit, any more than she had liked the hallway.

My impulse was to show her back out the door. You start thinking you're better than me and you do so at your own peril.

And yet I paused. I had made a career out of chasing beautiful women from my life, only to be filled with regrets

10

once they were gone. Chase this one off and what would remain but more jaded feelings and the lingering scent of some very fine perfume.

Humbled by the memory of my abundant failures, I went ahead with pulling a chair away from my desk, thinking to play nice that morning, as much as was humanly possible.

"Please, Ms. Evergreen. You've come this far. You may as well tell me what's on your mind."

I made a quick swipe at the dust and ashes on the seat cushion, closed the door to the hallway and went around to my side of the desk. Ms. Evergreen was perched on the edge of her chair as I settled in. I smiled and she smiled back, but it was a pretty miserable effort and segued to another nervous look around my office. A doe in the woods could not have looked more ready to bolt.

Oh Christ, I thought and reached for a pen and paper, ready to throw in the towel.

"Look, Ms. Evergreen. I really think one of these larger agencies would be a better fit for you. You know, where they have splashy offices and dozens of operatives?"

I looked up from having scribbled some names on my notepad to find Ms. Evergreen now distracted by a photo of me on the opposite wall, a photo taken some twenty years earlier in Africa, with me standing Hemingwayesque over a cape buffalo, one leather boot atop the vanquished beast and a Mauser 98 upright at my side. I had gotten lost in the photo too when Ms. Evergreen grew enthralled again, this time on a photo of me at a black-tie dinner, shaking hands with a recent president. When her gaze finally resettled on me, it was with what any man could rightfully construe as a renewed interest in my existence.

Okay, so she liked them rough. She liked them unshaven, with mustaches and big guns. She was seduced by the trappings of power. I wasn't and shoved the piece of notepad paper across my desk.

11

"That's the names and numbers for three big agencies. I'll gladly vouch for any one of them."

Ms. Evergreen took the piece of paper, had a cursory look and resumed staring at me. At a loss for anything better to do, I tried another smile and was modestly surprised when her eyes crinkled up sweetly in return.

But something else was at work there, some great unspoken grief, hidden not all that well behind our sudden detente.

I was about to break the silence when Ms. Evergreen did it for me, and with a fetching tilt of her head as she did.

"Please, Mr. Devlin. Perhaps you could tell me a bit more about how you work."

My fingers reflexively began to drum away at my desk. Something didn't add up here. First, she's Ms. Hoity Toity, holding up her nose at my operation. Then suddenly she's Mata Hari, preparing to seduce me. Anyone but a fool would want to know what was behind her sudden change of heart.

That I was once a big game hunter? With a mustache?

Whatever it was, had you tossed me into a tiger pit right then...with the tiger...I could not have felt more uneasy. Ms. Evergreen and I shared a common space. I wasn't so sure we shared a common interest.

That said, the woman had my curiosity up. Add in her enchanting beauty, and apparent wealth, and I decided, what the hell. We may as well see where this thing is headed, and Ms. Evergreen was the model of attentiveness as I spelled out my usual terms and conditions, nodding her head throughout and otherwise making it clear that she was sincerely listening.

"Of course I would update you regularly as we went along," I said, concluding my summary. "That's assuming, of course, that you'd want to hire me in the first place."

She remained staring and searching my eyes. Then, as if some unseen cog and gear had fallen into place in her mind, she nodded with her now signature tilt of the head.

"No. Your terms seem quite reasonable to me, Mr. Devlin. Let's go forward."

And there I was, pacing back and forth at the bottom of my tiger pit.

"Very well," I said, settling back in my seat. "Why don't we start with you telling me what brought you here today."

And with that, Ms. Evergreen was fumbling for tissues inside her St. Laurent purse. I watched as she tended to her now misty eyes.

"Sorry, but it's my daughter…She's run away."

Ms. Evergreen made a final dab at her tears.

"I assume that's the sort of thing you do? Find missing people?"

I nodded while continuing to drum my fingers. I had never been fond of such cases, especially when they involved runaway children. Parents often gave their kids good reasons for wanting to disappear. Never mind that Ms. Evergreen's grief registered somewhere on the wrong side of authentic to me.

All of that was on one side of the ledger. On the other, missing daughters were missing daughters. And I couldn't imagine any good reason why someone would want to run off on such a lovely woman, unless she pretended to cry a lot.

"What's your daughter's name?" I asked.

"Holly."

"And how old is she?"

"Sixteen…almost seventeen."

"Almost…as in?"

"As in…well…it's now ten days and she'll be seventeen."

"I see. And I assume you've gone to the police about this matter?"

"Oh no. That's the last thing I'd want, getting them involved."

"Why? Your daughter could be in danger."

"No. I'm sure she's just mad at me."

"I see. Then I take it the two of you had been fighting."

Ms. Evergreen's lower lip quivered a bit in considering my question.

"Mr. Devlin. What sixteen year old girl doesn't fight with her mother?"

I gestured to say, okay. Fair enough. Point taken.

"So when was the last time you saw Holly?"

"A week ago Saturday. She left home sometime that afternoon. I know because I had gone out to run some errands and when I returned, she was gone. I've called and called this past week but she just won't pick up."

"So she's sixteen and missing and you have no idea where she might be."

Lila nodded. I glanced at her hands. No ring on the left one but what appeared to be a wedding ring on her right. That usually signified a widow. That or Lila was seeing how she liked separation.

"And your husband?" I asked. "Or is there one?"

She shook her head as if she hadn't liked that suggestion one little bit.

So, we could assume an abundance of money. The St. Laurent leather purse alone told you that much. A lot of folks in this world didn't make in a year what that item had put her out. Add to that a missing father figure and you probably had a spoiled kid on your hands. And one that gravitated towards older men to make up for the missing father figure. Sometimes that meant danger, sometimes it didn't, but you could count on the attachment being a powerful one. Prying Holly loose would be difficult under the circumstances. And that's if you could find her before she turned seventeen, at which point, Ms. Evergreen would be legally powerless in California to drag her daughter back home, or keep her there.

That meant we had ten days to accomplish nothing, in all likelihood. Because even if we succeeded in returning Holly back home before the clock ran out, she'd only mope around the house until it did, and then disappear again.

I had thought to say as much but decided, oh well. Hope was hope. And Ms. Evergreen appeared to have no end of money.

14

A gust of wind blew up just then, sending a fresh flurry of ashes through my office.

"Sorry," I said and leaned back to crank the casement windows closed.

Ms. Evergreen touched at her piles of luxuriant hair.

"I probably have it all over me."

"A bit," I said with a smile.

She touched her hair a second time as if self-conscious now over my comment. I was getting lost in her lovely eyes and red lipstick again and caught myself.

"I'm sorry. Where were we?"

"I'm not sure."

"Oh, I know. I was going to say. Any friends you can think of where Holly might be hiding?"

"There is one close friend, Charlotte, but I've been trying to reach her all week too, with the same results. My calls just go to voicemail."

"And do you happen to know Charlotte's last name?"

"Yes, Huntington."

I stared, trying my best not to look like I was ready to fall out of my chair. I had a client named Huntington, who just happened to have a teenaged daughter named Charlotte. Were there two teenaged Charlotte Huntingtons in Orange County? Maybe, but I doubted it.

Ms. Evergreen glanced at my drumming fingers.

"Did that name mean something to you?"

I started to explain myself but stopped.

"No. Just thinking...By the way, have you spoken to Charlotte's parents about this matter?"

"No. I...it's like I said before. I'd rather keep this private. At least for now."

I nodded, not at all satisfied with her answer, but then I wasn't particularly satisfied with anything about this woman. For one thing, I knew there was no Mrs. Huntington and had to assume Lila Evergreen knew this too, but she hadn't said a word about it.

15

I rubbed my forehead, trying to gather my thoughts.

"So, a mobile phone? I assume from what you had said that Holly has one?"

"Of course. What teenager could live without a phone these days?"

"And in your name?"

"Yes. She had to have the latest so we both got an iPhone 14."

"And have you tried the 'find phone' feature?"

"Yes, but she's obviously turned hers off. Or changed the SIM card or whatever it is you do to hide things."

"Mind if I try?"

Ms. Evergreen pulled a sleek looking leopard print case out of her purse.

"Oh, sorry," she said as we fumbled the exchange.

I was now holding onto both the phone and one of her perfectly manicured hands.

"Let me turn it on," she said and touched the start button with her index finger. The screen came to life and we slowly parted flesh.

"Holly's number?" I said.

"It's there. The last one I called."

I copied it, went into the 'find phone' feature and checked the settings.

"I suppose I could get the phone records," Ms. Evergreen said. "If you think it would help."

I shook my head and handed her back the phone.

"No?" she said.

"No. You're right. There's no signal. Try it late at night. She's might be making calls when she thinks you're sleeping."

Ms. Evergreen put the phone away and we were back to staring at each other.

"So, finding your daughter," I said.

"Oh yes. Well, I'm in your hands, Mr. Devlin. You tell me how you'd like to proceed."

"I usually start with the paperwork."

"Yes, of course. That's fine."

16

I spun around to the oak filing cabinet behind me and spun back to find Ms. Evergreen wearing a pair of black framed reading glasses and looking downright legal all of a sudden. I situated a standard contract on my desk and watched while she thumbed through the duplicates of a monogrammed checkbook. When Mrs. Evergreen looked back up to meet my gaze, I smiled.

"What do you say we fill in the contract first, Mrs. Evergreen? Then we can get to the matter of money."

"It's Lila, and whatever you wish."

Very well. Lila, it was. We seemed to be getting somewhere.

I reiterated my hourly rate, one hundred dollars plus expenses, and she acknowledged that without flinching. I filled in that blank and explained again what might constitute additional fees, such as obtaining records, extra operatives, legal fees, etc. She nodded and watched me fill in that blank.

We went on in this manner until I had signed the contract and slid it over to her side of the desk. Lila, still wearing her glasses, started to read. When her review of the contract dragged on, I offered that she could take it home if she liked.

"In fact, feel free to run it by your attorney."

Her eyes came up from the document and searched mine.

"It's all right, Mr. Devlin. I have to trust someone and it may as well be you."

I smiled again, as much as one does from the bottom of a tiger pit.

Lila signed the contract, slid it back over to my side of the desk and removed her glasses. I signed on my line and handed her a copy.

The question of my retainer hung in the air.

"Oh, your check," Lila said, saving me the need to ask for it.

The glasses went back on and she filled in the date.

"You did say five thousand dollars."

She looked up over the lenses and I nodded.

When Lila handed me the check, I set it aside without looking. She had money. No worries there.

I reached back into the file cabinet, retrieved a fresh notepad and slid it over to Lila's side of the desk.

"Please. Jot down Holly's mobile number for me, along with the names of any of her friends."

When Lila was done, I took the notepad and scanned through the list.

"I could probably come up with a few more of the numbers if you'd like but those are the only ones I know by heart."

"No, no. This is fine. I can track down the numbers if it becomes necessary. What about family members? Someone estranged? Someone you're not in regular communication with? Someone who might be willing to harbor Holly without your knowledge?"

She shook her head.

"No?" I said.

"No. There's no one like that."

"I see. And a boyfriend? I mean, Holly's?"

Lila's countenance soured visibly at the suggestion.

"I take it that's a yes."

"Well, to be entirely honest with you, I'm not sure. I wish I could say no. Holly has always gravitated towards the wild type. All I can say for certain is, a man called a few weeks back and asked to speak with her."

I stared.

"I'm sorry. I guess I don't understand. You're saying he called...but on your phone?"

"No, no. On Holly's."

I was back to drumming my fingers. Lila made a penitent face.

"I had taken it away for disobedience. And Holly just happened to be out with a friend when this man called."

"So, he called and you told Holly about it when she got home."

"Yes, and you should have seen her. Grabbed the home phone and bounded off to her bedroom like a gazelle. I had the impression that it was an older man. Late twenties or early thirties. Certainly not one of her high school heartthrobs."

"And did you happen to get his name and number?"

"Only his name. His number was blocked but he said that Holly would know how to get in touch with him."

I kept staring.

"Oh. It was Donald Potter. Donald Ray Potter. I found it odd that he would include his middle name and made a point of writing it down."

"Did he have a southern accent?"

"No, not at all."

"And anything else about him that stood out?"

"No. Other than his voice…I found it menacing. Quiet, but menacing."

"I see."

I looked back over the list, thinking.

"Oh, a photo of Holly?"

"Yes. I have one right here."

She pulled a wallet out of her purse and a photo out of the wallet.

"I had imagined a detective wanting one."

I took the picture with a nod. Holly was a sweet looking blonde with a sad looking smile. There was a Christmas tree and Christmas decorations in the background and a couple of opened presents on Holly's lap. Someone had given her everything she could ever want in this life, and it still wasn't enough.

"She's pretty," I said. "I take it this is current?"

"Last Christmas."

"Close enough. Same hair, same general appearance?"

"The last time I saw her, yes."

"And may I keep this?"

"Of course."

I set the photo down by the list of names.

"Then I suppose I should start with this Mr. Potter."

"Oh god. I shudder to think she's with that man."

"Sorry, Lila, but it often happens. A young woman becomes allured by an older man and runs away with him."

She dabbed at her eyes with a fresh tissue. I studied her, unable to shake a feeling that there was something phony behind the façade, but unable to put a finger on what that might be.

Otherwise, we had come to a place where there was nothing more to say, unless I wanted to tell Lila how beautiful she was, which I did not, at least not for the moment.

I stood up and Lila stood up with me. The tissues quickly disappeared into her St. Laurent leather bag. There was a pause as she reached for the list of rival agencies.

"I suppose I won't be needing this now," she said.

I took the list with a smile and followed her around to the door

We paused there.

"I'll get to work on your case right away."

"Thank you, Mr. Devlin, but just to be clear again. I'd prefer not having the police involved. Not unless it's absolutely necessary."

"Please. It's Michael, and that's your call. But just so you know. You're skirting a not so fine legal line here. I mean, if something should happen to Holly between now and the time she turns seventeen?"

"I understand. But imagine if the police drag her back home. What will I have accomplished?"

"That's true. What about her school? I imagine they've called."

"Yes. I apologized to them and explained that we had gone out of town on an important family matter for two weeks."

"And they bought it?"

"What are they going to say?"

"Yes. I suppose so."

I reached out my hand.

"I'll be in touch then. The minute I learn something, you'll know."

"Okay. I'll be waiting."

I lingered there by the door, mesmerized by Lila's lovely strut down the floral carpet, but slipped back inside before she had a chance to catch me staring.

Seated back at my desk, I jotted down Donald Ray Potter's name on the fresh notepad before I forgot it. The demon with a hillbilly name. You had to wonder how Holly had gotten involved with him.

Then I was back to Lila, my mind poring over her behavior. Something didn't pass the smell test. She comes in exuding the airs of the rich and famous and holding her nose at the sight of my operation. Then she's Mata Hari, preparing her deadly potion. What exactly had happened there?

Then there was Lila's aversion to involving the police. I wasn't particularly fond of them, either, but with a missing sixteen year old daughter, that aversion was puzzling at best, and damning at worst. Even I knew that the cops had their proper time and place in this world.

Three

I had been sitting there for a minute or so, getting nowhere with that puzzle when the phone rang. I glanced at the caller ID, saw it was Detective Whalen and answered the call.

"What's going on, Pat?"

"I'll tell you what's going on. The word is you've been running a tail on Dirk Vanderhof again."

"You're kidding, right? That son of a bitch called the station to snivel?"

"Don't you worry about that. You just keep your nose clean and leave the business of police work to us, got it?"

"Yeah, let me take a wild swing here, Pat. Vanderhof just wrote the Policeman's Association another hundred grand check and you're all down on your knees, fighting over who gets to give him the blow job."

"Why don't you come up here and say that?"

"No thanks. I like saying it from right here."

"Yeah, and if I wasn't due in the chief's office in a couple of minutes, I'd drive right down there and throw you out a window."

"It's always something."

"You son of a bitch. You just stick to your husbands and wives stabbing each other in the back business and try to stay out of trouble."

"Yeah right...You tell the chief for me. I just happened to be out for a leisurely drive yesterday afternoon and that prick just happened to get in front of me. Pure coincidence. End of story."

"Devlin. The man's paid his debt to society so let it go."

"Debt to society. He did what? Eighteen months of a three-year manslaughter sentence? When it should have been murder one? And two or three counts of murder one at that."

"You and your murder one."

"Yeah, me and my murder one...Look, if you boys up there at the police academy want to give him a pass, knock yourselves out, but don't come around here telling me how to go about my business. I've dedicated the rest of my life to putting that bastard back behind bars and that's that."

"Okay, Devlin. You've been given a fair warning. Lay off or you'll find yourself wearing stripes."

"Yeah right, Pat. Whatever you say. Have a nice day."

I hung up on him, shaking my head. Exactly when did that son of a bitch go over to the dark side?

Fuming over the call, I grabbed a pencil and did a quick doodle of Pat nailed to a cross. I liked that so much, I threw in a crown of thorns and tried impaling him on a pike before spinning back around in my chair. There were four bikini clad gals down at the shore, knocking a volleyball back and forth. I watched them while playing mental volleyball with Whalen and the rest of the Laurel Lagoon Police Department.

I was up 11-zip when Charlotte Huntington popped back into my thoughts. It dawned on me that I had never properly looked into her background and quickly had her Facebook page pulled up on my computer. She was not a dreadful looking woman, but by no means a beauty. There was something more masculine than feminine about her face, and the look in her eyes suggested that she knew as much. The game of life had dealt her less than a magical hand.

Knowing Charlotte had an older sister named Ida, I did a search for her page and quickly saw the threads of a story developing. Ida was the enchanting one, donning glamorous outfits while Charlotte scrubbed the floors around her feet.

I swiveled back around and looked out to sea. Was there a rivalry between the two? In my discussions with Mr.

23

Huntington, he had been reticent to discuss his daughters but it was not hard to imagine Charlotte being envious. And that was setting aside the vast fortune at stake, once the old man finally croaked.

The fact was, I didn't know if this was the same Charlotte Huntington and likely wouldn't know for certain without calling the old man. While considering whether or not to do so, it dawned on me that I had yet to book that flight back east and returned to my computer. So, red eye? Or first flight out in the morning? I decided to split the difference and booked a flight going out at one in the afternoon. It put me into Bradley Field around midnight. I'd lose a day but it afforded me a good night's sleep on both ends.

With that done, I called Kenny's number and spun back around in my chair. Kenny's head promptly popped up in one of his office windows across the street. There was a brief lull between his glance at the caller ID and his head turning in my direction. I waved. He waved back and put the phone to his ear.

"How did the hearing go?"

"Oh, swell. Cole Pritchett threatened to kill me. I think the clan in general has torture in mind."

"Did you get any of that on tape?"

"Better yet, I left the county courthouse with Cole pinned to carpets by two marshals."

"At least we'll know who to arrest."

"Yeah. That ought to bring me a final measure of peace in my casket."

Kenny's dry chuckle came through the phone.

"So, what's up?"

"Oh, I've got another job for you."

"Yeah? Should I be worried as usual?"

I winked and gave him Donald Ray Potter's name."

"Probably. See what you can find out about this heathen."

"What did he do?"

"Maybe ran off with a client's underaged daughter, for starters."

24

"Would that be the doll who just sashayed out your front door?"

"What? You running a sting operation on me these days?"

He chuckled again.

"She's pretty hard to ignore."

"Yeah she is. So, can you get on this for me today?"

"I'll see what I can do."

"Thanks. I'll be waiting…Oh, and another thing."

I read off Holly's mobile number.

"That belongs to the daughter. See if you can track down any calls and her location."

I was about to hang up when something else occurred to me.

"Hey, do a background check on this Mrs. Evergreen too, will you? Lila Evergreen." I gave Kenny her address. "Probably best to find out who I'm dealing with here."

"*That* will be a pleasure."

I shook a finger at him and spun around in my chair.

The latest news was scrolling across my computer screen as I got off the phone. A spreading pandemic in Asia was the big story of the day. The Asian markets were tanking and our president had just crowed with one of his tweets in response. Our markets were still skyrocketing, all thanks to him.

What kind of sick, narcissistic impulses drove the man? I had no idea but was praying for someone to shoot him.

Could you even think that without getting yourself arrested? Jesus. His very existence drove me mad.

Meanwhile, there had been another mass shooting, this time out in Arizona. Barbarians were at the gates. The fall of Rome was nigh.

The ad for an animal rescue operation popped up on my screen as I stared. They had saved a hairless, homeless dog in India and wanted my donation. How about a homeless son of a bitch on the streets of Detroit? Or LA? You never saw an ad for something like that. We'd walk right by another human being, wishing he wasn't there. But a dog? Oh yeah. Here's my credit card.

Some world. Some species.

I was about to check a weather website, hoping for rain again sometime this decade, when a headline at the bottom of the screen caught my eye.

Man Found Beheaded In Indio

I clicked on the link and quickly scanned through the article. The man had been a Muslim cleric out in Moreno Valley and an advocate for Muslim rights.

That would tend to get you noticed all right.

For unknown reasons, the body had been dumped out in Indio. Due to all the white supremacist symbolism spray painted on the walls of his mosque, the Feds were treating it as a hate crime. They were still looking for the head.

If I was reading this correctly, someone had sent a message. You behead our people, we'll behead yours.

I was logging off the internet when Betty came in downstairs. I knew the clip clop of her high heels like I knew the back of my hand.

A moment later, she knocked on my door and peeked in. She was still trying to be Barbie Doll at seventy with her smoky hair, smoky voice and face full of ancient acne scars. I glanced at the hair. Was it real? I had never worked up the courage to ask her.

"Good morning there, handsome," she said.

"Morning, Betty. What's up?"

"Some weather, huh?"

"If you're a jackrabbit."

"You probably want it to snow."

"I think it already is. Southern California style."

We both glanced out at the ashes dancing around in the gusts of wind.

"You try living back east," she said. "A few of those brutal winters and you'd be back out here in a heartbeat."

"Yeah, well, earthquakes, fires, drought and pestilence have never been my idea of four seasons."

"You're a real riot."

"Yeah. So what can I do for you this morning?"

"Oh, just wondering if you'd heard about the big blow up over at Presage?"

"Nope. Been too busy on the international front."

"Ha ha…So you really haven't heard?"

I shook my head.

"Anton applied to the Coastal Commission for a big pier and boat launch out in front of the resort. Behind the council's back."

"Hmm. Sounds like presidential material."

"Don't even get started with that crap," she said.

I gave her an acerbic nod. Betty had voted for the current resident of 1600 Pennsylvania Avenue. I would never understand it. Otherwise decent people, approving of the SOB. Would you offer him up as a role model to your kids? No. But vote for him? Sure.

Back to Anton, he had purchased an old trailer park along the coast two years earlier, promptly evicted all the artists and bohemians who had called it home since the '50s and applied to build his swanky resort. No question which way the city council was going to vote on that one. Just follow the money. A motley collection of bohemians versus ocean view rooms at a thousand dollars a pop? The powers that be couldn't green light the project fast enough.

Six months later, the trailer park was reduced to rubble and a sprawling, 15-acre resort was going up in its place. Then Anton goes and stabs the city council in the back. Oh, the irony.

But everything about Anton was scandalous. A few months after Presage's splashy opening, he had purchased a nine-hole golf course on the inland side of Coast Highway, and before the ink was dry on that contract, submitted plans to expand the golf course to eighteen holes, at the expense of an adjoining wildlife sanctuary.

The man had no shame.

"Can you imagine it?" Betty said. "Big power boats roaring around on a Sunday afternoon?"

"They already do."

"But now there'll be hundreds of them! Anyway, everybody in town's in a big uproar."

"Maybe 'you know who' will come to visit."

"I told you. Don't even get started with that crap."

"Well, what did you expect, Betty? Anton came flashing money and the council gave him a blank check."

"People are still furious. Aren't you?"

"Like I said, I've been kind of busy on the international front. Wars. Famines. Genocide. *Pandemics*? It's kind of hard to get worked up over a boat launch."

"You're a real card...So, have you seen Steve lately?"

"I saw him for a drink a few weeks back. Why?"

"Just wondering how he is...I know...You've been kind of busy on the international front."

I winked.

"He's fine. What? You want to see if he'll drop off Butch for a couple of days?"

"Yeah. Could you check with him?"

"Sure."

She smiled her smoky smile.

"Off to work."

"Give 'em hell," I said.

She disappeared, trailing the scent of cigarette smoke.

I looked out my windows to the east. The dry desert winds were gusting with smoke and debris, high up into the sky, as high as the distant San Gabriel Mountains.

What the hell had happened to this place? It was supposed to be an El Nino year but you had a better shot of seeing rain down in Guerrero Negro, five hundred miles south of the border.

That jogged my memory. I had driven down to Cabo a few years back, on another drought plagued year, and on my way home, while crossing over from La Paz to the Pacific side, ran into a full-blown gale. I had left Todos Santos that morning in balmy weather. By the time I reached Bahia Magdalena, thinking to do some whale watching, I was in the brunt of a squall. The seas in the bay were riding over my head. I found the fishermen huddled together in a shack alongside the docks, drinking coffee and Kalua and telling tall tales. Still knocking them back in those days, I had jumped right in. Coffee and Kalua on a blustery day? That was just this side of nirvana to a good drunk.

Maybe that's what I needed. Not a drink. Just a nice long drive down to Cabo.

Before I got too far with that idea, the phone rang. It was Kenny.

"Got those reports for you," he said when I answered. "Want me to walk them over?"

"Yeah, sure. I'm kind of busy with my feet up on my desk."

Kenny laughed.

A minute later, he tapped lightly on the frosted glass door and slipped inside.

"I'm charging double for this one," he said, dropping one of the reports on my desk.

I picked it up as he sat down.

"Why's that?"

"To pay for my participation in the witness protection program."

"That bad, huh?"

"Scary. Unless you're fond of pikes and severed heads."

I showed him my doodlings and Kenny laughed again.

"It's Whalen. The two of us were butting heads a little earlier."

I turned to the first page of the report and started reading. My eyes opened wide with the first couple of sentences. Bruder Schweigen. Spawn of Satan. Names like that jumped off the page. I saw references to race-mixing Bolsheviks, flying saucers and Revelations.

"Wow. I had no idea these white supremacists were into this kind of crap."

"If it smells of conspiracy, they're all over it."

"Conspiracy about what?"

"About anything, really."

I scoffed. He shrugged.

"Laugh but it's actually a rapidly metastasizing cancer. You ever heard of Proud Boys?"

I nodded.

"QAnon? Oath Keepers? America First?"

I kept nodding.

"So there seems to be a new group like this popping up every week now. By the time I look again, there'll probably be a new conspiracy group somewhere."

"And what does this have to do with Donald Ray Potter?"

"Kind of everything and nothing. He does seem to be more old school."

"Old school, as in?"

"Like on this one website post, he swears allegiance to the Phineas Priesthood."

"What's that?"

"Nothing, really, at least not in any organizational sense. It just assumes you've read a book by a guy named Richard Kelly Hoskins and subscribe to his beliefs."

"Which would be?"

"He called it a Christian identity thing. His main beefs were taxation, abortion, interracial marriage and homosexuality."

"They get me all worked up too."

Kenny chuckled. I continued reading the report.

"Who *is* this Phineas character?" I said, having come to the name.

"The grandson of Aaron."

"The grandson of Aaron? As in the Old Testament!?"

"Yeah."

"Okay. I guess I should have paid better attention at Sunday school. Explain."

"So, in the Old Testament, Phineas catches a fellow Israelite doing a Midianite woman and runs a spear through both of them for racial intermingling. And for which zealotry, Phineas is commended by Yahweh and granted everlasting priesthood down through his seed."

"I thought these people hated Jews."

"I guess it's different if you're in the Bible. Just don't come around in the flesh."

I had to shake my head.

"And we give these Muslim zealots a hard time."

"Yeah…Anyway, Hoskins cites the passage about Phineas in his book and all these Phineas Priesthood fanatics cite Hoskins and that's basically it."

"So they're racists."

"I guess."

"Yeah, well, I'm definitely going to go with that one."

"Yeah…Anyway, there's more. Flip the page."

I did.

"Yeah? What am I looking for?"

"That Boogaloo business."

"Yeah? What's that? Their party site?"

Kenny smiled.

"No. It's kind of a catch-all, umbrella term these right-wing extremists are using these days. A way of saying we're all on the same mission. Violent insurrection. Death and mayhem to the system. Tear down the deep state. Their motto is, I became unreasonable."

I shrugged.

"I guess that's kind of mine too."

That got another smile out of Kenny. I read on in the report about Potter's upbringing. It was the story of a young man going from foster home to foster home, and all the while growing more alienated from the society around him. A stint in juvenile hall was followed by one in the slammer at nineteen for grand theft auto. It was all downhill from there. Potter had been convicted of just about everything but murder, which wasn't to say he hadn't committed one. He simply hadn't been caught for it yet.

Potter's mugshots alone told a story. He had acquired more and more facial hair and tattoos along the way, until, at 33, he was channeling Charles Manson, on one of Manson's wilder days. Why lost young girls like Holly fell for that kind of mystique, I would never understand, but they did.

"And this Abigale Potter out in Apple Valley? You know if that's his real mother?"

"As far as I can tell. Her past's a bit murky but it looks as if she gave up Potter for adoption when he was a little kid."

"Yeah, bummer."

I looked back at the report with a smidgeon of sympathy now. It wasn't hard to imagine yourself in that position, abandoned by your real parents, then punished again and again for the hurt and anger you'd naturally feel. Hell, any one of us could have turned into a monster.

Then, it wasn't my job to pity Donald Ray Potter. My job was to find Holly Evergreen and bring her back home

"What's with the three names, by the way? Mrs. Evergreen said he didn't have a southern accent."

"Don't know. Just giving Billy Ray Bob a run for his money?"

I looked up from the report with a smile.

"And that in your hands there? Would that be the report on Mrs. Evergreen?"

"It would."

"Looks like you're having a hard time letting go of it."

Kenny drew it close to his chest before tossing onto my desk.

"She was a real firecracker back in the day. If you didn't already know it."

"It wouldn't surprise me. I got the impression from talking to her that the acorn hadn't fallen far from the tree."

I opened the report and started reading. It was the portrait of a young woman living her life on the wild side — stripper, nude modeling gigs, etc., etc. — then an early marriage quickly cast aside before Lila moved on to a cold, calculated second act of marrying and burying rich old men. Lila had already placed two of them in their graves, neither of whom had anything to do with Holly's existence.

Lila was forty-one, Holly sixteen, so painting Lila in the most favorable light, she had gotten herself knocked up as a young woman and done what she thought was necessary to look after said daughter. No one could blame Lila for that. What it had done to her soul was another question.

"I would have paid to see her," Kenny said.

I looked up at him.

"Would have been something."

"Still would."

"Yeah…The truth is, Kenny. I think she's dangerous."

"Most women are."

"Whoa. Don't think I've ever seen this side of you."

Kenny smiled.

"Dangerous, how?" he said.

I explained that initial encounter in my office.

"I mean, she did everything but hold her nose at my little operation. Then all of a sudden, she's Mata Hari, sizing me up for the sacrifice. Something happened there."

"Probably hiding something. Most women are."

"Your girlfriend run off on you or something?"

Kenny smiled. I looked back at the report. Lila had buried the last old man up in Pueblo Hills, which was where I had grown up. I made a mental note to call my old friend Teri. She still worked as a secretary in the local police department and just might know a thing or two about Lila's past.

I looked back at Kenny.

"And this address for Potter out in San Berdoo? That's his current domicile?"

"As far as I know."

"Okay. Guess I'd better take a ride out there and see what I can see."

I stood up and grabbed my shoulder holster out of a desk drawer. Kenny stood up too and watched me putting it on.

"I'd take rations and a water supply with you."

"Yeah. These fires, huh?"

We both looked out the windows at the smoky sky.

"Say, you didn't happen to see that article about the Muslim cleric getting beheaded out that way, did you?"

"Sure did."

"You don't think...you know, Bruder Schweigen and all that?"

"Boogaloo," Kenny said.

I shook my head.

"Jesus. The world's coming apart, Kenny."

"At least we have front row seats."

"Funny...Oh, did you need money?"

"I'll send you a bill. Once I figure out how much this witness protection program is going to cost me."

Kenny smiled and started out the door.

"Oh, the daughter's phone?" I said.

"Nothing yet," he said and left.

I stalled there behind my desk, considering whether or not to call Mr. Huntington. His daughter Charlotte likely knew Holly Evergreen and might have knowledge of her whereabouts.

I decided to put that on hold for the moment. Best to look into Donald Ray Potter before I opened my mouth.

I grabbed my Smith & Wesson, went down to my Impala and was soon headed east out through the canyon. With the gusting winds trying to toss my car off the road, a line from one of my favorite poets popped into my head.

Tossing things into the fire. Tossing things into the fire. How long have I been tossing things into the fire?

The poet had experienced this revelation while burning old brush around his Sierra Madre ranch some years back.

It was a simple line that had left me gazing into the maw of eternity. Over and over and over again, we were all headed back into the fire.

Four

Fifteen minutes later, while loping out through the dry, chaparral country along the backside of Irvine Lake, my thoughts turned again to Steve's wife Connie. The unreal quality of her death wavered in the wild winds.

There was no doubt in my mind that Vanderhof had killed her, but the DA had failed to prove the case beyond a reasonable doubt and Vanderhof had walked. The eighteen months he did in Lompoc was for the death of his infant daughter a decade earlier. And that still left unresolved the murders of Cliff Black, Dan Colby and Rick Duncan. Of course I wanted to see Vanderhof back behind bars. The question was, why didn't Whalen? The confluence of money and corruption and our local politicians had never ceased to amaze me. But Pat? I had always taken him to be an honest cop. A pain in the ass most of the time, but honest. The idea that he had gone over to the dark side turned my stomach.

While on the subject of cops, I remembered Teri and gave her a call. It took the receptionist a minute to get her on the phone but Teri was absolutely effusive in answering.

"Michael! So good to hear from you! I swear to god, I was just thinking to call! We're planning our 35th reunion next year and you've got to come!"

"Oh god, Teri. I'm already feeling old these days. No need to remind me."

"Oh come on. We're all getting old!"

"Well, some of us are getting older than others."

She laughed.

"Come on. It won't be the same without you!"

"Okay, okay. We can discuss that in a minute but I've got something else on my mind."

I explained about Lila Evergreen.

"So I'm wondering if you could look into it for me. I've got a feeling there's something sketchy about her past."

Teri was ominously silent. Then I sensed her cupping the phone.

"I don't have to look into it," she whispered. "I already know. Her husband was murdered. Shot once in the heart. But it was all swept under the rug."

She lowered her whisper even more so.

"I shouldn't even be telling you this. No one was supposed to find out. It was filed under seal. Death by natural causes. But everyone around here pretty much knew otherwise."

"Jesus, Teri. Are you telling me that Mrs. Evergreen shot her husband?"

"Sssshh...I don't know. I can't swear to it but I guess that's what everyone's always thought. I can tell you this much. A lot of money went into keeping this thing quiet."

"Wow."

"Yeah. I don't know if you remember but Mr. Evergreen was one of the founding fathers."

"Oh sure. I remember him. The mysterious old man who used to hang around our football games and stuff."

"He wasn't that old."

"He seemed like it to me at the time."

"Yeah. Anyway, he was pretty quiet about the money but turns out he came from a big industrialist family back east. An only child. Inherited the whole fortune. He was always the nicest man to the staff around here. Cheerful and gracious. He'd stop by every holiday with Christmas presents. People cried when they heard the news. And of course gossiped…But not a word," she added in a whisper.

"No no. I won't say a thing."

"So," Teri continued in a normal voice now. "Can we count on you coming to the reunion?"

"Yeah, I guess. Just give me a call when we're getting closer and I'll find a way."

"Okay. I'd better get back to work."

"Yeah, same here."

There was silence.

"Not a word," Teri reminded me.

"No, no. Not a word."

"Okay. I'll talk to you in the spring, once we have all our plans sorted out."

"I'll talk to you then."

I got off the phone with my mind racing back through my encounter with Lila. Her air of disdain when she first darkened my door, the sense that she saw me as a two-bit operator with a messy office. Then the sudden change of heart as she stared at those photos of me on the wall, as if she had seen some form of raw male power that she thought she could harness. But to what end? To kill again? Or to help with hiding her previous sins? Lila's aversion to the police certainly made more sense now, but what did that have to do with Holly's disappearance?

I had come to the 91 freeway and turned east, hardly noticing the succession of bedroom communities passing by, the nearby hills combed with row after row of new cookie cutter houses. I was too busy pacing back and forth at the bottom of my tiger pit.

It wasn't until I neared the outskirts of San Berdoo that my trance broke and I noticed the mountains peeking out from above the nearby hills, their summits delicately capped with snow from a brief storm two weeks back. In blowing all that smoke down towards the coast, the desert winds had dragged the smog along with it, leaving the view looking east as clear as a bell.

At the southern outskirts of town, near Cook Canyon, I bore left and headed out a long dead-end road called Highland. Potter's place turned out to be the last house on the block. I pulled up well short of his driveway and parked with the car idling. The curtains of an adjacent house parted and a woman stared out briefly before letting them drop back into place.

I returned my attention to Potter's place. In keeping with the rest of the neighborhood, it was trashed. Holes had been punched into the stucco walls and pieces of the wooden wainscot below it were missing. Even the roof fascia was warped and falling off. An old washer and dryer sat to one side of the house, being swallowed by weeds. Potter could have run a meth lab out of the place for all the landlord knew. If not for a truck, an old travel trailer and one Harley parked in the driveway, you would have thought the place was abandoned. On the upside, the neighborhood came with spacious lots and an abundance of trees. Potter's place was tucked away nicely under an old oak and two pines.

Figuring I had a long wait ahead of me, and with Lila Evergreen still on my mind, I called Kenny.

"I think you were right," I said when he answered. "Most women are hiding something."

He laughed.

"What? Your girlfriend run off on you or something?"

I smiled.

"Look, you've got to keep this quiet but here's what I just learned about Ms. Evergreen."

Kenny listened to me relate the story of Lila's rich, old and now dead husband.

"Wow," he said when I was done.

"Yeah, wow, indeed…So what was the name again of that first old man she buried?"

"Oh, yeah. Just a second…Uh, Lowell Cabot. Looks like he came from one of the original colonial families and that's evolved into a global business over the years. Rubber, plastics, paints and inks."

"Yeah. We know the bastard was rich but how did he die?"

"Without a death certificate, I wouldn't know. I'm guessing from natural causes."

"Yeah. Just like old man Evergreen."

"I take it you want me to dig into this a little deeper."

"Please. I may be next in line."

He chuckled.

"I'll see what I can do."

"Thanks."

I hung up and watched the house. The wind had blown up and was swaying the trees wildly around it. The minutes ticked by. Lila's past kept turning around and around in my head.

An hour later, a young woman popped out the side door of Potter's house. It was Holly, with a Lab puppy at her feet. The puppy looked to be about two months old and was falling all over itself with youthful exuberance. Holly sat down on the side steps, playing with the dog but draped in gloom. The bruises on her arms told a story.

A few minutes later, a man's voice barked out and Holly sulked back inside. The puppy followed along, still falling all over itself with youthful exuberance.

I bristled to think of Holly under Potter's thumb. Every young woman ought to have her time of dreams, before someone like Potter came along and stole them away from her.

I was weighing what to do next when a faint roar carried on the wind. I checked my rearview mirror. A pack of Harleys had come into view, far back down that long street. As the bikers drew near, I slid lower in the seat. A few seconds later, they flew by, every one of them having a look in the direction of my tinted windows. I put the Impala in gear, just to be on the safe side.

It did not take long for my fears to be justified. The minute those bikers had parked, a handful of them started drifting down the street my way. I made a quick U-turn and glanced in my rearview mirror. Two of them had started running down the street, shaking their fists and shouting after me.

Then Potter flew out the front door with a shotgun in his hands, in full messianic mode. From Kenny's report, I had already gathered that Potter was a middleweight. I now knew he had no qualms about fighting above his class. He was the image of a man giving up seventy pounds to Foreman in his prime and going after him anyway, without a second thought.

I stepped on the gas before he had a chance to blow out my rear window and did not let up until I was pulling onto the freeway. Seeing that pack of Harleys race up on my tail would not have surprised me.

It was a long drive back to Laurel Lagoon with Lila's checkered past doing laps in my head. Kenny's report was still lying open on my desk when I walked into my office. Initially, it had inspired visions of G-strings and spangles. Now I was more inclined to picture Lila with a loaded gun in her hand.

I sat down and gave her a call.

"Oh, thank goodness," she said upon hearing the news. "Now all we need to do is convince Holly to come back home."

"Look, Lila. If you're thinking we can arrange a moment of reconciliation, forget it. We're not talking about choir boys here. These are dangerous men."

"But couldn't you run a stakeout and wait for a moment when she's alone?"

"Sure, we could run a stakeout, but let's say a moment did present itself where Holly was alone. I don't have any right to force her back home. What do you want me to do, tie her up? They'll be dragging *me* in for kidnapping."

"Then you tell me, Michael. What do you propose we do?"

"I already told you. Call the police and you'll probably have your daughter back by the end of the day, happily or not."

"And I thought I had already made myself perfectly clear. I don't want them involved. Not unless it's absolutely necessary."

"Oh, you've made yourself perfectly clear, Lila, but that doesn't make it right. Your daughter's in danger and what? You're just going to leave her out there?"

I sat there in the silence, waiting for her to go on, and she did.

"Michael, I'm paying you handsomely to do my bidding. My reasons for doing what I do ought to be my own."

"Fair enough, Lila."

There was more silence.

"What?" she said.

"What? I just don't get it, that's all. It seems to me that you're more concerned about keeping your name out of the papers than you are about your daughter's safety. I'm sorry but these are not the normal instincts of a mother."

I waited again for Lila to go on, and she did, only with a cold vengeance now.

"Michael. I believe it would be best if we concluded our professional relationship right here. I thank you for locating my daughter but I'll be moving forward in another direction now."

"Fine. We'll need to sign a termination of services agreement. You tell me when you can get down here to my office to do that. In the meantime, I remain professionally bound and in your employment."

"Very well. I'll try to get down there later today. In the meantime, please give me the address of this residence where Holly is staying."

Reluctantly, I read it off to her, unable to get past this lousy feeling that Lila was a threat to her own daughter.

Having passed along the address, we were back to silence.

"Then whenever you can get by here to sign the necessary paperwork, Mrs. Evergreen, just give me a call."

When she did not respond, I hung up.

An uncomfortable question hung in the air. Was Lila on to me? About me being on to her? But on to what? Perhaps the shooting of her former husband had been purely accidental and the ensuing scramble to cover it up perfectly understandable. I could think of a number of innocent scenarios for his death, but I could also think of some really lousy ones.

41

And that left to the side the question of old man Cabot. I was increasingly curious to know how he had bought the farm.

A few seconds later, the phone rang. It was Lila again.

"Yes," I said.

"Michael. Please accept my apologies. Naturally this news left me distraught and I was being rash."

"Okay."

"Please, Michael. I can't explain things right now but I promise I will. As soon as we have a quiet moment together."

I was silent.

"Okay, you're mad."

I sighed conspicuously.

"Michael. I just want to make sure that Holly's safe for now. And hopefully find a way to reconcile with her. Do you think she is? I mean safe?"

"If you're asking me if Potter would take your daughter's life, no. In fact, I suspect he'd kill to defend her. He's just not much of a gentleman when it comes to the opposite sex. And it's just not a very safe environment for your daughter to be in, generally speaking."

"But can we just run a stakeout for a few days and see what happens? At least we know where she is now."

I shook my head. In the annals of protective motherhood, this stunk to high heaven.

"Michael?" Lila said.

"Yes."

"Can you do that for me?"

"Yes, I can do that. But then what?"

"I'm just hoping a moment presents itself where I can meet with her alone. I feel certain that I can get her to come back home."

"Fine. I'll set things up but have to warn you. A stakeout like this can become quite expensive."

"I don't care about the money."

"Fair enough. It's just my job to inform you."

"You have free rein, Michael. Just keep me informed and let me know the minute anything changes."

"Of course."

"Thank you. And I am sorry about the way I acted earlier."

"That's fine, Lila, but we still need to clear the air. There's something going on here that you're not telling me and I don't like being left in the dark."

"As soon as we can find a moment to talk privately, I'll explain everything, okay?"

"I'll be waiting. In the meantime, I'd better get to work on this stakeout."

Having ended the call, I dialed Mr. Huntington's number. He answered after several rings.

"Mr. Devlin, sad to say but I was about to call you. I'm afraid there's been more mischief with my son-in-law Nicholas."

"Christ. What is it this time?"

"A Picasso and some jewelry."

"That son of a bitch...Sorry, sir, but when did you notice them missing?"

"Just today. The Picasso's a minor work but of great sentimental value to me. My first wife and I bought it in Europe on our honeymoon. The jewelry he can have, if it comes to that."

"All right. I'll look into things right away."

There was a pause.

"I'm getting to be a forgetful old man, Michael, but not that forgetful. You called me...With something on your mind, I presume."

"Actually, it's your daughter Charlotte, sir. Her name came up in another case I'm working."

"Oh dear. I hope she's not gotten herself into more trouble."

"Not that I know of, but I wonder if you'd mind answering a few questions for me."

"Go right ahead."

"Well, first of all, have you seen her lately?"

There was a sigh and another pause.

43

"Not recently. I'd say it's been almost three weeks. Please get to your point."

"I'm wondering if you know a young lady by the name of Holly Evergreen. It appears she was friends with your daughter."

"Was?"

"It's just a manner of speaking, sir."

"I see. Well, I do in fact remember Ms. Evergreen. A fetching young lady, and very sweet. Her mother wasn't bad looking, either."

That coaxed a smile out of me.

"If you're wondering, I met Holly's mother at a parent/teacher conference. How I hate the damned things. Always a grim reminder of how an old man went bat house loco and married a young woman. Never do it, Michael. They always run off with your heart, and half of everything you own."

"I don't own that much, sir."

"And that should keep them at bay right there."

I smiled again.

"But you have no particular knowledge of where Holly might be."

"Michael, as you well understand, I hardly know where Charlotte is half the time. It's cost me a small fortune, just keeping the local school district at bay. She comes and goes as she pleases. God only knows how she's maintained a straight A average. There's a brilliant mind in there somewhere. Naturally, I've thought to discipline her, but she'd only have more cause to stay away. I tried that course of action with her sister Ida and you see where it's gotten me..."

I didn't, not really. As with Charlotte, the old man had been reticent to discuss Ida in much detail. I knew this much. Ida had gone off to attend an Ivy League college, which had led to a sojourn in Paris and her prodigal return home one Christmas with a French anarchist boyfriend. How Ida had gone from

Jacques the revolutionary to marrying Nicholas was a mystery to me.

Huntington had confided this much more to me during one of our meetings in his study, his gaze wandering off among the late afternoon shadows, leaden with barely disguised grief. Neither of his daughters appeared to exhibit the least bit of interest in his existence, beyond the prospect of his death and the associated fortunes they both hoped to reap.

Did the daughters view each other with the same feelings of avarice? It certainly seemed within the realm of possibility.

"Michael," Mr. Huntington said, interrupting my thoughts.

"Oh, sorry, sir. Yes?"

"About Ms. Evergreen? I presume from what you were saying that her daughter has run away?"

"You would be correct in that assumption, sir."

"Oh dear. Well, if I hear of anything, I'll be sure to let you know."

"Thanks, and I'll start looking for that Picasso right away."

"Be discreet, of course."

"Of course."

"However, if the opportunity presents itself to shoot Nicholas, please don't hesitate on my account. I give you my blessing."

I smiled once more.

"I'll be in touch, sir."

I got off the phone, thinking he always sounded so sage. Then, when you had Huntington's kind of money, everything you said tended to sound sage.

Getting back to business, I pulled up Zillow on my computer. It was a long shot but I needed some kind of rental out on Highland Road. Running a stakeout of Potter from the curbside would be akin to suicide.

With scant hopes, I miraculously found a house for rent, and, going by the number, both on the opposite side of Highland and not all that far down the block. I quickly had the owner on the phone and arranged a meeting at his property for that afternoon.

I was about to call Bennie, this fast-talking Puerto Rican kid I had hired to do some leg work for me, when he called me.

"What are you doing?" I said in answering

"You know, boss man, if I didn't know any better, I'd swear you weren't happy to hear from me."

"Please, Bennie. Don't start."

"Me start?"

"Look, I've got a job for you so please shut up and listen."

I held the phone away from my ear while he went off in Spanish."

"Are you done?" I said with the first pause.

"Yeah. I'm reporting in like a good guy and you have to give me shit."

"Jesus Christ, Bennie. Sometimes I wish you'd just go back to Puerto Rico or Queens or wherever the hell it is you came from."

He went off in Spanish again and it was quite a while before he finally shut up.

"I was thinking you might choke there for a minute."

"Don't get me started again. Just tell me what you got."

"It's actually two things."

I explained about Holly first.

"So what I want you to do is take Billy, go meet this landlord, rent his dump and leave Billy out there on a stakeout. Then come back here and we'll get working on this other case."

"Which is?"

"More work for Mr. Huntington."

"You mean his dip shit son-in-law Nicholas has been at it again."

"Yeah. A painting's come up missing, along with some jewelry so I need you to follow him around and see what turns up. And don't make any waves doing it. As always, Huntington wants things kept hush hush."

"No problemo. What am I'm looking for?"

46

"A painting and some jewelry."

"Yeah, real cute."

"The painting's a Picasso. The jewelry's a couple of rings and a diamond brooch."

"That's still a pretty wide field."

"Just keep an eye on him and see if he tries to fence anything."

"How long ago did this shit disappear?"

"Huntington doesn't know for sure but sometime in the last three days."

"Meaning, the shit could be anywhere by now."

"I can't change reality for you, Bennie."

"Boss man. I already told you. Just by looking at shit, you're changing reality. We're living in a quantum mechanics universe. It's like reality's looking back and saying, oh yeah? You're looking at me? Then watch this shit. I'm over here now. Subject, object. It's all interconnected. Some kind of cosmic dance is going on so get with it, dude."

I gave Bennie a second to catch his breath again.

"You okay?" I said once he had

"Shit. You don't want to learn nothing."

"Well, you tell me what quantum mechanics has to do with us following Nicholas around?"

"Screw it, man. You're just another dumb gringo."

"Yeah, yeah. Just get to work, will you? You're giving me a headache."

"See? It's all interconnected. You…"

"Just get to work!" I shouted into the phone.

"Dude, chill out. You seriously need to get to a meeting."

"I'll chill out the minute you get your ass in gear!"

I hung up and looked around to see if the furniture was moving. Christ. That Bennie really had a way of screwing with my head.

47

Five

All that day and into the night, the wild winds continued gusting out of the desert, the next day the same, the sky still choked with smoke and ashes and caravans of refugees pouring down towards the coast. On my way out the canyon that afternoon, I had seen the fires raging here and there among the distant hills, none of them yet under control and the sense of an ongoing apocalypse still upon the world.

On the Holly front, not a single opportunity to approach her behind Potter's back had presented itself. Whether by chance or design, he had not left her alone for one second.

Late on that second day, I gave Lila a call and tried to impress upon her again the virtue of notifying the police. The minute Holly turned seventeen, there would be no dragging her home, but Lila refused to budge. In fairness to her, a police confrontation with Potter might well have led to his personal Armageddon, with everyone going down in a blaze of bullets, Holly included.

As to our promised summit, wherein Lila would confess all, she had failed to raise the subject again and I had been too busy with other matters to really press her about it.

On Wednesday morning, shortly after dawn, my phone rang, awakening me from a lousy dream. I searched frantically among the bedcovers for the phone, saw that it was Bennie from the caller ID and cursed.

"Yeah?" I said, still draped in dark dreams.

"She's gone."

"Who's gone?"

"Holly."

"Shit!"

I sat upright in bed.

"The one goddamned thing I asked you not to let happen."

"You aksed me to do a lot of things."

Bennie sometimes got his 'k's in front of his 's's and it made my brain stall.

"Well, the most important one. Goddamn it, Bennie! Ms. Evergreen's going to have my head."

"Sorry, boss."

"Yeah. I'm sure you are…So when did this happen?"

"Overnight, I guess."

"What do you mean, you guess?"

"I mean, Potter and his biker friends were moving their shit all night. Then they made one last trip early this morning and Holly wasn't with them."

"Moving their shit to where?"

"To a couple of cabins up in Crestline."

"And you didn't call me…because?"

"What would it matter? You weren't going to drive out there last night."

"Goddamn it, Bennie. Quit thinking for me."

Needing coffee, I got to my feet and shuffled off to the kitchen. There was a glimpse of myself in a mirror along the way. Hair disheveled, dark rings under my eyes, death on my trail. A man starting to look decrepit in his fifties.

Jesus. I hurried to make the coffee.

"So when was the last time you saw Holly in all of this?"

"Around noon yesterday. She went for a ride with Potter on his Harley."

"And you're absolutely certain she wasn't with them this morning."

"No man. Unless they snuck her out in a rug or something."

I stalled there with the coffee beans in my hand.

49

"Snuck her out in a rug or something? What do you think this is, the story of Cleopatra?"

"What do you talk? Don't be a gringo loco."

"Well, did you see them sneak her out in a rug...or something?"

"No. I'm just saying. If she was with them, they had to have snuck her out somehow. Either me or Billy, we've had that hole staked out night and day and she ain't gone nowhere, other than for that ride with Potter but they came back an hour later."

I started the coffee grinder and spoke above the din.

"Then how do you know they're gone for good?"

"Look, this is how it went down. Billy called me about one in the morning, saying something was up so I drove straight out there and we sat around for hours watching those dudes load up all their shit. But we never saw Holly and when they took off for good, she wasn't with them."

"Damn it..."

I sat down and watched the coffee brew.

"And you're sure they're living in these cabins up in Crestline now?"

"Yeah. When we could kind of tell, okay, this is the last trip, we followed them up the mountain. I left Billy up there to keep an eye on things."

"You left Billy up there all alone?"

"Yeah. Why not? He's been sitting in that house all day and night by himself."

"Because sitting out in the open is a lot different than sitting inside a house."

"He'll be fine."

"Everything'll be fine with you, Bennie. Meanwhile, I get to call Ms. Evergreen and tell her I've lost her daughter."

"Don't worry about it. We'll find her. Shit happens."

"Jesus, Bennie. That jive may cut it on the streets of Queens but it's not going to cut it here. We're talking about a million-dollar client who's expecting million dollar results."

"I'm telling you. Chill. She'll show up again."

50

"Yeah, right…And the house on Highland? Did you go back and check it out?"

"Yeah. I drove by there on my way down the mountain but there wasn't shit to see but a bunch of trash that was even trashier than the shit they took with them."

"Jesus, what a mess."

I poured a cup of coffee, beside myself.

"And what's happening with Nicholas?"

"The same old shit. Hanging out at bars until all hours with his prick buddies in their MAGA hats. Then on to a coke and bullshit session at somebody's house until dawn. Then crawling home and crashing all day. Which is where he is now. He ain't tried to fence nothing, if that's what you're wondering."

"It was on my mind."

Bennie unleashed a few of his favorite swear words in Spanish.

"So, what are you up to?"

"Christ, I don't know. I'd better drive out and check on Billy."

"I already told you. He's fine."

"Yeah, yeah. I'll be the judge of that. Meanwhile, keep an eye on Nicholas and let me know the minute anything changes. And that would include in the middle of the night, thank you."

I hung up before Bennie could go off on me again.

There in the speckled sunlight, that lousy dream went on haunting me. What bizarre stuff. I had been driving a big rig somewhere in the French countryside and ended up with it parked alongside a barn. Then, while asleep inside the barn, the big rig had gone up in flames.

It was a metaphor for my whole life. Bridges burned. Everything torched and up in smoke.

What had happened to me? I couldn't remember having a zippity doo dah day. It was always this feeling of the apocalypse first thing in the morning, like my destiny had taken a seriously wrong turn back down the road somewhere.

51

I had made the mistake of opening up about these feelings to an old timer named Tom one night after a meeting. Half blind, round like a Buddha and cheerily happy, Tom had suggested that I get down on my knees every morning and turn my will and life over to the care of God as I understood Him. Ask for His will to be done that day, not mine. Then see what I could do to help a fellow human being.

I had nodded. Sure. I'll get on that first thing.

I took to the idea the way a dog takes to a rolled up newspaper.

Anyway, humility was a big theme around the meeting circuit. Surrender to win. I heard it all the time, but the thought just made me feel rebellious, especially when Bennie joined the chorus. 'It's time to do this deal, boss man. The elevator to sobriety's broken. You gotta take the steps.'

Yeah, yeah. Have Caitlin call me. When that happens, then maybe we'll talk about surrendering.

But of course, it never did.

I went off to shave, muttering to myself.

Fine, I thought while lathering up. Please help me to stay sober today, and to be of the greatest possible service to You and my fellow human beings. That's my best shot. Take it or leave it. I'm not getting down on my knees.

It just seemed like the whole universe would be watching.

As expected, nothing changed. Just that black, ethereal hole of consciousness staring back at me, like the great black void of the universe itself sucking me in.

After a shave and a shower, I got dressed for a casual field day — Levi's, boots and a blue dress shirt — and called Billy on my way into town. He gave me the address of his location. I told him I'd be up his way in a bit.

Having checked on things down at the office, I packed my satchel and headed out the door. The Impala was beginning to look apocalyptic with its coating of ashes. The same with the streets and sidewalks. The wind had let up a bit, but not the fires.

The downtown was eerily quiet at that hour. I saw a guy surf fishing down at Main Beach and a couple of seniors strolling along the shore. Otherwise you would have thought it was the rapture.

A short while later, I was loping out through that dry chaparral country again, and with Steve's ex-wife Connie back in my thoughts. Vanderhof, that bastard. Back on the streets with a big grin on his face, figuring he had gotten away with murder. Hell, if it was that easy, maybe I'll put a few slugs in him.

Out in San Berdoo, I took the exit onto Waterman Avenue and drove up through the old downtown district. About a mile farther on, Waterman jogged right and turned into State Route 18. Soon, I was zigzagging up the rugged mountain, up past all the smog and smoke from the fires. The world grew as clear as a postcard; the way it would look if everyone in LA parked their car for a few days. I could make out individual pine trees from five miles away. It was beautiful — hot, dry and restless — but beautiful.

I found Billy parked up a quiet, dead end street on the high side of Knapps Cutoff. He had backed into the driveway of an unoccupied cabin. A cluster of pines shrouded the van. I looked up and down the street before knocking and slipping in the back door.

The surveillance van had been customized inside with a bed and a bank of four monitors. Four hidden cameras outside provided a view in all directions. The van also had a storage cabinet, a small fridge towards the front and a port-a-potty in back. Billy was seated in front of the monitors, focused on the image of a house farther up the hill. He glanced up at me, all serious like. He always looked that way. We were about to hit the beach on D-Day.

"How are you doing?" I said.

"Good."

His dark eyes remained fixed on me. Next stop, Omaha Beach.

I was reminded of Ralph Kramden whenever I saw him, a taciturn young Ralph Kramden. Billy had the same thick frame, the same black, greased back hair and jowly face, but he was a good-looking kid behind it all, and a lot more intelligent than he let on at first glance.

New in recovery, he often spoke of being insecure. To look at him, you were more worried about having your neck broken.

I leaned in for a closer look at the house in the monitors.

"That's it up there?"

"Yeah," he said with another intense look my way. "Both those cabins."

"Is anybody up there right now?"

"I don't think so. They went off on their Harleys about half an hour ago. I think they all went. I haven't seen anyone come outside since."

"And Potter was with them?"

Billy nodded.

"But no sign of Holly."

Billy shook his head.

"And you're sure you're okay up here all alone?"

"For tonight. I bought a couple of burgers and stuff." We both glanced over at his makeshift pantry. "Is Bennie coming up to relieve me in the morning?"

"Yeah. I'll make sure he does."

"Then I'm good."

"All right. I can spell you for a while if you need to run into town for something."

"No. I'm good."

"Just be careful," I said while staring at the image of the house.

Our eyes met.

"And get your ass out of here at the first sign of trouble."

Billy nodded. I patted him on the shoulder.

"I'm heading back down the hill. Just wanted to make sure you were good."

"You didn't have to drive all the way up here for that."

"I'd have been worrying all day if I didn't."

"Thanks, boss."

"Sure. Thank you."

I patted Billy on the shoulder again and slipped out the back. It was a nice, quiet street but it wouldn't be for long, not once those bikers got to partying.

The drive back down the mountain would normally have come with glorious views of the coastline, from Ventura down to Newport Beach. Instead, I was looking at a land enveloped in smoke. A towering plume of it from the Malibu fire was dissipating in high winds out over the Pacific.

At the bottom of the hill, I turned left and headed back over to Highland Road. Potter's old place looked even grimmer now with everyone gone. Not that I pitied the landlord but it figured he wouldn't know that his tenants had moved out on him until the rent check failed to show up at the end of the month.

I found the front door unlocked and let myself in. My nose crinkled up at the stench. Something more than rotting food was involved. I stepped around a minefield of debris on the floor and peeked out the kitchen window. There it was. Dog shit. It looked as if no one had cleaned it up for years. What a life. I imagined even the dogs had dreaded going out there.

I glanced around at the kitchen sink and countertops. They were overrun with dirty dishes and rotting food. It was enough to keep you moving.

In the wide passageway between the dining room and living room, chains had been bolted to the header. I had seen a similar setup years earlier, in a case involving a cult; handcuffs attached to the end of the chains and the young female victim left there hanging for everyone to enjoy when things got wild. It made my ears burn to think of Potter doing that to Holly.

In the living room, I stopped again. White supremacist symbolism had been scrawled all over the walls. Swastikas. SS bars. The same symbolism I had seen in that article about the beheaded cleric. Maybe it was a coincidence and maybe not. Moreno Valley was not all that far down the road.

I took a picture with my phone and moved on to the back of the house.

A long hallway led to four bedrooms and a bathroom. I pushed open the first door. Spent fast food wrappers, empty booze bottles and other bits of trash littered the threadbare carpet. The bed looked like it belonged under a bridge. All the bedrooms presented more or less the same snapshot.

I was ready to move on from the master bedroom in back when something on the carpet caught my eye. Carefully navigating the debris on the floor, I squatted down and picked up a business card. Embossed on the front were some of the same symbols scrawled on the living room walls. The name printed at the bottom of the card was Donald Ray Potter. Phineas Priesthood was printed under his name. Flipping the card over, I found a Mexican name scribbled on the back.

That's odd, I thought. Potter's dealer? A hitman? Or just a bit of Bruder Schweigen he had planned to exterminate?

I placed the card in my pocket and was starting to stand up when the edge of a small photo caught my eye. I squatted back down and fished it out from beneath the rubbish. It was Holly, clipped from a string of carnival booth photos. She was smiling, but through a shitload of fear and uncertainties. You could see bruises peeking through her powder makeup.

Vengeance was now converging with the thought of Potter in my mind.

Slipping the photo in with the card, I headed back out to the living room and stood there thinking. Curiosity got the better of me so I went to have a better look in the kitchen. It was a lab experiment, from the piles of dirty dishes to the inside of the refrigerator. I tried the freezer door and found a bag of peas, a TV dinner, some party ice and an opened box of frozen waffles. I looked inside the box. One waffle left, with freezer burns.

I returned to the living room and stared out the sliding glass door. What now? A grove of trees was visible over the rear fence. Hills rose up on the far side of the trees. Something told me to go out there and have a look.

I headed out the front door and around to a strip of land between Potter's place and the house next door. That led to a field overrun with mustard plants. That brief storm a few weeks back had been enough for them sprout up nearly over my head. Lemon grass carpeted the ground around my feet. The days of my youth whispered in the wind, wandering home from school, sucking on lemon grass stalks, wild beasts out there in the woods.

I came to the grove and had wandered in among the trees a short ways when a deep arroyo halted my progress. I walked along its edge for some distance and was about to turn back when I noticed flies swarming in a small clearing. I went to investigate and was soon lurching in the direction of the nearest tree.

It took me a minute to gather myself and return for a closer look. A decomposing arm jutted out from the soil, with the tips of the fingers and thumb crudely clipped off, as if by a pair of dikes. The coyotes had dug the body out and eaten things down to the bone, including the arm. Why they had left the hand intact was a mystery to me. It definitely belonged to a woman. That much you could tell at a glance.

Using a branch, I brushed aside some leaves and lurched away again. Christ. The body had been decapitated. That left DNA as the only likely means of identification.

I backed away and weighed the situation. This wasn't Holly. That much seemed obvious. The timeline didn't fit. This body had been here for at least a week, if I knew anything about corpses.

The question was, should I call the cops? I could think of several arguments against the idea. Mainly, I hated getting myself involved, especially out here in San Berdoo. Sure as hell, these local boys would start eying me like I was a possible suspect. Then there was Lila's aversion to them. Either way, we'd be opening up a hornet's nest, with little hope of keeping Holly's name out of things.

All that was on one side of the ledger. On the other side was my legal exposure. I was now witness to a likely murder, with my tracks all over the crime scene.

Not in the mood to be anyone's fall guy, I pulled out my phone and dug up the number for the San Bernardino Police Department.

With the call ended, I had started back towards Potter's house when I noticed something shiny among the dead leaves and crouched down to have a look. It was a ring. I glanced back at the woman's hand and the middle finger had the associated indentation. The killer must have removed the ring while clipping off her fingertips, knowing it would help to identify the body, then accidentally dropped it and gave up the search. That suggested the killing had taken place at night. Or someone had been in a great hurry. Or both.

I slipped the ring into my coat pocket and called Billy on my way out to the street.

"Pack up and get out of there," I told him when he answered.

"But they just came back from their bike ride."

"I don't care."

I explained what I had found.

"Oh man. That's some really fucked up shit."

"Yeah it is and your place is going to be swarming with cops real soon now so get your ass out of there."

"I'm cool with it."

"I said get out of there! Don't argue with me, Billy!"

"All right," he said like he was sincerely wounded.

"Hey, I'm just looking out for you, okay?"

"I know."

"Then get a move on. And I mean right now."

Just seconds after we hung up, I heard sirens in the distance. To be on the safe side, I slipped Holly's photo and Potter's business card into my wallet.

A minute later, I had two squad cars barreling down the street at me. I pulled out my PI license and held it up, along with both hands. The two squad cars skidded to a halt and four cops jumped out, one hand on their unclipped holsters, all ready to pump me full of lead if I made the wrong move.

The badge on the sergeant read Rodriguez. Aztec blood bled through his high cheekbones and receding forehead. One of the cops was black. He had a shaved head. So did the Mex-Asian mix next to him. The lone white kid looked almost bubbly at the prospect of trouble. All of them were buffed out to varying degrees, all of them a few pounds overweight, except for the white kid, and aside from him, could just as easily have had their photos hanging on a post office wall. It looked like a gang line up from South Central.

"What's your business here?" Rodriguez said.

"Missing girl. The last time I saw her, she was with these boys."

"A minor?"

I nodded.

"Then why didn't you call the police?"

"That's not the way her mother wanted it. She'll be turning seventeen in a couple of days."

"And you say the body's out back?"

"Yeah. In the woods. Just beyond that field out there."

Rodriguez nodded.

"Dempsey, Robinson, check the backyard and secure a perimeter."

The white guy and black guy headed for the side gate of the house. I didn't envy their detail much.

"Okay, show us," Rodriguez said.

Tanaka, the Mex-Asian fell in with us and we headed back out among the mustard plants. Whether or not it was my imagination, I thought I could smell the stench of the body from two hundred yards now.

Rodriguez and Tanaka both paused at seeing the body. For what it was worth, neither one of them lost their lunch.

Six

While we stood there, the sound of more sirens tore at the sky.

"We'd better get back out there," Rodriguez said with a nod at Tanaka.

The three of us walked back across the field. Two more patrol cars were parked out in the street when we arrived, and more were coming. Dempsey and Robinson had rolled out enough yellow caution tape to circle a football field. Most of the neighbors had come out to gawk; women holding babies, one of them in hair curlers, a guy in white socks with a beer in his hand. It was a snapshot of lower middle-class America, with a bit of the outlaw spirit thrown in.

Rodriguez dispatched a couple of men to safeguard the body. Instructed to hang around, I got comfortable in the front seat of my Impala. Another cop car soon braked to a stop out in the street, then another one. It was starting to resemble a train wreck out there. No one wanted to be left out of the fun.

The desert winds served as a backdrop, swaying the trees wildly and kicking up dust a mile high in the sky.

Several times I tried reaching Billy without any luck. Finally, he called back.

"What the hell, Billy? Where have you been?"

"Boss, you wouldn't believe what happened up here. It's a full-on war zone."

"Goddamn it! I told you to get your ass out of there!"

"I know, boss, but I thought, what if Holly's inside?"

"I don't care! When I give you an order, you follow it!"

"Okay, man. You don't have to beat my balls."

"Well, Jesus, Billy. Do as I say next time."

"Don't worry, man. I moved down to the bottom of the hill where it was safe and zoomed in from there."

"Yeah? So, anything?"

"You mean about Holly?"

"Yeah?"

"No, I didn't see her. Good thing, man. She probably would have been wasted. I saw three or four of those bikers go down and one cop. I'm telling you. It was a full blown battle scene."

"Goddamn it, Billy. Next time I tell you to do something, you do it, okay?"

"Okay. I'm sorry."

"Yeah, me too...So where are you now?"

"Down at a 7/11 grabbing an ice coffee. The cops have the roads blocked going down the hill. I saw them stopping everyone. Checking ID's and opening trunks and shit. Half the town's out on the streets, gawking."

"Yeah. The same down here with the neighbors."

There was a pause.

"You think Holly's still alive?" Billy said.

"God only knows. I hope so."

"So, what do you want me to do?"

"Oh, go home. Take the rest of the day off. With pay."

"I can keep working, man."

"No, no. Go home. Hit a meeting. You've earned your keep for one day."

"Thanks, boss."

"Sure. Just check in with me before you crash tonight."

"I will."

While I was sitting there, two plainclothesmen pulled up in an unmarked car.

"Okay, I'd better go. Looks like two detectives just pulled up and I'm sure they'll be wanting to talk to me."

They sauntered up as I was getting out of the car. One of them looked ex-military — sixties era military — right down to the butch haircut. The other one looked as if he had seen one too many Tom Selleck movies. He had the mustache and good looks to pull it off. I'd give him that much. The ID clipped to his coat pocket read Barnes. He did the talking.

"You the PI who broke in?"

By way of answering, I flipped open my credentials.

"I didn't break in. The door was unlocked."

He glanced at the license and nodded.

"Hang loose. I may have some questions for you."

Barnes and his partner left me prisoner and ducked under the yellow caution tape. After a quick look in the house, they headed out to the field.

The second they were out of sight, I pulled out my phone and dialed Lila's number. It wasn't a call I relished making. First of all, there was having to admit I had lost her daughter. Then there was the matter of a corpse. The minute I mentioned a dead body, there would be no getting on to the part about "but I don't think it's Holly" fast enough.

Either way, I wasn't sure what to expect from Lila. Would she chew me out for losing Holly and getting the cops involved? Or fall apart? Or both?

"Hi," she said in answering my call. "Do you have news?"

When I hesitated, she said, "Oh god no."

"No no. It's nothing like that."

I did my best to get ahead of the story — likely time of death, last time I saw Holly — but it still required me walking her back from the grim news.

"Trust me, Lila. It's not your daughter. That body's been out there at least a week now. Maybe more."

"Well, thank god for that but you lost her. How could you lose her?"

"Look, I'm going to make an educated guess here and say she snuck off. The way Potter was watching her, she couldn't have just walked out the front door. She must have found a moment to slip out the back way when he wasn't looking. Anyway, as much as I feel like hell about it all, it's probably for the best."

I explained about the shootout up in Crestline.

"If she was still with that gang, she'd probably be dead."

"Oh god. What a mess…Okay, so what does this mean to me, Michael."

"It means there's no way of keeping Holly's name out of things now so you'd best hire an attorney. Everything points back to her being a witness."

"Can't you just make up some excuse for why you were out there?"

"No, Lila. I'll go out on a limb for you, but not over a dead body."

"Oh god, okay. And I suppose you're going to tell me you know an attorney."

"I do. A good one. Jim Harrison. Shall I have him call you?"

"Yes, please. What else am I going to do?"

"Nothing. Just expect to hear from him shortly. Best to get this attorney business out of the way quickly. Two detectives have me waiting around here and I expect the next thing they'll want to do is talk with you and Holly."

Lila let out a big sigh.

"I'm here. Have your attorney call."

"I will. And I'll let you know if there's any delay."

I got off the phone with her and immediately called Jim. It took a moment for his secretary to get him on the line.

"Trouble?" he said without saying hello.

I had to smirk.

"My reputation precedes me."

"What can I say?"

"Well, I definitely have a situation going on here so let me explain."

Jim listened without interrupting.

"Yeah," he said when I was through. "I could see that going south in a number of different ways."

"Yeah…So look, Jim. There's more."

I went on to explain that initial encounter with Lila at my office and a feeling that something didn't smell right, and then what I had learned about the shooting up in Pueblo Hills.

"You know what I mean? Like she thought she could use me somehow? And then I find out about this shooting and my friend's belief that it was all covered up?"

"Yeah, I usually trust my gut instincts in situations like that. If you don't mind me asking, why did you go ahead and take the job?"

"Let's just say you'd have to see her."

"Nice?"

"Yeah, pretty heavenly. Plus, she's got plenty of dough."

"That never hurt."

"Or as I like to say, almost never."

"Yeah, I appreciate the warning but I can take care of myself."

"I know you can. Just thought it was my duty to give you fair warning."

"Consider me warned."

"So you mind giving her a call?"

"Not at all. Are you okay in the meantime?"

"I think so. You'll hear from me if not."

Jim and I ended the call. I had been sitting there for a good fifteen minutes before Barnes reappeared from around the back of the house, alone and heading my way. The look on his face said that he was weary of trouble and considered me part of it.

"What made you go out there?"

"My sixth sense."

"Don't get cute."

"Well, the truth is, I don't have a better answer for you. Something just told me to go have a look."

He studied me with his head slowly nodding.

"Fucking mess."

"Any luck up in Crestline?"

He scoffed.

"Another fucking mess. Four of them dead and one of ours in critical condition with a bullet in his neck. He's alive but he may never talk again."

"Sorry to hear it."

Barnes nodded.

"What do you know about these bastards?"

"Not much. I've only had them staked out for a couple of days. They came and went, doing the usual crap. The kind of stuff you wouldn't want to write home to mom about. But beyond my client's daughter being with them? I had no overt proof of anything illegal going on."

"She's a minor. That's illegal enough right there."

"I already told your sergeant in there. It's not what her mother wanted. You can take it up with her if you want, but fair warning. She's got all kinds of money."

"Yeah? And what else do you know?"

"I wasn't around to see it myself but one of my men told me they booked out of here late last night, like they smelled trouble. Maybe they just got tired of their own stench. Anyway, that's all I know."

Barnes' attention had drifted off down the block while I was talking, his head slowly nodding the whole time. Then he looked back, his head still nodding.

"You have any idea who that is out there?"

I shook my head.

"Think it's your Holly?"

I shook my head.

"You'll have to check with the coroner on the time of death but I'd say no. I saw her myself just two days ago and that body looks to have been out there a good deal longer than two days."

"And you didn't touch anything out there? Or while you were fishing around inside?"

"I poked around a bit inside, sure. There's some frozen peas in the freezer. One waffle left, with freezer burns. That's about as far as I got. All that dog shit in the backyard was enough to keep me moving."

Barnes stared at me like I was playing a pair of deuces for a straight flush and he knew it.

"You got a card?" he said.

I pulled out my wallet, careful to keep the contents pointed discreetly away from his view. He took my card and gave it the once over. I tucked my wallet safely back out of sight.

"And this Holly. I assume you know how to get in touch with her mother."

I nodded. Barnes pulled out a little note pad and pen and stood there with an expectant look. I rattled off the name and number.

"Why don't you give me five minutes," I said. "It's probably best if I give her the news first."

"Fair enough. And then hang loose here until I've had a chance to talk with her. And try not to leave planet earth until I've gotten to the bottom of this."

He waited for me to nod before slipping back under the caution tape. I waited until he had disappeared again before calling Lila back.

"Did you talk with Jim?" I asked her.

"Yes, he called right away."

"And you hired him?"

"Yes, of course."

"Good, because the police want to talk to you."

"Oh god. Then shouldn't I refer them to Jim?"

"No. You should call Jim and ask him what he wants you to do. Right now. I've stalled this Detective Barnes for five minutes. Then he's going to be calling you."

"Okay. I'll call him right now."

"I'll be here. If I don't hear back from you in the next few minutes, I'll know Jim gave you the go ahead to talk with this detective and I'll have him call."

"Okay."

"Either way, call me back once you're done."

"I will."

I got off the phone with Lila and stood there watching police business. It wasn't unlike a county road job. One guy doing the work and three guys leaning on their holsters.

When a few minutes had passed without a call back from Lila, I flagged one of the patrol cops. He went inside to grab Barnes. Barnes met me back out at the caution tape.

"I talked to her. She's waiting for your call."

He nodded, pulled out his notepad with the phone number and drifted away several paces. I went to wait in my car.

Old Tom came to mind as I sat there. He had become my unwelcome conscience, a reminder of how many little lies I told every day. Could anyone get through an hour in this world without bullshitting someone? Maybe, but not in my line of work. Telling white lies was a vocational hazard. It was with this detective in any case.

Five minutes later, my phone rang. It was Lila again.

"So? What happened?"

"Jim told me to take the call."

"And?"

"That detective wants me to drive out there and see if I can identify the body."

I cursed under my breath.

"And Jim gave you the go ahead on that."

"Yes. He said it was best to play along. That I didn't have much choice in the end. Just keep my mouth shut as much as possible, and refer the police back to him if I started feeling uncomfortable in any way."

"Then you're headed out here now?"

"Yes. I'll be on my way in a few minutes."

"Then I'll stick around and wait for you."

"Will you?"

"Sure. I'll go grab some lunch. Just call me whenever you're getting near."

"I will."

"Then I'll talk with you in a bit."

I ended the call and asked a cop to get Barnes' attention again. Barnes came back out, trying not to look perturbed.

"Mrs. Evergreen asked me to stick around for her. I'm thinking to go grab some lunch while I wait."

He checked his watch and headed back into the house. I headed back to my Impala, feeling a bit like a school kid with a hall pass.

Over a chicken Caesar salad, I called Kenny. He answered after a few rings.

"I'm looking across the street."

"Yeah, I'm out here in San Bernardino."

"Bummer."

"In more ways than one."

I explained what was going on.

"Really big bummer."

"Yeah…Take this down."

I had Potter's card out and read off the name scribbled on the back.

"See what you can find out about our Latino friend."

"My witness protection fees just went up."

"I assumed as much. Just add it to my bill…And how about Holly's phone? Any sign of that?"

"Nothing."

"Yeah. That thing's in a dumpster somewhere."

"Yeah."

"And Cabot? Nothing new there?"

"Just that, whatever happened, it happened back in Ohio. I tracked him down to a big estate in Indian Hill."

"Indian Hill."

"A suburb of Cincinnati. Anyway, I'm guessing that's where he met Lila."

"And where Lila killed him."

"Maybe."

"Well, keep digging. And get back to me on this El Chango character as soon as you can. I'll be out here holding Mrs. Evergreen's hand."

"Lucky you."

"Yeah, maybe. Or maybe not."

Kenny laughed and we hung up. I got back to my chicken Caesar salad. It was lousy, and a lonely choice out in these parts. Deep fat fried was your sweet spot. One glance at the surrounding clientele told you that much. The handful of 'heart friendly' options were buried at the back of the menu.

I was reading the obituaries in the local rag and about to try the want ads when my phone rang. It was Lila. She had just pulled off the freeway.

"You locked in on where you're going?"

"Yes. I have it up here on GPS."

"Then go ahead and head that way but park well down the street. I'll meet you there and we'll drive in together."

I hung up, paid for the lousy salad and headed out to the parking lot. Paper and debris were swirling all around in the dry wind. The mountains towered over the land.

On my way up Highland, I spotted Lila at the side of the road and slowed down long enough for her to pull in behind me. At Potter's old digs, we parked in tandem. I got out and opened her door. She slipped out of her Jaguar wearing a sleeveless beige dress with matching colored high heel pumps and her face half hidden behind tortoise shell glasses. Every cop in sight gave her an eyeful. Something about her made you want to sell your soul, even if it was going to kill you. As far as I knew, no one had survived her yet.

"Are you all right?" I asked.

She sighed deeply.

"I guess. What are we doing?"

"Heading way out there into that field. Don't you have something to wear besides those heels?"

She shook her head

"Then we'll have to make do."

I offered her my arm and we headed for the house. All eyes were on us as we approached the caution tape. I stopped there and asked the nearest cop to bring Barnes out again. He appeared a minute later, looked Lila up and down and slipped under the caution tape.

"Bob Barnes."

She shook his hand.

"I don't understand why you're making me go through this. From what I was told, we already know it's not my daughter."

"Protocol, Mrs. Evergreen. We just have to check every box."

"Oh god...Okay, which way?"

Barnes pointed. When I started to follow, he held up a hand. "You wait here."

"I'm not going anywhere without him," Lila said.

Barnes frowned, seeing his little cake party blown all to hell. I received a grudging nod to follow. Lila gripped my arm as we started across the field. Several times, I had to catch her from falling.

When we neared the buzz of forensics people, Barnes stopped.

"Sorry but there's just no easy way of going about this."

I gently urged Lila around a tree. When the remains of the corpse came into view, she threw herself at my shoulder. Barnes stared. Lila darted a look his way and shook her head.

"No?" he said. "It's not her? Or you can't tell?"

"Oh God, how are you supposed to tell from that?" Lila looked one more time at the corpse and shuddered. "It can't be her. It can't."

"Do you know if your daughter was wearing a ring on her right middle finger?"

Lila shook her head again.

"No, she didn't wear one?"

"I never saw her wearing one."

"Well, whoever that is was wearing one, but not anymore."

Barnes settled his gaze on me for a moment before looking back at Lila.

"You're sure about the ring."

She nodded and urged me to take her away.

Barnes fell in beside us as we re-crossed the field. Then, back out on the street, he motioned for me to get lost. I headed over to Lila's Jaguar and watched as he gave her a grilling. The prick appeared to be playing it rough. Then, from what I remembered, Lila tended to like her men that way.

She eventually rejoined me and said she needed a drink.

"I know a quiet place nearby. Just follow me."

Seven

I guided her back out to a small commercial strip by the freeway. It was home to a liquor store, a manicure shop, a barber, a small appliance repair outfit and a bar called the Cock & Bull. Lila parked next to me in front. I got out and walked over to her door. She hit the window button with her engine still running.

"This place?"

"Sorry. The Waldorf closed last week."

"Please don't joke right now."

"Well, I didn't know a place like this was beneath you."

"It's just...I don't know."

I figured I did. There was a time, not all that long ago, in a bar not all that different from this one, where Lila had strutted her stuff wearing spangles and a G-string.

"I can try Googling someplace else if you'd like."

"Oh, never mind."

She hit her window button, turned off the Jag, pulled down her visor, did a bit of housekeeping in the makeup mirror, pushed the visor back up and climbed out.

"How did you find this place, by the way?"

"Just passing by on my way to the freeway. Full confession, it did look like my kind of place. Nice and dark and hidden away from the world."

She feigned a look of disapproval and took hold of my arm. I led her up to the door and pushed it open. Bright sunlight heralded our entrance and quickly vanished as the door closed behind us.

It was a quiet afternoon at the Cock & Bull. A businessman in his thirties sat alone at the bar, scrolling through his phone. He had a quick look at Lila and returned to his phone, but with divided attention now. A middle-aged couple occupied a booth off in the corner. That was it, besides the two of us and the bartender. There were no dancing girls.

I led Lila to a secluded booth and helped her scoot in. The businessman stole another glance at Lila. Jack Jones crooned in the background.

Lila noticed me noticing the man noticing her.

"I hate it when men do that," she said.

"What do you want? You're a beautiful woman."

She gave me a look, the one that beautiful women give you when they want to pretend they're ignorant of that fact. I looked to get the bartender's attention but he was already on his way over.

"What can I get you two?" he said while setting down the obligatory cocktail napkins.

"I'll have a Tom Collins," she said.

"Club soda with a splash of cranberry and twist of lemon, not lime."

He took both orders with aplomb and retreated to his workshop. I looked back at Lila.

"You don't drink?" she said.

"Oh, when I really want to let my hair down, I have them throw in a dash of bitters."

She shuddered.

"What?" I said.

"I can't get that image out of my mind."

"Understandable. What was Barnes grilling you about?

"Oh, wanting to know when I last saw my daughter and why I hadn't reported her missing and all that."

She played with her cocktail napkin.

"Tell me you're sure it's not her."

I shrugged.

"I already told you. The time frames don't fit."

Lila shuddered again. The drinks came and we backed out of the way.

"Run a tab," I told the bartender.

Lila swished her Tom Collins around, dispensed with the stir stick and took a stiff drink. I sipped at my club soda.

"I wish you'd drink with me," she said.

"I am."

"You know what I mean."

"Look, this is a workday for me. I still have business to attend to."

She sighed deeply.

"I just wish you hadn't lost my daughter again."

"I already told you, Lila. She ran off, and it's a damned good thing she did."

She put a hand on my forearm.

"I'm sorry. I'm just worried. You think she's all right?"

"I'd put my money on it. She's clearly resourceful."

"Oh god. What a mess."

She took another good slug from her drink and had a look around the dimly lit bar. The two lovers were having a good laugh over in their corner booth. The businessman stole another glance at Lila. She played with her hair.

"I hate this kind of place." She took another drink from her cocktail. "So? Do you really let your hair down once in a while?"

"Sure. Late at night. When no one's watching."

"You're just being a card now."

She finished her drink and held up the glass for the bartender to see. He quickly got the message and went to work on the next cocktail. Lila played with her empty glass.

"I could just kill her for running away in the first place."

"Yeah, but what are you going to do? Kids do that sometimes. And then they come home when they're good and ready."

Lila's next cocktail arrived. She smiled for the bartender, in a way that wasn't really a smile, quickly dispensed with the stir stick and tossed back a goodly portion of that drink.

I felt her staring at me and glanced that way.

"I suppose you think it's all my fault."

"I never said that, Lila."

"But it's crossed your mind."

I shrugged.

"Look, I don't claim to know much about raising kids, but there's one thing that's always puzzled me."

"And that is?"

"How, at a certain age, communication always seems to break down between parents and their children. Why does it always turn into a war of the generations? I just don't get it."

"If you've never had kids, you wouldn't understand."

She was right. I had no standing on the subject. But Lila wasn't finished.

"Let me tell you something, buster. It's no easy task being a parent. You buy them new clothes, fix their teeth, clean up after them every time they make a mess, indulge them with every little thing they want and next thing you know, they're in front of you with another demand. 'Oh Mom, can I get this?' Or another complaint. 'Oh Mom, why didn't you do that?' It's never ending, and mostly thankless, so please don't pretend to lecture me about raising my daughter."

She knocked back more of her drink.

"Well?" she said.

"Well, as I remember it, it wasn't easy being a kid either."

"Well. Don't we have all the answers."

Lila moved on to playing with her nearly empty glass. I waited until she looked back at me.

"I asked a question, that's all. And a pretty legitimate one, in my humble opinion, but it wasn't meant to indict you."

"It certainly sounded that way."

She knocked back the rest of her drink. I nodded at her glass.

"A few more of those and we'll be wrestling on the floor."

Lila gave me a look and resumed playing with her glass.

"Oh god," she said suddenly. "What a giant fucking mess."

I raised my eyebrows.

What?" she said in response. "My potty mouth?"

I shrugged, and nodded.

"Oh yes, I have one at times. I can be incorrigible too...It's probably where Holly got it."

I looked back at my drink.

"Okay," she said. "We know where Holly got it but I've tried to give her everything in this world. Everything I never had and to see it turn out like this..."

Lila was suddenly pulling tissues out of her purse again. I did my best to mind my own business. After a spell, she did a bit of housekeeping on her makeup and turned to face me.

"I believe you had wanted me to confess all my secrets, right?"

"Something doesn't add up."

"Fine, I'll tell all. Mind you, this isn't something you confess to just anyone. In fact, I haven't spoken about it for years."

She knocked back the rest of her drink, dabbed at her nose and heaved another big sigh.

"I was given up for adoption as a child."

She reached for another tissue. Al Green was crooning about romance in the background. Lila looked up at me.

"Well, say something."

Hell, what was I going to say? This wasn't even remotely close to what I had expected.

"There's no sin in being adopted," I offered.

"How would you know?"

"Yeah, you're right. I don't."

"No. And the truth is, you're abandoned, not adopted. Flung aside like an unwanted piece of trash. Can you imagine how that feels, to know your own parents didn't want you?"

"I'm sure it was awful."

She dabbed at more tears.

"That's right. Think of Christmas and birthdays, watching the other kids get better presents than you. Of course I indulged Holly with everything she could want. But it was never enough to stop the questions as she grew up. 'Where's my Dad?' and 'How come you don't have any brothers and sisters?' and 'Why don't I have a Grandma and Grandpa?' God, to think of the stories I told her. Holly thinks her father ran off to South America, her grandfather died in Vietnam and her grandmother was killed in a car accident. I used to take Holly to this gravesite, hoping to god the real relatives never showed up while we were there. And that's just my side of the family. Whenever she asked about her father's side of the family, I made it clear, it was better not knowing."

Lila gave me a look.

"And trust me, it was."

We sat there quietly for a spell with our separate thoughts. I still didn't know what to tell her. I had been expecting a murder confession.

"So, if you don't mind me asking, what really happened? I mean with your parents? Or do you know?"

Lila shook her head.

"Not really. The people at the adoption agency lied to me. It wasn't until I was in my twenties that I learned my mother had drunk herself to death. Or so I was told. I would have been nine years old when she passed away, if that's true. I have no idea what happened to my father. I vaguely remember a face but who knows? All I know is, he ran off about the time we were put up for adoption."

"We?" I said.

"Oh, yes. I have three siblings. God only knows what's happened to them. We were separated after a few months and shipped off to separate foster homes. I ended up with this Italian family. No one was overtly cruel to me but it might have been easier that way. The teasing never stopped. Their real kids called me peanut because I was so small and played tricks behind my back. And of course the parents always doted on their own in a way that they never doted on me. I always had this feeling of being second class. That I didn't really belong."

Lila bit her lip.

"I guess that part haunts me the most, not knowing about my real siblings. I have no idea where they are or what they're like. I just find myself thinking of them on special occasions. And then go off and cry alone. I've always wondered if Holly had figured this out. Maybe, huh?"

I shrugged.

"I'm sorry. I'm boring you," she said.

After a long look her way, I waved to the bartender and motioned at Lila's drink. He went to work. I looked back at her.

"Oh, I see. Now you're really going to get me snockered."

"What the hell? What's one more drink at this point?"

She smiled painfully.

"Come on, Michael. Have a drink with me."

"I can't."

She shook my hands.

"Why? What's the harm in a cocktail or two?"

"Lila. You don't want to see me drinking alcohol."

"Oh…I see…It's like that."

"Yeah, it's like that."

"I understand then. But you'll make sure I get home safely, yes?"

"Of course."

We stared.

"How many brothers and sisters?" I said.

Lila bit her lip, the image of a sad little girl.

"Two older brothers and a younger sister."

"Lila…We need to find these people."

Whatever props had been holding her up to that point completely collapsed and she fell against my shoulder in grief. I noticed the bartender coming with Lila's drink and waved him off.

Some minutes later, Lila gathered herself and headed off to the ladies' room. I caught the bartender's attention again and asked him to bring two cappuccinos. When Lila returned, she sat close to me and wrapped both hands around one of the mugs.

"Thanks."

I nodded.

She took a sip and set it down.

"Oh god. This is everything I had dreaded. The police involved and my daughter out there god only knows where."

"Have you tried tracking Holly's phone again?"

"Several times. Late at night, like you had suggested."

She tried again while we were sitting there, but nothing. I had my money on Potter having destroyed the SIM card first thing. He would understand the importance of such things.

"Look, Lila. I'm going to say this again. It's probably best that Holly stole away before Potter and his gang moved up to Crestline. Trust me, I feel like hell about the situation but it could be a lot worse."

"I know, but now we have no idea where she is again."

"We'll keep looking. She'll turn up. I promise you."

Lila nodded and played with her mug. I looked at mine, hoping those weren't hollow words.

Lila kept working at her coffee and was reasonably sober half an hour later. Absentmindedly or not, she had come to be playing with my hand.

"You going to be okay driving yourself home?" I asked her.

"I guess, Michael. I just don't feel like being alone tonight." She looked up from playing with my hand. "It would be nice to have someone around."

"I can probably call you later, Lila, but there are things I need to do. Finding your daughter being foremost among them."

Lila searched my eyes before gathering things back into her purse.

"I'd better let you go then."

"You're sure you'll be all right driving home?"

She nodded. I threw some money on the table and we headed for the door. Day had turned to dusk during our sojourn in the bar. Rush hour traffic rushed past us in the fading light.

We stopped at the door of Lila's Jag. She stared up at me. The wind was doing a ballet with her lovely locks.

"You know, you're awfully handsome, Michael. And kind. I hadn't expected that part." I stared back at her. "I'm sorry. I know. I shouldn't be making a play at my detective."

I continued staring. She searched my eyes for a long moment before reaching up to touch my cheek.

"Thanks for comforting me today...You will call tonight if you can."

I nodded.

"And don't make too much out of what I just said."

"I won't."

A shadow passed over Lila's countenance with those words. She searched my eyes for a moment before climbing into her Jaguar. I waited as she did her patented housekeeping in the mirror, fussed with the radio and pulled on her seat belt. There was a final look my way before driving off. I climbed into my Impala and headed for the freeway, torn even more so now over my feelings for the woman. Sympathy, of course, over her having been abandoned. And swayed by her beauty. What mortal man could ignore it? It grabbed you by the heart and dragged you in. To consume you in the end, I assumed. I knew that once I had tasted the drug of Lila, I would never be able to get her totally out of my blood. But someone had put a bullet into her last husband and I had every reason to believe that Lila was the one who had pulled the trigger.

Remembering everything, from her look of disdain upon walking into my office that first day, to her curious attitude towards her missing daughter, to her pass at me just now — You're awfully handsome, Michael — to her ensuing look of disappointment when I had failed to take the bait, I could not escape a sick feeling that I was being played somehow.

Well, I'm nobody's fool, Lila. Not anymore. No more of this having my guts kicked in over a woman. I trust no one, and least of all you.

And still I wanted her badly.

Driving along, a carousel of all the beautiful women I had loved over the years made a pass through my head. So many lovely ladies, so many wonderful memories, and all of them gone.

Naturally, Elfie did a lap of her own, and with one more stab of regret. I had beat myself up abundantly over that decision. A silky blonde doll with no end of money? Never another care in the world?

We had seen each other several times after my return from that trip down to Baja, encounters that had been intelligent, playful and wonderfully carnal, but it was just as she had said. Elfie couldn't forget the death of her little girl and I had been unable kick the other woman. In the end, Elfie had gone off to live in Switzerland, leaving behind an invitation to join her, an invitation I had failed to accept.

Then there was Audrey. Even now, just the thought of her long red hair and pale skin swept me away. But the truth was, that romance never stood a chance. Audrey and I were cut from different cloth, forged in different fires. It had become clear to me after only one date. She would never understand who I was, and I could never really love what chasing after money had done to her.

Add it all up and a tragic streak seemed to run through my romantic impulses. A man would be dumb to think otherwise.

I came out of my reveries to find a grim industrial area alongside the freeway. Low slung concrete buildings backed up against a chain link fence, with stacks of empty pallets and trash stuck to the fence everywhere.

Hating all that had become grim about this world, I switched to my '40s station and found Glen Miller swinging away. Visions of that faraway time settled over my day. Long ago, in another time and place, Lila was waiting in high heels and apron at the end of the day.

"Cocktail, dear?"

We had a forties kitchen, forties sofa, forties everything. The two of us would live happily ever after.

Until she put a bullet in me.

A mile or so past Corona, my phone rang, dispersing Glenn Miller and my pleasant visions. It was Bennie. I answered.

"What's up? And please don't give me any shit about not liking you."

"Boss man, I figured out a long time ago that you don't like me, so don't even go there with that shit."

"Goddamn it, Bennie. Just get to the point. If I want to argue, I'll get a wife."

"Boss, with your shit, you ain't never gonna have a wife…"

"Just get to the point!!!" I yelled in the direction of my phone.

"Wow, dude. Chill out. You seriously need to get to a meeting."

I rubbed my forehead.

"Please, Bennie, just tell me why you called before I have to drive over there and shoot you."

"Okay. I started following said son-in-law around this morning and he led me out to some kind of meth lab or crack house on the backside of Baldy."

"What are you talking about?"

"Just like I said. I followed him up into those shit forsaken hills above Pear Blossom Highway and he eventually parked at this rundown looking stucco ranch house. Nothing around it for miles. I saw a sign for The Devil's Punchbowl so that ought to tell you some shit right there."

I almost laughed. Bennie and his conspiracies.

"And why do you figure it was some kind of meth lab or crack house?"

"Come on. Way the fuck out there? With a bunch of Harleys parked out in front?"

"Well, you hadn't mentioned the Harleys."

82

"I was getting to that."

"Then please cut to the chase. What the hell would Nicholas be doing out there with a bunch of bikers?"

"What do you think? He was fencing something."

"Fencing what? The Picasso?"

"No, man. Those dudes don't want no Picasso."

"Then just describe what you saw. And any time today will do."

Bennie got in his daily dose of Spanish. I happened to be taking a sweeping turn onto the toll road right then, with what was left of the Santa Ana River in my rearview mirror. In my youth it had been a wild place, where my friends and I had rafted down through the bamboo groves on lazy summer afternoons.

I was still lost in those memories when Bennie finally shut up.

"So?" I said.

"So, I'm taking a deep breath and saying the short version of the serenity prayer."

"Which is?"

"Fuck it."

I laughed.

"I don't know how we get going like this, Bennie, but please just finish your story. What did he have and why do you think he was fencing it?"

"Well, for starters, I had to hang back and park, so by the time I got up on this knoll to scope things out with my binoculars, Nicholas was already heading up to the house but he had something wrapped in a towel. About the size of a shopping bag so I'm guessing it was an ancient artifact or something. It wasn't no Picasso, I can tell you that."

An ancient artifact.

"And then what?"

"Then he knocks on the door and this Mexican biker looking dude answered it."

"Whoa, wait a minute. Mexican biker dude?" I told him about the card I had found at Potter's place. "So you think this could be our El Chango?"

"Could be. They're definitely Mongols."

"Okay. So then what?"

"So then that biker dude invited Nicholas in and about half an hour later, Nicholas comes back out looking real stoned and with just the towel."

"So you think he traded whatever this thing was for some drugs."

"That's my thinking."

"And where is he now?"

"Doheny Beach. I'm down here right now, staking out his place. Nice view of the coast. I think I can see the Mexican border. Makes me want to head that way. I was going to say, you'll have to invite me down to your place someday but I know that's never going to happen."

He was right, but I wasn't about to say as much.

"Yeah, I knew it," he said. "So what do you want me to do here?"

"Keep an eye on him. Are you good for tonight?"

"I'd be a lot better off if I had the van."

"I'll drop it off later."

"Why not Billy?"

"Because I told him to take the rest of the day off."

I explained what had gone down out in Berdoo and up on the mountain.

"Man, why do I always miss out on the action?"

"Consider yourself lucky, Bennie."

"Yeah, right. You don't know shit. I was nearly special forces in the army."

"So I've heard."

"Yeah, go ahead and yank my chain...And by the way, I don't ever remember you giving me the day off with pay."

"I can't remember the last time you had bikers shooting at you."

"Well, if that's what it takes, I'll see what I can do."

"I'm just going to leave that one right there, Bennie."

"Yeah, go ahead, boss man. Yank my chain. That's what you're good at."

"Come on, Bennie. You don't think I appreciate all your good work?"

"Yeah?"

"Of course."

"Well, what do you know? A benny for Bennie."

"Yeah...So back to those Mongols dudes. You think there could be a connection between them and Potter?"

"No way. You can forget that shit right now. A white supremacist? Those dudes would turn his ass into beef jerky."

"Well, there has to be some reason why Potter wrote El Chango's name on the back of his card."

"Probably planning to dust his ass."

"Maybe...Okay, I need to run. I'm coming up on my turnoff to Jack Oliver's place."

"I thought you took him dinner on Thursday nights."

"I do, but I'm already driving right by his exit. Figured I'd save myself an extra trip tomorrow."

"How's he doing these days."

"Oh, still the same old cranky bastard."

Bennie laughed.

"Hey, how about bringing me some grub and sodas when you come."

"No problem. I'll stop at Huffie's down at the harbor."

"So when should I expect you?"

"Sometime early tonight."

"I'll be hanging."

"I'll be by as soon as I can get free...And, hey. Get a bug on Nicholas' car as soon as it's dark, in case we lose him."

"Consider it done.

Eight

Our call ended as I was coming up on Santiago Canyon Road. I took the exit and turned right at the stoplight. Thirty years earlier, I would have been greeted with rolling hills and untamed country. Now, strip malls and car dealerships crowded the roadside. In Southern California, you could go home again, but the places of your youth were no longer there.

Three miles farther on, I arrived at the long grade leading down into El Modena. The Broasted Chicken restaurant with its strutting rooster neon sign came into view as I made the last turn, and with it, more memories. So many times on our way home from the beach or after school, my friends and I had driven over there to gorge on the chicken and talk away an afternoon.

I parked in back, went in to order two dinners and headed up to Jack's place. There had been talk among his kids of placing him in a nursing home but Jack put the kibosh on that idea straight off. Said he'd blow his brains out first. So the kids lent a hand, an LVN came around three times a week to help him bathe and prepare some meals and I brought him dinner every Thursday, while listening to his interminable rants. He had given me a key to let myself in.

"Who the hell's that?" he called out when he heard the door opening.

"Your Aunt Gertrude."

"What the hell are you doing here? It's Wednesday."

86

"I was driving by and thought I'd save myself a trip."

"You might have warned me."

"Up yours too," I said and headed out to the kitchen.

I got the meals arranged on two plates and carried them out to the living room. Jack had a TV dinner stand in front of his recliner. The TV was blaring on his favorite conspiracy news channel.

"Turn that thing off," I said about the TV.

"Yeah. You ought to listen. You might learn something."

"Yeah. I'll learn why you're nuts…Come on. Turn it off."

He muted the sound. I got his meal set up.

"You want a beer or what?"

"A beer, yeah."

I set my meal down on the coffee table and went to grab one.

"So what the hell brought you out here?" Jack said as I was opening it.

"Working a case out in San Berdoo, chasing after a runaway girl. And then a dead body turned up."

That got Jack's attention.

"No shit. Tell me about it."

I settled in on the sofa and explained things.

"Any leads?" he said when I was done.

"No. I was hoping you'd have some idea. I don't know anything about these right-wing conspiracy nuts."

"Christ, Devlin. I don't like being overrun by Mexicans but these guys are in another league altogether."

"Yeah. You know anything about this Mr. Evergreen?"

"I've heard stories but I don't have the inside contacts anymore. I know this much. The old man would have fucked a poodle if it had lipstick."

That got a look out of me. I stared for a long moment before returning to my meal.

"So this Lila's a real firecracker, huh?" he said.

"Yeah. I'm torn between wanting to nail her seven ways from Sunday and fearing a knife in my back."

"Yeah. You were always letting your brains go out your pecker."

"Like you never screwed the clientele."

He chuckled.

"Yeah. That's the ace of being a detective. You never know when it's going to jump in your lap...I remember this one time, back in '57 or so, when I was first starting out. I had nailed this guy for cheating on his wife and went over to collect the final payment. She comes out wearing a negligee and high heels. A real pinup doll. Told me she just wanted her revenge and did I mind? Holy Jesus. When we were all done, she walks me to the door with a final kiss. 'I hope you liked your bonus, Mr. Oliver.' Oh yeah, honey, I liked it just fine. I went on banging her for another year before she finally moved on."

"Yeah. All your brains went out your pecker."

He laughed and had another bite of his meal.

I cleaned up when we were done and stopped in the living room.

"Clueless as usual," Jack said.

"I have the ring."

"Check with your jeweler buddy."

"Yeah. I was planning to do that."

We stared.

"Is it just me, Jack, or was it really a better world back then?"

"Oh, hell. Way better. Too many people now. I remember having to drive down to Huntington Beach or something and passing through nothing but farm country. The world was all young and wide open and full of potential."

"Makes you want to cry, huh?"

"Yeah, we'll both be gone soon enough but you think of the young kids these days."

"We've left them a bag of shit, haven't we?"

"Yeah we have."

"Who do you blame for that?"

"Fucking liberals, who do you think?"

I scoffed.

"Does that mean you're going to start sending back your Social Security checks and get off of Medicare?"

"Up yours."

"Yeah yeah. You're just like the rest of your nut jobs. Not an ounce of intellectual integrity among you."

"Yeah, you just wait until we have the revolution."

"Revolution, my ass…The only way you bastards can stay in power is by staging a junta."

I started to leave.

"I'll see you next week."

"Yeah. Thanks for the warning."

I flipped him off on my way out the front door.

Half an hour later, at dusk, I was motoring down from the hills into lush farm country. The scent of crops and orange blossoms bled through the smell of burning brush.

Up ahead, I came to the corridor of high-tech industry along Interstate 5. A minute later, I was cutting through a gap in the coastal hills. In the last sylvan light, a nature preserve now surrounded me. Herons and cottontails dotted the rippling marshes.

Fifteen minutes later, I was pulling into the backside of Laurel Lagoon and headed for the police station. The gay guy who had been manning the front desk for the past five years was now on parking enforcement. I saw him from time to time around town, making people miserable. He had nailed me twice.

The new cadet looked fruity too. Maybe being gay had become a prerequisite for manning the front desk at the Laurel Lagoon Police Department. At least the new guy was pleasant. I received a smile and a prompt buzz of the gate when I asked to see Whalen and showed him my license.

Whalen glanced up from the file in his hands when I appeared. It struck me how little he had changed over the years — graying but still the buffed-out lifeguard type.

"Hello to you, too," I said, sitting down.

"I'm still pissed at you for hanging up on me."

Whalen's eyes remained focused on his file.

"You can throw me out a window now if you'd like."

He gave me a quick review.

"No new battle scars, I see. I'll assume you've been staying out of trouble."

"Mostly."

He nodded and looked back at his file.

"So, to what do I owe the pleasure?"

"I came to warn you about a terrorist attack."

That got Whalen's attention.

"Don't ever say something like that. Not unless you really mean it. Or you'll find yourself in the gray bar hotel."

"Yeah, right. I've been thinking to shoot the president, too."

Whalen stared for a moment and looked back at his file.

"Go on. Spill it."

"Oh, a client had some things lifted and I wondered if you could keep an eye out for them."

"Yep, the usual. Devlin down here wanting me to do his job for him."

I smirked.

"I'm just saying, Pat. If something resembling this stolen property crosses your desk, please let me know."

"Why doesn't your client just file a police report?"

I rubbed my thumb and fingers together. Whalen glanced up.

"Who?"

"I probably shouldn't say."

"Same old shit."

"Come on, Pat. Let's say this client did file a report. It's not like you'd send out the cavalry looking for it."

Whalen stared.

"And what are we looking for?"

"A Picasso. Minor work but of sentimental value. And some jewelry."

I described both the painting and the jewelry.

"How long has the jewelry been missing?"

"Three or four days."

"It's probably been fenced by now."

"Yeah."

Whalen returned to ignoring me. I drummed my fingers on his desk.

"Do you find this kind of stuff usually stays in the area. Or gets shipped off to distant shores?"

"I don't find anything usual in this world. Except for you being a pain in the ass."

I stared until Whalen looked up from his file.

"It usually doesn't go far. Maybe up to LA, or down to Dago. Maybe as far as Vegas or the Bay Area. Depends on how valuable it is. Are you going to take a Picasso on a commercial flight with you?" he asked rhetorically. "Or ship a two thousand dollar brooch overseas? You're either talking big time money and private jets or it's still in the area."

I nodded.

"Don't I remember you having a jeweler friend?" Whalen asked.

"Yeah."

"Check with him on the jewelry. Most pawnshops are a bust. Some jewelers may not be so picky. Anyway, they usually have a network of contacts."

"Thanks for the tip," I said, standing up.

"Yeah? What do you have for me?"

"Seabiscuit in the third at Santa Anita."

"Prick."

I smiled and started out the door.

"Hey," Whalen said. I stopped and looked back. "Were you serious about this terrorist attack?"

"No. But maybe about shooting the president."

"Son of a bitch. Go on, get out of here before I lock you up."

I went out to my car, somewhat reassured. Yeah, Whalen was a prick, but it did not appear that he had gone over to the dark side, at least not completely.

91

Back at my office a few minutes later, I unlocked the door to find the afternoon wind had scattered papers all over the floor. As I went about gathering things up and closing the windows, I noticed what appeared to be a huge cruise ship parked off the coast. What in the world?

Before logging online to see what that was all about, I called Billy. No answer. I hung up and stared out at the ship, concerned on two fronts now. Billy and his sobriety, of course. But cruise ships? Had Laurel Lagoon become a port of destination? I smelled Anton's fingerprints on this one somehow.

I got back to worrying about Billy. He had been in and out of recovery so many times over the past two years, I had lost count. It was day to day with that boy, and sometimes minute to minute. Meanwhile, I was left to track down the van.

While listening to voice messages, I tried to get online and received an error message. I tried several more times with the same results. I checked my phone and saw it was still on the network. Shit. Somewhere in Sudan, a mother and child were starving, but I was ready to blow a gasket over my internet.

With the modem rebooting, I called Betty but she was gone for the day. I hung up and stared at the modem. Horizon and their cheesy equipment. There had been nothing but trouble since I switched over to them.

Once the modem booted back up, I tried logging on again, and again received an error message. I looked around the office for something to throw.

It took me five minutes to navigate Horizon's automated phone system and get an actual human being on the line. I explained the situation and was told to reboot the modem.

"I've already done that."

"Wait a minute, then."

While I waited, I remembered Bennie's words. 'You need to get to a meeting or something.'

And maybe I did. Or maybe I just needed a good romp in the hay with Lila. That ought to fix all my problems. Or maybe it would just create a whole new set of them. I kind of knew the answer to that question before I had asked it.

"It looks as if your modem is bad," I heard the tech gal saying.

"Great. So what do we do?"

"You can either go out and buy a new one or buy one from us."

"Buy one? I'm leasing the goddamned thing from you."

"Please don't talk to me like that, sir."

"Well don't tell me you don't warranty your own equipment."

"If you read your contract, you…"

"And don't tell me to read my contract! I'm leasing this modem from you and expect you to warranty it!"

"Sir. I asked you to please not talk to me like that."

I sat there stewing.

"As I was trying to say, when you signed your contract, you were offered a choice. Buy a modem from us or go out and buy your own and you chose to buy it from us. You're not leasing it. You're just making monthly installments."

Great. I wanted to strangle her.

"Let's get this straight," I said with all the restraint I could muster. "I don't care if I'm buying this equipment from you or leasing it or whatever. I consider it your crap, all right? So either you warranty it or I'm calling your competitor."

"I'm sorry but I don't have the authority to replace it for free."

"Then I'm cancelling my account!"

"Fine. I'll transfer you over to billing."

She was gone before I could scream at her again. I beat the phone on my desk a few times for good measure. Meanwhile, their canned messaging system was telling me what a great company they were.

The accounts gal finally came on the phone and I gave her a piece of my mind. She tired of my harangue and offered me up to customer loyalty.

"Customer loyalty?!" I said. "You're kidding, right!? You have a department that you only reveal to people once they go postal!!!?"

I shut up to find that this woman had disappeared on me too. Oh man. I really needed to shoot someone.

A minute later, a rep with this super-secret customer loyalty department came on and succeeded in calming me down a bit. The long and short of it was, she would replace the modem for free but couldn't get a tech guy out there until the following Monday.

"Monday! I need my internet right now!"

"Calm down. If you're in a rush, go out and buy one and call me back. I'll credit your account for whatever it is."

I hated her a bit for taking the air out of my rant.

"Fine," I said.

I jotted down her direct line, hung up the phone and stared out at the coast. I had heard people talk in meetings about emotional hangovers and thought I might be having one.

I had another idea and called Kenny.

"I've got that report on your Latino hitman," he said in answering. "And my witness protection fees have really gone up."

"Fine, whatever. I've got bigger fish to fry right now."

I explained about the modem.

"I gather you want me to come over and rescue you."

"Please. Before I find myself wanted for murder."

He laughed and said he would be right over. I hung up and tried calling Billy again. Still no answer. He might have been sleeping, but I doubted it. Something didn't smell right.

While waiting for Kenny, I considered all the apologies I now had to make, to various phone reps around the world, that I would never see or hear from again. Kenny slipped in through the door before I got too carried away with that idea, a modem in one hand, a report in the other. He plopped the report down on my desk.

"This guy makes Potter look like a cream puff."

94

I opened the report and found a ruthless looking man staring back at me, dark hair down to his shoulders and the fierceness of a cornered jaguar in his eyes. He was strangely handsome, despite his face being heavily scarred by acne.

Kenny was trying to squeeze in to where the modem was connected under my desk so I rolled my chair out of the way. While he worked, I explained about my struggles with Horizon.

"I'm thinking to sue. I've always found it the best way to initiate negotiations."

Kenny popped back up with a smile and took control of my mouse. A minute later, he had my internet up and running again.

"Want to see if your rant is trending on Twitter."

I smiled and nodded at the ship parked out there off the coast.

"You have any idea what that's all about?"

"District Nine?"

I imitated his dry laugh.

"But seriously. A cruise ship?"

"Yeah, it was just heading back to San Diego from a cruise along the Mexican Riviera when some of the passengers tested positive for that new virus."

"I thought they had contained it in Asia."

"Guess you haven't been checking the news lately."

"Not today. Why?"

"Outbreaks in five more countries. And on several of these cruise ships. The Dow tanked four thousand points before closing."

"Great. I'm guessing Der Fuhrer is in a state."

"On a tweet bomb all afternoon."

I shook my head.

"God help us."

Kenny smiled.

"Any news on Potter and Holly?"

I explained what had been happening and looked back at the report.

"Armando 'El Chango' Villarreal. I don't get it. Why in hell would Donald Ray Potter have a phone number for this bit of Bruder Schweigen?"

Kenny shrugged. I flipped the page to El Chango's rap sheet.

"Holy Jesus. You're right. Potter's a creampuff compared to this guy."

I flipped another page and swore out loud.

"What?" Kenny said.

"Bennie followed Nicholas out to a place near Pear Blossom Highway earlier today, so if that's El Chango's last known address, it sounds like it might be the same biker gang."

"It's all becoming clear, my dear Watson."

"Yeah. I wish it was."

Kenny headed for the door.

"Hey, you need money?" I called after him.

He paused there.

"Yeah. I'll put together a bill and send it over."

"Don't forget about the router."

"And the witness protection program."

"I'm afraid to ask how much that's going to cost me."

"You should be."

"Yeah…Anyway, thanks for rescuing me. I really appreciate it."

"No sweat."

Kenny started to leave again.

"Oh, hey," I said before he could completely disappear. "I almost forgot. I'm looking for Mrs. Evergreen's long-lost siblings. Two brothers and a sister."

I scribbled the names down on a piece of paper and handed it across my desk.

"That's the paternal name, the mother's maiden name and the names of the three siblings. See what you can find out."

"Will do. Any idea where to start?"

"Well, as you had suspected from this Cabot business, Lila grew up in Ohio. And the last place she saw her siblings."

"It's Lila now, huh?"

"Yeah. I think she's going to stab me in the back any minute but we're cozy."

Kenny smiled and started down the hallway. I remembered one more thing and called out again.

A moment later, Kenny reappeared.

"Yeah?"

I was scrolling through my iPhone and held up a finger.

"Just a second. I forgot to show you this."

Once I had the photo from Potter's place pulled up, I showed it to him.

"Remember that business with the beheaded cleric?"

"Yeah."

"It's the same shit."

"Yeah, well, it's pretty common to all these white supremacists."

I stared.

"I hate it when you take the air out of my paranoid conspiracies." He chuckled. "So? Do these symbols mean anything to you?"

"I know that one," he said, pointing. "It's the Othala rune."

"Sounds like something out of the Lord of the Rings."

"Kind of is. It comes from the Norsemen."

"Why them?"

"Because they liked making up runes."

"Funny."

"Yeah...Anyway, then the Nazis came along and coopted it."

"They ruin everything."

Kenny laughed.

"Go on," I said.

"So, the Norsemen believed these runes had powers and this one was meant to maintain balance between the physical and spiritual realms. Then the Nazis somehow turned that into their superior race thing."

"They really do ruin everything."

"Yeah. Just text me that pic and I'll look into the rest of it."

"Oh hell. I'll look into it. I just figured you'd know something off the top of your head."

He smiled and headed out the door again.

"But nothing more on Cabot?" I said.

"Nothing yet."

"Okay. Keep me posted."

"Will do."

"And thanks again."

He disappeared. I stalled there behind my desk, wanting to call Detective Barnes about El Chango but not having a good reason why I'd know the first thing about him. I couldn't even think of a good reason why I'd know so much about Potter, except to say that I had been hiding things.

I picked up Donald Ray Potter's card again. What would tie Potter, Nicholas and some Mexican gangbangers together? Jack was right. I was clueless.

I decided to let the matter rest another day and headed out the door.

Nine

On my way up the Third Street hill, I noticed a forest-green Audi A8 hugging my tail. When I turned right onto Legion, the car followed. The same when I turned left onto Glenneyre. I stepped on the gas and jockeyed around traffic but the car kept pace with my every maneuver, and followed me again when I turned left up Bluebird. With the windshield being heavily tinted, I was unable to make out the driver's face but could tell it was a man, with hair down over his ears.

When I made the final turn onto my dead-end street, I saw the car slow to a crawl in my rearview mirror. I braked to a stop in front of my garage and jumped out. The driver raced away as I started up the block towards Bluebird on foot.

I stood there, fuming. Naturally Cole Pritchett came to mind. It had been the right length of hair, but I struggled to picture him driving an A8. Number one, it wasn't his kind of ride. And two, I seriously doubted the man could afford one. The last I had seen Cole, he was driving an old stripped down Camaro.

Beyond Cole Pritchett, the list of people who'd love to see me six feet under was a long one. I had helped to put a lot of folks behind bars over the years. But why now? Nothing added up in my brain.

The only other possible explanation was Vanderhof. I had been on his tail since he got out of prison, and he had been known to return the favor, but an A8? To Vanderhof, that was a junker.

I waited several minutes to see if the car came back down Bluebird and finally gave up.

Up in my home office, I tried reaching Billy again. No luck. He had been crashing at his parents' place off and on over the past few months so I tried their home number.

After several rings, his step-father answered. I asked if he had seen Billy. He told me Billy had run off with his old girlfriend that afternoon.

That was bad news; really bad news. Every time Billy got near that woman, his life careened off a cliff. There were car wrecks, overdoses, fistfights and arrests. If Billy woke up with his car missing and his wallet gone, that was getting off easy. The results were usually far worse.

Meanwhile his step-father had gone off on a rant. Of course Billy went out. He's an idiot and would never amount to anything. It was a common riff by normal people about alcoholics. Just show a bit of backbone. Try to control your drinking. To them, booze was a choice, not a fix. They couldn't understand a man drinking himself into the gutter.

As soon as there was an opening, I interrupted his rant.

"I trust he didn't take my van."

"Oh no. It's parked right out there in the driveway."

"Good. I'll be over in a little while to pick it up."

Before the old man could get going again, I told him I had another call coming in and hung up.

While changing clothes, I called a taxi company. A thirty dollar cab ride later, I was in possession of the van and headed down the coast towards Bennie's stakeout. No sign of that A8 on my tail but it was still leaving tire tracks in my brain.

Along the way, I called Mr. Huntington.

"Yes, Mr. Devlin," he said by way of answering. "What have you learned?"

"Sorry to say, nothing about the Picasso and jewelry but I think you may have something else missing."

I explained about Nicholas' sortie out to the biker's den.

"Very well. I will have a look at what was readily within his grasp and return your call."

I hung up, feeling like hell for Mr. Huntington. He had enough money to live like a king for a thousand years, but it was useless against a world now going mad. Barbarians were at the gates. Rome would soon be sacked.

Still, I'd take his money in a heartbeat. Knowing you could live like a king for a thousand years? I had no earthly idea how that would feel.

Down by the harbor entrance, I pulled into a fast food drive-thru and bought Bennie the works. He was slumped down in the front seat when I walked up to his car, his back to the driver's side door.

"Don't even think you're sneaking up on me," he said with a glance my way.

"Oh yeah. There's no getting one past Bennie 007 Morales."

"Damned straight, boss man. Ain't nothing going on around here without me knowing about it."

Bennie poked his head up far enough to see over the seat. With his pencil mustache and perfectly coifed hair, he looked like Cesar Romero.

"Where's the van?" he said.

"I had thought to parade it around out here for the idiot son-in-law to see but a strange premonition came over me."

"Real funny."

Bennie sat up now.

"Did you bring some food?"

"It's in the van."

"Where's Billy?"

"MIA."

"Shit. Don't tell me he ran off with that floozy again."

I nodded. Bennie shook his head in disgust.

"He's going to kill himself over a piece of pussy."

"He wouldn't be the first man to do it."

I pointed my chin back up the street.

"Come on, let's do this. And leave the keys in your ignition. I took a cab over to Billy's place."

I walked back up to the corner and watched Bennie park his car behind the van. As soon as he had moved the van around to Nicholas' street and was settled in place, I called him.

"What's up?" he said.

"Nothing. Just giving you a heads up. I'm off to get some shuteye. As soon as I'm back on my feet, I'll call you."

"You got it. And thanks for the food. Let's see. A couple of burgers, an extra-large fry, a large coke and a coffee. Wow. Even an apple turnover. You're a pretty decent guy for a dick."

"Yeah, thanks. Just keep an eye on what's his name down there. I'll be back in a few hours. And don't call me unless guns are going off."

"You got it."

I hung up and started Bennie's hotrod Honda Civic. It made you want to hide. He had lowered it, added flames and installed a spoiler on the back. The tires had one inch of rubber on them. It sounded like a juiced up vacuum cleaner and rode like a covered wagon. At every stoplight, I stared straight ahead, pretending I wasn't there. Pushing a shopping cart down Coast Highway would have been less embarrassing.

There was one upside. It gave me cover from that A8. Just for the hell of it, I drove a mile farther up Bluebird, looking for any sign of it, but nothing.

Back at the house, I walked in with a strange feeling that someone had been there. It was a feeling I had experienced before, and had almost always dismissed. It was just me and my imagination, but the feeling remained.

Famished, I nuked some leftover lasagna, gobbled it down and crawled into bed. The phone rang before I had a chance to doze off. It was Mr. Huntington.

"It is as you had suspected, Michael. A bronze figurine of Osiris is missing."

"Shit," I muttered. "Sorry, sir, but I'm just disgusted to hear it."

"Oh, don't worry yourself too much. 26th Dynasty. Not terribly valuable. Enough to buy some drugs, I presume."

"Well, and I'm speculating a bit here, but it does appear that that's exactly what Nicholas did. Fenced it with some bikers."

"Do you happen to have photographic evidence of this transaction."

"No. At least not of the item itself. One of my operatives observed Nicholas taking something into a house but it was wrapped up in a towel. I'm just putting two and two together here."

"I understand."

I was silent.

"You have something else on your mind, Michael."

"I do, sir. Not that it's any of my business, but why do you keep allowing Nicholas access to your belongings? Especially when you say your daughter's already divorcing him."

"No, you're perfectly right to question my behavior. I had just thought it best to keep my reasons private. Out of respect for your wellbeing, mind you. Shall I explain?"

"Please."

"Well, you see, my daughters have no vested interest in my fortune while I'm still alive. Misguidedly or not, I provide both of them with a monthly stipend, but there's nothing of real substance that Nicholas can attach in a divorce proceeding. So, in view of his desperate financial position, my presumption has been, give him enough rope and he'll eventually hang himself. He's certainly tried but I've yet to obtain the hard evidence I need to assist in that endeavor."

I was silent.

"You believe I should have apprised you of my scheme, is that correct, Michael?"

"It would have helped."

"My apologies. In the future then, I won't play my cards so close to the vest."

"I'd appreciate it."

"Apology accepted?"

"Of course."

"Very well. What do you propose we do next?"

"That's really up to you, sir, but given your intentions, there's not much point in me confronting him."

"No no. Messy business. Plus, Nicholas might hang himself yet."

"Then did you want me to continue poking around for the other missing items, or would you prefer me to stop altogether?"

"I would say yes to that question if I weren't so fond of my Picasso. The rest he can have, for all the grief it has caused me."

"I'll continue looking. Discreetly, of course."

Mr. Huntington thanked me again and hung up. I had been close to slumber before his call. Now I was unable to turn my mind off. The lines of that poem popped into my head again. For all eternity, tossed back into the fire. But what did it mean to be alive in this universe? I had no idea. I had no idea why I'd be alive anywhere, in any universe.

The last I looked, the clock read a quarter to ten. I reawakened at a bit past midnight from another frenzied dream about Caitlin. In this edition, I had tried to worm my way back into her life disguised as a door to door salesman. Of course she was immediately on to me and quietly closed the door in my face. Adding insult to injury, Caitlin's new man had been viewing all this from over the back of her sofa.

How many different ways could a man torture himself over a woman?

I checked my phone and saw that Bennie had texted me. Nicholas was on the move and had settled into a nightclub called Zanzibar in Laurel Lagoon. At least the bastard had saved me the trouble of leaving town.

I texted Bennie back to let him know I was up and jumped into the shower. While drying off and getting dressed, it dawned on me that I had forgotten to call Lila. Should I still bother at this hour? I decided that at the very least, a text was in order and dashed one off.

Sorry, Lila. Working late. Just didn't want you to think I had forgotten you.

I glanced at the phone several times while pulling on my socks and shoes, but nothing. She was probably already asleep. Or mad at me. Either way, she had failed to text me back.

Fifteen minutes later, I was parking behind the van on Coast Highway. That A8 was nowhere in sight. Maybe I had been imagining things. He wouldn't have been the first driver to get lost in Laurel Lagoon. But no. His tailing me had been no accident. I remembered how the car had slowed to a crawl as I pulled onto my street.

Down on the highway, I found Bennie parked on the ocean side with the van pointing south, a hundred yards north of the Zanzibar and adjacent to an inn that would have been a Motel 6 if not for its view. I slipped in through the back door. The club was up ahead and opposite us.

"What do you know?" I said, settling in next to Bennie.

"Nothing. He headed up here about an hour ago. He was out there on that second story veranda a little while back. With a pretty nice looking babe. Both of them smoking cigarettes. Then they went back inside."

"Is he driving the same red Cayenne?"

"Same one."

"All right. Go get some sleep. I'll give you until dawn."

"Come on, boss. I may as well sleep in here."

"Suit yourself."

"How about if I slip in there and see what's going on?"

I eyed Bennie and looked back at the club.

"I don't know. Has he ever made you?"

"No way. That fucker doesn't know me from Adam."

I eyed Bennie again.

"Is that how you guys say it down there in Puerto Rico?"

"Él no me conoce desde Adán. Don't mess with me, boss man. We're more gringo down there than you are. You forget we're the fifty-first state."

"You're right. I'd forgotten."

"So?" he said.

"Sure. Go ahead. Just don't start any trouble."

"Don't start any trouble."

Bennie was talking to himself in Spanish on his way out the back door.

I watched him wait for traffic to clear and dash across Coast Highway. A minute later he disappeared into the club. I stared at the front entrance, remembering the old days, when the Zanzibar was a Mexican dive catering to artists and bohemians. The drinks were cheap, the food good. Then big money arrived in Laurel Lagoon, with splashy décor and big prices. Now, there was no place left for a student or starving artist to go. Not that money necessarily ruined everything, but it had done much to ruin this town.

I checked my watch, growing concerned. Then Bennie finally reappeared and hustled across Coast Highway.

"You're not going to believe this shit," he said, climbing in and closing the door. "He's in there with that Vander fuck character."

"Vanderhof?"

"Yeah and I'm going to tell you something right now. That big shot has a harem of dolls draped around him that ought to be waving pom poms at a high school football game. He's making the Pritchett brothers look like saints. Seriously. I can't even believe they're serving those chicks drinks."

"Money," I said.

"Yeah, I guess."

"Okay. Let's put that on the back burner for the moment. What's with Nicholas? Where does he fit into all of this?"

"Oh, he's just hanging around the scene like a lap dog. You know that prick. He has the moral bearings of a virus."

I flashed a look at him and turned my attention back to the monitors. Well, if any of my theories had been bordering on neat and pat heretofore, they sure were blown to hell now.

Vanderhof and Nicholas. What would bring those two together? You had to write it off as a toady trying to mingle with money. Nothing else made sense. And that still left the question of how they had met.

I looked back at Bennie.

"Think you can get a tracer on Vanderhof's rig right now?"

"Shit, boss man. Does my father have a dick?"

"I'm going to go with a maybe on that one."

Bennie stared at me stone faced. I did my best not to smile.

"Look, Vanderhof usually drives a blue Bentley at night. If you don't see that or a yellow Ferrari, give me a call back."

I watched Bennie hustle back across the highway and make his way to a side street adjacent to the club's parking lot. He waited there until all three valets were otherwise distracted, then dashed over to the parking lot and disappeared out of sight. A minute later he was dashing back across Coast Highway.

"Here you go."

Bennie gave me a serial number for the tracer and watched as I typed it into the program. A moment later, I had it pinging on my screen. I logged everything into my laptop and closed it.

"I'm calling it a night."

"Oh yeah. Now that it's your turn, we're packing it in."

"That's why they call me the boss man."

That got Bennie going.

"What the hell?" I said. "We're going to sit around and wait while those two clowns stroke each other? I'll take the van and give chase if warranted but from the looks of things, they're planning to close the bar."

I glanced at my watch.

"That's another hour and a half. Anyway, I can't see where this has anything to do with Huntington's stolen property."

"Maybe he fenced that Picasso to Vanderhof."

107

I looked back at the club and drummed my fingers.

"Maybe. But it still doesn't change things for tonight."

Bennie was staring at the club and playing with the tuft of hair under his lower lip.

"What, Einstein?"

"What? I say fuck all this waiting around. Let's just march those two dudes over to what's his name's place and put a gun to their heads. You know. 'Show us the goddamned Picasso, motherfuckers, or you're dead.' Get some results. That's what."

"We'd get some results, all right. Both of us in jail and me out of business."

"Come on. Just like in the movies. Why not?"

"Because it's not the movies, Bennie."

He smiled.

"Come on. Admit it. You'd like a little taste of that action."

"Oh sure. I'd like everyone in this world doing exactly what I want them to do, and when I want them doing it. It just doesn't work that way."

Bennie looked at the club on our monitors.

"How about just this once?"

"Shit. Talk about needing a meeting."

I stood up and stretched.

"I'm going home to get some more shut eye and you do the same. We'll both need to be bright eyed and bushy tailed tomorrow morning."

"To do what?"

I looked back at the monitors.

"I don't know yet. Probably take on some bikers."

"Now you're being loco. We'd need an army for that kind of shit."

"Maybe. Or maybe we'll just go bearing gifts."

"What do you mean?"

I clicked my tongue in thought.

"I don't know. I'm working on it."

"Well, bikers or not, we're going to need some more bodies. You know, with Billy gone?"

"Yeah. You can forget about him for a while." I looked up from the monitors. "Probably for good."

"Yeah. That dude needs a spiritual awakening. I aksed him the other day if he believed in God and you know what he said? No...I mean, real serious like. Like he wanted to believe real bad but he just couldn't bring himself to do it. What do you do with a sick fuck like that?"

"Pray," I said.

Bennie smiled.

"Hey. Now you're talking program, boss man...You know what? I'm going to go home and pray for you."

"Good. I need it. In the meantime, your hotrod's a few cars back up the highway and the keys are in it."

"Okay, but look. That ain't no shit about needing some extra bodies and I know a perfect guy for the job."

"Yeah? Who?"

"Someone in the program. I see him down at the San Juan club all the time. A real type-A personality. I think he irons his shirts twice before going out the front door. Used to be an accountant for this tech company but got fired for drinking and cooking the books."

"Great. Just the kind of operative I need."

"Hey man. We all got here with some wreckage."

"Yeah? And how long's he been sober?"

"I think three, four years."

"Yeah?"

"Yeah. He's solid. I know this much. He could watch a monitor all night without blinking."

Bennie sat up with his back as straight as a ruler.

"Just like a sphynx in the meetings."

I gave him a look.

"I'm serious. This guy is all serio mundo. Staring straight ahead like he's made of stone or something. I can picture him keeping a log on which way the last alley cat went."

"Okay, okay. What makes you think he needs a job?"

"Because he shared in a meeting the other night about getting pissed at his last boss and walking out."

"Oh for Christ's sake, Bennie."

"No, man. It's cool. He just needs a gig where no one's telling him what to do all the time."

I drummed my fingers in thought.

"You know how to reach him?"

"Yeah. He aksed me for my number the other night after I shared."

"That's cause for concern right there."

Bennie stared.

"Don't kid yourself. I'm a rock star at meetings. People quote my shit all over town."

I scoffed.

"What happened to humility?"

"Hey, I'm humble before God but when I talk shit, people listen."

"With the emphasis on shit."

Bennie stared. I rolled my hand.

"You say you know how to get in touch with this guy? What the hell. Talk to him and see what he says…What's his name?"

"Morey."

"Short for Maurice, I assume?"

"Don't even call him that. He flips out. He's real particular. You know, every hair in place, everything perfectly pressed."

"I got it, Bennie, but maybe you've forgotten that this can be a messy business."

"Hey, we give him a shot and if he can't handle it?" Bennie gestured. "Out the door."

"All right. I'll talk with you tomorrow."

"Yeah, later."

Bennie gave me five, gathered up what remained of his fast food and sodas and started out the back door.

"Oh, hey," I said. "Was it the blue Bentley."

Bennie nodded before disappearing. I sat there staring at the monitors. Nicholas and Vanderhof. Nicholas and the Mongols.

What was it with this guy? Next thing I knew, he'd be hobnobbing with Betty.

Ten

I was there for another minute in thought before opening the door to the front and climbing behind the wheel. The back streets were eerily empty at that hour, the hills up behind town black save for a few window lights.

I parked in my garage and got out with the scent of burnt eucalyptus in the air. The wind had let up a bit over the past several hours but I still heard it calling to me, beckoning to that far off horizon somewhere.

I paused inside my front door, remembering the A8. It had been nowhere in sight. There was the good and bad in that. You did not want to leave such things to my imagination.

In bed, I tossed and turned for a spell, with no new revelations about Nicholas or Vanderhof, or about any of it. Then Caitlin was back in my thoughts. I could hardly remember her kindnesses. The memories of her were all laced with uncaring looks and dismissals of my devotion.

Maybe this was where you went back to see Sylvia the fortune teller. Voodoo was in order, amulets and incantations. If things didn't change soon, the grief of it was going to kill me.

I finally found sleep but was reawakened a few minutes past two by a beep on my laptop. Nicholas and Vanderhof were headed up into the hills behind Laurel Lagoon. I assumed to Vanderhof's place. He had purchased sixteen acres up there while still serving out his manslaughter sentence. What amounted to a mansion soon followed, done up in a mission revival style. The estate included a sprawling guest house, bigger than most homes around town, and a garage big enough to swallow the guest house. Vanderhof spent millions the way I bought new shoes.

When it became clear that the party had settled in at Vanderhof's place, I went back to sleep. At a little past four, the software program beeped me again. Nicholas was on the move. I kept one eye on things until he was safely back home in Doheny Beach, then closed the laptop, hoping Nicholas was done for the night. I was weary and could have slept for a thousand years.

I was just starting to doze off again when that business with Vanderhof and his underaged girls popped back into my thoughts. From investigating him for his ex-wife Elfie during their divorce three years earlier, I already knew that Vanderhof liked them young. He had barely escaped with his scalp for sleeping with a sixteen year old girl.

So why flaunt his sins in public, given the notoriety? And with a whole coterie of underaged girls, no less. That seemed rash. Then maybe he saw safety in numbers.

I made a mental note to look into it further. I'd rather nail the man for murder, but anything would suffice, if it put him back behind bars.

Then Ida Huntington was in my thoughts. She returns home from Paris with an anarchist boyfriend, then goes off and marries Nicholas? From a Molotov cocktail throwing radical to a rightwing MAGA nut? Maybe that's why she was divorcing Nicholas, but it was one more thing that didn't add up. What on earth had brought those two people together in the first place? I made a mental note to dig into her life, too. If nothing else, Ida might lead me to Charlotte. Charlotte may have resented Ida's beauty but that probably would not have stopped her from reaching out to Ida, if and when she needed help.

As I lay there trying to make sense of it all, Holly returned to my thoughts. Where in the world was the poor thing? With all the distractions, I had nearly forgotten about her. I pictured her all alone out there with her fears and bruises and abandoned dreams.

The following morning, I was cleaning up the breakfast dishes and still deliberating over the previous night's events when a large moving van passed by my front fence, backing down the block in reverse. The driver hit the air brakes with the cab adjacent to my driveway.

It had to be the new neighbor moving in. Glenn from across the street had told me she was a middle-aged divorcee. That was cause for concern. The previous owner had been as quiet as a mouse. Now there was the prospect of ditzy girlfriends coming and going at all hours of the day and night. The neighbor's house was at the end of our cul-de-sac, thus at a right angle to mine, and effectively below street level, save for the garage. Plus, there was a sizable, pie-shaped plot of land separating our two lots, along with a towering jacaranda, but the house was still next door.

A dry wind stirred in the eucalyptus trees just then, whispering of Zen. A release from bondage was near. Reflexively, I tried to grab hold of it, and as always, the feeling promptly vanished into thin air.

Hell.

Captive of this world again, I grabbed the phone and called Bennie.

"Please come pick up the van," I said when he answered.

"And do what?"

"Stake out Nicholas."

"Where is he now?"

"At home."

"What happened after I left last night?"

"They went up to Vanderhof's mansion."

"And did what?"

"Oh, I'm guessing they brought in Taylor Swift for a bit of entertainment."

"Did anyone ever punch you in the nose for being a dick, boss man?"

"Once or twice."

"Didn't learn nothing, huh?"

"Not much. Just come get the van before I feel the urge to shoot you again."

I put the phone down on the counter while Bennie let off a bit of steam. When there was silence, I picked up the phone again.

"If you're done, head this way."

"Fucker."

"Yeah, yeah."

I started to hang up but called out again.

"Hey."

"Yeah, what?"

"What about this Morey guy?"

"I called and left him a message but he hasn't called me back. I'll have to chase him down at a meeting. That's if I can ever get some time off from work."

"You have my blessings to attend a meeting."

"Yeah? You ought to try it sometime."

Bennie hung up before I had a chance to go off on him. The little prick. But he was right. I hadn't been to a meeting in over a week and whenever I got too far away from them, paranoia crept in. Enemies were everywhere. I was Bogart in The Treasure of the Sierra Madre.

Nobody messes with Fred. C. Dobbs if they know what's good for them.

I moved on to preparing for work with Bennie's snarky comment doing laps in my head.

Out in the garage and seated in my Impala a short time later, I hit the garage door opener, only to find that moving van blocking my driveway. I backed out to where I could see the new neighbor's place and tapped on the horn a few times. When that effort failed to rouse anyone, I laid on the horn. Presently, three movers came rushing up from her below street level home. They were Middle Eastern in appearance and headed my way, ready for jihad.

I had gotten out to confront them when the new neighbor appeared and rushed over to get between us.

"Hi, I'm Fitzy," she said with a breezy laugh.

You would have thought we were heading off to the beach that day. All we lacked were some sand pails and an umbrella.

"Michael Devlin," I said with a glance at her movers.

They stood restlessly behind Fitzy.

"It's okay," she told them. "Let's go ahead and get your truck moved out of his way."

In a kaleidoscope of nervous energy and more breezy laughter, Fitzy played traffic cop and soon had the van backed up twenty feet. I eased my car onto the street and the movers pulled the moving van back into its previous position.

"Thanks, you guys," Fitzy told them.

They had a few more looks my way while heading back down to her place.

Fitzy stood over my open window with a smile. She had rose petal skin and beautiful brown eyes, but the eyes had prominent dark rings beneath them. I chalked that up to the recent divorce.

I noticed a very expensive SUV in Fitzy's perfectly organized garage. Given that she had just paid a few million for the house, you had to assume an abundance of money. On a day of work, she was wearing silk like it was cotton and had an air that only the well-to-do can pull off.

"I am so sick of this smoke," Fitzy said with one of her laughs.

"It's practice for purgatory."

"God, don't even say that..."

I shrugged.

"Oh, one of the neighbors mentioned that you're a private detective."

"Yeah, which one? I'll have to have him investigated." Fitzy laughed. "Welcome to the neighborhood, by the way. It's just you then?"

"No. I have a teenage daughter…"

We stared.

"Divorce," she added.

"Sorry to hear it."

"It's okay. He was a bastard."

Fitzy blithely filled me in on the dirt while keeping an eye on a neighbor watering his lawn up the block. My participation in the conversation did not appear to be of any great importance to her.

I learned from Fitzy's rambling monologue that her ex had bought himself a new red Porsche before running off with a young tart. Of course Fitzy was suing the crap out of him. When she mentioned that she was a life coach and personal organizer, I feared for the world.

With her back to the house, Fitzy failed to notice that her teenage daughter had made an appearance at the top of their stairs. The daughter was barefoot, wearing shorts, torn from a pair of old jeans, a jersey blouse that had been ripped up to look punk and was staring petulantly in our direction. Her long, silky brown hair was a bit unkempt, but with a face like hers, a man could forgive the sloppy housekeeping.

The daughter quickly grew bored and disappeared back down the stairs. Desperate to make my own escape, I told Fitzy that I had some pressing business downtown and drove off without too many bruised feelings.

Things could have been worse, I thought. Ditzy Fitzy might benefit from a basket weaving class or some other such meaningful diversion, but she wasn't the type to throw wild parties and upend our quiet neighborhood. At least that did not appear to be the case on the face of it.

On my way down to the office, I noticed that the A8 was back on my tail and cursed. Son of a bitch. Who was this guy?

At the first opportunity, I pulled to the curb, thinking to get his license plate number going by but he noticed my maneuver and made a quick right on the cross street behind me. Now hemmed in by traffic, I waited impatiently for it to clear, then sped up to the next cross street and turned right up to Catalina. With no sign of the car in either direction, I doubled back to Glenneyre, but still no sign of him. Half mad over the whole thing, I headed on to my office.

There at my desk, I checked phone messages with that A8 doing more laps in my head. Nothing you can do about it now, I reminded myself, but it went on dogging me.

With a number of calls to make, I weighed which one to tackle first. I was still itching to talk to Barnes about El Chango but had yet to come up with any good reason why I would know about him. Everything pointed to me tampering with evidence. At the very least, I was keeping secrets.

I leaned back in my chair. This rigorous honesty business was starting to give me an ulcer. I could picture a nervous breakdown up ahead. I consoled myself with knowing that if I told the truth in every instance, I wouldn't have a business, but it wasn't much of a consolation.

I had been sitting there for a spell longer, trying to see through the mist when I decided to hell with it. I needed answers and Barnes probably had them.

A desk sergeant at the San Berdoo police station answered my phone call.

"Is Detective Barnes in?" I asked.

"Yeah, he's around," I was told and placed on hold.

Most of a minute went by before Barnes came on the line.

"Any news on your end?" I asked after identifying myself.

"Not much. I have half of Potter's gang behind bars. The other half are dead or scattered to the wind. Mostly dead."

"And no word on who that was, buried out in the woods?"

"They have a DNA sample. Now all we need is a match."

"What about Potter? Anything on him specifically?"

118

"Listen, Devlin. How about you coming clean? I've got a funny feeling you know something you're not telling me."

"I don't know a thing, Barnes. All I have is a client with a daughter who was hanging out with Potter until a few days back and now they're both missing. Naturally Mrs. Evergreen would like to know if Potter's dead or alive and on the run. Whatever you can comfortably tell us, we'd appreciate knowing."

I pictured Barnes' brain working overtime in the silence. He didn't trust me as far as he could throw me, I felt the same, and we both knew it.

"On the run," he said finally. "You have any reason to think he's with Holly?"

"I don't have a better theory right now but I can't find her. What do you think?"

"Like I said. I think you're holding out on me."

"I'm just here trying to make a living, detective."

"Sure, and if I find out that includes withholding evidence, I'll make your life a living hell."

"Fair enough. You'll be the first to know if I learn anything."

"Good. So, are we done here?"

"Well, actually, there's one more thing. I've got a name here and was wondering if it meant anything to you."

There was a pause.

"Go ahead. Shoot."

"Armando Villareal. I guess he goes by El Chango."

There was another pause.

"Maybe. How do you know about him?"

"A report I had done on Potter. Back before you boys got involved. Anyway, I was thumbing back through the list of Potter's known contacts and the name jumped out at me."

"And just like that. It jumped out at you."

"Hey, given recent events, and Potter's obvious dislike for people of color, it doesn't seem to fit."

"And you just figured that out."

"Hell. It's a long list and I've been busy. What can I tell you?"

119

I waited.

"Look, Barnes. A mother is sitting at home right now, worried sick over her missing daughter. I don't know what you think is going on here but there's nothing more to it."

"Yeah, well, next time I'm chatting with El Chango, I'll be sure to let him know you're concerned."

Christ. I wanted to slap the guy around but went with diplomacy instead.

"Look, Barnes. I appreciate the info. I'll keep you posted and please do the same."

When he failed to respond, I ended the call.

I grabbed Kenny's report from my desk and thumbed back to the listings of Donald Ray Potter's former residences. Joshua Tree. Hesperia. El Mirage. A man living along the fringes of society, anywhere that offered him a quick escape if he smelled trouble. And there had always been trouble in Donald Ray Potter's life.

I turned my attention to Abigale Potter. Driving out to Apple Valley was the last thing in the world I wanted to do, on that day, or on any other day. They could call it Apple Valley if they liked but there wasn't anything akin to apples or a valley about it. It was just another dusty, lifeless desert town, with an ever increasing blanket of smog drifting in.

Having another thought, I grabbed the phone and called an old number. After several rings, a familiar voice answered.

"What's the matter, Vanderhof?" I said. "You get nervous, seeing me in your rearview mirror?"

"Well, I'll be damned," he said after a pause. "So what? Did someone down at the police station yank your chain?"

"What did you expect when you went sniveling to them?"

"And how did that go?"

"It didn't go far. I told Whalen to go screw himself. I think we left off with him gnawing on my ankle."

Vanderhof laughed.

"So how the hell are you?"

"Still alive, no thanks to you. How's things with Dick and Tom?"

"Don't know about Tom but Dick has a parole hearing in '24 and is looking forward to a reunion with you."

"I'll bet. You be sure to tell him I said hello."

"Will do. You still down there in your little hole in the wall?"

"That's me, Vanderhof. I'm a hole in the wall kind of guy."

"Yeah you are."

"Yeah I am…"

"Yeah. So I'm guessing this isn't a social call so what's on your mind?"

"Just letting you know that you're heading down a dangerous path."

"How so?"

"Buying Picassos on the cheap from one of your sycophants."

In support of Bennie's theory, Vanderhof grew silent.

"The point is," I continued. "As an agent working for the man who owns the Picasso, you're just putting yourself right square back in my crosshairs."

"Who said I have any Picassos?"

"You did just then, when you paused."

"Think you're pretty smart, huh, Devlin?"

"Let's not waste time, Vanderhof. What do you say? The sooner I can retrieve the Picasso, the better for all concerned. And please don't tell said sycophant that we're on to him. We're still trying to track down some missing jewelry and an Egyptian figurine from the 26th Dynasty. Imagine that. The 26th Dynasty. Anyway, we believe he stole those items too."

"I don't know anything about any jewelry…Or the 26th Dynasty."

"I didn't think you did. Gold and diamonds, you can buy anywhere. And as far as I know, the figurine made its way out to the high desert. Maybe you noticed your buddy still had sand on his shoes last night when you ran into him."

Vanderhof grew silent again.

"So, about the Picasso," I said.

"Like I told you. I don't know anything about a Picasso."

"But you'll look into it for me."

"Oh, sure," he said facetiously. "I'll poke around among my contacts."

"Because your contacts are the kind of people who'd know where to find a stolen Picasso."

"You're a real prick, Devlin."

"Right back at you, Vanderhof."

"And now that we've gotten that out of the way, what's next?"

"Nothing," I said.

I had considered mentioning Vanderhof's penchant for underaged girls but decided not to play that card quite yet. Better to keep him guessing.

"I'll be waiting for your call," I added and hung up before he could answer.

With another glance at the clock, I decided to hit the noon meeting. I had over an hour to kill and turned my attention to a stack of paperwork on my desk. There had often been a thought to hire a full-time secretary, but that thought always died before I could act on it.

I had started to open envelopes when the phone rang. It was Bennie.

"What are you doing?" I asked.

"Hanging around waiting for Nicholas to get out of bed. What are you doing?"

"Opening envelopes."

There was silence.

"Want to know what I think?" he said.

"Not really, but I'm guessing I'm going to hear it anyway."

"I'm still betting my ten inch dick that Vanderhof has the Picasso."

"Well, you've certainly put your money where your mouth is there."

There was a menacing silence.

"Sorry, Bennie, but you kind of set that one up on a T."

"Yeah. I don't know why I let you get under my skin, but fine. Don't listen to me."

"Bennie, let's get something straight. I'm just as eager as you to find out if Vanderhof has the Picasso but I'm not about to break the law in order to do it…"

"Bullshit. We put tracking devices on people's cars all the time and I already know that shit's illegal."

I busied myself with organizing things on my desk.

"Yeah. I figured you'd have a whole lot of nothing to say about that shit."

"Look, Bennie. There are risks and there are risks and breaking into Vanderhof's place is not one I'm ready to take at this point. Certainly not with what little we know. And even if I was willing to do it, I wouldn't involve you, so please get that notion out of your head."

"I'm a big boy, boss man. I can handle myself."

"I'm sure you can, but hell. We may as well put a gun to Vanderhof's head."

"Now you're talking."

"Oh for Christ's sake, stop. What I need you to do is find this Morey character and get him doing what you're doing so I can have you focus on something else."

"And what would that be?"

"I don't know. I'll think of something."

"And what are you doing for the rest of the day?"

"Not sure yet but I am going to the noon meeting."

"Whoa! A miracle!"

"Yeah, yeah. Anything to get you off my back…Besides, I'm also hoping to run into Jake. You know, that ex-biker?"

"Yeah, I know him. We're tight."

"Yeah?"

"Yeah…So what did you want with him?"

"To see if he maybe knows something about the Mongols."

"Shit. I know all about them."

"Oh, yeah. I'd almost forgotten. Bennie 'El Gato' Morales."

"Screw you. Anyway, at least you're thinking now."

"Yeah. I've always said I'd try it once or twice before I was through."

"Yeah? How you liking it so far?"

"It kind of hurts."

Bennie chuckled.

"You're a real card, boss man."

"Yeah…By the way, I talked with Barnes and I guess they have most of Potter's gang in jail or dead, but no sign of him."

"Well, Holly ain't with him. I can guarantee you that."

"Yeah? Then where is she?"

"I don't know but we'll find her."

"I appreciate the optimism. Now can I get back to opening envelopes? I'm hoping to find a check in here so I can pay you at the end of the week."

"Fine, but you don't need Jake to deal with the Mongols. I can do that. I know just how they think."

"So you said. In the meantime, please find this Maurice character and get back to me the minute Nicholas starts moving again."

"I know you don't believe this, boss man, but I've got your back."

"No. I know it, Bennie. You're a good man."

"Hey, another benny for Bennie."

"Yeah. But don't let it go to your head."

"Dick."

"I know."

We ended the call. I opened the next envelope. Another bill. Another reminder of a life lived on the edge. It had always been that way with me. I had never known how it felt to be on easy street.

When I was done with the mail, I made a few phone calls. Caitlin kept dancing in and out of my thoughts. Maybe that's why she had moved on. Looking for an alpha male, not a guy who was always one step shy of disaster.

I glanced up at the Hemingwayesque photo of me on the wall. There was a thought. Send her a copy. I've got your alpha male right here, sweetheart.

I sat there trying to feel young and brash and daring again — the way it had been back in the day — but failing. I had made a wrong turn somewhere back down the road. If only I could remember where that was. Maybe Sylvia the fortune teller was right. Someone had placed a curse on me three thousand years ago and I had what remained of a lifetime to get that yoke back from around my neck.

Eleven

When it was finally nearing time for the meeting, I threw a few things into my satchel and headed out the canyon. A line of bumper to bumper cars was heading into town the other way, people still funneling down towards the coast, like a wildebeest migration, flocking in the direction of fresh pastures. You could easily spot the refugees by all the crap tied to the roof of their rigs.

With the wind having died down overnight, the smoke from the fires had settled over the town like a thick blanket. The heat had not relented, the air still kindling dry. Hell was right around the next corner.

Three miles up the road, I turned right onto a gravel driveway, crossed the creek on a wooden bridge and parked to the left of an expansive stucco building. When it came to meeting places, this was the Taj Mahal, its existence set in motion when a member of the local fellowship passed away and left behind a goodly sized plot of land. Then, true to the nature of their disease, said group of recovering alcoholics went completely overboard, seriously leveraging the land in order to erect this veritable cathedral, which had left the group up to its neck in debt and in an endless hustle for money to pay off the mortgage.

I was no expert on recovery but could see that once you started mixing sobriety with money, things would quickly go south. What would a newcomer think, walking in for the first time and getting a whiff of all the raffles and yard sale announcements? I entered the voluminous foyer through a glass front door, having decided it was none of my business.

A coffee bar was off to my left, the meeting room to my right, bathrooms straight ahead. I turned right and acknowledged various smiles and hellos on my way through the self-closing double doors.

This grand old dame named Gigi waved me over to her spot by a sliding glass door in back. I liked Gigi, and liked where she was sitting. Gigi had the door opened to the meager breeze. A fountain gurgled out there against a backdrop of native plants and two picnic tables. A mockingbird had parked on one of the picnic tables and was letting everyone inside know what he thought of them. Sitting down next to Gigi, I whistled back and he added me to his list.

Gigi reached out with one of her elegant hands and patted mine. She had been a dancer in New York back in the day and still looked the part. Lean and upright, with a long neck and a face that would have left young men tripping all over themselves.

"Hi, Michael," she said.

"Hey there, beautiful."

"Oh, you're a charmer."

"Trust me. I would have been chasing you all over Manhattan."

She smiled and rubbed my hand.

"And how are you doing?"

"All right. I was kind of feeling humble this morning...but it passed."

Gigi laughed.

"You're right on schedule."

"So I've heard."

"You just keep coming back," she said with another pat on my hand.

We had gotten on to chatting about the fires and that pandemic business when I heard the roar of a Harley out in front. It was Jake. He strolled into the meeting a minute later looking the part of an ex-biker. Goatee. Chains. Tattoos. Nobody offered Jake a smile and he didn't offer any in return.

There was an old saying around the fellowship. When you sober up a horse thief, what do you get? A sober horse thief. And Jake now appeared to be a sober biker.

Someone read the preamble and the 'brown bag' meeting got under way. Per the name, there were a number of business people working on their lunches. The rest of the crowd was a mix of retirees and lost souls. Some of the lost souls appeared to have made a career out of not having one.

I had been cautioned about taking other people's inventory but this guy Phil drove me up a wall. A native of Brooklyn, he had perfected the art of looking half comatose. Sitting upright appeared to be a chore. I pictured him on the government dole. Then maybe he was independently wealthy. That thought had the power to send me over the edge.

The topic of the meeting turned out to be humility. I tried working on that instead of Phil's program.

One of the old timers raised his hand and shared on the topic. Humility started with surrendering, and surrendering started with getting down on your knees every morning. Until you had turned your will and life over to the care of a higher power as you understood it, you'd never find lasting sobriety.

That got Jake to raise his hand.

"You know, people around here keep telling me that I gotta get down on my knees and pray. Well sorry, but that ain't gonna happen. So what? My woman can see *her* higher power down on his knees to *his* higher power?"

That got a good laugh out of the men in the room, the women not so much.

Jake continued his harangue for another minute before shutting up.

At the end of the meeting, I followed him out to the gravel parking lot. He was seated on his Harley and securing a Nazi looking helmet to his head. I held out my hand.

"Michael."

Jake shook it with a hard look into my eyes. I explained about being a private detective. Jake kept staring.

"Anyway, I'm working a case where some bikers are involved and was wondering if you'd be willing to act as a go between. You know. Get in touch with these folks for me without guns going off? I'd be more than happy to pay you for your time."

Jake kept staring. If he liked me at all, it was pretty well disguised.

"What do you want from these dudes?"

"Some stolen goods back. If I'm right about what went down, they took an ancient Egyptian figurine in exchange for some drugs. The client is willing to pay whatever it takes to get it back. No questions asked."

Jake nodded.

"You know which gang and chapter?"

"I believe it's the Mongols, and this shit went down out near Wrightwood. Does the name Armando 'El Chango' Villarreal mean anything to you?"

Jake nodded and started his Harley.

"Maybe. I'll look into it."

I decided to press my luck.

"I'm working on another case that involves some white supremacist dudes. Does the name Donald Ray Potter mean anything to you? He was hanging out with the underaged daughter of one of my clients and now they're both missing. We're hoping to find the girl."

Jake revved his Harley.

"I'll look into it."

"Thanks. You want money? I'll be happy to pay you up front."

Jake stared at me like I had just confessed to screwing his teenaged daughter.

"I don't take money for helping a fellow alcoholic."

129

I handed him a card. He stuck the card in his pocket without looking at it, revved his Harley again, pulled the kickstand up and roared off.

All things considered, I thought the encounter had gone fairly well.

Out of courtesy to Gigi, I went back inside to say goodbye and found her surrounded by a coterie of women, most of them newer to sobriety and clinging to Gigi's skirt like bear cubs to their mother. When someone had her kind of serenity and grace, you wanted to steal a bit of it.

I was starting to grow impatient and turn away when Gigi noticed me and reached out a hand.

Good for you," she whispered. "Reaching out to your fellow alcoholic. God knows Jake needs a friend."

"Yeah. Anyway, I just wanted to say goodbye before I left."

"Thanks. And see you here tomorrow?"

"Maybe. I'll try. I just never know with my business."

"At least you made one meeting." Gigi gave me a hug. "Hurry back," she added before returning her attention to the other women.

I was chewing on Gigi's words on the way out to my car. 'At least you made one meeting.' It sounded like she had been talking to Bennie.

I glanced in my rearview mirror while pulling out onto Canyon Road. Clusters of people chatting away, everyone part of something but me.

What did you expect, Devlin? You've spent the last seven years turning into a lone wolf, until nobody knows you, or much cares about your existence. Your best friend is Bennie, and even that's in question.

I had parked out in front of the office and was marching upstairs when he called me.

"Any news?" I said.

"Not much. I'm down here watching Nicholas drink beer with his buddies in the harbor. Some job for an alkie."

"Sorry, Bennie. I can take your place if you're troubled."

"Wow. You really worried about me, boss man?"

"Sure, Bennie. The last thing I'd want to see is you losing your sobriety."

"Thanks. That's real white of you, but I'm cool. Watching these guys get fucked up in the middle of the day is actually the best thing that could ever happen to me. I keep thinking, wow, that was me six years ago. Blah blah blah. I knew everything. When I was just full of BS."

"Nothing changes much in this world, does it?"

"Man, I can't even believe I bought into your nice guy routine."

"Hell, Bennie, we're all half nuts. I was thinking that today in the meeting. I don't even know how to be a human being anymore. I feel more lost than I ever did when I was drinking."

"That's why you gotta work the steps, bro. The elevator to sobriety is broken."

"So you've told me. Many times now."

"It's true, dude."

"Fine. Let's get back to this Morey guy? Were you able to track him down?"

"Oh yeah. I was going to tell you before you started beating my balls. He called me back and wants to meet us tonight down at Hennessey's."

"Hennessey's? I thought he was sober."

"He is but I guess he does a karaoke gig down there every Thursday night."

"And we have to listen to him sing as part of the deal?"

"He says he never misses it."

"Oh brother."

"It's cool. We can chase him down tomorrow."

"No, no. We'll go see his gig. What time?"

"He said any time after eight. He likes to do his set early. Before everyone gets drunk."

"Yeah, and starts throwing pickled eggs." Bennie laughed. "I've got to run but I'll see you down there around eight."

131

As I was opening the door to my office, I remembered Betty's request and called Steve.

"Michael," he said in answering the phone. "How are you doing?"

"Okay, man. How are you?"

"Oh, you know. Still struggling with acceptance."

"Yeah, I know."

"Yeah. The bitch of it is, I never get to find out if it would have worked out between Connie and me. Like maybe we weren't meant to be together but..."

"Yeah," I said.

I had no answers for him. I had the same feelings for a woman who still walked the face of this earth.

"Sorry," Steve said. "I know I'm always saying the same shit."

"It's all right, brother. Any time you need to get things off your chest."

"Thanks, man. So what's going on?"

"Oh, I ran into Betty and she was asking about Butch. I guess she wants to babysit the little monster for a few days."

"Oh, man. You know what? That'd be perfect. I made plans to go skiing for a few days and was just wondering what to do with him."

"Skiing? On what? Rocks?"

Steve laughed.

"No. We're heading up to Mammoth. They had several feet of early snow this week. I'd take Butch but I'll be up on the slopes most of the time."

"Well, Betty's dying to see him."

"Cool. Should I bring him down right now?"

"Sure. Why not. You know she'll take him in a heartbeat."

"Cool. I'll be down in a bit."

I had hardly hung up the phone when it rang again.

"Michael Devlin here," I said.

"Yeah, dis be Motation DX. Motation wid a reputation. You hep to it, bro?"

"Can't say that I am."

"Then I'm gonna tell you all about it."

And with that, I had this soul brother going off on a rant. Motherf#!*%#!g this and Motherf#!*%#!g that. You know what I'm sayin'?

I sensed some kind of drugs involved. Maybe it was just an overabundance of testosterone. The man was amped up on something.

From what I could gather, he had an online, get rich marketing scheme and some pimp ass soul brother was trying to horn in on his brand.

I could imagine his pitch.

'Listen here, bro. The only reason you ain't rich is because of you. You too can live like a gangsta, and let me tell you how.'

Lots of dolls and furs and a Ferrari in the background. For $99.95, he'd get you laid on a leopard skin rug.

I had been looking for an opportunity to bow out gracefully when he thankfully came to his own denouement.

"So, what you think, man?"

"Think about what?"

"About putting this dude in his place for me. What d'yu think I want?"

"I don't know. That's not really the kind of work I do."

"Look, bro. I can get you all this dude's info. Where he lives, what he drives, anything you need. Now all I want you to do is follow his ass around until I know every goddamn thing about him. Now is that something you do?"

"Yeah, maybe."

"All right, bro. I see your contact info here online. I'm going to send all that shit over so you can get to work. We cool?"

"Sure, sure," I said.

"Then I'll be back at your ass soon."

I hung up the phone and weighed the proper course of action. Patience, probably. Chances were, he'd be amped up about something else by tomorrow and forget the call.

I had been sitting there for a couple of minutes longer, still unsettled by the exchange, when I heard the front door open downstairs. That was followed by the sound of paws and nails sprinting up the wooden stairs and down the carpeted hallway. Butch skidded to a halt at my open door and got down in the play position.

"Yeahhhhhhhhhhhhhhh, I'll GET that guy," I said and off he bolted down the hallway, ears flying. A moment later, I heard Betty calling out his name. Steve poked his head in my door about the same time. I got up and gave him a hug.

"He'd forget about me in a New York second," Steve said.

"He definitely has a thing for the ladies."

"Yeah, he does. He falls all over himself."

I smiled and joined Steve down the hallway. Butch and Betty were just inside the door when we walked up, Butch on his back and getting the treatment. Leonard looked up from the paperwork on his desk, a pair of oversized reading glasses perched on the end of his nose, as always.

"Thanks," Betty said to me.

"Sure."

"Perfect timing too," Steve said. "A bunch of us are heading up to Mammoth tomorrow and I was reluctant to take him with us."

"Well, we're just going to have ourselves a little party, aren't we Butchie? Did you bring all his stuff?"

"Yeah. It's down in the car. I was thinking to take him for a walk and drain him before I brought it up. Wasn't sure you really wanted him."

"Did you hear that, Butchie? He wasn't sure if I really wanted you."

Butch lay there with paws up and tongue out, oblivious to all things human, save for petting.

"Guess I'd better get back to work," I said.

"Thanks again," Betty said.

"Yeah, thanks," Steve said.

I patted him on the shoulder and headed back down to my office.

Seated at my desk, I recalled gangsta man with a shudder. Then my thoughts turned towards Caitlin. In a world filled with venality, my love for her was as pure as gold. How could I make the woman understand?

Then I remembered the pendant I had commissioned my friend Sal to make the previous year. I had gone as far as to pick out one of Caitlin's birthstones, along with a delicate gold chain, and there things stood. Sal had called me back a week later to say that everything was ready, but I had never returned. Something inside of me had said, face it, Devlin. The woman doesn't want you.

Having already paid for the pendant, I had assumed it was no sweat off of Sal's back.

A breeze rustled the papers on my desk. I sat there staring out at the cruise ship without really seeing it.

Butch raced down the hallway and skidded to a stop at my door, bringing me back to the moment. I grabbed the dead woman's ring out of my top drawer and was out in the hallway locking the door when Steve walked up

"You're off?" he said.

"Yeah. Something just came up."

We headed downstairs together. Butch had his snout to the front door, ready to dash outside. Steve got a leash on him.

"Thanks again," he said out on the sidewalk.

"Sure."

I petted Butch and gave Steve another hug before jumping into my car.

Fifteen minutes later, I was five miles inland and driving down a long, narrow dead-end road. A chain link fence and railroad tracks bordered the road on my left, a row of aging, Spanish style commercial buildings on my right. The interstate freeway was a quarter mile to the other side of the buildings.

135

Sal had a shop down at the end of the road, tucked away in the last little cul-de-sac. I parked there and climbed out of the Impala. The drone of the freeway whispered off in the distance.

Sal's shop was one in a line of drab office fronts and his interior was right in line with the nondescript exterior. He had a glass display case facing the front door, a huge safe off to the left and a desk over to the right, piled high with papers. He was an artisan, not a retailer. You could see his workshop through an open door behind the display case.

Sal was standing behind the glass case when I walked in, right out of central casting...if you were looking for Mexican bandits. The Wild Bunch came to mind. Sal had dark, scraggly hair and a waistline that had gotten way out of hand. He wore T-shirts the way overweight women wore muu muus. There was a blend of comedy and grief in the man that I had never been able to articulate properly.

"What's going on?" he said as if I had come to sell him a bum horse.

That was Sal. Always figuring you were out to screw him.

With a flick of his head, a set of jeweler's glasses came down so he could have a better look at a ring in his hands. Then, with another flick, the glasses were back on top of his head. Sal kept glancing at me while fiddling with the ring.

His big black cat appeared from in back and made a few passes at my legs. It was a handsome fellow with white spats and jowls. Finally, it jumped into the display case and stared up at me with oversized eyes through the glass.

"What's up?" Sal said again.

"I came to get that necklace for Caitlin."

"Shit. I figured you'd forgotten about it."

"No, just taking a break."

"So what? You guys back together?"

"Not really. She won't make time for me but I wanted to give her the necklace anyway."

Sal did a double take.

"It's okay, Sal. No need to pity me."

136

"Who said I was pitying you?!!! Don't say shit like that!!!"

"Yeah? What about you? Still fighting the divorce?"

"Shit," he said and started fishing around among the papers piled on top of his display case. "See!" He showed me a ledger. "Here's everything I've sold in the last two years! It's nothing! She thinks I'm rich! How do I convince these people?!"

Sal's once docile wife had filed for divorce the previous year and her attorney had hired a CPA to go through his books. That, more than anything, had pissed Sal off. For twenty-five years the woman had been the model of spousal submission. Now she wanted the house and lots of money.

Sal's response had been to move into his shop and erect the ramparts.

"See?!" he'd say every time the subject came up, waving a piece of paperwork. "I don't have any money! These people are crazy!"

I was reminded of Lenny Bruce towards the end, reading transcripts of his trials in place of a standup routine.

Who knew what had gone wrong with the marriage? The usual stuff; too many years, the passions gone. It was depressing.

I got back to my business.

"So, do you still have the pendant?"

"What do you think?"

"Sorry. I just didn't know what to do?"

Sal went to his safe and fished around inside for the necklace. He kept things in tiny manila folders. It took him a minute to find the right one. I watched him pull out the chain and pendant.

"I'd better polish this again," he said.

I followed him back to his work bench. A twin bed and TV occupied one corner of the workshop. A countertop and mini fridge represented his makeshift kitchen. A quart of good Scotch sat next to his microwave. Sal had gotten himself quite comfortable there during the divorce; maybe too comfortable.

137

While he worked, the jewelers' glasses went back and forth from the top of his head.

He looked up at me at one point.

"You really love this chick, don't you?"

I shrugged and nodded. Sal smiled.

"Shit, man. You're just like me. A hopeless romantic."

I almost laughed. Both of us hopeless romantics. We weren't even in the same galaxy cluster.

Twelve

Finally satisfied with the polish job, Sal waved me back out front. He found a black gift box in his safe and carefully arranged the pendant inside.

"What are you going to do?" he said, handing it to me. "Just show up with this?"

"Yeah."

"And what if she shuts the door in your face?"

"I don't know. The whole world's going mad. What the hell does one more hurt feeling matter?"

"Man, don't talk like that!"

Sal had gotten back to working on his ring and glanced up at me with a bum horse look.

"What?" he said in response to my stare. "What?!" he said again.

"Nothing. You asked me and I told you. The whole world's going mad. What does one more hurt feeling matter?"

"Well, fuck, you can't think like that!"

"Like what?"

"Like it's all over because of a woman!"

"I'm not trying to convince you of anything. I'm just telling you how I feel."

"Shit, you're talking like there'll never be another woman! You want problems, think of all the people starving in this world! And if you feed them, they'll just have more babies and make things even worse!"

He looked up at me from the ring, nearly out of breath.

"I mean it! It's just one big evolving state of calamity! You solve a problem and a worse one takes its place! And you're sitting here worrying about a woman?"

How depressing. If you weren't already thinking to shoot yourself, Sal would lend you a hand.

"Shit," he went on. "I saw this program on PBS the other night about all these rogue plant and animal species hitchhiking around the globe. All this modern transportation's supposed to be making our lives easier but all it does is drag this alien shit everywhere and screw everything up!"

"Yeah?"

"Yeah! Don't look at me that way. I'm telling you the truth!"

His bum horse look made me smile. It was part anger, part wounded dog.

I leaned down to pet the cat at my feet. It was twenty pounds if it was an ounce, a male, and having a thrill with my legs again.

"He's my buddy," Sal said.

"Yeah," I said.

Twenty-five years of marriage, a nice home and Sal was down to living in his shop with a cat. The man made me look like a piker.

Still working on the ring, Sal got back to his diatribe.

"I'm telling you the truth, man! All we do is fuck things up! Like these new species taking over the indigenous ones. Then some idiot scientist comes along and introduces the next foreign species, thinking it will get rid of the first one, only to find out we've made things even worse!"

He was out of breath again.

"What does this have to do with me being in love with Caitlin?"

"Nothing, man! Everything! There's just all this shit we can't control!"

Half an hour and the man had finally said something irrefutable.

"What?!" he said with me still staring at him.

"Are you saying that Caitlin's an indigenous species?"

"No! Fuck! Quit saying shit like that! I'm just saying, you probably shouldn't go over there. You want to control this woman and you can't!"

"I just want to let her know I love her. That's all"

"And let her kick you in the balls again."

I glanced around his shop.

"What?!" he said.

"Nothing, Sal. Nothing."

I pulled out the ring and moved on to my other reason for being there.

"What's this?" Sal said.

I explained.

"Shit, man! What are you dragging this thing around here for?!"

"Just wondering if you can help me figure out who made it."

"It could be a million different jewelers!"

"Just look at the dedication, will you?"

Sal's jeweler's glasses came down and he had a closer look. The jeweler's glasses went back up.

"Yeah? So what?"

"So. 'Charlotte's Web'? Does that mean anything to you?"

"No."

"And what about the initials, SOS?"

"No! Why are you asking me all this shit?!"

"Christ, Sal. I'm just taking a swing in the dark here. No need to get all worked up."

He had another look at the ring.

"I could ask around. Are you going to leave this with me?"

"I'd probably better not."

"Then why are you asking me all this shit?!"

Oh brother. I explained about Huntington's missing jewelry.

"Shit! You're the private investigator!"

"Quit being such a prick, Sal. Just keep your eyes open, okay?"

141

Sal gave me his bum horse look.

"Get me a description."

I grabbed a pen and piece of paper and jotted down what I knew about the jewelry. Sal watched me leave like I was a fool. I was just relieved to get away from his energy.

A few minutes later, I was winding down a country road. Off to my right, a farmhouse was nestled at the backside of a persimmon grove. Hills rose up behind the farmhouse, growing dark under the late afternoon sky.

I passed a Christmas tree farm, then a firewood lot, all of it bringing back a flood of dear memories. Caitlin and I had driven along this same road numerous times in the past, always hand in hand, always dearly in love.

Sal's observation kept turning over in my head. I wanted to control all this shit I couldn't control. Old Tom would have told me the same thing. Wanting something always led to frustration. Your lack of serenity was directly proportional to your expectations, and good intentions were no better than bad ones in that regard. The pendant had become a symbol of mankind's eternal drama.

I said Bennie's short version of the serenity prayer and pressed on.

Five minutes later, I was parking across the street from Caitlin's house. My heart beat wildly as I climbed out of the car.

Part of me said run. Part of me said, you have to do this. It's your destiny.

I went up to the door and knocked. Nothing. I knocked several more times but it was as if the woman had sensed me coming and gotten out of Dodge.

Before leaving, I fished around her enclosed front garden area, found a twig and plastic bag and used them to hang the pendant from her door knocker.

On my way home, I felt as empty as a box. All my good intentions, and all for naught.

Back at the office, my every attempt to refocus on business failed miserably. Every other thought was of Caitlin. I pictured her arriving home, finding the gift on her door and shoving it into a drawer somewhere, hardly a look inside.

Christ. What a fool. She didn't want you. Let it go.

Restless in spirit, I called Kenny but he had already gone home for the day. I stared at the phone, hoping for someone to call. Even Bennie would do.

Reminded of the ring inside my pocket, I pulled it out and tried to make sense of the riddle. Who was the poor young woman and why had someone wanted her dead? The ring turned around and around in my hand as I stared out to sea.

Maybe Barnes knew something by now. I thought of calling him but decided to check in with Lila instead.

"Any news from the police?" I said when she answered.

"Oh, you bet. Detective Barnes called again, with a million more questions. Actually, the same ones, from a million new directions. When did Donald Potter first call? Had Holly ever spoken of him? Did she ever mention his hideouts? Was there anything else I knew? Meanwhile, I have the school district and child service agencies breathing down my neck. And all thanks to you for losing my daughter...Well?" she added.

"It's fine, Mrs. Evergreen. I'll take the hit."

"Oh, here we go again. It's back to Mrs. Evergreen."

I sat there in silence, regretting the call.

"Well? Say something."

"What's there to say? You start drinking like this and it's impossible to reason with you."

"Oh, it is, is it? And I suppose you still think I have something to hide."

"It's occurred to me."

"Fine. Why don't you drive right over here and we'll get all our cards out on the table?"

"I can't. I'm meeting a potential new operative here in a bit."

"Of course."

"Lila, please. Call me when you sober up. If I drive over there now, we'll end up wrestling on the floor."

"And wouldn't that be the worst thing that ever happened."

I was silent.

"Fine," she said. "You know where to find me."

There was a brief pause before she hung up.

I set the phone down and rubbed my forehead. The only way I wanted that woman was hard and rough. Slap her across the face a few times. Rip off her bra and panties. All my feelings for her were below the belt.

Then, hell, at least she had invited me over. The minutes ticked by without a word back from Caitlin. Five o'clock came and went, then six, then seven. I was ready to lay my life down for the woman but she couldn't be bothered.

Half mad with frustration, I wandered up to the English Cottage for a bite to eat in the bar, only to find myself seated at same table Caitlin and I had shared on our second date, lo those many years ago. Amidst the warmth and glow of that Friday evening, I could still see her smile and hear her laughter.

What gladness it had been, falling in love. And there I was now, a prisoner of things that could never be again.

At a quarter to eight, I headed down to Hennessey's, feeling thoroughly abject. I kept picturing Caitlin being annoyed by my gesture. The last place I wanted to be right then was Hennessey's. It reeked of stale beer and broken hearts.

I found Bennie commandeering a table out by the sidewalk patio. It was as far as you could get from the stage and still be inside the bar. The karaoke was in full swing with a sixty-ish woman up front singing *Moondance*. I took a seat and gave Bennie a look.

"Don't give me no shit. I didn't pick this scene."

"Karaoke," I grumbled. "I'd rather spend an eternity in hell."

"Maybe this is eternity in hell."

I gave him another look.

The cocktail waitress stopped by and took my order for a club soda. When she left, I turned my attention back to the singer. The song evoked some kind of spiritual nausea for me. *Moondance* had been enjoying something of a renaissance on the airwaves when I was a kid in puberty, so everything associated with puberty came with it.

Another act followed. I was drumming my fingers and checking the clock.

Promptly at eight, Morey sauntered in, medium height, lean as a whippet and as serious as Dirty Harry. In fact, his hair was done up in the same style.

Dirty Morey.

He stopped at our table and gave the current act a once over before taking a seat. Bennie introduced us. Morey shook my hand with barely a look. His eyes were laser beamed on the singer. I guessed he was giving her a D. Maybe worse. When her song ended, Morey abruptly stood up

"Excuse me. This is my set."

I gave him a thumbs up and glanced at Bennie. Where did you find this guy?

When Morey lit into an early Dylan song, my eyes opened wide. I had not seen that one coming.

'...and you thought that they were all kiddin' youuuuuuuuuu...'

Morey topped off his set with *Long Cool Woman In A Black Dress* and rejoined us to a smattering of applause. The look on his face said he knew he hadn't nailed it.

"Not my best set," he said with complete gravity. "Channeling Dylan is usually my A stuff."

I nodded. Those were the breaks. I'd give him a C+. Maybe.

"So, Bennie tells me you're looking for work."

"Yeah, maybe. Tell me more about your gig."

My gig. Oh boy. I went ahead with the presentation.

"So, it's mostly watching and observing and making notes," he said.

"There's a lot of that, yeah. A lot of late hours. Sometimes there's action. Sometimes it's as boring as hell. The upside side is, you're mostly your own boss. No one's looking over your shoulder."

Morey's eyes narrowed as though peering through a sandstorm. He seemed to be far away now, weighing things from another dimension.

"Yeah," he said. "I could do that gig."

"Yeah?"

"Sure. I'm an accountant so I'm good with details. But I was also an amateur boxer coming out of college so I know how to handle myself."

Morey feinted with his fists, real serious like. I nodded. Kid Morey.

Bennie agreed to set up Morey on the Nicholas detail that night and Bennie would get back to keeping an eye on the Mongols. I welcomed Morey aboard and made my exit. At least we had a body to replace Billy. Only time would tell if the 'Kid' could cut it.

Back at home, I checked again to see if there was any news from Caitlin, but nothing. No phone calls on my land line. No emails. Nothing. Had a swarm of crows invaded my soul right then, I could not have felt bleaker. A thousand pound stone sat on my chest.

Not knowing what else to do, I sent her a brief email.

> I adore you with all my heart, darling, hence the pendant.
> Now, I'm ready to jump off a bridge, to think it didn't matter
> to you.

Some minutes later, while staring off into space, an email arrived in my mailbox.

From Caitlin.

I rushed to open it but paused with my hand on the mouse. What if it's a rejection?

Oh hell. It is or is isn't.

I opened the email and nearly cried out.

> What a lovely gift, Michael, and sorry I failed to respond
> sooner. Work, you know. Anyway, it was very Boy Scouty,

146

the way you hung it from the door knocker and please don't jump off a bridge. Why don't you come over tomorrow night instead and help me make some fancy chicken?

I sat there reading Caitlin's words over and over, a wreck. Oh, the milk of human kindness. Once I had gathered myself, I dashed off a return note, doing my best not to sound overly eager. Sure, I'd love to stop by and help you make fancy chicken. Was there anything I could bring?

She wrote back a bit later, saying no, just myself.

I remained seated there, staring at her words, utterly helpless. With the flick of a hand, the woman had lifted me out of blackness, a blackness that would not have existed without her.

I went to bed, dreaming of Caitlin, but with Lila dancing around the edges of my thoughts. We had left off with her hanging up on me and the prospect of us wrestling down on the floor. Somewhere in all of that, I knew I would have to talk with her again and was rather dreading it now.

In the morning, I went out to grab the paper and found a plate of homemade gingerbread cookies wrapped up on my front porch. There was also a gift certificate for a free espresso and muffin at a downtown coffee joint. The note was signed Fitzy. I assumed it to be atonement for the forty-foot moving van having blocked my driveway the previous day.

I wasn't a big fan of gingerbread cookies but nibbled on one and found them to be quite delicious. And the colored sugar glaze had been done up cleverly to evoke various cloak and dagger figures, in keeping with my profession.

Classy lady, I thought and made a mental note to return the favor.

Sometime later, while eating a bowl of cereal at my breakfast nook, I noticed storm clouds barging in from the Pacific and quickly checked a weather site on my phone. Rain was forecast for that evening. What serendipity. It brought to mind my first winter in love with Caitlin, the two of us hastily rearranging

147

schedules day by day in order to sync our soirees with every impending storm.

It seemed completely unreal. That after all these years apart, we would be seeing each other again in but a few hours.

Down at the office, I scanned through emails and phone messages while absentmindedly rolling the young woman's ring around in my hand. Finally, I was back to staring at it. How horrible it must have been, those last seconds of her ill-fated life. No, no, no, please. I don't want to die.

And all for the thrill of riding on the back of a Harley.

There was yet another impulse to call Detective Barnes. It was none of my business, really, the mystery of her death, but it went on haunting me and I had little hope of solving it without another clue. The fact was, I had no proof that Donald Ray Potter and his gang were at all involved. Maybe it was pure coincidence that the body had been dumped out behind their place. I doubted it, but unfounded assumptions had led me down more than one investigative box canyon in the past, leaving me to retrace my steps and start all over.

Either way, the thought of that poor woman's fate would not leave me alone. It seemed to be symbolic of every act of cruelty and barbarism exacted by our species upon itself.

Finally, I stuck the ring back in my drawer, said a prayer of thanks for Caitlin and called Bennie. He was out keeping an eye on the Mongols.

"Hey, boss man. What's the plan for today? I know, watch and wait."

"Yep, the same thing as always. Anything new?"

"Nope. I figure that statue of Tutankhamen could be anywhere by now."

"Yeah? You all up on Tutankhamen, are you?"

"You bet your ass. I do my homework."

"Would that include keeping an eye on Morey?"

"What do you think?"

"Just checking."

"Well, if you're dying to know, he's been calling me about every hour. I can't wait to see his notes. If an alley cat happens by, he logs it."

"Maybe you can learn something."

"Is that it? Just called to beat my balls a bit?"

"No, Bennie, you're right. I should be working on my own character defects."

"Yeah. That ought to keep you busy for a couple of lifetimes."

I pretended to go off in Spanish and that got Bennie laughing.

"Good one. So what else is happening today?"

"Actually, I'm getting ready to pull the trigger on another van."

"Now you're talking."

"And then hit the noon meeting again."

"Hey! He's on a roll."

"Not that I really need it."

"Not that you really need it. You're self-will run riot."

"Maybe. And then I have a date tonight."

"Whooaaaa!" Bennie said.

"Yeah, so I'm hoping you can hold down the fort in my absence."

"You bet...So what? Are we talking some babe from the program?"

I was silent.

"Oh man. Don't tell me it's that old flame."

I still didn't answer him.

"Boss man, when are you going to stop letting that woman pussy whip you?"

"I don't know, but apparently not today...Just keep an eye on things, please, and report in if you have any news."

"Will do...And hey."

"Yeah?"

"Good luck."

"Yeah, thanks."

149

I hung up and looked out at the suddenly autumn-like sky, feeling more and more like a leaf in the wind as the hour of our soiree drew near. I loved that woman too much for my own good, but could not have turned away if I tried.

I got back to business and called the van customizer. He answered after several rings, heard me out and said he could have his end done in a couple of days. He just needed the van.

I called the fleet manager at a local dealership next and talked price. Bottom line, with the customizer's bill thrown in, I would be out close to forty grand. I weighed the pros and cons and decided to pull the trigger. If business died, I'd be filing for bankruptcy anyway.

The manager said he'd take care of getting the van over to the customizer. All I had to do was stop by and sign the paperwork. I told him I'd be by later that afternoon. As kismet would have it, the dealership was just a few miles down from Caitlin's place. All roads in life seemed to be converging.

With a glance at the clock, I grabbed my keys, headed downstairs and was soon driving out the canyon, chased by the approaching storm. Trees stirred wildly in the wind. Charcoal clouds barged across the blue sky. It was impressionism come to life, the unbearable heat and smoke of the past week gratefully gone.

Gigi was at her usual table and waved me over as I walked in.

"Hey, you made it back, handsome."

I gave her a kiss on the cheek and sat down.

"You already got a guy, Gigi, or do I stand a chance?"

She waved a hand at me. Had the timing been otherwise, no question I would have been chasing her around Manhattan.

"And how are we feeling today?" she asked.

"Like James Brown."

"How's that?"

"I feel good."

Gigi laughed.

"Oh, that's good. Mind if I use that in a share?"

150

"Not at all. I haven't licensed it yet."

Gigi laughed again and was about to go on when a distraught looking middle-aged woman came over and leaned into Gigi's ear. Suddenly, there were tears. I discreetly backed out of the way and tried not to listen. The poor woman was new to sobriety and anguished over everything.

God, the grief. Then, who was I to talk? But a few hours earlier, I was ready to jump off a bridge.

The meeting started and the topic turned to gratitude. Every other day it was gratitude.

Yesterday, I would have groused. Now my heart was ready to burst with it.

Towards the end of the meeting, Gigi nudged me with her elbow. I frowned at her and looked away. She nudged me again, and again.

Oh hell, all right. I raised my hand and introduced myself.

"Michael, alcoholic."

The group greeted me back and I shared a bit of what was going on in my life.

"So, I've been thinking lately, the serenity to accept the things I cannot change, sure, and the courage to change the things I can, okay. Now will somebody please grant me the patience to wait for the wisdom, because most of the time, I feel like Donald Duck...on one of his bad days."

There was laughter. I thanked the group for letting me share and shut up.

After the meeting, a young woman came up and introduced herself.

"Kayla. I really, really enjoyed your share."

"Oh, please. I was all over the place."

"No, no. It was really sincere. I especially loved that part at the end. The patience to wait for the wisdom. I'm going to add that to my prayers."

Her compliments left me feeling awkward. Compliments always had.

I was relieved when she finally went away, then felt lost on the way back out to my car. Again, everyone around me was chatting away with friends. I peered back through the mist of time, back to when I had been a gregarious soul, always out on the town with friends, able to see that person but for the life of me unable to understand what had happened to him, or to find my way back there again. When had I become this grizzly bear, living his solitary existence up above the timberline?

Thirteen

On the way back to my office, I remembered Holly with a feeling of helplessness and guilt. She was out there somewhere and I couldn't find her. Maybe it would be best to have Lila hire one of those big-time agencies, with snazzy offices and dozens of operatives. Maybe she'd forgive me all the money we had already spent.

I parked in the alley and went in through the back door. Halfway to the stairs, it struck me that I'd forgotten about the Audi and poked my head back outside. No sign of it. Who would be driving an A8? It was driving me half mad.

Back at my desk, I called Kenny and watched while his phone rang. As usual, he glanced at the caller ID first and then at me.

"What's up?" he said in answering.

"Any news on Potter."

"Nothing. I take it he doesn't use credit cards."

"Who'd give him one?"

"New Parole Visa?"

"Funny…How the hell do we track this guy?"

"Stake out every known former residence?"

"Yeah. I was just beating myself up for not having twenty more operatives."

"I'll try digging a little deeper."

"I'd appreciate it. I should probably be hanging out in one of those QAnon chat rooms. See what kind of mayhem those madmen are cooking up."

"I can do that."

"Would you?"

"Sure. Give me a chance to buff up on my conspiracy theories."

"Thanks…And what's going on with everything else?"

"Oh yeah. On the long-lost brothers and sisters front, I'm waiting for a call back from the original orphanage. It's not like the old days. You can do a freedom of information request if they refuse to cooperate."

"And old man Cabot?"

"I'm still waiting for a copy of the death certificate. Not the easiest thing in the world to get your hands on. But on the face of it, there doesn't appear to have been any foul play."

"Yeah. Just like with old man Evergreen."

"Yeah, well. There's that."

"And what about the estate? Any squabble between Lila and the family over who got what?"

"Haven't found anything yet but I'm still looking."

"Okay. Thanks."

I got off the phone, feeling adrift. I tried Bennie, in hopes that he had news.

"Anything?" I said.

"They went out for a bike ride this morning. Now they're back at the house. Probably fucking each other's old ladies."

"You paint a lovely picture."

"What can I tell you? They're definitely dealing meth or some shit because they don't do nothing."

"Yeah. But no sign of Potter."

"Nothing. You got any leads?"

"Nothing."

"I'm cool. All stocked up and kickin' ass on online poker."

"Great. I'm paying you to gamble."

"Shit, if I just sat here staring at the monitors, I'd nod out."

154

"Yeah, good to know. I'd hate to think I was wasting my money."

"It's physics, dude. You see, they did this study and..."

"All right, Bennie. I've got to go."

"Shit, you don't want to learn nothin'."

"You're right. Just remember. I'm going to stop by and sign the papers for that new van later this afternoon. Then I'll be at Caitlin's place tonight. You text me if anything comes up."

"You got it."

I started to hang up but heard Bennie's voice again and pulled the phone back to my ear.

"Yeah, what?"

"Good luck."

"Yeah. You already said that."

"I mean it. I hope you get a little lovin' man. We all need a little lovin'."

"Yeah, thanks."

I hung up and dug into correspondence and paperwork. I hated correspondence and paperwork. It was always a feeling of time wasted. Two hours flew by with it seeming as if I had accomplished nothing.

Sensing the shadows of late afternoon, I checked the time, saw it was going on four and headed out the door with another pang of guilt about Holly. I should have been doing everything in my power to find her, not having a date.

Five miles down the coast and two miles inland, I was at the dealership signing papers for the new van. Then I backtracked up the coast a mile to Morey's location. Late afternoon was now turning to dusk.

Not wanting to surprise Morey, I phoned ahead.

"Yeah, what's up?" he said like I was a nuisance.

"Just giving you a heads up. I'm headed your way."

"I'm here."

"I'll be there in a minute."

I found Morey parked up the street from Nicholas' place in an old yellow and white Bonneville. He had given it a new

155

paint job, with little attention to the body work. It looked like a sack of walnuts down the side.

A convertible I could see. A hard top not so much, not even when the price of gasoline was 27c a gallon.

Morey gave me his 'peering through a sandstorm' look as I slipped into the shotgun seat. I took note of the interior. It was the original white upholstery, soiled by the years and showing cracks. Otherwise, everything was as orderly as a drill sergeant's desk.

"What have you got?" I said.

Morey handed me his notes.

"I would have been more thorough but a lot's been going on."

I scanned through them quickly. Christ. Bennie was right. Morey had logged everything short of passing alley cats. I was surprised to see he hadn't included them. I stole a glance his way. He was staring straight ahead, still on the job. I didn't have the heart to tell him that most of this information was useless.

One plus on Morey's ledger. His penmanship was worthy of a Franciscan monk.

"Good job," I said, flipped the page and felt the hair stand up on the back of my neck. With the next entry, Morey had described a young woman going into Nicholas' apartment.

"And this woman, she's in there right now?"

"Unless she slipped out the back way, yeah."

I pulled out my wallet and showed him the two photos I had of Holly.

"Is that her?"

Morey studied them.

"It could be. I didn't get that good of a look and the hair's shorter, but yeah. I'd give it 50/50 odds."

"And she just walked up out of nowhere."

"She came around the corner back there and walked past my car. Then this this guy Nicholas answers the door and acts none too happy about seeing her. You know, standing there with one hand against the opening, like he wasn't going to let her in."

"And they didn't make you?"

Morey shook his head.

"She went right by like I wasn't here and he never looked this way."

"Then keep your eyes on this place and if she leaves, follow her. And call me. I'm going to call Bennie and tell him to get his ass down here."

"I can cover this guy," Morey said. "He tries anything and I'll break him like a pencil."

I climbed out of the car and ducked my head back in through the open door.

"Don't take it the wrong way, Morey. I just want to make sure we've got both entrances covered. If it's who I think it is, we've been looking for this chick big time."

"Yeah? She wanted for something?"

"Not really. Just on the run from her mother. And probably from a biker now too. Like I said, keep a sharp eye out. Especially for this biker. He's dangerous. Enough for both of us…I'm going around to the back street while I call Bennie."

"Anything?" I asked when Bennie answered.

"Nada."

"Okay. I think she's here."

"Who? Holly?"

"Yeah."

"At Nicholas' place?!"

"Yeah."

"What kind of crazy shit is that? How did she get involved with that clown?"

"I don't know and I don't care. Just get your ass down here. I need you and Morey staking out both ends of the house. We'll figure out the whys and wherefores later on."

"I'm jumping behind the wheel right now. What are you going to do?"

"I don't know." I looked at my watch. "I'm due over at Caitlin's place in ten minutes."

"Well go, sucker. We have his car tagged. He's not going anywhere without us knowing it."

"I'm not worried about him. I'm worried about her. Morey said she just walked up. She could just as easily walk out the back way."

"Naw. She ain't jumping no fences, boss man. Go see your lady. I'm already on my way to the freeway. You tell Morey to stay on his toes and I'll be there in 45 minutes."

I drummed my fingers, weighing things.

"All right. I guess this is where you're supposed to turn it over."

"There you go, brother. Enjoy your evening and I'll let you know the minute anything happens."

"I will, but call Morey to let him know you're on your way. And text me as soon as you get here."

"You got it."

I hung up and started the Impala. There was a thought to call Lila but I decided against it. Best to be solid about the intel before saying a word. I had no proof it was Holly at this point.

A few blocks shy of Caitlin's house, a big raindrop splattered against my windshield. Then several more hit in swift succession. Gray clouds rushed overhead, a few hundred feet above the treetops.

It was kismet, the memories of our first winter in love rushing back at me: our first dinner, our first kiss and all the wonderfully silly laughter, the many barren years preceding Caitlin's entrance into my life washed away in an instant. At last, the woman of my dreams had arrived, my one and only, my everything, a love affair for the ages that had slowly faded away, Cheshire catlike, into nothingness.

And yet, despite the passing of years and Caitlin's absence, I had found myself unable to fall in love again, the way I had fallen in love with her. How could I? To do so would have made a mockery of everything we had shared. I was a man both

158

blessed by and a prisoner to undying devotion, so what were you going to do?

Having arrived at the curb outside her front porch, I parked there and stared. Everything was exactly as it had been — her door slightly ajar, a glow of lights seeping out into the shadows of dusk, dinner for two lovers on a stormy night — except that we had been apart. And even that did not seem real now. It felt like only yesterday, the last time I had walked out her front door, never knowing in that instant that it would be seven long years before I saw her again.

I quietly opened the small front gate, walked up to her porch, removed my fedora and sighed deeply before poking my head inside. A fire was crackling in the fireplace and laid-back jazz was playing, a retro Norwegian trio that Caitlin liked to call her Swedish guys.

"Hello," I called out and immediately little Senan came barking.

He had aged greatly, and it took him a moment to recognize me, but once he had, he hardly knew what to do with himself. Back and forth he went, round and round.

"Hey Senan," I said.

Finally, he came and fell against my feet. Caitlin appeared from around the corner a moment later, a big smile on her face and a wooden spoon in one hand.

"Is it okay to come in?"

"Suurrrre," she said with a laugh.

With Senan scampering around the foyer, Caitlin came and cupped my face with both hands.

"Look at that handsome guy."

I completely fell apart at hearing those words. We embraced, the two of us sharing tears of joy together.

"Sorry," I said in pulling back. "It's just a little something in my eye."

She brushed at my tears, and then her own.

"But it's the good kind of something," she said.

"Oh Caitlin," I said, biting my lip. "I have missed you so. The world has not been the same without you."

An errant moth flew in and she waved at it comically.

"We'd better close the door before we get attacked by giant moths."

I laughed and closed the door. Caitlin pulled on my hand tenderly before starting back towards the kitchen. I set my hat down on her credenza, hung my leather jacket up in the coat closet and followed, thinking it only proper to say something about our long separation but knowing to keep mum, knowing that Caitlin disdained any such discussions. To her, the past was a fool's errand. Zen dictated that you stay in the moment.

I had other ideas on the matter but kept my mouth shut.

"It smells wonderful," I said, walking into the kitchen.

She grabbed her bottle of chardonnay and started to pour me a glass.

"No?" she said when I held out a hand. "Maybe just some club soda then?"

"Suurrrre," I said, the same way she liked to say it, charmingly drawn out and sensuous. "Pour me some zeltzer, doll."

She waved at me before going to the refrigerator and fishing around amongst the chaos inside. Out came an already opened bottle.

"I think it's been around since the sixties," she said.

I laughed. When she unscrewed the cap, the bottle barely fizzed and we both laughed.

"That's some zeltzer you got there, dear."

"Maybe if I shake it up."

She did and got a hint of carbonation, to more laughter.

"Thanks," I said as she poured some into the wine glass.

I held up my glass to her.

"To the woman I love with all my heart."

She stared into my eyes while touching her glass to mine.

"But enough with all this mushy crap," I said after a drink of flat seltzer.

160

Caitlin guffawed and went to check her fancy chicken. I followed and put my arms around her waist from behind. There were sundried tomatoes, artichoke hearts and other garnishes with boneless chicken in a thickening sauce.

"You can cut the bread, if you'd like."

"Sure. I'm a big bread cutter from way back."

Caitlin responded to my kiss on her cheek with a tender touch of my face and headed over to work on her salad by the sink. The bread was already sitting on the countertop between the kitchen and the dining room, waiting to be sliced. I went over to the cutting board and pretended to be Art Carney in *The Honeymooners*, lining up a cue shot. Caitlin glanced my way with a laugh.

"Oh, listen," she said.

A flurry of raindrops had slapped at the metal roof jack above the stove. I went to the sliding glass door in back and opened it. Caitlin joined me and we peered up into the sky. Senan snuck by us and out into the rain.

"It's really coming down," she said.

"Yeah. Just for us."

"Yeaahhhh."

She pecked me on the cheek and called to Senan before returning to her salad. I saw the fire getting low and added a log before returning to the bread.

"I'll bet you're going to vote for the nutty President," Caitlin said to me over her shoulder.

I made a so-so sign with my hand.

"It's touch and go. The way I see it, he combines entertainment with politics and I'm all for streamlining."

She laughed.

"That's so stooooopid. But then I like stupid stuff."

"Well, then, you must really love the nutty guy."

Caitlin's mood darkened with those words.

"I can't even believe he's our president."

"I know. It's no longer a backwards world. It's upside down."

161

"It's even worse than that." Caitlin had dried the red lettuce and was tearing it to pieces over a bowl. "Have you watched the debates?"

"Oh, about two minutes of it before I was ready to scream. I was screaming."

"Yeah. I can't stand his lies."

"Hell, I can't stand the sound of his voice."

"Yeah. I've been volunteering down at the party headquarters, making calls and sssssstufffff for the election."

"God. You're making me feel guilty. I've been so caught up in my work, I haven't done a thing but complain."

"But you'll vote."

"I already did. Absentee. Not that it matters much in a blue state."

"We need to move to a battleground state."

"Yeah, when you can think of one where we'd want to live, give me a shout."

She laughed.

The Swedish guys had stopped playing so Caitlin went to change the CD. A moment later, I heard Cannonball Adderley's *Dancing In The Dark* come on. The CD was a mix of straight-ahead jazz that Caitlin and I had put together one night while lying in bed and dreaming up things to do.

I grabbed Caitlin on her way by and slow danced her around the kitchen.

"I love this song. It always sounds like they're in an old nightclub somewhere."

"Yeaahhhh," she said.

We were eye to eye, nose to nose, and kissing.

"I could do this forever, you know."

"Yeaahhhh," she said.

I sensed Caitlin growing anxious over the unfinished meal preparations and let her go with a final kiss. She checked her fancy chicken and returned to tearing up the lettuce. I returned to cutting the bread.

I took a bite of a crust end.

"Hmm," I said. "I want butter."

Caitlin laughed and mimicked me.

"I want butttterrrr."

"I do."

She brought it from the refrigerator and we had a minor orgy, buttering up several thick slices. Then Caitlin went to check on her chicken again.

"It's ready. Did you want to grab the salad?"

"I'd rather grab you."

She swatted playfully at me and got on with her chores. I took the bread and salad over to the table, then poured both our glasses full. A few moments later, we were toasting and digging in.

"Hmm, delicious," I said.

The chicken dish had been ladled over rigatoni. When the wind and rain gusted at Caitlin's windows, we both paused with our forks in the air. She smiled sweetly and touched my hand.

"So, you were saying about work?"

"Oh, yeah. I was checking on my guys just before I came over here."

"You're probably spying on the nutty president."

"I wish."

I explained about Holly, being careful to leave out anything sordid or grim. Caitlin suffered the grim part of this world the way Jesus did the cross.

"But shouldn't you be over there right now trying to rescue her?"

"There's really nothing we can do but watch and wait." I reached out and touched Caitlin's hand. "Honestly. My guys have it covered."

"But what if the bikers come?"

"They won't. Anyway, I can't just go busting into people's homes. And I'm not even a hundred percent sure it's her."

Caitlin stared down at her meal. I squeezed her hand.

163

"Look, I know how you feel, honey. It frustrates me too. You want to bust in there and nail the bad guys, but sometimes you can't."

"But maybe this Nicholas guy's in there hurting her."

"No, no. Nicholas's not that type."

"I'm sure. How do you know?"

"I know. Honestly, sweetheart. This guy's just a big puff ball. A crooked one, yeah, but definitely not some biker type."

Caitlin was now rearranging her meal with her fork.

"Hey, did I tell you about my new guy Morey?"

Caitlin shook her head, still playing with her food. I explained how I had met Morey at the karaoke gig and did my impression of him doing Dylan.

"How does it feeeellllllll...to be on your owwwwwnnnnn."

She dropped her fork, in stitches. I took hold of her hand again, laughing with her. It took us most of a minute to gather ourselves.

"Seriously," I said. "Early Dylan?? I never saw *that* one coming."

"I'm kind of liking this Morey guy now," she said.

"Yeah. I figured he'd be your type."

She swatted at me playfully and took a bite of her meal. I ate too, but with wary glances her way, the question of Holly's safety still lingering in the air. With Caitlin's brilliant mind and her clinical depression, she had mastered the art of compartmentalization in a way that most people would find unimaginable, but when those walls broke down, oh boy.

When it got down to the two of us stabbing at the last Kalamata olives in the salad bowl, I suggested a walk.

"Suurrrrre," she said.

Caitlin got up and opened the sliding glass door. The storm had let up, leaving the concrete patio puddled with rain.

"I can see the moon peeking through the clouds."

I got up to look with her.

"Oh lovely."

We shared a moment before closing the door and starting to clear the table. We quickly had everything in the dishwasher and were grabbing our coats and hats in the foyer. I went out to the sidewalk and waited while Caitlin got Senan leashed.

My phone vibrated while I was standing there. I looked and saw it was Bennie, letting me know he had arrived. I texted him back with a thumbs up and put the phone away.

Caitlin came out through her front gate and closed it. I reached for her hand and we turned right down the sidewalk. At the next corner we turned right again with Senan straining at the leash out in front of us, marking everything of interest.

We eventually arrived at a park with rolling lawns and pepper trees. The trees were dark from the rain, their boughs sagging.

Following a winding path, we exited the park onto a long, narrow street shrouded over by Douglas firs and hemlocks. There was one streetlamp along its entire length.

"Sherwood Forest," I said as we walked in the darkness.

"We'll probably see Robin Hood pop out of the trees any minute."

"Yeah."

The moon peeked through the clouds again, washing the treetops with moonlight. I became aware of Caitlin's delicate little hand in mine. My heart was as high as the stars.

At the end of Sherwood Forest, we turned right again and were soon back at Caitlin's front door. Inside, we hung up our coats and hats and Caitlin went off to use the bathroom. I added a log to the fire. When Caitlin returned, she stood with her back to me and we watched the roaring fire. I wrapped my arms around her waist. Her red hair was aglow from the flames.

"I love you," I whispered in one ear.

Her arms encircled mine.

"Eternity would not be long enough to hold you in my arms."

She pulled me closer.

Standing there together, lost in our spell, Senan got up on his hindlegs and tried to involve himself in the fun. Caitlin reached down to pet him.

"Come, let's sit," she said.

I flopped down on one end of the sofa and pulled off my boots. Caitlin sat opposite me with her feet in my lap. Senan found a place in the middle and curled up.

We stared.

"So listen, doll," I said. "I've been wanting to talk to you about something. You know, just to say I'm sorry? I don't know why I lost my temper the way I did sometimes. I just never knew what to do when you…"

Caitlin gently reached out a hand to stop me.

"No, please, honey. I really need to get this stuff off my chest. I mean, there were times when the littlest stuff would get all blown out of proportion and I just didn't know how to deal with it. I just couldn't understand why you got so anguished over…"

Caitlin was suddenly waving her hands around her head. It was the image of someone being attacked by bees, and would have appeared playful to the uninitiated, but I knew better. This was being done in desperation.

I let out a big sigh. She pretended to ignore me and grabbed her copy of *Finnegan's Wake* from the coffee table.

"Why don't you read to me."

Reluctantly, I opened the book to a random passage and started reading.

This is Roo-shious balls. This is a ttrinch. This is mistletropes. This is Canon Futter with the popynose.

"Oh please, Caitlin," I said, shutting the book in frustration. "I really need you to understand. This is important to me."

She looked off at the fire. I continued staring at her. We sat there with horns locked. The silence dragged on.

"All right, forget it," I said finally.

I was getting ready to leave when Caitlin spoke up out of the blue.

"Maybe we could take the train down to San Diego again."

"Oh sure," I said with dramatic flair.

Caitlin laughed.

"Real funny," I added.

"We can sit backwards like on our last trip," she said as if we hadn't locked horns at all. "We'll be teenagers by the time we get there."

That was Caitlin. Only in her magical world could facing backwards on a train take you back in time. And only in her world was it impossible to discuss your feelings.

Still grousing, I doubled down on the dramatic look and Caitlin laugh ed.

"Fine," I said. "We'll take the damned train down to San Diego. Do you care which weekend?"

"No. Just buy the tickets and give me a week or so to plan."

I nodded and we were back to staring at each other, with all the things I wanted to say still bottled up in my chest.

Love In A Dying World

Fourteen

Deciding that sex would fix everything between us, or at least allow me to take out all my frustrations, I had leaned forward to kiss Caitlin when my phone vibrated. With a quick glance, I saw it was Bennie calling and held up a hand.

"I'd better grab this. It's one of my guys…What's up?" I said, answering the call.

"She's on the move."

"Alone?"

"No. She jumped in the car with Nicholas. I'm on their tail and it looks like they're heading for the freeway."

I quickly had my boots on and was heading for the back slider.

"But you're sure it's her?" I said while slipping outside.

"Oh yeah. No doubt about it. She cut her hair short but it's her."

I closed the door and wandered away from the glass.

"So? What's going on now?"

"Oh, he just took the loop onto Coast Highway instead and we're cruising south below the palisades."

I looked back to find Caitlin staring out at me with Senan in her arms. I waved to her and got back to Bennie.

"What's Morey doing?"

"I told him to stay put, just in case something else went down while Nicholas was gone."

168

"I'm good with that. You stay on Nicholas and keep me posted. I'm heading your way right now."

"You got it."

I hung up and went back inside.

"Is it her?" Caitlin said.

"Yeah."

"What's she doing?"

"I don't know for sure. She got in the car with Nicholas and they're heading south on Coast Highway. I'm guessing to San Clemente. Anyway, Bennie's on their tail and I'm heading that way now."

When I went to kiss Caitlin goodbye, she waved like she was being attacked by bees again and herded me towards the front door.

"Come on, Caitlin," I said while grabbing my coat and hat. "Just one kiss goodbye."

"No no, you've got to hurry. Before something terrible happens."

When I attempted to kiss her anyway, she waved her hands even more frantically.

Good lord. When things went sideways with Caitlin, they really went sideways. And I was a stubborn fool to think I could fashion a happy ending from one of these moments, when nothing of the sort could be had.

"Okay, I'll call you," I said from the front porch.

Caitlin had the door parted just enough to show her face.

"Okay, go," she said. "You've got to hurry."

"I love you," I added.

She waved and gently closed the door. I went out and kicked a tire. Christ. You may as well try to get in the last word of an argument. Like one kiss was going to end the world.

Climbing into the Impala, I heard old Tom saying, accept, accept, accept, but I couldn't. The harmony between us had been broken.

I called Bennie with that image of Caitlin's rejection stuck in my head.

"Where the hell are you now?"

"Whoa, dude. Chill. I'm guessing things went south with you and the doll again."

"Just tell me where you are!"

"Jesús Cristo. Okay, I'm down at the south end of San Clemente. You know where all those seedy apartments are alongside the freeway?"

"Yeah, what? Did they go inside somewhere?"

"No. We're still rolling…Oh wait. He's parking now."

I waited.

"So, what?"

"So, I'm parking too."

"And what?"

"They're talking in the front seat…And now he just got out."

"Just him?" I said.

"Yeah. She's still in the car…I've got my money on this being a score because he just looked over his shoulder…Now he's disappearing into the courtyard of one of the apartment buildings. It's got to be a score. Why else would that prick come down here?"

"I don't know. You don't see him anymore?"

"No. Should I go in and stake things out from a bit closer?"

"No, just hang loose until I get there. What's your address?"

He read it off to me.

"Got it. I'll be there in five minutes max. Call me if he comes back out before I get there."

I was just then careening onto the freeway and hit the gas, quickly doing ninety and darting in and out of traffic. That episode at Caitlin's place kept playing over in my head. I hit the steering wheel and cursed out loud. Why did I let this crap drive me mad? She wouldn't even remember it the next time we talked.

I made the Christianitos exit in just over four minutes, still fuming. Two wild right turns and a left turn later, I was pulling into a maze of aging apartment buildings. Bennie called back.

"He's coming out now."

"I just pulled into the 'hood. Let him get behind the wheel but if he starts to take off before I get there, hit your lights and cut him off."

"You want me to take him out?"

"Cut it out, Bennie. Just keep an eye out and do as I said."

I hung up and stepped on the gas. By the time I turned the last corner, Nicholas had his lights on. Bennie hit his but I flashed mine and raced up to the side of Nicholas' car, blocking him in. Nicholas tried muscling his way out until he saw me flash the cop badge I kept in my center console.

When Bennie pulled in behind me, I got out with my Smith & Wesson pointed at Nicholas. He was checking his rearview mirror as I approached. I motioned for him to roll down his driver's side window.

"Hands on the steering wheel," I said when he looked up at me.

He did. Bennie came up from behind.

"Go keep an eye on that courtyard," I told him. "Make sure no one tries to get away before our backup arrives."

Bennie headed off across the grass and disappeared into the courtyard. I opened Nicholas' door.

"Okay, get out with your hands on the car."

"What the fuck, man? You got no right to be searching me."

"Just get your hands on the car."

I peeked in at Holly. She looked both wretchedly strung out and furious to see their drug deal had gone south.

"Don't try anything funny," I told her.

Patting Nicholas down for weapons, I felt something in his coat pocket and pulled out what looked to be a quarter ounce. With the gun at Nicholas' back, I had a quick look. It was quality cocaine, pure flake. I tucked it away and took his wallet.

"You can relax."

I stepped back and opened the wallet.

"So, Nicholas Chalmers. What are we doing out here tonight?"

"Just minding my own business until you came along."

"Yeah, I can see that."

I poked my head back into the car.

"Your ID," I said to Holly.

She dug around in her purse. Our eyes met as she handed it to me. I had expected a pleading look but saw only anger. Holly was too fierce to beg.

Bennie reappeared by the entrance to the courtyard and held up his hands. I waved him over.

"Run these two IDs."

"You got it."

"Just a second," I said as Bennie walked away.

I held up a finger to Nicholas.

"Like I said. Don't try anything funny."

I joined Bennie several paces away and whispered.

"Let's pretend we have a missing persons bulletin on Holly and cut Nicholas a deal. The mother doesn't want her daughter's name in the papers so it's his lucky day. We keep the coke and the girl. He gets to walk. Just mention the missing person bulletin when you come back."

Bennie nodded and went to the van. I returned to Nicholas.

"Any priors?"

"You're the cop. You tell me."

"Tough guy, huh?"

He looked off. I stood there staring at him. Bennie came back a minute later.

"There's a missing person bulletin on the girl."

We moved away again several paces and whispered back and forth before I returned to Nicholas.

"She here against her will?"

"What does it look like it to you?"

I motioned to Bennie.

"Get her out here."

Bennie went around and opened the car door. Holly followed him back to my car and leaned against it, sulking.

"All right, Nicholas," I said. "Looks like it's your lucky day. Apparently Holly's mother pulled some strings downtown because I'm being told to cut you a deal. We take the coke and Holly. You walk and none of this gets into the papers. If you don't like that, I'll take you in for possession with intent to sell and let you rot for a spell. So what's it going to be?"

"Fuck it, take her," Nicholas said. "She wanted to get high and I was just trying to be a nice guy. I didn't ask for this shit."

I smirked.

"A regular Sir Lancelot...Go on, get out of here. And try to keep your nose clean. I know where you live."

I handed him back his ID and waited until he had driven away, then walked over to Holly.

"Looks like you're going home, kid. You can thank your mother."

I opened the passenger door of my car. Still sulking, she pushed away from the hood and slid into the seat.

I motioned Bennie some distance away from my car. Holly kept staring straight ahead.

"Now what?" Bennie said.

"I don't know. Get her cleaned up and take her home. She turns seventeen in a week or so, after which no one can make her do anything."

"I'll tell you this much. I know a junkie when I see one and that chick is totally strung out. Coming down is going to be a bitch."

"Yeah, well, we'll have to cross that bridge when we get to it. Right now, I just need to stash her someplace safe, before Donald Ray Potter finds her, and me."

"And you can bet your ass he's looking."

"Yeah, I know."

"So what am I doing?"

"Oh, go back out and watch that biker house. I still owe old man Huntington his 26th Dynasty Egyptian figurine. And a Picasso."

"I already told you, boss man. That Vanderhof prick has your Picasso."

"Yeah, yeah."

"See? You don't want to learn nothing."

"Come on, Bennie. Let's not get started."

"I'm not getting started. I'm just saying. Didn't I tell you we'd find Holly?"

"Yeah. So quit while you're ahead."

"You don't want to learn nothing."

"Oh shut up and get your ass back out there to the Devil's Punchbowl."

"Yeah, you got that shit right."

"Hey, before you go, what's up with Morey?"

"He's still watching Nicholas' place. You want me to leave him there?"

"Yeah. I guess he can't get into too much trouble. Kid Morey."

Bennie did a couple of lefts and a right.

"I could see him in his prime."

"Yeah. He'd have given Marciano a run for his money."

"That's him."

I sighed.

"We'd better get moving. Just keep me posted."

"I will. And hey. Dump that coke. You don't need the temptation."

"You don't think she might be needing some of it before we're through?"

"Yeah, there's that…You're sure you're okay?"

"Yeah, I'm not going to put this shit up my nose."

"Good. You don't want to get started again."

"Like I would."

"Hey, I've got to keep an eye on you newcomers."

"Get out of here."

He smiled.

"I'm going to grab some grub and I'll be back out there."

"Thanks. You're a good man, Bennie."

He playfully pumped a fist.

"Another benny for Bennie."

"Yeah. Just don't let it go to your head."

"Hey, no worries. Because sure as shit, you're going to be busting my balls again before I know it."

"No, I've turned over a new leaf, Bennie. No more ball busting. I'm tired of ball busting. I just want to be a decent human being."

"No shit, boss man? That's some spiritual shit."

I gave him the so-so sign.

"I'm working on it…so don't push me." I glanced over at Holly in my car. "I'd better deal with her before she falls apart."

"Yeah. I can tell she's already Jonesing big time."

"Yeah."

Bennie started to walk away but stopped again.

"Hey. Did you, you know? With the doll?"

"Don't even talk like that. I don't expect you to understand it, but this is love on a spiritual level."

"Wow, okay. Con respecto. I didn't know."

"And now you do."

He tapped his heart with his right fist and headed back to the van. I returned to my car and climbed in. Holly met my eyes when I looked her way. She was a mess.

I opened my PI badge and set it on the seat. While she took that in, I started texting Caitlin.

"You fucker," Holly said.

I held up a hand to let her know, chill, while I finished the text. Holly's impulse was to bolt, but as long as I had that coke in my pocket, she wasn't going anywhere.

The text to Caitlin was simple. I've got her and she's safe. You can sleep easy now. I'll fill you in tomorrow.

With that done, I looked over at Holly.

"Yeah, I'm working for your Mom."

"Cop. Fucking liar."

"Holly, maybe you ought to count your blessings. Because if I was a real cop, you and your pal there *would* be on your way to jail right now."

"Yeah, some luck. I don't suppose you know what it's like to come down from meth."

175

"Not from meth, but I know about coming down."

The fierceness in her eyes turned to a pleading look. I knew what she wanted. I also knew that I'd be committing several crimes, giving it to her.

"Please," she said. "I'm dying here."

I glanced in the rearview mirror.

"Please," she said again.

I gave her a quick look. No doubt about it. She was going to be a mess detoxing cold turkey from meth.

I looked again in the rearview mirror.

"So here's the deal, Holly. I'll make this coming down as easy as possible for you, but I want answers in return."

"Answers about what?"

"About a lot of things."

I pulled the coke out.

"Whatever I ask, you give me a straight answer. Okay?"

"Okay."

"I mean it, Holly. No bullshitting. The minute I feel like you're not being honest with me, boom. I'm cutting you off and you can come down cold turkey...Deal?"

"Yeah."

"Yeah?"

"Yes!!!"

I nodded my chin at the glove box.

"Go on. Grab the warranty booklet."

She did so while I got a credit card out.

Holly was mesmerized as I chopped up a big fat line for her. I kept glancing in the rearview mirror and every which way as I worked.

With the line ready, I took a hundred dollar bill from my money clip and rolled it up for her. She did half the line with one nostril, savored the effect with eyes closed and quickly vacuumed up the rest. The sense of her being crushed by the world slowly slipped away as we sat there. Finally, she exhaled and settled back into the seat as if having an orgasm.

"Thanks," she said and held out the hundred dollar bill.

"You may as well keep it for now."

She tucked the bill into her bra. I stared until she looked my way.

"So, let's get down to business."

"What? You mean going back home to my Mom?"

"There's that part, yeah."

"I'd rather go see the cops."

"Yeah right. It can't be that bad."

"No? Does she still have that pervert Desmond hanging around?"

"I don't know a thing about Desmond. Who's that?"

"Her boyfriend. It figures she wouldn't mention that part."

"So fill me in."

"He's a child molester."

I scoffed.

"He is. He's always trying to get me in bed. At least when he's not trying to play the *Dad* role."

"That's a pretty serious allegation, Holly."

"Well, it's true. He's always coming up to my bedroom like he needs to lay some fatherly shit on me, when all he wants to do is to stare at me in my pajamas."

"Has he ever touched you?"

"See? You're just like my Mom That's all she ever says. 'Did he touch you?' No, but I have no doubt the fucker would screw me front ways, sideways and backwards if he ever had the chance."

I shrugged and looked forward. Hell, what did I know? I guess a woman could sense when a man was after her scent.

Feeling Holly's stare, I looked over. She gave me another pleading look.

"What? More?"

She nodded.

"Christ. That last one would have killed a horse."

"No way. That just took the edge off."

"That's the general idea. I'm here to help you to come down, not rocket you into another dimension."

"Please," she said again.

I shook my head in disgust. It wasn't hard to picture a similar scene playing out with Desmond. A flirting look, an enticing bit of leg exposed, anything to get what she wanted.

I looked back at Holly and had to smirk. God. The look.

Then, what the hell, anything to build trust. I needed answers and she probably had them.

I looked at her several times while chopping up another good line. When she was done with it, she threw her head back, in another dimension now.

"Wait," she said when I went to return the warranty booklet to the glovebox.

Holly quickly scooped up the loose coke dust with an index finger and used it to numb her gums.

"You done?" I said.

She nodded. I put things away.

"Okay, back to business."

"Sure, whatever. Can we go get a drink now?"

I eyed her while starting the car. Can we go get a drink now.

I worked my way back out of the neighborhood and headed north on Coast Highway. The road was still wet from the rain and mostly empty. Gossamer clouds drifted by against a starry sky. Holly was busy pointing out every bar we passed along the way. I was wrestling with what to do next. I knew alcohol would be necessary to ease her down from the drugs and decided it would be best to take a bottle back to my place. We'd have to work things out from there.

"What's this?" she said when I stopped in front of a liquor store.

"I'm getting something to drink and taking you back to my place. What do you like?"

"You don't want to go out partying somewhere?"

"Don't even get started, Holly. We're going home to my place, where you're going to start answering my questions. And then we're both going to get a good night's sleep."

"I do kind of like you."

"Knock it off. What do you want to drink?"

"I like piña coladas. They're really good with coke."

"Oh, they are, are they? You'll be lucky to get some warm Budweiser."

She made a face. I went into the liquor store and returned with the Jimmy Buffet bar kit; rum, pineapple juice, coconut cream and a bag of crushed ice.

Remembering Morey, I gave him a quick call to make sure he was okay.

"This Nicholas guy came back about 30 minutes ago without the girl. Then he took off again. I wasn't sure what you wanted me to do."

"Why don't you go home. I can track him for the rest of the night from the bug on his car."

"Whatever you say."

"Yeah, it's fine. We'll pick things up in the morning. I ordered a new van and it should be ready in a couple of days. Then you'll be all set up in style."

"Yeah. I was going to say. This sitting around in my own car isn't exactly what I'd call professional. Anyone passing by could spot me in a New York second."

Well, I'll be right down with a cocktail and your foo foo slippers, Morey. He should have been around in the old days, when you had to run to a phone booth every time you needed to make a call.

But I shelved the rant, acknowledged his complaint and got off the phone. No need to make trouble. The man was dependable and that was worth its weight in gold.

"What?" Holly said once I had hung up. "That's probably some guy you've got watching Nick's place."

I shot her a look.

"And I don't need any more trouble from you, either."

"Oh, like you're my Dad now or something?"

"Somebody ought to put you over their knee."

"Oh, sure. I'd like to see you try it."

Again, I held my tongue. Better to think long and hard about my game plan for this young lady.

Fifteen

On the way home, Holly resumed her survey of every bar we passed along Coast Highway. When she wasn't doing that, she was pestering me about being a detective. It was well past midnight when I parked in the garage. I was ready to send her back to Nicholas.

"Cool place," she said as we crossed the creek.

I opened the front door and hit the lights. Holly immediately flopped out on the couch like she owned the place.

"Are you going to make me a drink?"

"You know what, kid? You really have a way of getting on my nerves."

"Kid. I'm almost an adult."

"Oh yeah. All ready to run for Congress next week."

"Okay, Daaaaaaadddd."

I took the Jimmy Buffet bar kit out to the kitchen. Holly sprang to her feet and followed me.

"Do you know how to make them?" she said.

"I know how to order them. That's about as far as I ever got with the thing."

"Here, I'll show you," she said, muscling her way in.

"No, no," I said when she grabbed two glasses from the cupboard.

"What? You don't want one?"

I shook my head

"Is that like in 'never'?"

"Just make your goddamned drink."

She laughed.

"You're so funny…So you're one of those, huh?"

"Yeah. I'm one of those."

"You're sure you don't want just a little one?"

"Just make your drink."

She laughed again and went merrily about her business. I sat down at the kitchen table and waited.

When she was done with her concoction, she took a long sip and put the mix away in the frig. I waited until she was seated opposite me.

"Okay, business."

She gave me another one of her pleading looks.

"Just a little one? Before we get started?"

"This isn't a party."

"Please? I'm starting to feel rotten again."

"Yeah, I can see you're really suffering over there."

She doubled down on the 'pity' look.

"All right. Go on. Get a plate."

She sprang to her feet like a gazelle before lions.

I got the bindle out and a credit card. Holly sat back down and watched hungrily as I dumped a modest bit of coke onto the plate.

"Come on," she said when I started to close the bindle.

Exasperated, I dumped a bit more onto the plate and tucked the rest of the coke away in my pocket. She would have snorted up the entire quarter ounce in one sitting if I had let her.

When Holly was done with her line, she dabbed at her nose real lady like and followed that up with another long pull on her piña colada.

"Okay, I'm ready," she said.

I shook my head.

"What?" she said.

"What…So for starters, I'll help you come down easy, but you're coming down, and then you're going home."

"With Desmond the pervert."

"Look, if this guy's really trying to get you in bed, I'll personally knock him around."

"Fine, I'll go home. And then I'll leave again. As soon as I'm seventeen."

"Fine, but your mother's paid me handsomely and I'm damned well going to fulfill my part of the bargain." I patted the coke in my pocket. "You know what happens if you don't cooperate."

"God, okay. How many more rules are you going to lay down?"

"None. You just answer my questions and we'll be fine. Or I'll flush the rest of this shit down the toilet."

She propped her chin up on both palms, pretending to be all ears now.

I wanted to smack her.

"Look, Holly. Let's start with a little heart to heart here, all right?"

"I thought you weren't going to lecture me."

"Just shut up and listen. I just want you to know that I get it. Most parents are a disaster at raising their kids."

"Like my Mom."

"Yeah, well. I'm beginning to think *her* biggest mistake was spoiling the crap out of you."

"Ohhhhh," Holly said sarcastically and had another sip of her piña colada. "You don't happen to have some grass lying around, do you?"

"Oh Christ. Can we just try to stay on message here?"

She blew a raspberry at me.

"Fine. There's always the toilet."

"Okay, okay."

"Okay, so all I'm trying to say is, I get it. I grew up with that crap too. 'Don't do this. Don't do that.' Parents can be a real pain in the ass."

Holly nodded sarcastically.

"Yeah, well, I wouldn't gloat. The older you get, the more you realize that in most cases, they were just doing the best they could. Your mother included."

Holly rolled her eyes.

"Hey, I've seen her cry over you so don't give me that crap."

That seemed to give Holly pause.

"Really?" she said.

"Yeah, really…I'm wondering why she would, but yeah."

Holly made a face and I made a face back.

"Look. The last thing I'm going to do is tell you how to live your life. I know it's pointless, but at least take a long, hard look at where you're headed. I wonder if you get it. That you're actually making choices with your behavior and some of those choices can lead to some really bad places."

"Is this the lecture you give all your kids?"

"I don't have any…"

She looked askance at me.

"You're not gay, are you?"

"Oh for Christ's sake. Just try to stand back and look at your life, Holly. You want to be a junky at twenty-five and living on the streets? I mean, your mother may not always be around to bail you out."

"I get it."

"Yeah?"

"Yeah. Can we get on to your questions?"

"Let's start with Nicholas. How did you come to know him?"

"He knows some other people I know."

"You mean Potter."

At the sound of his name, all of Holly's party balloons seemed to pop. She had another sip of her piña colada. I kept staring at her until she looked back.

"What?" she said.

"What? I was watching you out there on Highland Road. Until you disappeared." I pointed at the bruises on her arms. "I know how he treats you."

She had another sip of her piña colada without answering me. I waited until she looked back.

"How did Nicholas come to know Potter?"

"I don't know. I guess Nick's older brother was in the Army with this guy named Zeke and Zeke belonged to Don's gang."

"And Nicholas got involved...how?"

"Drugs. I mean, that's how I met him. He came one day with a kilo of meth."

"And how did you get his address?"

"He gave it to me at the beach one day when we were all down there partying."

"And just like that, you decide to show up at his front door?"

She took a sip of her drink. I waited. When she failed to answer me, I headed for the bathroom.

"All right!" she said.

I slowly returned to my seat and stared.

"Nick had told me that if I ever got into trouble, he knew a man who would help me. Give me a place to stay and all that. Someone really rich, I guess."

"Did you get a name?" I said.

She shook her head.

"You're sure?"

She nodded.

"Then explain to me why Nicholas was so unhappy about seeing you at his door. My operative said he wasn't going to let you in at first."

"I don't know. I guess Nick was kind of freaked out because Don had gotten in touch with him. Said he'd kill anyone who helped me get away."

"And do you happen to know where Nicholas was getting his meth?"

"This guy named Chango."

I nodded.

"What?" she said.

"Nothing...So, Potter. Where did you meet him?"

"At a concert."

"A concert where?"

"At the Orange County Fair this past summer. There were a bunch of biker type guys hanging out and my girlfriends and I started partying with them and then Don and I kind of hooked up."

"And then?"

"And then I went for a bike ride with him the next day and then…you know."

"And then?"

"I don't know. We were texting back and forth a lot for a while. When I was in school and couldn't see him. And communicating some online."

"Online where?"

"On chat rooms and stuff."

"What kind of chat rooms?"

"I don't know. He was always directing me to this stuff he had posted on 8kun and places like that but I…"

"8kun? What's that?"

"You don't know?"

I shook my head.

"It's where a lot of these white supremacist guys post their stuff. It used to be 8chan but the servers stopped hosting that site so everyone migrated over to 4chan. Then they stopped hosting that site too so now everyone's on 8kun."

"Everyone."

"You know what I mean."

"Yeah, I get the idea…And are you into that crap?"

She shook her head.

"Okay. I guess I'll have to do my homework. In the meantime, what about your mother. Do you think Potter knows where she lives?"

Holly shook her head.

"No? Or you're not sure?"

"He never asked me and I never told him."

"But he threatened you, right? Like, if you ever try to leave me, I'll find you, no matter where you go?"

She nodded and looked away.

"Do you have any idea where he is now?"

She shook her head.

"Think, Holly. A place where he might have gone to hide. This is really important. You and your mother's lives are in danger."

"I can think of a dozen places."

She slurped at the last of her drink. I went to my satchel and returned with a pen and notepad. Holly had made another drink while I was gone. When I sat down, her eyes darted to where the coke was tucked away in my pocket.

"I'm kind of coming down."

"Yeah? Well you're not going back to your mother's place all coked out."

"Please."

Reluctantly, I pulled the bindle out of my pocket. A minute later, Holly was in the general zip code of nirvana.

"Start anywhere you want," I said with my pen ready.

"There was this cabin up in Big Bear, for one thing. A friend of his owned it."

"Address?"

"I don't know. It's way out on the end of Sand Canyon Road. The last place. That's all I know. I don't even think it has an address."

I jotted all that down and looked back up at her.

She shrugged.

"There was a place we visited out in Joshua Tree."

"Describe."

She did.

Over the next fifteen minutes, she laid out a collection of dives and crash houses that Potter had frequented over the three months Holly had known him.

"Is that it?"

"That's all I can think of."

"Well, please. If anything else comes to mind, let me know."

She sipped at her drink. I pulled Potter's card out of my wallet, along with the photo I had found at his place and waited until our eyes met.

"I found these out on Highland Road. After they had booked up to Crestline. Did you know they were headed up there?"

She nodded.

"Is that when you got out?"

She nodded.

I turned the card over and showed her Chango's name.

"I'm going to guess from what you told me that Potter got connected with Chango through Nicholas somehow."

Holly nodded.

"Do you have any idea what they were up to? I mean, besides drugs?"

"I don't know for sure. I just heard that Chango was ex-military too and was supposed to be helping Don get a bunch of weapons and stuff."

"Weapons and stuff. Like what?"

"I heard them talking about bombs and rocket launchers and stuff like that."

"But you don't know what for?"

She shook her head.

"Something up in LA, I think. He never discussed it in front of me. He always made me leave the room."

Holly had more of her drink and stared.

"Charlotte Huntington," I said. "Do you know where she is?"

Holly shook her head.

"No?"

Holly shook her head again and had another sip of her piña colada.

I stared until she looked back at me.

"Do you know that a young woman was killed and buried out behind Potter's old place on Highland?"

Her eyes flickered as we stared at each other.

"No?" I said.

188

She shook her head.

"I know this isn't pleasant, Holly, but sooner or later you're going to have to tell the police everything you know. They're going to sit you down in a room with a little table and the bare lights and all that BS and they're going to put you through it, so you'd better get your story straight right now."

"I don't know anything about someone being killed."

I kept staring.

"I don't!"

"You know how the law works, right? If you witness a crime and don't tell the police about it, you've become an accessory?"

She looked down and played with her hands.

"All I know is, they came home with this girl one day and the next day she was gone."

"Her name?"

"Crystal."

"Last name?"

Holly shook her head.

"We talked a bit but never got that far."

"Did you find out where she's from?"

"She said something about the Midwest."

I kept staring.

"That's all I know!"

"So, she's there one day and the next day she's gone and that's it."

"Yes."

"And you didn't sense that something had happened to her?"

She shook her head.

"A bunch of the guys went off on their bikes one day and when they came back, she wasn't with them. I thought they had just dropped her off at the freeway or something."

"And Charlotte Huntington. She never came out to visit you."

"No. Why would you think that?"

"Because she's your best friend and she's missing too."

"I don't know what you're talking about."

I kept staring. My gut told me she was lying, but what the hell were you going to do? She wasn't going to talk and I wasn't ready to wring the truth out of her. At least not yet.

"One last question," I said. "This rich guy that Nicholas said would take care of you. You really don't know who it is?"

"No. Nick just said he lived here in Laurel Lagoon."

I stood up.

"I need to get some sleep."

"Can I stay up."

"Yeah. Just don't leave."

"I won't."

"And I know why."

"Can I have a little more?"

"Yeah, but this is how it's going to be. I'll leave some on the plate now. And maybe a bit more in the morning, but then you have to start coming down. You're not going through this entire quarter ounce, I can tell you that much."

"Where am I sleeping?"

"There's a guest bedroom behind that door over there. Or you can sleep on the couch. The TV's in the living room."

"I'll sleep there."

She flopped out on the couch. I went to grab some bedding out of the linen closet. Holly already had the TV on when I returned.

"Keep it down. I don't want it blaring while I'm trying to sleep."

Holly looked at me hopefully. In response, I went back out to the kitchen, dumped a half gram of coke onto the plate and set it on the coffee table in front of her.

"Use it wisely. Like I said, tomorrow it's..."

I pointed down. Holly stared back coquettishly, no doubt expecting she could con me into more.

"You know. You really are a pretty decent guy after all."

"Yeah, well...I *am* reluctant to pull the fatherly card on you, Holly, but there are people in this world who just want to see you have a good life. You know, with a happy future? Not one where you're all strung out on that shit. I know this life sucks sometimes but you can't always change it. It's something you learn over time. Sometimes you just have to deal with things the way they are. Maybe you'll look back someday and understand what I'm trying to say here."

"I do," she said. "I know you're just trying to help me."

Without warning, Holly jumped up and gave me a kiss on the cheek.

"Thanks. I feel like you're the first real friend I've had in months."

That tugged at me a bit. I gave her a kiss on the forehead and started up the split-level stairs to my bedroom.

"Oh," I said, looking back. "What's Desmond's last name?"

"Ducot."

"French, huh?"

"He likes to think so."

I smiled and continued upstairs.

"Hey," she called out. I stopped again. "Can I use your phone?"

"No."

She made a face.

"Sorry, Holly, but I'm not taking any chances of you calling Potter and having him figure out where I live."

She looked frustrated but seemed to understand. I heard the chop chop chop of my credit card on the dinner plate as I stepped into my office.

Going online, I started down the rabbit hole of Potter's conspiracy world. The 8kun website quickly led me further underground. QAnon. #WWG1WGA. #TheGreatAwakening. 1488. Follow the White Rabbit.

In this alternative reality, the deep state was behind every government agency and conspiracy behind their every harmless action. The deep state was out to take them down and they were there to take out the government first.

My flesh was crawling by the time I was through.

Last thing, I did a quick background check on Desmond Ducot.

B.A. from USC, 2003. A stint on the professional tennis circuit that quickly flamed out. Dabbling in what looked like a number of ventures — a hip bistro, an art gallery, an online art auction — all of which had failed. Then somehow, he had come to know Lila Evergreen. When and how, there was no clear evidence but one thing jumped off the page. Desmond had lived in Pueblo Hills, from 2012 until three years ago, and now lived in Doheny Beach, his exodus directly paralleling that of Lila Evergreen. You did not have to be a conspiracist to see that connection.

He was still alive, from all appearances, which was something, knowing Lila.

Before going to bed, I checked my email and, among the several messages, there was one from Motation DX. Opening it, I was met with flashy animation and a blaring soundtrack, and that was just the background email template. He had included the info on his rival and a not so subtle suggestion that I should get to work on this right away. Oh boy. How did I get rid of this guy? I didn't dare mention it to Bennie. He'd be all over this like ants at a picnic.

I crawled into bed but lay there with eyes wide open. A million thoughts. A million theories. A million dead ends.

My mind kept coming back to one thing Holly had said; a very rich man who'd give her a place to stay and make sure she'd never have to worry, and a man who also happened to live in Laurel Lagoon. Add to that what Bennie had described at the Zanzibar the other night and my thoughts naturally turned to Vanderhof. I could think of only one explanation for why that son of a bitch would surround himself with a coterie of beautiful teenage girls and it wasn't a good one.

Once in the middle of the night, I got up to use the bathroom and heard the TV still on down in the living room. At least Holly had it on low. Whatever her failings, she understood

192

respect. There was a thought to go check on things but I left it alone.

In the morning, I found her sitting at the kitchen table, wrapped in a blanket and with a coffee mug in her hands. The coke was gone. Her mascara was streaked. She had what was left in the bottle of rum on the table.

"How are we feeling this morning?" I asked on my way to the coffee pot.

"Lousy. How do you think?"

"Sorry. There's just no easy way to kick drugs."

She gave me a pleading look. The disheveled mascara lent a clownish touch. I almost laughed.

"Can I at least have one?" she said.

I doctored up my coffee and sat down at the table without answering her. She stared. I glanced at the rum. There were about three inches left in the bottle. Enough for a couple more piña coladas.

"Maybe," I said.

"Come on," she said. "You promised last night."

"No. I said, maybe."

Her response was dismal.

"Look. I know a little bit about this shit so here's what we're going to do. You go ahead and polish off the rum. I'll go out and buy you some beer. Then we start tapering off. You'll be hurting by tonight but you'll be through the worst of it by tomorrow morning."

"What are you going to do with the coke?"

"Flush it down the toilet."

"Come on. I'm fucking dying here."

"You're detoxing, Holly, and you're going to keep detoxing. It's that or I turn you over to the police as a missing person and let them deal with you."

"Fucker. I'm sorry I said all those nice things about you last night."

"Yeah, yeah."

I sipped my coffee and returned her stare.

193

"And what am I supposed to do after I detox?"

"I told you. Go home. That's my deal with your mother. Deliver you safely back home."

"That's all you care about. Your money."

"You don't know a goddamned thing about me Holly so don't start."

"Well, I'm suffering and you don't seem to give a damn."

I bit back a smile.

"Oh, real funny," she said.

"Well? We're being a bit overly dramatic, aren't we? I mean, people starving in Africa, that's real suffering. You're going to feel like you have a cold for a couple of days. I don't see much comparison."

"And *you'd* know all about it."

"I already told you. I do."

Unable to get what she wanted, Holly grabbed the bottle and poured a bit of rum into her coffee.

"I suppose you go to those meetings and all that stuff."

I nodded.

"Please," she said.

I nodded slowly while studying her.

"I'll give you one before I go buy your beer, but that's it."

Holly looked abject — about detoxing, about the thought of me flushing all the coke down the toilet, about having to wait for her snort, about everything — but it didn't change what I planned to do. She was going to detox, and then go home. My only concern was whether or not she would need medical care.

"Some breakfast?" I said, standing up.

She made a sound that suggested nausea. I scrambled up three eggs and made some toast. She did her best not to watch while I ate. When I was done, I placed my dishes in the sink.

"I'm going to take a shower and go grab your beer."

"Great. Can I at least have my line now?"

I stopped and stared at her.

"Just wait another fifteen minutes, will you? It's going to have to last."

She made a face. I went up to my bedroom and locked the door behind me.

Sixteen

When I returned, Holly was wrapped up on the couch and watching cartoons. I knew the drill. Detoxing always made me think of the Flintstones.

I sat down and pulled the bindle out of my pocket. Holly looked up from her cartoon.

"What?"

"One more question."

"What?"

"I want to know what happened up in Pueblo Hills."

She looked back at the TV.

"I don't know what you're talking about."

I put the coke back in my pocket.

"I don't!"

I stared.

"Your step-father was killed up there and you don't know a thing?"

"Not really. All I know is, one night, my Mom and one of her friends woke me up in my bedroom and rushed me off to the friend's house. The next day I heard my step-father had died from a heart attack or something but when I got home a few days later, nothing more was said about it, except for the funeral and stuff. After that, we went on like nothing had ever happened. A couple of times, I brought it up but my Mom made it real clear. She didn't want to talk about it."

"Was he nice to you?"

"I guess."

Holly looked to where I had tucked the coke away.

"Please."

Holly watched dismally as I dumped out enough for a modest line.

"Come on. If it's going to be the last one."

Sympathizing with her a bit now, I pulled the bindle back out and added a goodly amount more.

"Thanks," she said.

I went out and poured myself a last cup of coffee and grabbed my keys.

"Try taking a shower," I said at the door. "You'll feel better."

"Sure."

"You will. In fact, I'd say take it while you've got that buzz going. You won't feel like doing it later on."

"I don't even have any fresh clothes."

"There's a washer and dryer. You can wear the sheet while doing your laundry."

"Aren't you going to ask me what kind?"

"Of beer?"

"Yeah. I like Fosters. Or Becks."

"I'll bet you do."

"Yeah. You'll probably bring back Budweiser."

"Actually, I was shooting for Millers, but I could do Bud."

"Bastard."

I couldn't help but laugh. She was such a spoiled brat. I had been thinking to buy her Heineken. I knew how much it hurt when you started jonesing.

"Just clean up, will you?" I said. "And let me worry about the beer."

On my way out to the garage, I heard Fitzy yelling from inside her house. Then her daughter was yelling back. Then a door slammed.

Who did your life coach call when *her* life was falling apart?

I was nearing downtown when I received a return text from Caitlin.

Thanks for letting me know about Holly. I hope she's okay.

I had been thinking to stop by the office anyway and called once I was there.

"How is she?" Caitlin asked after we had said hello.

"She's fine. She was pretty drugged up when I found her but she's starting to come down."

I explained about the beer and tapering off.

"I'm out to grab some right now and then we'll see how it goes. If things get really bad, I'll have to find a detox joint."

"What was she doing?"

"Coke."

I thought it prudent to leave out the meth part. Caitlin wanted to hear all about how I had rescued Holly so I related the basic details.

"I made her an offer she couldn't refuse. Me or the cops."

Caitlin laughed.

"But you think she'll be okay now."

"I think so…So what are you doing?"

"Oh, stuuufffff."

"Yeah? Stuuufffff?"

"Yeah."

"Okay, I'll let you get back to doing stuuufffff. I need to call and find out what bozos number one and two are doing."

Caitlin laughed again.

"Do they know that's what you call them?"

"Bozo number one probably does. That's Bennie, the Puerto Rican. He goes off in Spanish every time I piss him off. It's like I have a bitchy Ricky Ricardo working for me."

We both laughed.

I paused over what I wanted to say next.

"It was awfully nice seeing you last night. I hope we can do it again soon."

"Yeahhhhh. Maybe it'll rain again this week."

"Yeahhhhh. We could take another stroll through Sherwood Forest."

"Yeahhhhh."

"Okay. I'll call you soon…I love you."

"Stop! You're not supposed to say that!"

"Oh. Okay. Then I mxyzptlk you." She laughed. "A lot."

"Let me know how she's doing, okay?"

"I will."

I got off, shaking my head. You're not supposed to say that. Christ. The woman had more idiosyncrasies than Hindus had gods, and still I adored her.

I called the car detailer next, learned the new van would be done that afternoon and called Bennie to let him know.

"Any news?" I asked him first.

"Nada. Morey called me from home and said he'd spell me any time."

"You two work that out. Meanwhile, the new van will be ready later today so arrange where you and Morey want them to drop it off. Can you handle that?"

"Can I handle that."

Bennie had a conversation with himself in Spanish and then asked me about Holly.

"Oh, I left her making piña coladas and doing the last line."

"You're enabling her, dude."

"Yeah, yeah. She's coming down, Bennie. Have you forgotten how it feels?"

"No way, bro. That's why I'm sober."

"Then don't lecture. I'm out grabbing some beer and was thinking to check with Gigi before I head back. It's probably best to have some sober ladies hanging around over there. She'll be jonesing big time by the time the sun goes down and I don't know if I'll be around to keep an eye on her."

"Did she tell you anything new about Potter?"

"Yeah. The addresses to a shitload of hideouts and that he's been gathering up a cache of weapons."

"For what?"

"She didn't know exactly. Apparently he was careful not to discuss the details around her but she had a feeling it was something big. Something that would get him on the evening news."

"Shit, boss man, you're talking domestic terrorism. Isn't this where you're supposed to call Homeland Security or something."

"Maybe, but I'd like a few more answers before I do."

"Answers, like what?"

"I don't know. Get Morey situated in the new van and we'll talk more when I see you."

"Sure. Play it close to the vest. See if I care."

"Oh Christ, Bennie. Let's not get started."

"Well don't treat me like a kid."

"Bennie. There are things I don't tell you for your own damned good. Now please deal with the new van and we'll talk later."

I carefully placed the phone back in its cradle, then banged it a few times for good measure. This was where you executed a few men, just to maintain proper military discipline.

Butch must have heard the ruckus because his snout poked through the partially opened door a minute later, sniffing. Then the head appeared.

"Yeaaahhhhhhhhhhhh, I'll get that little GUY!" I said and off he bolted.

He was making his second lap down the hallway as I got Gigi on the phone.

"You okay there, handsome?" she said.

"Just fine, beautiful, but I've got a wet one on my hands. A young lady who's going to need some help before the night is through."

"Where is she now?"

I explained the situation.

"I'll be heading back with some beer shortly. I'll give her about four hours before she starts bouncing off the walls."

"How about if I bring some gals over after the noon meeting?"

"That would be great. I'm not exactly sure where or when but I'll probably have to head out of town for a spell tonight and don't dare leave her alone."

"You don't worry about a thing. We'll take it from here."

"Great. Thanks. You're a treasure."

I gave Gigi my address, ended the call and was dialing the next number when Betty walked in the door. Butch was right on her heels. I held up my hand.

"Just a second there, hot stuff…Yeah, Kenny. Michael. I have another list of addresses I need you to check out."

I looked across the street at his office window. He smiled back.

"Send it over," he said.

"It's written down on paper."

"So, use the clothesline."

"Oh yeah. Almost forgot about the clothesline…You know what. Give me a second and I'll scan it to file."

Betty waved at Kenny and he waved back. I lurched at Butch on my way to the printer and he barked. Kenny laughed.

"Grand Central over here. Put a rush on this if you can," I added and hung up.

I looked over my shoulder at Betty while scanning the document.

"What's up?"

"Have you heard from Steve?"

"No, why? Were you expecting him back already?"

"Yeah. He was supposed to be in last night."

"He's probably having a good time. You getting tired of Butch?"

"Of course not. Just a little worried about Steve."

"Yeah?" I said while opening a new email and attaching the document. "Did you try texting him?"

"I did."

201

"I'll bet there was a lot of fresh powder from the storm and they decided to stick around for an extra day."

I glanced up from my computer.

"You're busy," she said.

"A little. Give him until tonight. If my assumption's correct, he's up on the cornice right about now, going airborne."

"I'll let you go," she said and started out the door.

"You're always welcome around here!" I called after her.

She didn't answer. Oh Jesus. Another wounded soul. We were all on the verge of unraveling these days. I had to stop worrying before I came unglued.

I leaned back in my chair and tried to still the static between my ears. It felt like oak up there. Just give me some serenity, please. Why is it so hard to find?

I reached for my phone and pulled up some Koto music on YouTube. It worked like a drug. Breathe in. Breathe out. Yin yang. All of life is in passing.

I had been at peace for a few moments when the phone rang. I glanced at the caller ID. J. Richards. That didn't ring any bells. I answered anyway.

"Michael Devlin here."

There was a pause.

"It's Jake. You hit me up the other day about putting out some feelers."

"Oh yeah, Jake. Thanks for calling back. What do you know?"

"I know you can talk to the Mongols. They're cool. As long as you don't want no trouble, they don't want no trouble. This Potter dude's another story. I hear that fucker's crazy. I guess there's some dude down San Diego way with money, wanting to finance some crazy blow up the world shit and Potter's in with him."

"With blowing up the world?"

"That's what I heard."

"Do you have any idea where in San Diego?"

"My source didn't know for sure. Just San Diego somewhere…So, are we cool?"

"Yeah, Jake. We're cool. Thanks a lot for looking into this for me."

"No problem. Keep on trudging."

"Yeah. Same to you."

I got off the call, thinking maybe it was time to get the FBI involved. Blowing up the world was definitely above my pay grade.

I had been weighing the pros and cons of that decision when another message from gangsta man appeared in my mailbox. As before, the message opened with party poppers going off. I had grown so captivated by the animation, I nearly missed his harangue at the bottom of the page. Was I working on his case or what? Everything he did was like a finger in your chest.

Christ. How did I get rid of this guy?

I was chewing on that question when I remembered Holly's beer. Best to take care of her before she came completely unglued. I could picture her tearing the house apart, in search of the motherlode.

I headed out the door and made a quick stop at a liquor store. To my surprise, Holly was asleep on the couch when I walked in. The coke plate on the coffee table looked as if a dog had licked it clean. The TV was on low to an old episode of Friends.

I went out to the kitchen. The empty rum and mix bottles were sitting by the sink. I quietly put the bulk of the beer in the refrigerator and three of them in the freezer. When you were trying to jones on beer, the colder the better.

Back out in the living room, Holly sleepily opened her eyes.

"I'm dying," she said.

I sat down on the coffee table and poured one beer into a mug. She quickly guzzled down half of it.

"Thanks," she said, noting that it was Becks.

I nodded.

"Can I have just a little one."

"I'm sorry, Holly. I threw it all out."

"You fucker."

"I know. I'm sorry but it's time to come down."

She shuddered.

"The beer helped. Did you buy lots of it?"

I nodded. She downed the rest of the mug.

"Can I have another one?"

"You can have as many as you want, but try to pace yourself. Wait until it hurts again."

I squeezed her hand and stood up.

"Did you shower?"

"Yeah. My clothes are in the dryer."

"Okay. I've got a few beers icing down in the freezer. When you're ready, shout and I'll bring a fresh one. I'm going to clean up in the kitchen in the meantime."

I tossed all the bottles first thing and went to work on the dishes. As I was wrapping that up, the dryer dinged. I folded Holly's clothes and delivered them to the living room. She was in the bathroom. There was no sound of her retching.

She came out a minute later, wearing the blanket.

"You all right?" I said.

"Yeah. Just peeing."

"Your clothes."

"Thanks. Another beer?"

"Sure."

I rotated another beer from the frig into the freezer and brought a freshly iced mug with the cold beer.

"Thanks," she said as I poured the beer. "I can see you've done this before."

"You bet."

She downed half the mug. I sat down on the coffee table again.

"What's it like being clean and sober?" she said.

"A bitch."

Her smile was more of a grimace.

"It's just easier than being messed up...And you get to do fun stuff, like helping old Holly Evergreen sober up."

"Some fun."

"Trust me. It's worth all the cheap drunks I've ever had, seeing you get well."

She stared.

"Did you really flush it all?"

I nodded. She quickly downed the rest of the beer.

"I kind of hate you right now."

"You'll feel differently in a couple of days."

"I doubt it."

I stood up.

"Just holler when you're ready. I'm going up to get some work done."

She curled up tighter in her blanket and stared at the TV. I headed up to my office.

Over the course of the next hour, I worked without distraction, save for several beer runs to the kitchen for Holly. Then I heard voices outside, assumed it was Gigi with her entourage of ladies and headed back downstairs to greet them. Holly looked anxiously at me as I passed through the living room.

"Who's that?"

"Reinforcements."

"What do you mean?"

I winked and went to open the door. The ladies were just coming over the bridge as I did.

"What a wonderful home you have here!" Gigi said. "A creek and a bridge! My god, it's magical!"

I gave her a hug and greeted the other three women. We had all crossed paths at various meetings without being formally introduced.

"Welcome. Come on inside and meet Holly."

"Oh, this must be our little warrior princess," Gigi said, marching across the living room with an outstretched hand. "Hi, I'm Gigi."

Holly looked at me as though wanting to be rescued.

"These are your new sober friends, Holly. They've all been through it before. She's on a beer detox right now," I told Gigi.

"Of course, of course," Gigi said. "We've got to do this nice and slowly. The last thing we want is for you to end up in the emergency room."

As Gigi introduced the other ladies, Holly darted another desperate look my way. I got the message and returned with a fresh bottle of Becks and mug.

"Well, he's certainly bringing you home in style, young lady."

"Yeah. Here's the drill," I said. "I have a couple of beers in the freezer, along with a second mug. Just keep rotating the beers and the used mug as you go along."

"Quite a system you have," Gigi said.

"A lot of practice."

"I see."

"So, if you gals have this situation under control, I'll be upstairs working."

"Oh, we have this entirely under control," Gigi said.

I winked at Holly and headed up to my office. In the background, I heard Gigi asking Holly all about her life story. There was a thought to call Lila but I decided to put it off again, at least until that night.

Back at my desk, I found that scene at Caitlin's place doing more laps in my head. 'Go. You have to go.' Then the door quietly closed in my face.

In talking with her earlier on the phone, you would have thought it never happened. I loved the woman with all my heart, but she drove me mad. I could not think of one other adult who behaved in this manner. As if the world would come apart over a quick kiss goodbye. You couldn't really call what she had done a tantrum, but the effect on me was the same; worse maybe. There was no earthly way to explain it, save for madness.

Unable to restrain an impulse to fix things, I reached for the phone, called a florist near Caitlin's house and dropped a 'C' spot on an autumn bouquet with red and orange roses. They said it would be stunning.

I leaned back in my chair, remembering Old Tom. He would have told me that everything was just the way it was supposed to be in this universe, right now. Acceptance was the answer to all my problems. But no. I had to control things. Forever trying to wrest order from chaos.

I had been sitting there for a spell, cuffing that conundrum around when Potter returned to my thoughts. He was out there somewhere hunting for Holly, and planning god knows what kind of destruction.

I was reaching for the phone, ready to call the Feds when Gigi tapped on my partially opened door.

"Come in," I said.

She did so smiling.

"She's agreed to come over to my place...What do you think?"

"Sure. I just need to deliver her back to her mother's place tomorrow some time. She turns seventeen next week."

I made a sarcastic face.

"Have you called her mother?"

"No. Not yet."

"Oh, Michael, you should. She must be worried sick."

"You don't know the history."

"Bad?"

"There's been worse. Anyway, Holly doesn't want her around so I figured, let's get her through the worst of this detox first and go from there."

"You're not giving mothers enough credit. And Holly is still a minor."

I shrugged and leaned forward with a whisper.

"Did Holly tell you that she was strung out on meth? And that I've been feeding her coke to help bring her down?"

"She mentioned the coke. And is pretty pissed off about you flushing it. In fact, she's pretty sure you still have it lying around somewhere."

Gigi raised her eyebrows at me.

"Yeah, it's still here, if that's what you're wondering. I wasn't sure if she was completely out of the woods yet."

Gigi gave me a concerned look.

"Did you want help with flushing it?"

"I can handle it."

"You're sure?" she said.

I held up a hand.

"Gigi. I can handle it."

I wasn't about to explain that I might have other plans.

"So, were you thinking to leave now?" I asked.

"That was the idea. Just wanted to run it by you first."

"No, that's great. She's in good hands. She was a captive audience, as long as she thought I had the coke lying around. Now? I don't know if I could control her."

"And her mother?"

"I don't know. I'm still thinking about that one."

"Well, Mrs. Evergreen is your client, so I best leave that to you."

I nodded.

"Did you want to take the beer with you?"

"Sure. She'll no doubt need a few more before it's all through."

"Yeah."

I stood up and followed Gigi back down to the living room. The three ladies had Holly dressed and sitting up. She looked miserable.

"You're in good hands," I said. "Just hang in there. You'll feel a thousand times better in a few days."

"Yeah. I just wish I could have one more."

"I told you. It's gone."

The look on her face wanted to break your heart, but I wasn't about to give in. I led Gigi out to the kitchen and helped her load up the beer. Gigi gave me a kiss on the cheek.

"Get rid of it, Michael," she whispered. "You don't need the temptation."

"I know. Don't worry."

"I'm worried."

"I'm fine."

She shook a finger at me. I gathered up the bag of beers and headed back out to the living room with her.

"Are we ready, ladies?" she said.

Holly was less than thrilled about the mission but stood up. I gave her a hug.

"Look, I have to call your mother."

Holly shook her head.

"I'll give it until tomorrow, Holly, but she's got to know."

She made a glum face.

"Let's just hurry. I feel like I need another beer already."

As I was escorting them out the door and across the bridge, my phone rang. It was Bennie.

"Hey, Bennie, hang on a minute, will you?"

The ladies helped Holly into Gigi's old Jaguar. I handed them the bag with the beer. Gigi paused with her door open.

"Such a lovely place, Michael. I'm always amazed to find there's another magical street in Laurel Lagoon I didn't know existed."

"The dead-end ones are the best."

"Indeed they are."

Gigi gave me another peck on the cheek and climbed into her car. As I was closing the door, I noticed Fitzy's daughter standing inside their opened garage, stealing glances our way. Her hair was unkempt, as before, and it appeared as if she was wearing pajamas. She was giving Holly a run for her money.

I waved and she halfheartedly waved back.

Gigi had started her engine and rolled down the window.

"We'll see you down at the club again soon?"

I was still busy watching Fitzy's daughter.

"Hello? Earth to Michael?"

"Oh, sorry, Gigi. Yeah, I'll definitely be back down there soon."

"You be careful," she added and backed out into the street with a final wave.

Holly stared out her window at me like she was being taken to the gallows.

Seventeen

I had been staring after her for a long moment when I realized I still had Bennie on the line.

"Oh shit, Bennie. Sorry. I was saying goodbye to Gigi. She and some other gals in the program came by to take Holly home with them."

"Yeah, it's cool. I got nothing better to do than to sit around and listen to you schmooze with some bitches."

"You know, I was almost feeling sorry for you there. Then you had to go and be a jerk."

"Me a jerk? You should talk, boss man."

"All right, Bennie, let's get down to business. What's going on with Morey and the van?"

"He's got it but had to go over things real careful like before he was satisfied."

"Yeah, I can picture that one…And you?"

"I'm out here watching these fuckers shoot jackrabbits and toss them to their pit bulls."

"Fun. Anything else?"

"A couple of their bitches drove off a little while ago and came back with a bunch of groceries. And they are some pretty nice looking bitches."

"Jesus, Bennie."

"Oh. Sorry. A couple of their *ladies* went off a little while ago. What's the big deal? Their old men call them bitches. They probably call themselves bitches."

"Okay, okay. What's your point?"

"My point is, this shit's going nowhere fast."

"Bennie, you know the drill. All we can do sometimes is watch and wait."

"For what? That 26th Dynasty figurine to go somewhere? Shit, for all we know, they unloaded it last night while I was gone."

"Could be, but I doubt it. I picture them setting it on the coffee table and staring at it while they get high."

"Meanwhile…"

"Meanwhile, just hang in there. I have a funny feeling that Potter's going to show up there soon."

"And then what?"

"Shit, I don't know. Start shooting someone. That's what you're dying to do."

"Fucker."

The whole time Bennie and I had been talking, Fitzy's daughter had remained up in the garage, pretending to be busy with something at their work bench. I headed in towards the house with a final look back. She was staring my way as I closed the gate.

"And what are you going to do?" Bennie said.

"I don't know. I was thinking to go check on this Abigail Potter out in Apple Valley and then come see you. I'm guessing I won't be but twenty, thirty minutes from your location."

"And then what are we going to do?"

"Bennie, if you want to turn this into CSI: Hell's Angels, knock yourself out."

"I just want some action."

"Then why don't you march right up there and tell those Mongol boys, 'Give me my 26th Dynasty figurine or else'."

"I think I will."

"And if you don't stop beating my balls, I'm going to pay you to do it."

I let Bennie have a moment in Spanish before interrupting him.

"Look, you son of a bitch. I'm going nuts here too. I feel like I've got a million balls up in the air and I'd just as soon shoot someone as look at them right now. But that's life, isn't it, Mr. Program Guru?"

"You don't know shit. You're supposed to change the things you can and I can see us changing all kinds of shit right now, like putting a gun to Vanderhof's head."

"Christ, Bennie. Please. March in there and pull a gun on those Mongols. It'll save us both a whole lot of grief."

Bennie went off again.

"You done?" I said when he was through.

"Fucker."

"Well, just hang loose. I need to make some calls and then I'll head your way and we'll put our heads together."

"Fine. You know where to find me."

"I'll see you soon."

I had started to hang up when Bennie called out.

"Yeah, what?"

"How much did you say this Egyptian thing is worth?"

"I didn't, but from talking with the old man, I'm guessing he wouldn't pay more than five or ten K to get it back. Why?"

"I don't know. Just wondering."

"Yeah, well, don't go doing anything stupid."

I hung up but immediately felt an impulse to call Bennie back, worried that he might actually be planning something. People in the program were always talking about character defects and I was beginning to think that micromanaging was one of mine. I headed back into the house, wondering what was behind the impulse but not really wanting to know.

Anyway, I had bigger fish to fry, like whether or not to call Lila about Holly. Part of me thought it was a lousy idea. Part of me knew that I had no right to keep her in the dark any longer so I sat down to make the call.

"I've been wondering if you'd ever call back," she said without saying hello.

"Sorry. I've been busy on your behalf."

213

"And?"

"I have your daughter."

Lila gasped. Then I heard muffled sounds, as if she had fumbled the phone. I pictured her reaching for tissues again.

"Oh, thank god, Michael. Thank god. So where is she now?"

"Here in Laurel Lagoon. Detoxing at the home of an old gal I know. Someone who understands recovery very well. Sorry to say but Holly was pretty drugged up. Drugs and booze so she's not in the best of shape right now.

"Oh god. All right, give me the address and I'll drive right over."

"Look, Lila. I got Holly to agree to go home but I think it's best if you give her a few days before trying to see her."

"Michael. Are you seriously telling me how to deal with my own daughter?"

"Those are her terms, not mine, Lila."

There was a brief pause.

"Well, I'm sorry, but as her mother I insist on seeing her."

I was silent

"Well?" she said.

"Well, I seem to remember someone saying that dragging Holly home against her will was the last thing she wanted to do."

"Well, this is different."

"Fine, but with the way things are between you two, she'll just walk back out the door the minute she's seventeen."

There was more silence.

"And just exactly what has she been telling you?"

"Oh, a little of this and a little of that. About Desmond, for one thing."

"Oh, she's always in such a snit about him. There've been times when I've just wanted to take her over my knee."

"Your family problems aside, Lila, you might have mentioned him."

"Michael, I'm not obligated to tell you every little detail about my personal life...What?" she said when I failed to answer her.

"What? 'Michael, you're awfully handsome.' 'Why don't you come over and have a drink with me?' 'I really don't want to be alone tonight'."

"Oh, for god's sake."

I waited.

"Fine, Michael. Just call me a confused woman who doesn't know which way is up but it was never my intention to hurt you...I didn't, did I?"

Oh Christ. The acorn never fell far from the tree.

"Mrs. Evergreen, let's just get back to the business of your daughter."

"Fine, Mr. Family Counselor. What do you propose I do?"

"Give Holly a few days to detox, for starters. She's agreed to come home after that. Then, I don't know what. You two obviously have a history to sort out and that is definitely none of my business."

"God, I really hate you right now. I hate her. I hate everything."

I would have smiled, if I wasn't so fed up with her.

"Look, you're free to hate me all you want. There's a long line. In the meantime, your daughter's safe and you'll be seeing her soon enough."

"When?"

"Tomorrow night. The next day at the latest. She just started detoxing this afternoon."

I heard Lila working on her sniffles.

"You know, Michael. It really hurts that she doesn't want to see me."

"I understand but you're just going to have to try and rebuild trust with her."

"And how do you propose I do that?"

"Quit bossing her around for one thing? She's not a kid. She's a young adult with all the hopes and dreams and

215

complications of any other human being...That, and maybe quit siding against her with Desmond."

There was a pause.

"God, I really do hate you right now."

"Yeah, I can feel it."

"You bastard. Can you at least tell me how you found her?" she said after another pause.

I did, got off the phone and stared out to sea. Women. If life hadn't already sent me over the edge, they would definitely get the job done in short order.

I headed out the door a minute later, still struggling with this trip out to Apple Valley. Here and there along the highway, I caught glimpses of the coastline and Catalina Island on my left. A patina of brown smog had gathered out there on the horizon. So much for that feeling of autumn. The wind had shifted in from the desert again and completely blown it away. At least the sky had stopped raining ashes. The last I had heard, three of the five fires were now mostly contained.

On my way down the 3rd Street hill, I caught sight of the cruise ship. It was still anchored a mile off the coast. The news had said the infection rate was out of control so it was being denied permission to dock. From a Disney World high seas adventure, the passengers had descended into the first level of purgatory. One could only imagine the mutiny onboard.

I soon reached the freeway and pushed seventy-five with one eye on the rearview mirror and was winding down the backside of the Cajon Pass an hour later. You had to wonder who had come up with the name. Apple Valley was just a flat expanse of desert with a mishmash of stop lights and power lines, the original settlement layered over by some newer, cookie cutter stucco homes.

In chasing down Abigale Potter's address, I arrived out to a crisscross of gravel roads, well past any recent efforts to make Apple Valley look respectable. The homes were now spread far enough apart to keep your neighbors at bay. A chain link fence

216

surrounded each house, in case anyone got a wild notion about stopping by for a cup of sugar.

By the time GPS landed me at Abigale's driveway, the houses had all acquired a trailer trash quality to them. Her roofline was low enough to make it seem as if it had collapsed. There was not a welcoming thing about it. Even the driveway was guarded by chain link fencing.

In the course of that hour drive, I had developed this image of Abigale Potter as a frail little old lady who liked to knit. I got the 'little' part correct. The minute I opened the gate in her chain link fence, a small, wiry woman came flying out the front door, wearing polyester slacks and a plaid blouse and wielding a twelve-gauge shotgun like she knew how to use it.

"Take one more step buster and I'll send you back to your maker."

"Mrs. Potter?" I said.

"Who wants to know?"

I very gingerly reached for my ID and held it out to her.

"That don't mean nothing to me 'cept trouble."

"I don't mean any trouble. I was hired by a woman to find her daughter and the daughter was last seen in the company of a Donald Ray Potter."

She stared.

"I'm guessing from the records that he was your son?"

"He weren't no son to me."

"Then you wouldn't know how to find him?"

"Hell no. And how the hell did you find me? That's what I want to know."

"Public records, Mrs. Potter. It's something anybody could find...Look, I'm just trying to locate a missing daughter. Anything you share with me won't go any further."

"I ain't sharing a goddamned thing with you, boy, 'cept for some buckshot. Now get the hell off my property and close that gate behind you."

Mrs. Potter leveled the shotgun at my chest.

I cautiously pulled a business card from my wallet and dropped it on her walkway.

"In case you change your mind…"

She cocked the shotgun.

"I said get the hell out of here."

I retreated to my Impala, having no doubts now about this being Potter's real mother. Abigale was not the type to sign up for the foster home program.

On my way back out to the interstate, I called Kenny.

"You again?" he said by way of answering.

"Yeah. I'm on a roll."

I related my encounter with Abigale Potter.

"Like mother, like son."

"Yeah. So look, please do a deep dive into her background for me. I'm guessing she has her own checkered past."

"Any particular hurry?"

"No, not really. I'm more interested in that death certificate for old man Cabot."

"Oh, yeah. I almost forgot. I got it this morning."

"You almost forgot, huh?"

"Sorry. You're not my only client."

"Well, that hurt."

"Sorry."

"I'll let it pass. So what did it say?"

"He died from a broken neck."

"Oh Jesus. And any word on how that happened?"

"No. That would be in the police report."

"So why don't you have one of those?"

"Uh…I'm only human?"

"How come?"

Kenny laughed.

"I'll work on it and get back to you…I hope you have life insurance."

"Yeah, right…So what else do we know?"

"Oh, on that list of Potter hideouts?"

"Yeah?"

"It reads like a list of the usual suspects but nothing in Potter's name."

"And anything else?"

"Not right at the moment."

"Okay. Just remember to look into that estate business with Lila. I'd like to know how many enemies she left back in Ohio."

"You got it."

I started to hang up and called Kenny back.

"Hey, how old was this Cabot geezer when he died?"

"Uhhhhhh, let's see...eighty-six."

"And this happened, what? About ten years ago?"

"Eight, actually."

"Which would have made Lila thirty-four at the time."

"Sounds like true love to me."

"Yeah, well, there has to be some reason why Lila went off and married the next old geezer so let's find out."

"Maybe she likes old geezers."

"Or maybe she didn't get enough dough out of the first estate and felt like she needed more."

"Brilliant deduction. You should be a detective."

"Just get that police report, please."

"I'm on it."

I ended the call, still chewing on that shotgun in my chest. Then Lila's suspect past was back in my thoughts. Her husbands kept having terrible accidents. Sure, any eighty-six year old man could have fallen down a flight of stairs and broken his neck, but everything about Lila was rotten with suspicion.

About five miles down the road, my phone rang. It was Bennie.

"What's up?" I said.

"I'll tell you what. Bring five grand cash with you out here to Pear Blossom Highway."

"What are you talking about?"

"Just what I said, boss man. You want your 26th Dynasty figurine back? Bring five grand."

"Bennie, what in hell did you do?"

"I went in and talked with my home boys." Bennie rattled off something in Spanish. "See? You speak la lengua and you get a long way with these people."

"I don't believe this."

"You don't believe what? That I'm getting some shit done? Just bring five grand."

"Yeah, right. They'll probably take the money and shoot us both."

"You don't know shit. This is a Latino thing, dig? These guys are solid. You don't fuck with them and they don't fuck with you."

"Fine, Bennie. What am I supposed to do? Come in with my hands up?"

"No. Look. I'll ping you my location. You bring the cash and I'll take it from there."

"Okay, big shot."

"Shit. You're just jealous."

"Yeah, right. I'll see you in a bit. I need to find a Bank of America."

"Well hurry up. I've got my dick in my hand over here."

"I thought you were all bros."

"They still want to see the money."

"Fine. Tell them I'm on my way."

I got off and said the serenity prayer. Bennie was just one more thing I could not control.

With a quick Google search, I found a branch in Apple Valley and turned around. When I asked to withdraw five grand in cash, they called down to the Laurel Lagoon branch and had them fax over a copy of my signature card. And even then they didn't seem to believe me. I finally left with fifty $100 bills in a banker's envelope.

Plugging Bennie's location into Google map, I was directed north on Phelan Road, then over to 138 on Sheep Creek Road, then up towards Wrightwood on Angeles Crest Highway and left where the road split onto Big Pines Highway. The Devil's Punchbowl was straight ahead.

Eventually I was guided onto a dirt road and went along with dust kicking up in my wake. Where the road jogged hard right at a sign for the national forest, I spotted Bennie's van. He climbed out as I pulled to a stop. Before we had time to discuss the weather, five guys popped out of the surrounding brush, all bearing shotguns. One of them was Armando 'El Chango' Villarreal.

I looked at Bennie. Nice going, home boy.

El Chango watched as I was frisked for weapons. Another guy searched my car and quickly had the Smith & Wesson out of the glove box. El Chango said something in Spanish and the gun went back. While that guy closed up my car, Chango came over and got in my face.

"I don't like cops staking out my place."

I stared back.

"Did you hear me, gringo?"

"I'm not a cop and I don't care if you gentlemen fuck elephants out here. All I want is that figurine back."

Chango nodded.

"Okay. Bennie here says you're cool. Did you bring the money?"

I nodded.

"Then let's do this."

Armando motioned for Bennie and me to follow him. He and another guy led the way. The other three guys brought up the rear with shotguns over their shoulders.

Inside, a dozen or so bikers were scattered around the living room, their women draped about them like trophies. A couple of the women would have looked nice on the cover of a magazine, if you liked bleached blondes or dyed black hair with tattoos and nose rings. Altogether it was den of thieves, and a pretty rough looking one at that. The pit bulls definitely didn't look happy to see us, the little monsters ready to pounce at the wrong word. One of the men had said something to them in Spanish and they sat back down where they were.

Chango pointed me to a chair and said something to his lady. She got up with a sultry air and left the room. I sat there with everyone staring at me. I had one eye on them and one eye on the pit bulls.

A minute later, the woman returned with something wrapped up in a towel. Chango took it from her and revealed a figurine. It looked like it had come from the 26th Dynasty to me.

"Is this what you're looking for?" Chango said.

"Looks like it."

"Then five grand and it's yours."

With all eyes still on me, I reached into my coat pocket and pulled out the envelope. Chango held out his free hand and I tossed the envelope his way. He tossed the figurine back. There were laughs as I juggled to keep the thing from hitting the floor. Meanwhile, Chango did a quick count of the money.

"We're good. So are we done here?"

I decided to push my luck and mentioned Donald Ray Potter.

"I've been looking for him and wondered if you happen to know where he is."

If anyone in that room had been distracted heretofore, they weren't now. All eyes became laser focused on me.

"What the fuck do you want with Donald Ray Potter?" Chango said.

"He had a thing going with a client's daughter. The daughter got away and I figure Potter's going to come looking for her. And I'm thinking to find him before he finds her. And me."

Chango exchanged looks with his people around the room. I was thinking to take back what I had said but it was too late.

Chango nodded at two of his men and they got up to leave the room with him. Chango pointed at Bennie and me before disappearing.

"Make sure these dudes don't go nowhere."

With that, Bennie and I had a sizable munitions cache pointed our way. One of these days, I thought. I'll learn to keep my mouth shut.

Bennie and I exchanged looks. It didn't take a rocket scientist to figure out what he was thinking.

When Chango returned, he barked out something and four of his boys were quickly hustling Bennie and me towards the back door. Nothing good was going to come of this adventure. We were cattle now, being taken to slaughter.

Bennie was talking fast in Spanish the whole time. I picked up on a few of the words, enough to have a vague idea of what he was trying to convey.

The back screen door was about to slap us in the ass when Chango barked out something else and we were led back into the room. I promptly had Chango in my face again. His buddies were still supporting me by both arms.

"All right, gringo. Bennie makes a good point here. Killing you could make big trouble for me. But so could leaving you alive. So give me one good reason why I shouldn't bury you out in the desert back there."

"I can't think of any."

Chango went off in Spanish. It grabbed your attention, considerably more than Bennie's version did.

"You got a death wish or something, gringo?" he said.

"No. I just don't like being pushed around. And then expected to grovel."

Chango sized me up.

"You've got balls, fucker. I'll give you that much."

"My one sin is not knowing when to keep my mouth shut."

Chango said something to his minions and pretty soon they were all having a laugh. Then just as suddenly, Chango was back in my face. A knife at my throat would have had the same effect.

"The truth is, gringo. I could give a shit about Donald Ray fucking Potter but some shit's going down and that fucker could make real trouble for me if he ends up behind bars."

223

"Then I'm guessing we're all on the same page here."

Chango nodded slowly.

"What are you trying to tell me, gringo?"

"I'm just saying, if Donald Ray Potter no longer walks the face of this earth, that would be in both our interests."

Chango continued nodding his head while staring, then finally motioned for his boys to cut me loose.

"You lay low, fucker, and I'll see what I can find out. And I mean real low, comprendez?"

I nodded.

Chango spoke to Bennie in Spanish and looked back at me, not all that happy about the deal we had just made

"Go on. Get the fuck out of here before I change my mind."

I had started to leave when I remembered something and reached into my coat pocket. Every gun in the room was quickly leveled at me again as I did.

"Peace offering," I said, pulling out what was left of the quarter ounce.

Chango nodded for me to bring it to him. I tossed it instead.

"What the fuck is this?" he said.

I gestured for him to look. A smile crossed Chango's face as he opened the bindle.

"Would you look at this fucking shit," he said to his nearest buddy. "Pure fucking flake. Where did you get this, gringo?"

I grabbed the figurine.

"Chasing down the guy who stole this."

Chango nodded approvingly and gave me a thumbs up. Bennie and I left them putting their noses to roughly five grams of pure Peruvian flake.

Eighteen

On our way back through the brush, Bennie and I shared a look but held our tongues until we reached our rigs and were certain no one was listening.

"Next time you're trying to get me killed, boss man, how about a little heads up."

I shrugged.

"Yeah, maybe that wasn't one of my best moves."

"Maybe…That shit rates right up there in the top ten worst of all time. I can't even believe you said that. You almost got our asses dusted."

"Yeah, well. It's done now so let's get back to business."

"Yeah. If I fuck up like that, you're beating my balls from now until next Sunday. But when you fuck up, it's always 'let's get back to business'."

"Yeah. So let's get back to business."

"Fucker."

I placed the figurine on the front seat of my car and joined Bennie in leaning against the van.

"What else was he saying back there? Did he tell you how to get in touch with him?"

"No. He was telling me how they cut your dick off and shove it down your throat before they shoot you. And that's if they're in a good mood."

"And if they're in a bad mood?"

"You don't even want to know that shit."

"I suppose not…Anyway, Jake finally called back and told me roughly the same thing about these boys."

"You might have told me."

"It was out of concern for your safety that I didn't. I had been planning to approach them myself."

Bennie scoffed.

"They'd have roasted your dick for marshmallows."

"Maybe."

I gazed off towards the backside of Mt. Baldy. The tallest peak was volcanic looking and streaked with fingers of snow.

"Abigale Potter was pleasant, by the way."

"Yeah? And how did that shit go?"

I explained.

"Wow, okay. At least now we know where that dude got his personality."

"Yeah…" I sighed. "So let's get back to planning our day."

"You already got my vote. March over there and put a gun to Vanderhof's head. Get the old man's Picasso back and we're down to some jewelry."

I rubbed my forehead.

"Let's not press our luck, Bennie."

"I'm telling you. I have a sixth sense about that painting."

"Yeah? Bennie friggin' Cayce over there?"

"Bennie Cayce? What's that shit?"

"You don't know? He was a famous Mexican clairvoyant."

"Yeah, bullshit. I don't know why I bother with you. You don't want to learn nothin'."

I returned my gaze to the backside of Mt. Baldy, trying to be clairvoyant, and getting nowhere. I pushed away from the van.

"Go ahead and get back to staking out Nicholas' place. You and Morey take shifts. If you need me to spell you, give me a call."

"I still say it's a bunch of bullshit. I should be staking out Vanderhof's place."

"Can you just do as I ask this once, Bennie? Please?"

Bennie opened the door to the van and climbed in, muttering to himself. I stood there until he had started the engine and hit the window button.

"And what are you gonna to do, boss man?"

"I don't know. Maybe go stake out Vanderhof's place."

That got Bennie going. I had to laugh.

"But seriously. I've been thinking to go have a talk with Nicholas' wife."

"His wife? What for?"

"She married the idiot, didn't she? Who's to say she's lily white in all of this?"

That got a shrug out of Bennie.

"Maybe you got a point there."

"Yeah?"

"Yeah. It's pretty little but I'll give you a couple of points."

"Go on. Get back to work."

He hit the window button and drove off. I climbed into the Impala and grabbed a notebook out of my satchel, looking for Ida Huntington's address. She lived in Doheny Beach, 1104 Cambridge Court, the last house on the block. There was a passing thought to call ahead but I dismissed it as quickly as it had popped into my head. I'd only be giving her a chance to get her ducks in a row, or dodge me entirely.

On my way back down to the coast, I dialed Gigi's number. It rang several times before she answered.

"Just checking in, Michael?"

"Yeah. How's our little soldier doing?"

"She's seen better days."

"Yeah. Off the beer yet?"

"She has three left. By the time it turns dark, she'll be shaking."

"Yeah. Sure glad I don't have to go through that again."

"We are blessed, aren't we?"

"Pretty much."

"So?...Did you?...You know?"

"Oh yeah. It's gone."

227

"Good, good. I'm so glad to hear that…Anything else I can do for you right now?"

"No. Just wanted to let you know. I spoke with Holly's mother. I had to knock heads with her a bit. Naturally she wanted to rush right over."

"Well, she is Holly's mother."

"Yeah, and like I said, there's a history there…Anyway, you can tell Holly that I bought her at least another day before her mother drags her home."

"I'll let her know."

"Thanks. She hates me enough already."

"She doesn't hate you."

"It's close." Gigi chuckled. "Okay. I'd better run but please keep me posted on how she's doing."

"I will."

"Thanks."

I hung up and continued my drive down to the coast, juggling balls as I did. Potter. Nicholas. The Mongols. Vanderhof. If I ran out of things to worry about there, I had Betty's power boats and beheaded clerics and Bert's funeral to keep me busy, and behind all of that was Caitlin, dancing in and out of my thoughts. A word of thanks for the flowers would have been nice, but no. I reached for my phone, wanting everything to be all right between us, but stopped. Women were hardwired to look for the alpha male. They saw the wounded coming and got out of Dodge.

I had just turned south on Interstate 5, headed for Doheny Beach, when my phone rang. It was Lila.

"Detective Barnes just called me again," she said when I answered.

"And?"

"He asked if I had seen or heard from Holly."

"And what did you tell him?"

"I told him no but I have a funny feeling it's going to come back and bite me."

"Lila. Have you seen Holly?"

"Well, no…Not when you get right down to it."

"Or talked with her?"

"No."

"Then you gave him an honest answer and that's your cover. She was in detox and I never told you. I'll take the heat for keeping Holly under wraps and make sure to cover your butt whenever I talk to him, fair enough?"

"Fine. *You're* in charge."

"Look. I already have half the world beating me up. I don't need you piling on."

"I understand, Michael."

There was a pause.

"And I am sorry…About Desmond and all that."

"It's water under the bridge. I don't hold grudges."

In the ensuing silence, I sensed danger coming, and it came.

"And I suppose you're going to tell me that there's no one else in your life."

I didn't answer.

"What?" Lila said. "Cat got your tongue?"

"Lila, have I ever made a play on you?"

"No."

"No…Now if I had, I would consider my personal business your personal business, but I haven't, so I don't. Am I making any sense to you?"

"Fine. Whatever."

"Christ, Lila. This is serious. The cops are going to want to grill the crap out of your daughter about that young woman being killed, so she and Jim need to sit down and have a long talk. We all need to sit down and have a long talk before we let the police get anywhere near her."

"Oh god. I can't believe this is happening. What was she thinking, hanging around with bikers?"

I looked to the heavens.

"Lila. Are you going to tell me that your past is as pure as driven snow?"

There was a long pause before she said, "Go to hell," and hung up on me.

Great. I wasn't sure why I put up with her crap. I had driven several more miles down the road, steaming over Lila's impudence, when I remembered Mr. Huntington and called him.

"Good news, Michael?"

"Some, yes. I have your Egyptian figurine."

"Splendid. Did it by any stroke of luck involve shooting my son-in-law?"

"Sorry to say, but no, sir."

He laughed dryly.

"Very well. I won't ask how you recovered it."

"I wouldn't."

"And I take it no luck on the Picasso yet."

"No, sir, but I'm still working on it…How about if I drive by tomorrow sometime and drop off this figurine?"

"As you wish."

"Any particular time that's good?"

"Afternoon or evening. I'll be out in the morning doing some banking."

"Got it. I'll call before heading your way."

"Very well. We'll talk tomorrow then."

"Sir?" I said before he could hang up.

"Yes?"

"There's one more thing."

"Yes, what is it?"

"I'd like to question your daughter Ida."

"About what, if I may ask?"

"It has to do with another case."

"Would that be the one involving Holly Evergreen?"

"That would be correct, sir."

"Have you succeeded in locating Holly yet?"

"No," I lied.

"But you think Ida may have knowledge of her whereabouts?"

"Not directly sir, but I'm still hoping your daughter Charlotte might and that Ida might know of Charlotte's whereabouts."

"I see. That seems like quite a lot of conjecturing but you know your business better than me, so feel free to go ahead. You have my blessings."

"Thank you, sir. I just thought it only proper to run it by you first."

"Thank you for the courtesy."

"You're welcome."

I got off feeling lousy for having lied to the old man, but I would have felt even lousier, casting about my suspicions without any proof. I had no evidence that Ida was up to no good. It just felt that way to me.

Thirty minutes later, I was pulling onto Cambridge Court in Doheny Beach. An undeveloped hillside rose up steeply from Ida's street and dropped off just as steeply below it. Cambridge Court died out on a point and had a view looking south from Smuggler's Cove down towards Trestles and the Mexican border. Ida's home was the last place on the block. I got out to the sound of lanyards clanging down in the harbor. Ida's backyard would have a direct line of sight to it, roughly half a mile away. Take away the view and the house wasn't much to look at — a nondescript ranch with tidy landscaping and a crisp new paint job — but the view and seclusion pretty much made up for whatever the house was lacking.

Given the nature of divorce law in California, it wasn't surprising to find Ida comfortably ensconced in the house and Nicholas relegated to a rented condo across town. How the couple had come to own the home in the first place, I had no idea. The old man had never mentioned buying it.

I walked up to the front door and knocked. A few moments later, a woman's form appeared through the raindrop privacy glass next to the front door. Ida opened the door and stared at me like I was selling vacuum cleaners. She was wearing black silk slacks, a sleeveless, patterned blouse and open toed slides.

Her hair was pulled back severely, but she was still beautiful. All in all, she looked like the kind of woman who found men wanting, and my presence did not appear to have changed her opinion in that regard.

"May I help you?" she said with one hand on the doorknob. I flashed my ID.

"Michael Devlin. I'm working for your father."

Ida took in my PI license and resumed staring at me.

"So? What do you want from me?"

"I'm looking for a missing young woman. Holly Evergreen. It's another case but I understand that Holly is friends with Charlotte and wondered if you had seen your sister lately. Your father hasn't for at least two weeks now."

Ida hesitated before answering my question.

"What makes you think I'd know where Charlotte is?"

"She's your sister."

Ida searched my eyes with her mind working away.

"Sorry but I rarely hear from her these days. I can't even remember the last time she called or came by."

"Holly was last seen in the company of a man named Donald Ray Potter. Do you happen to know him?"

Her eyes flickered.

"No," she said finally.

"Your husband apparently did. You don't remember Nicholas ever mentioning the name."

She hesitated before shaking her head.

"Do you know Holly?"

"I've met her a few times," she said after weighing my question.

"And her mother, Lila?"

"We've met," Ida said after another pause.

I pulled a card from my wallet and held it out to her. Ida took it without looking.

"Please call me if you hear from Charlotte."

She stood there, still barring the door.

"Is that it?"

I nodded. There appeared to be scant prospects of extracting more information from Ida, short of torture. She let her return silence serve as a goodbye and closed the door.

Her form lingered for a moment behind the raindrop glass before disappearing. I headed back to my Impala, digesting what I had just learned. Ida and Charlotte Huntington weren't cozy. That much I had already suspected, but the mere mention of Potter's name had given Ida pause. Did she know him personally? That I couldn't say, but I'd put my money on her knowing *of* him. From what Holly had told me about the Nicholas and Potter connection, it would hardly be surprising. Ida knew something. She had made a point of looking opaque, and that alone spoke volumes to me.

More importantly, Ida had admitted to knowing Lila. What did that mean? My brain was ruminating on that question all the way back to my office.

Arriving there, I locked the 26th Dynasty figurine in my safe and checked phone messages. There was another one from Motation DX. On and on it went, telling me what was what in a mélange of bluster and braggadocio.

Why couldn't the guy just start a legitimate business? But no. There was a fool born every minute and Motation was in the business of finding them.

I sighed and gave Sal a call.

"What?" he said without me saying a word. "Calling to beat my balls again?"

"Beat *your* balls? You're the king of ball beaters from way back."

He laughed.

"How did it go with your gal?"

"She had me over for dinner."

"No shit? See? I knew that necklace would knock her out."

"Knock her out. You spent most of an hour telling me not to give it to her."

"I did not! I just said one thing!"

"Oh, okay. I mistakenly thought the whole diatribe was interconnected."

"Fuck! You don't want to learn anything!"

His comment caused my mind to stall a bit.

"Hey, you don't happen to have a long-lost brother named Bennie Morales, do you?"

"What are you talking about!? I don't know anyone named Bennie! Quit saying shit like that!"

"Chill, Sal. It's just an innocent question."

"But she really liked it, huh?"

"Yeah."

"And invited you over for dinner?...See? I got you laid."

"Oh Jesus."

"See? You don't want to learn nothing."

"All right, that's it. Either admit to being related to Bennie Morales or I'm doing a background check."

"Background check!? Don't even say shit like that! It makes me nervous!"

I gave Sal a minute to hyperventilate.

"Who's Bennie, anyway?" he asked after a long pause.

"A guy who works for me. Never mind. It doesn't matter. I called to see if you had learned anything about that jewelry. My cop friend says it was probably fenced."

"I don't fence jewelry!"

"I didn't say you did."

"Well don't say shit like that!"

"Jesus, Sal. I'm just asking if you've heard anything."

"No and don't talk to me about stuff like this over the phone. My wife's lawyer's probably listening. For all I know, you're working for them!"

"Oh Jesus, Sal. Never mind. I'll let you get back to your conspiracies."

"Well, I just got another letter from them this morning! They want to do another audit! They won't stop looking into my shit! Of course I'm paranoid."

"Hey, look. I'm sorry. I didn't mean to add to your grief."

There was more silence. I pictured the jeweler's glass going up and down.

"Did you check the pawn shops?" he said.

"Not yet. I was going to do that next. Any ideas?"

"Yeah. Try Tony's down in San Clemente…But don't talk to Eric, the son-in-law. He's a prick."

"Yeah, I know."

"You know him?"

"I know he's a prick."

"Yeah. Talk to the old man. He was a cop back in Jersey and knows all the old networks. Maybe he can tell you something."

"Thanks."

"But don't tell him I said anything!"

"Jesus, Sal. What? Are you working for the mob now or something?"

There was silence.

"So you really got laid, huh?"

"Stop saying shit like that!" I said, imitating him.

He laughed.

"You going to see her again?"

"I hope so, but I'm taking it slowly. I was just happy to be around her and she seemed happy to be around me. We'll see how it goes from there."

I looked at the time.

"I've got to run, Sal, but thanks again for the tip. I'll keep you posted."

"Sure. You don't want to hear about my fucking problems."

"Oh stop. I've listened to your problems until my head hurts. Give her the house, keep the business and start over. Just get her out of your hair before you go mad."

"I tried! She wants everything!"

"Okay. I'll be praying for you."

"Fucker."

"Yeah, I know."

"Come by for a drink sometime."

"Fat chance."

Sal laughed.

"Let me know if Tony takes care of you. If he doesn't, I might have another lead."

"You're the original ball buster," I said and hung up.

What to do next? I swiveled around in my chair and gazed out at the cruise ship. You could make out the tiny bodies gathered along the railings. No doubt swimming to shore had come to mind but the ship was just far enough out at sea to dissuade you of the idea. You'd be shark meat before you got a hundred yards.

A pandemic. Good god. Maybe it was the end of times. I knew enough about the demise of civilizations to know that perception became reality towards the end. It would feel as if order had turned to chaos, long before barbarians arrived at the gates. And so they would read about us in two thousand years, scratching their heads. The solutions to all our problems would seem so obvious in hindsight. How could we have failed to do something about them?

Lost in that melancholy, the days of my youth suddenly popped into my thoughts. I had never imagined those glorious times coming to an end, had not realized that there was no escaping the second law of thermodynamics, that the ensuing disorder was always inevitable and sat there now, haunted by those magical hours and longing to have them back again.

Restless and getting nowhere with my thoughts, I walked down to Coast Highway and crossed over to Main Beach when the light turned green. At the north end of the wooden boardwalk, I started up a series of steps and winding pathways. That led me to a blufftop park and glorious views of the coast. The sea was navy-blue in the blustery afternoon, framed here and there by spikes of orange aloe blossoms.

Person after person passed by me along the trail, their attention glued to a phone screen, oblivious to the beauty around them. Good god. We really had entered the virtual phase of humanity.

I continued down the coast for a mile, brooding over that poor young woman, my thoughts plagued at the fringes by something I could not seem to see. My best shot was to question Holly again. She knew something. I felt certain of it.

Why don't you fold up your tent and call it a day, Devlin? That woman's fate is none of your business.

Having gotten nowhere with the puzzle, I headed back to my office and home. Twenty minutes later, I was stopped in front of my garage door and waiting for it to open when an odd sensation came over me. Something was wrong in the universe. Then it hit me. The towering jacaranda straddling the open space between my driveway and Fitzy's house was missing. Someone had whacked it down, leaving the area as naked as a field after harvest.

Goddamn it. I parked in my garage and marched down to Fitzy's front door, girded for battle. I had pounded on it several times before she finally answered.

"What the hell happened?"

"What?" she said.

"The tree?"

"Oh, that," she said with one of her flippant laughs.

"Yeah, that."

"Well you don't have to be sarcastic."

"Well you don't have to go cutting down trees around here without asking first."

"Actually, I had the property lines checked and it was on my side."

"Bullshit. I happen to have known the original owner and his family planted that tree when they first built the house."

"Well they planted it on the wrong side of the property line. Anyway, it was dead."

"No, it just looks that way every time we've had a couple of dry winters."

"Oh well," Fitzy said with another one of her flippant laughs. "Those stupid purple flowers were making a big mess on my driveway so I'm glad it's gone."

"Well I'm not and I'd really appreciate you checking with me before taking a chain saw to anything else around here."

"Fine. Have a nice day."

With one more of her flippant laugh, Fitzy shut the door in my face. I watched her silhouette linger for a brief moment through the stained-glass before she moved away. I stood there, weighing various forms of homicide.

Having marched back up to my place, I threw Fitzy's gift certificate into the trash, along with the rest of her gingerbread cookies.

Nineteen

Still beside myself, I jumped into my sweat suit and ran a 5K up into the hills, only to arrive back home in the same furious state. The minute I saw the empty space between our two properties, I had Fitzy up in front of a firing squad. I showered and sat at my desk, unable to work. I went to bed still chewing on my anger.

Early the next morning, I went out to grab the Sunday paper and found a decorative tin on my doorstep, along with an opulent looking greeting card. I opened the tin and found another batch of Fitzy's homemade cookies. I opened the card and read Fitzy's note. In it, she conveyed her abundant regrets and asked if I would please accept her apologies.

Hardly. I now viewed Fitzy as a sailor does calm seas.

As with her previous offerings, the card and cookies went into the trash. I didn't want to owe that woman a goddamned thing.

After breakfast, I went out to the garage to check for supplies in my spare refrigerator and found a gardening crew installing a row of tall junipers in the area where the jacaranda had been. Jesus Christ. On a Sunday? And junipers? I hated them. They were a place for spiders to spin webs. And I hated Fitzy even more now. She kept doing things without my consent.

A short while later, as I backed out into the street in my old 3.0, headed for the market, I saw Fitzy idling in her SUV with Allison. They were arguing again.

239

When Fitzy noticed me, she waved. I stared back as one would, meeting an adversary on the courthouse steps.

Seeing Fitzy start to back out of her driveway, I dropped the BMW into first, sped up the street and left some rubber turning onto Bluebird Canyon Drive. The last thing I wanted was to have her pull up alongside me at a stoplight.

Back from the market, I quickly disappeared inside the house and spent all day stewing. I tried not to hate Fitzy, but I did. The serenity prayer came to mind, but I found revenge a far more satisfying pastime.

As day was turning to dusk, the phone rang. I glanced at the display screen, saw it was a blocked number and answered, relishing the opportunity to chew out some marketing son of a bitch for violating my privacy.

"Yeah, what do you want?" I said.

There was silence. Then a gravelly voice said something indecipherable and the phone went dead.

Goddamn it. Potter must have found me. My mind raced through all that it would imply.

I quickly had Bennie on the line.

"Hey, boss man," he said. "Just calling to beat my balls on a Sunday?"

"No time for screwing around Bennie. I need you to get over to Gigi's place and I mean right now."

"Jesus. I was just lying down to catch a few Z's. I was up all night."

"It'll have to wait. I just got a call from Potter."

"Holy shit. Are you sure?"

I explained the call.

"I don't know who else it could have been. Anyway, if he knows about me, he probably knows about Caitlin."

"Man, you'd better get your ass over to her place right now."

"Where do you think I'm headed?"

"And Morey?"

"I'm calling him next and dragging him with me."

"Something tells me we're going to need some more bodies."

"Yeah but just get your ass in gear for now. And check in with me the minute you're down there."

"You got it."

I tossed some things into my satchel, raced out to the garage and was speed dialing Morey's number as I backed the Impala out onto the street. He answered the call with me careening onto Bluebird.

"What's up?" he said.

I quickly explained the situation and gave him Caitlin's address.

"Please get over there right away."

"Don't you worry," Morey said. "If this clown's dumb enough to show up at her place, I'll snap him like a pencil."

The desperate nature of the situation aside, I almost laughed. Morey, the terminator, off to give the lords of the apocalypse a good shellacking.

I thanked him and called Caitlin next. Her phone rang and rang.

Come on, sweetheart. Answer my call.

She finally did so after numerous rings, and with a sweet but puzzled voice.

"Helllllooohhh?"

Yeah, right. Like she had no idea who it was. I had watched her screen calls and knew she never picked up the phone without first checking her caller ID.

"It's the Fuller Brush Man," I said, not wanting to set off any alarms.

"You're underwater," she said with a laugh, referring to the sound of my voice while on the road."

"Yeah, I was almost in my polar bear bathrobe and baked potato slippers but got called out on a job."

"Doing what?"

"Stuufffff," I said, imitating her.

"Yeah?"

"Yeah. Just wanted to hear the sound of your voice."

"Yeah?"

241

"Yeah. It's like wind chimes, only the magical kind."

That made her purr a bit. I could hear it over the car speakers.

"Hey, I was checking the weather and it looks like there might be rain this Wednesday."

"Yeah. Unless the cone of drought comes along and wrecks everything."

"Yeah, well, if it doesn't, maybe we could get together that evening?"

"Suurrrre," she said after a brief pause.

"Yeah?"

"Suurrrre."

"Okay. I'd better get back to doing nuttin'."

She laughed.

"Yeah, me too."

"I'll call you on Tuesday then to check in. I'm praying for rain."

I did my version of an Indian rain dance and she laughed again.

We said one more goodbye and hung up.

That was some measure of relief. Whether or not Potter knew of Caitlin's existence, he had yet to darken her door. I cursed the fact that the man existed and stepped on the gas.

There was a clown doing twenty-five in the fast lane so I darted around him, then quickly left a few more dawdlers in my wake. Horns were honking behind me.

I had just run a red light when the phone rang. With a glance, I saw it was Detective Barnes. What the hell would he want on a Sunday evening? Nothing good, I imagined. I hesitated but ultimately answered out of a misguided sense of duty.

"Burning the midnight oil, detective?"

"Maybe. And you?"

"Just out for a drive. What's up?"

"Oh, not having much luck with running down Holly Evergreen and wondered if you knew anything."

I considered everything that had gone down so far, including his recent call to Lila, and decided it was time to stop playing dumb. I had already veered way too close to perjury and obstruction for my own tastes.

"Yeah, she showed up," I told him.

"Yeah? You're saying you know where she is?"

"Yeah."

"So why didn't you call to tell me?"

"Because I only tracked her down late last night and hadn't pictured you working weekends. I was figuring to call you tomorrow morning. Anyway, Holly was strung out on meth so I got her into detox."

"And what about Mrs. Evergreen? She all up on this news?"

"I just called her a few minutes ago to explain the situation. She knows Holly's in detox but not where. Holly made it clear that she didn't want to see her mother. There's a bit of a history there."

"I don't care about their little family drama, Devlin. I just need to question Holly. I've got my little notepad here, all ready to write."

"Sorry, Barnes, but no can do."

"Bullshit, Devlin. What do you think this is, Horizon collections?"

"I'm just following orders, Barnes."

"Whose orders?"

"Mrs. Evergreen's attorney."

"Look, I don't know what kind of bullshit game you people are playing but *you* know where Holly is and that's good enough for me, so spill it. It's that or I'll be down there bearing warrants and subpoenas in about an hour."

"And like I already told you, you'll have to go through Mrs. Evergreen's attorney. He happens to be my attorney too, so you can kill two birds with one stone. I have his name and number right here if you'd like."

"Look, Devlin. The girl's a material witness to a crime, maybe a couple of them, so she's talking."

243

"You don't know if any of that's true."

"The hell I don't."

"You don't."

"Bullshit. On a drug charge alone she's up to her ass in it."

"Good luck on that one, but as far as anything more serious? We were watching that house 24/7 and I can assure you that nothing akin to murder went down. Not on our watch. Just bikers being raunchy. You don't think I would have called the police if it had?"

"I don't know what you'd do, Devlin."

"Yeah, right. A big pain in the ass."

"It's getting to be that way, yeah."

"Then fine. Bring your warrants and subpoenas but you'll be locking horns with Jim Harrison, attorney at law, not me."

I read off Jim's phone number.

"Feel free to call him anytime."

Barnes was silent for a moment.

"Okay, pal. Let's hear it. What's your plan?"

"Get Holly cleaned up and safely back home first. Two or three days at the most and then you can question her all you want."

There was more silence.

"I'll give you twenty-four hours and then I'll be up your ass."

"Yeah. You ever detoxed, Barnes?"

"Hell no. What do you think I am, a junkie?"

"Cute."

I had pulled into Caitlin's neighborhood and slowed to a crawl, searching for any sign of Potter.

"So?" Barnes said.

"So. You know how it goes with detox. Holly's useless right now. She probably has her head in a toilet, retching."

I pulled to the curb and turned off the Impala. Assuming Morey had followed my directions, he was parked in a cul-de-sac, roughly fifty feet up a wooded slope from where I sat.

Barnes had yet to say a word.

"So?" I said.

"So, I'm just looking over some paperwork here while you bullshit me."

"No one's bullshitting you."

"Yeah, right. So, here's the deal, Devlin. You tell me where she is and I'll give you an extra twenty-four hours. That's forty-eight hours total, after which you turn her over to me with no more BS."

"Fair enough, but you need to call Jim Harrison and arrange things with him."

"Son of a bitch. You know, Detective Whalen had warned me you could be a real pain in the ass."

That made my ears burn. Me a pain in the ass? Never mind that Whalen and Barnes had been talking behind my back.

I was inclined to go on a rant but stuck to business.

"Look, Barnes. This is no time for pissing contests. I think Potter may have found me so people's lives are at stake here."

There was a pause.

"Explain," he said.

I did.

"Have you ever coughed up the whole truth at once, Devlin?"

"I'm just a man trying to do his job, Barnes."

"All right. I'm on my way down there."

Barnes hung up before I could respond. I stared at my phone for a few seconds before setting it down.

Great. Now I had that SOB breathing down my neck.

I promptly called Lila and gave her the rundown.

"And what do you want from me, Michael? If the police show up here with a warrant, I'll have no choice but to tell them the truth."

"We've already been through this, Lila. Do you know where your daughter is?"

"No…Thanks to you."

"And do you see the wisdom of me not telling you now?"

There was a pause.

"Are you really thinking that far ahead, Michael?"

I let out a sigh.

"I don't know. Maybe. I know enough to keep my mouth shut until I can see where things are headed."

"And where are things headed, Michael?"

"Well, for one thing, Potter's out there roaming around, searching for your daughter, which means he's searching for you too, so you'd better get some added protection."

"I thought that's why I hired you."

"You hired me to find your daughter. This is a completely different matter."

"So your firm's not designed to do that sort of thing."

Oh man. I was definitely going to slap her around at some point.

"Look, Lila. Let's stop playing games. Just tell me what you want me to do and I'll do it."

"Protect me, of course. And my daughter."

"I'm already protecting your daughter. I have a man over there right now, watching the place where she's detoxing."

"And me?"

"I'll have to bring on another operative. Which means extra costs."

"I already told you. I don't care about the money."

"Fine."

"So, you'll do it?"

"Of course. I'll have someone over there within the hour."

"Thank you. And please let me know when your man is in place."

"I will. In the meantime, keep your house alarm on and lights off. And don't answer if someone knocks. And as far as Barnes is concerned, you tell him to contact your attorney. I already told him that you don't know where Holly is."

"That much is true."

"I've got to run but I'll call you as soon as my man is there."

"Thank you."

"No problem. Talk to you in a bit."

I hung up, feeling a pang of conscience over my suspect professionalism. I had two of us here, keeping an eye on Caitlin, when Potter was far more likely to show up at Lila's place.

I climbed out of the Impala, reflexively checked to make sure the Smith & Wesson was in my shoulder holster and started up the steep, wooded slope. Thick clutches of oleander and other undergrowth blocked the way. At the top of the slope, I spotted the new van through a wrought iron fence, parked on the other side of a cul-de-sac. Good old Morey.

All looked to be calm so I called Bennie first.

"I was just going to call you," he said.

"I just got here to Caitlin's place. Are you at Gigi's?"

"Yeah. Is Morey there?"

"Yeah. He found it all right."

"So now what?"

"I just spoke with Mrs. Evergreen and she wants me to station a man at her place."

"I'll take that assignment. Anything's better than this gig. Ain't nobody going to show up here."

"No. I wouldn't dare leave Gigi's place unguarded. If anything happened to her, I'd never forgive myself."

"So what?"

"So, I need to hire another operative. Which I plan to do, as soon as I'm done dealing with Bob Dylan here."

"I thought you were done with being a dick, boss man."

"Yeah, well. I had a slip." Bennie laughed. "Okay, if everything's fine on your end for now, I need to call the agencies."

"Hey, no need for that. I've got the perfect guy for you."

"Yeah, who? Morey's twin brother?"

"Having another slip, dude?"

"Yeah, what the hell. I'm already out..." Bennie laughed again. "Go on, spill it. What do you got?"

"Oh. I was talking to this guy named John at a meeting the other night and he said he was looking for work. This dude's got to be at least 6-6 and built like a linebacker. Ain't nobody going to mess with that boy, not even Potter."

"Let me guess. He's got, what? Two weeks of sobriety?"

"No, ninety days. A little more than that now."

"Oh, what a relief."

"Quit being a dick. I'm telling you. He's solid. He came out here from Massachusetts to rehab and decided to stick around. Sounds like he just got off a lobster boat but talks some straight shit. Funny guy."

"Great. Just what I need. A 6-6 comedian with ninety days."

"I told you. Stop being a dick. The guy's solid."

"Does he know how to use a gun?"

"Yeah, he did two years in the Army. Washed out from all the boozing but he's trained."

"Fine. If the guy can come to work right now, I'll take him. Do you have his number?"

"Seguro. I'm always thinking ahead. Always thinking ahead."

"That's my Bennie."

"You got that right."

"So give him a call and see what you can arrange. I'll call you back as soon as I'm done checking on Morey."

"Will do."

I started to hang up but brought the phone back up to my ear.

"Hey Bennie!"

"Yeah, what?"

"Just wondering what you want me to do with this guy if I hire him."

"Shit, seniority. Leave him here and send me over to Evergreen's place. I'd rather keep an eye on the doll."

"Okay, Romeo. I'll call you back in a minute."

I hung up and immediately called Morey.

"What's up?" he said.

"I'm here. Just didn't want to sneak up on you."

"Don't worry. I've got all four corners covered."

"Then see you in a second."

I looked both ways and jumped the fence. It was a clear, warm night dancing with stars. A few folks had already put their Christmas décor out. The neighborhood had a contest and prizes so there were some really serious light displays.

I glanced down at Caitlin's place, roughly a hundred yards off to my right. Everything seemed to be in order. She had the sheer curtains closed to her upstairs bedroom windows and a soft light bled through them into the darkness.

I stared that way for a long moment before slipping in through the back door of the van. Morey darted a look at me and returned his attention to the monitors. I sat down next to him.

"Anything?"

"Nothing to write home about. Mostly people out walking their dogs. Every clown in this neighborhood seems to have one. I've counted two dachshunds, a Corgi, a Collie, one Shih Tzu and a pit bull."

"Whoa, wait a minute. A pit bull? In this neighborhood? Does that sound right to you?"

Morey barely shrugged.

"So? Was it a guy? A gal? A couple? What?"

"A guy."

"How old?"

"Probably thirty-ish." Morey looked up from the monitors. "He seemed normal enough to me."

I had a photo of Potter that Bennie had taken while staking out his place and pulled it out.

"Does this look like him?"

Morey stared for a moment and shook his head.

"This guy was pretty clean cut."

I described Potter's size and build.

"That's about the right size but he didn't have all that hair."

"Go ahead and roll the film back. Let's see."

We watched a parade of people and dogs marching backwards at high speed until the man with the pit bull appeared. The recording had flown past that point some distance so Morey hit stop and fast forwarded on slow until they were back in the frame. I held the picture of Potter up to the screen.

"Hard to tell. What do you think?"

"Maybe," Morey said with his 'peering into a sandstorm' look.

I looked back at the monitor. It would have helped if the man had looked our way. All we had was his profile.

"Go ahead and run the film forward," I told Morey

He did and we watched the man turn the corner by Caitlin's front yard and onto the next street. That street ran along one side of her backyard fence. He could have jumped the fence for all I knew. I kicked myself for not positioning Morey on that street but then he wouldn't have been able to see the front.

"Maybe I should pull around to that street," Morey said.

"No. Just run the tape back. I want to see this guy again."

Morey did and we both stared at his image.

"Shit. I don't know, Morey. It could be Potter."

"Or not."

"Yeah."

I glanced at my watch. My impulse was to call Caitlin again but she rarely answered her phone at this hour. Plus, I couldn't think of any good reason why I'd be calling her back, except to say that I missed her.

I dialed her number anyway and motioned for Morey to keep quiet. His return look was that of a man who'd just had mud splattered on his white suede shoes.

I focused back on the monitors. The phone kept ringing. I was about to hang up when the silhouettes of a man and a woman appeared in Caitlin's upstairs bedroom window. The man had his back to us and was gesturing animatedly. Then he reached out and Caitlin appeared to fall over backwards.

"Son of a bitch!" I said and bolted for the back door. "Go ahead and pull around to that side street! I'm going in and need you to cover me!"

"With what? My dick?"

I paused at the opened door.

"I don't know. Just be there. We'll cross that bridge when we come to it."

Twenty

I jumped the wrought iron fence and scampered my way down the slope. Brush and thorn tore at my flesh. Above me, I heard the van start and Morey race away from the curb. I was focused on a point of entry. I had never seen Caitlin leave her front door unlocked for one second, not unless she was expecting me to stop by. My best shot was the dining room slider. With Senan needing to go out and pee every so often, she usually didn't lock it until it was time for bed.

One big plus to that option. All of Caitlin's second story windows faced towards the front so anyone up there would be blind to me approaching from the rear.

I hit the sidewalk hard, rushed around to the driver's side door and was speeding away from the curb moments later. There was a question of whether or not to call the cops. A sick thought crossed my mind while considering it. What if I was barging in on Caitlin and her date? After all these years, who was to say she wasn't seeing another man? I had never thought to ask her.

I raced around the next corner and past the neighborhood park with that potentiality gnawing at my guts. Then, if some guy was pushing her around, I didn't care who he was. I was taking him out.

Seconds later, I was careening around a corner and braking to a stop behind Morey. Both of us were now parked across from the side fence of Caitlin's corner lot. The fence continued up a steep slope and stopped at the side yard of the house above her. I jumped out, having pretty much decided to leave the cops out of this.

Morey had his eyes locked on me in the van's side mirror and hit the power window button as I approached. He took stock of the leaves and brush covering my clothing.

"What's up?"

I dusted myself off a bit.

"If you don't see me in five minutes, call the cops."

"What if I hear guns going off?"

"Do the same."

"Hey, what about a gun?"

I paused.

"I don't have another one on me. Just call the cops if you smell trouble."

I dashed across to Caitlin's fence, looked both ways, leapt over and crouched down inside. The waterfall in Caitlin's small fish pond gurgled quietly alongside the back slider. There were no other signs of life or activity under the starry sky.

The vertical blinds to the sliding glass door were pulled shut but in the open position. The chandelier was on low over her dining room table. There was also a lamp on in her living room, but no sign of Caitlin or anyone else.

I watched and waited for a minute before crossing the concrete patio and pausing again by the back door. The fish came to the surface at seeing my presence. A rusted iron frog figurine stared up at me. Both the pond and the frog had been my gifts to Caitlin on Valentine's Day, ten years earlier. She had gone on to do a bang up job with the surrounding shrubbery.

The genesis for the pond had been a flippant comment made by me during my first visit to her house. A patch of grass had stood where the pond was now and looked as if it hadn't been mowed for months.

"Wow, kind of looks like the African savannah out there," I had commented playfully

Caitlin's response was to go into an absolute meltdown, as if I had insulted her personally.

"I was just kidding," I said, trying to reassure. "Let's not make a big deal out of it."

I would have gladly gone over to mow the grass personally. But no. The meltdown continued.

"It's all wrecked now. It's all wrecked."

Lord, the grief.

It had taken me most of an hour to draw her back out of a funk, and still a cloud of gloom had hung over the entire evening. In fairness to me, the grass did have an abandoned property look about it.

Driving home that night, I had experienced my first reservations about our fledgling romance. Something wasn't right there. But I had already fallen so deeply in love by that point, the warning signs were dismissed and over Victoria Falls I went.

I came back to the moment with those memories still clinging to me. As always, terror and bliss were woven together in my feelings for Caitlin.

I shook off the distraction and reached out to try the sliding glass door. It was unlocked. I slid it open just enough to ease my head through and paused to listen again. Nothing. The lack of activity was troubling. A dog, even one like Senan, would prick up its ears at the movement.

Something was definitely amiss here.

I slid the door open a few more inches and slipped in past the blinds. Caitlin had placed my bouquet on the dining room table. As promised, it was stunning.

I moved quietly to the base of the staircase, picturing Potter upstairs with a gun to Caitlin's head. My only advantage was the element of surprise.

I was halfway up the stairs with gun drawn when I heard Caitlin laugh and a man laugh with her.

"Oh, he'll absolutely love it," she said.

Amidst more laughter, Caitlin appeared in the open doorway and shrieked. The man quickly appeared in the doorway with her. It was Liam, Caitlin's British brother-in-law, this Cockney software programmer from the southside of London. Caitlin had grabbed hold of his arm and was staring at me with a mixture of shock and fury.

"What the hell are you doin', mate?" Liam said with a glance at my gun.

I looked at Caitlin.

"I thought I saw somebody pushing you around through the curtains."

"So you're spying on me now!!!" she said with her hands to her ears.

"Caitlin, I wasn't spying on you…"

I looked at Liam and back at her.

"It's just that that guy Potter had called me and I was worried he might figure out where you live."

"Oh great. So now you've dragged your giant mess over here to my house."

"I was just trying to protect you, doll."

"And now everything's wrecked."

Caitlin buried her head against Liam's shoulder. Jesus, the grief. I was so thoroughly fucked up in the head by that point, I didn't know which way to turn.

"I'm sorry, Caitlin. I was just trying to look out for you."

"Look, mate," Liam said. "Maybe it's best if you go for now."

He took stock of my soiled clothing. I did too. The question of how that had come to be hung in the air, as did how I had gotten into the house in the first place. Liam nodded his head, as if to remind me. Best if you leave, mate. At least he was being sympathetic. Caitlin still looked as if I had come to rob the place.

Aware of my gun still being drawn, I slipped it back into my holster and turned down the stairs.

"Where's Senan?" I said at the bottom

"At our place," Liam said. "We didn't want the little bloke seeing his Christmas present."

I shook my head.

"So that's what you were…"

"Just go," Caitlin said. "Please?"

"But sweetheart, I was just looking out for you."

When she failed to respond, I started towards the still open sliding glass door.

"Please use the front door, Michael. I don't want you jumping over my fence again."

I halted alongside the bouquet before turning back towards the foyer. As I opened the front door, the faint sound of sirens carried on the night wind. They were distant but closing fast.

Out on the sidewalk, I looked back. Caitlin and Liam were standing in the doorway arm in arm like a couple.

I had turned at the corner of Caitlin's lot when three squad cars careened onto the street, coming the other way. I was promptly hemmed in by flashing lights and drawn revolvers.

"Face down!" one of the cops barked. "Hands on your head!"

I did as instructed and soon had a gun barrel at my back. Another cop frisked me. My wallet and gun quickly came out.

"A private dick," that cop said to the other two cops. "All right, up with you," he said to me.

I was handcuffed. The third cop had gone off to speak with Caitlin at her front door. Our eyes met as I was being led away to one of the squad cars. Her look had all the warmth of an inquisition.

I had been sitting there for several minutes when the third cop came back and motioned for his partner to open the back door. He leaned in and stared.

"What was your business here?"

"Didn't she tell you?"

"I'm asking the questions."

"I'm not fond of repeating myself."

"Just answers, pal."

"I'm working a case and thought her life was in danger. I had also mistakenly thought she was my girlfriend."

"In danger from what?"

"You see any crimes being committed around here?"

"Yeah, you. Breaking and entering."

"Fine. Haul me in and book me. Otherwise, I'm not legally bound to divulge the nature of my work."

"Smart guy."

"As smart as the advice I get from my attorney."

He stared for a long moment before nodding at his partner. I was freed from the back of the squad car, and none too gently. Uncuffed, I was left facing the cop who had been asking the questions.

"The fact is, your lady friend here already coughed up the name. Donald Ray Potter. Quite a character. I guess we can't fault you for trying to protect her but next time try calling us. That's why we're here."

I stared, knowing not to argue at this point. It would only be digging myself a deeper hole.

"Go on. Get out of here," he said.

Turning back towards my car, I glanced at Caitlin's front door. It was closed with the porch light off.

"Oh yeah," the cop called out.

I looked back.

"Your friend Barnes? He's on his way down to see you."

I continued up the block, gutted by what had transpired. Barnes was just salt in my wounds.

At least Morey had known enough to get out of harm's way. He and the van were nowhere in sight. I assumed that he was the one who had called the cops.

I was starting my Impala when he called.

"You okay?" I said.

"Yeah. You?"

"Yeah. Aside from being held by the cops for the past half hour."

"Hey. You told me to call them if I didn't see you in five minutes so that's what I did."

"No. You did the right thing."

"Then I heard the sirens coming and thought I'd better get out of there. I figured they'd be checking every parked car along the block."

"No, you did the right thing…So where are you now?"

"A couple of blocks over in this little cul-de-sac. What the hell happened in there, anyway?"

"Oh, false alarm."

I explained the situation, leaving out Caitlin's heartless reception.

"So what now?" Morey said.

"Are you good for tonight?"

"Yeah. I'm stocked up on food and drinks but I'll tell you this right now. I'm not about to crap in your little shit box toilet here."

"I'll see if I can get someone to drop off a port-a-potty for you."

"No need to get smart about it."

I was ready to clock him.

"Look, Morey. Let's stick to business."

"That's what I was going to say."

"Great. Give it five minutes and relocate to that parking area down past Caitlin's place. You know where I'm talking about?"

"Yeah. I think so. On the other side of that grassy knoll?"

"Yeah. I just realized walking by it that you can see both her front door and side yard from that location."

"Yeah. We should have thought of that in the first place."

"Yeah, Morey. I'll give you a shout once I'm walking on water."

"Hey. I'm just saying. We should stay on top of this stuff."

"Yeah…Hey, hold on a second."

The three cops had rolled around the corner from Caitlin's place and gave me a look going by.

"What's up?" Morey said.

"Just a second," I said again.

I watched in my rear-view mirror until the cops had disappeared around the next corner.

"Okay. It was just those three cops leaving. I wanted to make sure they were gone before you relocate. You're good to go now."

"Ten-four."

I rolled my eyes. Sergeant Morey.

"I'm heading out but keep me posted. I'll make sure somebody relieves you in the morning."

"Yeah. Just give me a heads up."

"I will," I said and hung up.

Rather than let Caitlin witness me slinking past her front door, I made a U-turn and headed up the block the other way. Her heartlessness went on eating at me like sulfur.

A mile or so shy of Coast Highway, I remembered Bennie and called him.

"Jesus, boss man," he said, answering my call. "I've been wondering what hole you fell into."

"Things got a bit complicated over there at Caitlin' place."

"Yeah? What happened?"

"Oh, no sign of Potter. What's going on with this guy John?"

"He's been waiting around for you to call him."

"Give me the number and I'll call right now."

Bennie rattled it off.

"So, am I getting off this chicken shit detail or what?"

"I already told you yes, Bennie, so quit beating my balls."

"Yeah. I'm getting a pretty good picture of what happened over there at the doll's place and it ain't pretty."

"Did anyone ever tell you to mind your own business?"

"Shit."

"Yeah, so let's not get started. What's happening over there?"

"Like I already told you. Nothing. I may as well watch paint dry."

"Welcome to the private investigation business."

"Yeah, yeah," he said, imitating me.

"Yeah, yeah," I said back. "So, we're good?"

"Yeah, we're good."

"Then let me call John. I'll call you back as soon as I've spoken with him."

I hung up and dialed the number. John answered after three rings. Bennie was right. He sounded like he had just fallen off a lobster boat. After the introductions, I explained a bit about how the investigation business worked.

"So, what do you think? Is that something you'd want to do?"

"Well, sitting around waiting for the furniture to move isn't exactly my idea of fun but if it gives me a shot at punching somebody in the nose from time to time, I'm all in for that."

"We try to steer clear of direct confrontation as much as possible but, yeah, you might get a chance to pop someone every once in a while."

"You know what I mean? Sometimes this world just pisses you off and to get paid for, boom, that would be a real plus."

I smiled. After dealing with Bennie and Morey, this guy was going to be a breath of fresh air. John made character defects sound like a virtue.

"So here's the deal," I told him. "I have three stakeouts going on tonight and only two men. Meaning, if you can come to work right now, that would be a great help."

"And you say it pays how much?"

"Thirty bucks an hour to start."

"Hey, yeah, sure. I'll punch somebody in the nose for that kind of money. So where do you want me?"

I gave him Gigi's address.

"You can hook up with Bennie over there. He'll be in a white van parked somewhere up the block a ways. I'll be over there in half an hour or so and we'll go over everything."

"You got it. Anything I should bring?"

"Do you have a licensed gun?"

"Not a pistol, if that's what you mean but I do own a 12-gauge shotgun and a 30-30."

"Licensed."

"Oh yeah. Not that there's much to shoot around here besides assholes."

I smiled.

"Bring 'em both."

"You got it. Anything else?"

"Whatever you think you'll need to eat and drink tonight."

"I already have some bottled water in the car. I'll grab a sandwich and some coffee."

"Sounds good. And hey, call Bennie and let him know we're all good."

"Will do."

"Thanks. I'll see you both there in a bit."

I hung up with that scene at Caitlin's place returning to plague my thoughts. What a nightmare. I had rushed to her side, ready to lay down my life, only to have her shut the door in my face. I should have known better than to think that things would ever be all right between us. I loved her wind chime voice and magical laughter, the warmth of her spirit and especially her discerning mind, but disaster of some kind was always waiting for us just around the next corner..

I went down the road with a sea of grief dammed up in my chest.

Five miles north on Coast Highway, I turned right up into the hills of Laurel Lagoon and eventually left onto a narrow lane. It snaked precipitously along the hills for half a mile with no sidewalks and only a handful of street lamps the entire length. Homes rose up a steep hillside to my right, each one with its garage on the street level and no driveway. The first floor was invariably up a long flight of stairs.

A handful of brave souls had built homes on the downside of the street, where the hill fell away in a nearly vertical plunge. Those garages were on the street level with the remainder of the structure clinging to the hillside somewhere out of sight.

Where no homes existed, that side of the street was girded by a white guardrail, with trees and shrubs growing up and around it from the slope.

The street was narrow enough that if two cars met from opposite directions, they would be hard pressed to squeeze past each other. Frequently, one or the other of them had to back up to an empty lot on the high side of the street. Laurel Lagoon had grown up around the horse and buggy, not the automobile.

Gigi lived at the very end of the road and shared her cul-de-sac with two other homes. Her home faced north and had a glorious view of the coast in that direction for fifty miles.

I spotted Bennie's van backed into one of the pull outs, roughly a hundred yards up the road from Gigi's driveway. An aging Rav was parked tight to the adjacent bank. I parked behind the Rav and stared down in Gigi's direction. One car was parked in her driveway with several more around the cul-de-sac.

I got out of the Impala and scanned the neighborhood before opening the rear door of the van. John was sitting beside Bennie when I slipped inside.

I closed the door and offered John my hand.

"A pleasure."

"Hey, yeah, the same. Bennie was just filling me in here on how things worked."

I sized John up while turning my attention to the monitors. Bennie wasn't kidding. The man was at least 6'-6" and 300 pounds if he was an ounce, and none of it flab. Even his sizable gut looked as hard as a punching bag. There was a sense of him taking up the entire van. Any bigger and his head would have popped up through the roof.

"Anything?" I said to Bennie.

"Yeah, some gals we know in the program coming and going but mostly quiet. Especially in the last half hour. I'm betting Gigi had a meeting down there and most of them have gone home now. Haven't seen her for one second."

"Who? Holly or Gigi?"

"Holly. Both."

John nodded his chin at me.

"If you don't mind me asking, how is this going to work?"

"Oh, I'm going to leave you here and send Bennie over to keep an eye on Holly's mother."

"Yesssssss!" Bennie said with a pump of his fist.

John looked at him and back at me.

"Here?" he said, deadpan. "Just me? Sitting around in my car?"

"Consider it the rookie initiation," Bennie said.

"Shut up," I told him.

John kept staring.

"But that's it?"

I shrugged.

"I only have two vans."

"Yeah, sure," he said facetiously. "I see how it's going to be. I get the Pinto while you guys run off in your tricked-out BMWs."

I smirked. The man was a regular comedian.

"Look, John. Maybe I'll get another van here soon but this is how we've done it for ages. Slink down in the front seat and try not to get noticed."

"Yeah, no problem. I'll just wave with my Slurpee if this Potter character happens by. Don't mind me, pal. I'm just the neighborhood watch dog."

A car passed by just then and John pretended to wave to it.

"Howdy, neighbor."

"Look, John. I'll understand if you don't want the work but I really need help right now and this is the only gig I've got."

"No, no. It's okay. I'm just blowing off some steam."

"You're sure?"

"Sure, sure. I'll just sit here and take some inventories. Fucking pricks with their tricked-out vans."

Bennie cracked up.

"Yeah, I'll get you, you greasy little Puerto Rican."

"All right, let's get serious here," I said. "This Potter's nothing to joke about. He'd skin kittens alive for laughs and he's determined to find Holly, or die trying. And I know he's trying. He found me. Who knows what the hell he'll do next?"

"Don't you worry," John said. "Give me a chance to pop the son of a bitch in the nose and that'll be the end it."

"He'll have a gun, John. Maybe several and he won't hesitate to use them, so don't figure he's going to take you up on an arm wrestling contest."

"So I'll blow his head off with the shotgun."

"You brought it?" I said.

"You bet your ass."

"And the 30-30?"

"That too."

"And they're both licensed and registered."

He nodded.

"Well, our policy is, we don't shoot unless we're being shot at, but if it comes down to your life or his, you go right ahead and blow his head off."

"You bet I will."

I stood up.

"Come on. Let's do this."

"Whoa, wait a minute, boss man. You still haven't told me what happened over there at your doll's place tonight."

"I believe I had told you to mind your own business."

"Shit. You can't bullshit a bullshitter. She fucked you around again."

"Bennie. Drop it or I'm going to toss you off that cliff over there."

"Oh man. That bitch's really got you by the huevos."

"I said shut up."

"Yeah, okay. I just hate seeing her treat you like this."

"I appreciate the concern. Now get your ass over to Mrs. Evergreen's place. And you, John, park your car here once Bennie's out of the way."

I opened the rear door and climbed out. John paused as he was climbing out.

"Prick," he said to Bennie. Bennie laughed and climbed forward into the cab. I closed the rear door but could still hear him laughing inside.

"He is a prick," John said to me. "You know what I mean?"

"He means well."

"You're a better man than I, Gunga Din."

I nodded while staring down at Gigi's house.

Twenty One

Once Bennie had driven off and John was parked in the same spot, he opened his door.

"Seriously?" he said. "I'm going to stick out like a sore thumb."

"Yeah, maybe. Look, here's what you can do. It's a little trick we used back in the day. Go ahead and jump in the backseat."

John stared.

"You're not hitting on me, are you?"

"Get in the goddamned backseat."

He laughed but did as asked. I took his place behind the wheel.

"Now lie down with your head on the shotgun side."

"Jesus. You really are hitting on me."

"Just lie down, you big son of a bitch."

He did. I got my hand on his rearview mirror.

"Now tell me when you can see the road behind you."

"Oh, I get it. Yeah, a little more down...Okay, a little more to the left. Hey! It really does sound like sex.

I shook my head.

"Just pay attention. Now which way?"

"A little more to the left. A little more down. Okay, that's it."

I looked over the backseat.

"Just keep your head up unless you see headlights coming. Potter's cagey enough to sneak up from the street below. I want your eyes on Gigi's house at all times."

"Sure, sure. That son of a bitch won't get by me."

"Want your snacks?"

"Oh yeah, thanks."

I handed everything over the seat to him.

"Maybe I should have brought a blanket."

"I'll see if Gigi has one."

"No, that's all right. You're not really going to tell her I'm out here, are you?"

"I'd rather not, but rigorous honesty and all that."

"Hey, far out. I've never thought of applying the program to real life. You know what I mean?"

"And where else would you apply it?"

John laughed.

"Yeah. I'll work on that one and get back to you."

"John," I said. "After Bennie, you're going to be a breath of fresh air."

"Jesus. Anything's a breath of fresh air after that guy, isn't it?"

"What? You don't like him?"

"No, yeah. He's cool. It's just that…you know…sometimes he gets up on his soapbox in meetings and I think I'm going to have to take him outside."

I looked away, reminded again of Caitlin. Nothing was ever going to cut through the grief of that episode.

I looked back at John.

"We probably shouldn't be taking his inventory."

"Yeah. You're right."

"And I'd better get in there to talk with Gigi. You're cool for now."

"Yeah, sure. I've never gotten paid for lying around before."

"Just don't fall asleep."

"No no. I'm good."

John gestured with his oversized cup of coffee.

"Good. And you have my number?"

"Yeah. It's in my phone from when you called."

"Just remember. You see anything that doesn't look right, you call me right away."

"Will do."

I gave him a thumbs up and climbed out of the car.

"And thanks again," I said before closing the door.

I started back towards my car but thought better of it. No point in turning over the engine just to drive a hundred yards.

On a warm autumn night, I walked along with that episode at Caitlin's place haunting my thoughts. The heartlessness of her stare was enough to gut any man. To her, I had been an intruder, not her gallant knight.

At the base of Gigi's driveway, I paused and dialed her number. While waiting for her to pick up, I looked down the street. John was sitting up and staring back at me.

"It's Michael," I said when Gigi answered.

"Hi. Checking up on our little soldier again, are you?"

"Actually, I needed to talk to you about something."

"Oh. Then go ahead. What's on your mind?"

"I was hoping we could talk face to face. I'm standing out here in your driveway."

"Oh dear. Then let me come open the door."

I walked up to the front porch. Gigi opened the door a moment later with a somewhat disconcerted look on her face.

"To what do I owe the pleasure, Michael?"

"Mind if I come in? This is going to take a minute."

She backed out of the way and waited while I stepped into the foyer, then closed the door.

"Did you want to say hello to Holly?"

"Yeah, but afterwards. Let's talk first. In private, if you don't mind."

Gigi raised her eyebrows and waved a hand.

"Right this way, then. We'll talk in my study."

Passing from the foyer into the living room, I caught a glimpse of Holly over the back of the sofa. She was watching TV. Curious, she looked over her shoulder, saw me, made a face and returned to watching TV.

Gigi waved me into her study and closed the door.

"So what's the big mystery?" she said once we were seated.

I struggled a bit with how to explain the situation but basically told it straight. Mainly I left out Potter's ostensible terrorist plot and the Mongols. I wanted Gigi to understand the gravity of the situation, not terrify her completely.

"Do you have any reason to believe he knows that Holly's here?" she asked when I was through.

"I don't know. I'd put those odds at very slim but he's resourceful. He found me. Assuming it was him. I don't know who else would call and breathe into my phone."

"Well, I can't pretend to be happy about the situation but we certainly can't blame you."

"I wouldn't blame you if you did."

"No, no. It's all part of helping others in this program. We all brought along our share of baggage with us, didn't we?"

"I definitely did."

Gigi leaned forward with a look of concern.

"Michael. You don't seem yourself tonight. What's wrong?"

"Nothing, nothing. I'm fine."

"Like hell you are. Now tell me what's going on."

I glanced at her.

"Come on," Gigi said, reaching out her hand.

I shook my head.

"No...it's just something better forgotten."

"Someone hurt you."

I glanced up again. The dam inside wanted to break.

"You know what they say, Michael. We're only as sick as our secrets."

I felt a flash of anger at hearing those words. I harbored so many secrets, I was like a nest of vipers in a dark cave. Gigi squeezed my hand.

"Come on, you."

Reluctantly, I went ahead and explained the events at Caitlin's place. When I was through, Gigi came around behind me and rubbed my shoulders.

269

"Oh, Michael. I can see how dearly you love this woman, but my god, how heartless."

"I've always tried to protect her, you know? I mean, she's clinically depressed. She can't help it. But this? I had rushed over there to be her gallant knight and she treated me like I had raped her."

Gigi came around and looked into my eyes.

"Michael. I know enough about depression to know it's just like dealing with a practicing alcoholic. She doesn't consciously mean to hurt you, but until she's ready to get help with her disease, she'll go on acting this way."

"Yeah, I know."

"Then it's probably best if you back off for a while. You can't fix her on your own, Michael."

"Yeah, I know."

And still I couldn't let go. You may as well have cut the heart out of me.

"Maybe we'd better get back to Holly," I said.

Gigi squeezed my hand and went back around to her side of the desk.

"And what do you propose we do?"

"Well, knowing that bastard has her mother's number, that's the last place I'd want to stash Holly right now. I'm worried enough about Mrs. Evergreen as it is."

"So you think we're better off leaving her here."

"I can't think of a safer place, but I have no right to drag you into this mess."

"No, no," Gigi said. "It's hard to imagine him showing up here."

"Probably not, but still…"

"Michael. I can take care of myself."

"Gigi. This is not a normal person."

"It's okay. You say you have a man down the block keeping an eye on things."

"Yeah. Big John. You know, just moved out here from New England and has a couple of months?"

"Oh god, yes. He's out there?"

I nodded.

"Well then. We don't have much to worry about, do we?"

"He's armed and no one to tangle with, but we're still talking about a psychopath on the prowl."

Having studied me for a long moment, Gigi stood up and waved for me to follow.

"Come. I want to show you something."

Gigi led me to a door adjacent to the kitchen. It opened onto a flight of stairs.

"I didn't know you had a lower level."

Gigi hit the light switch and whispered.

"It's not much, but there's a secret to it."

Before following Gigi downstairs, I glanced back at Holly and found her watching us intently.

On the lower level, I joined Gigi in a long sunroom. Chairs and end tables and a sofa were scattered about the hardwood floors. A small desk faced the windows. Lights sparkled north up the coast. It looked like a fine place to talk away the end of a day.

Gigi led me to the center of the room and pointed at a worn, Persian rug.

"Pull that aside."

I tried but found the rug was glued to the floor. One edge pulled back just far enough to reveal a brass pull.

"A hatch door?" I said.

Gigi smiled.

"Go ahead. Open it."

I did and found a stone staircase spiraling down into the darkness.

"Wow."

"Yes. It goes all the way down to the next street. The story goes, the original owner was a rumrunner and wanted an escape route, just in case the *coppers* ever came around looking for him."

"Funny. So you're thinking you have an escape route if Potter shows up here."

"I doubt he'd ever find this."

"Probably not. He'd be knocking down doors and checking the attic first."

"Feel better?" she said.

"It's some comfort. I'm just afraid he'll bust in here before you ever get this far."

"I have a pretty reliable alarm system."

"Then please keep it on."

"Yes sir."

I closed the hatch.

"Pretty clever, that."

"Yes. You'd be hard pressed to get the rug back in place from the other side."

"Indeed. Well, guess I'd better have a word with Holly and be on my way."

"She's a good soul," Gigi whispered.

"I know."

"A bit mixed up, but who wasn't at that age?"

"I'm still mixed up at this age."

Gigi squeezed my arm affectionately.

"You're a good soul, too, Michael."

"The story of my life, Gigi. All the best girls are already taken."

She waved a hand at me. My smile was quickly swallowed by the ongoing grief.

Upstairs, Gigi discreetly headed out to the kitchen. I sat down with Holly. She kept staring at the TV, pretending I wasn't there.

"I need your attention for a minute."

"I'm not listening."

"Yeah, real cute, but this is serious…I think Potter's found me."

Her eyes flashed my way.

"But that doesn't mean he knows about this place."

"He could have followed you."

"That's true, but I have the place guarded. Men with guns, and Gigi knows what to do if he shows up. I just felt it was only fair to tell you."

"Thanks for nothing."

"Quit being petulant. I'm trying to help you."

She stared at the television while I told her everything I had learned about Potter.

"The thing is, if I tell the cops what I know, I'll also have to tell them where you are."

"If you're asking me, I'd just as soon not talk to the cops."

"I assumed as much, but there'll come a point where we have no choice. Where I have no choice. I'm headed off to see what my attorney thinks right now. If it comes down to me going to jail or you talking to the cops?"

I shrugged.

"I hope you go to jail," she said, still being petulant.

I kept staring until she looked back at me.

"Did you really?" she said.

"Did I really, what?"

"Throw away all that coke?"

"Oh Christ, Holly. Let it go, will you? It's gone, all right?"

"I don't believe you."

"Fine."

I stood up.

"I know you're thinking that sobriety sucks, but maybe you'll get right with this disease before it kills you. It's not a given."

I left her sulking and went to say goodbye to Gigi.

Back up the block, I checked on John again before climbing into the Impala. On my way down the hill and out to Coast Highway, I called Jim.

"Hey, Michael!" he said with a din of voices in the background. "Just a second!" he added over a burst of laughter.

From the sound of things, he was out on the town. I listened as the din and hubbub slowly waned. Then it sounded as if a door had shut on the festivities. Wherever he was, it appeared that he had gone outside.

"Sorry," he said. "It's a bit of a madhouse down here at The English Cottage tonight. Sundays, you know. Folks getting in their last lick at the weekend."

"I know it all too well."

"Yeah. So how are you? Can I assume you've been staying out of trouble?"

"You can assume that if you'd like."

"Uh oh. What's going on?"

"Oh, that prick Barnes. He's breathing down my neck again."

"I believe we had expected that."

"I had been hoping for the best…Anyway, I figured I'd better get your counsel."

"And you were thinking now?"

"I was, but I don't want to spoil your party."

"No, no. It's fine. Things were about to break up anyway."

"I thought I heard Doris in the background."

"Perceptive of you."

"It's the laugh."

"Ah, yes. Well, actually, she drove down with some friends so I can send the lot of them packing."

"She'll hate me…but then pretty much everyone does these days."

Jim laughed.

"Having a bit of a persecution complex tonight, are we?"

"A bit, yeah."

"So? Are you coming down?"

"Sure, if I won't be getting in the way."

"Not a bit. The other couple at our table are about to pack it in anyway and I'm sure Doris will be perfectly happy trotting off with her chatty friends."

"Ooohhhh. So it's like that, is it?"

"Unless you have tapes, I never said it."

"I'll remember that the next time you're lecturing me."

"You do that."

"Okay. I'm on my way."

"ETA?"

"About ten minutes. I'm just now coming down from the hills on the south end of town."

"Look for me in the bar. We'll chat over a cappuccino."

"See you there."

I hung up, struck suddenly by how truly deep I was in the weeds. I knew too much about Potter not to have Barnes crawling up my ass, when in fact I had no idea where the bastard was or what he was planning to do next. All I had was a reasonably well-founded fear that he would be showing up in my life soon, and a sick feeling in my gut over that fact.

While considering all the other balls I was juggling, I realized I had forgotten to call Mr. Huntington about his 26th Dynasty figurine.

"I've been waiting patiently all day," he said in answering.

"I'm so sorry, Mr. Huntington. I've gotten myself into a bit of a mess here tonight and completely forgot about you."

"A lot of women have told me that over the years."

I smiled.

"It wasn't intentional, believe me. I've been dealing with a life and death situation and it's taken precedent over everything else, my sense of decency included, apparently."

"No need to beat yourself up on my account, Mr. Devlin. I'm just an old man worrying over the manifestations of his wealth. Hardly a life and death situation."

"It doesn't change things. I should have called."

"Well, we are where we are, so what do you propose?"

I glanced at my watch.

"I know it's late but I could stop by in an hour or so, if you think you'll still be up."

"Michael. I rarely sleep. In fits and starts, mostly. I haven't had a good night's sleep in over thirty years. Feel free to stop by anytime."

"Fine but I'll try not to make it four in the morning."

"When I say anytime, I mean anytime."

"Got it but you can expect me at a more reasonable hour. Probably around two. I have one more stop to make and I'll be on my way."

"The porch light will be on."

In the time it took me to dispense with Mr. Huntington's call, I had arrived downtown and found a parking spot behind the Cottage. The back entrance opened into one end of the bar. I made my way through the crowd and found Jim seated alone at a table. Doris was going out the front door with her chatty friends as I pulled a chair back.

"Good timing," he said as I sat down. "Oops...Or maybe a second too soon."

Doris had looked back for a final wave to Jim, spotted me and made a snooty face. I returned the favor and Doris shook a finger. There was a final frown for Jim before she slipped out the door.

"No. She doesn't hate me or anything," I said.

"It's calling in the middle of the night that gets her hair messed up."

'Do you remind her that it was I who introduced you two?"

Jim smiled.

"No need. Actually, she often worries about you."

"I know. That's why she set me up with her girlfriend Angie."

"Whatever happened with you two anyway?"

"Oh Christ. Two Corgis, three cats and four parrots?"

"A bit much?" Jim said.

I gave him a look.

"You think she would have left a little room in there for a human being."

"I take it you've never learned to say 'yes, dear'."

"No, I haven't. Just ask Lila Evergreen."

Jim smiled.

"She stopped by to sign a contract and leave me a check the other day."

I raised my eyebrows.

"Ready to sell our souls, are we?"

"Her smile's definitely something to behold."

"Yeah. Even if it's the last thing you ever see."

That got another smile out of Jim. With the two of us savoring our humor, the cocktail waitress arrived.

"Are we still talking cappuccinos?" he said.

I nodded.

"Actually, make his an Irish coffee. A double."

"No, no," Jim said and waved her off. "Two cappuccinos will be fine."

She left with our order. Jim looked back at me.

"And how is your...you know...?"

"You mean, drinking?"

He nodded.

"Oh, I'm fine without the booze. There are moments when getting bombed and forgetting the whole world does sound rather attractive, but I realize it's black and white now. I'm either on this new path, or I'm going for total destruction."

I tapped my temple.

"It's this little monster that gets me in trouble." I made eyes. "When all else fails, I go to a meeting and take someone's inventory."

Jim laughed.

"Trust me. That'll keep you busy for a couple of weeks at a clip. I've taken pretty much everyone's inventory around town...Except my own."

Jim laughed again. I raised my eyebrows at him again.

"Have a few drinks tonight, did you?"

"A few. Why? You thinking to drag me to one of your meetings?"

"It would give me a chance to take your inventory."

He laughed again.

"See? I can't remember you ever laughing twice in the course of a conversation, let along three times."

"Hmm. Good bourbon."

"Yeah. You'd have to remind me."

The waitress arrived with our coffees. We thanked her, saluted and had a sip. I was getting lost in some better forgotten memories when Jim interrupted me.

"So, you were saying about Barnes?"

I had another sip of my cappuccino and explained. Jim leaned back in his chair, his eyes closing from time to time while he absorbed the gist of my tale.

When I stopped to sip again at my cappuccino, Jim spoke up.

"This Potter sounds like a pleasant fellow."

"Oh yeah. We'll have to have him over for tea some afternoon."

Jim smiled.

"And the body you found? Still no idea who it might be?"

"A few wild ones, but nothing the least bit solid."

"And Detective Barnes. You want me to do *what* about him?"

"Make him disappear…For good, preferably."

"I suppose there's no point in me reminding you that you've broken the law several times along the way."

"You're right. I already know I'm breaking them. Your job is to help me get away with it."

"And I believe this is where I submit my resignation."

"You can't."

Jim stared dourly.

"Just tell me how I can keep him away from Holly for now."

"Look, your problem is, you know where she is. You'd be on safer ground if you didn't. Having knowledge of her whereabouts and not telling, Barnes? That can quickly turn into obstruction of justice, and/or contempt…Come on, Michael. Why do I have to keep repeating this crap?"

"I keep hoping you'll come up with a loophole."

Jim stared dourly.

"Look," he said. "I told Mrs. Evergreen the same thing. At some point, it's best just to cooperate. It's not going to kill Holly to testify."

"It might."

278

Seeing that Jim wasn't much sold on the idea, I leaned over the table.

"If she drinks and uses over it, that's as good as killing her."

"I can't speak to that. But as to this other business, you're courting disaster, as usual."

"What's the matter, Jim. You mad at me tonight?"

A reluctant smile crossed his face.

"Fine. Enough on that score," I said. "If it becomes necessary, I'll have Holly moved to a location unbeknownst to me. As to me testifying, what can I get away with not telling Barnes?"

Jim made a face and leaned back in his chair.

"What?" I said.

"What? You may as well do whatever the hell you're going to do. You're not going to listen to me."

"Jesus, Jim. I've been beaten up enough for one night. And you know I couldn't get a damned thing done if I didn't break the law here and there. It's not like I relish the idea."

"You could have fooled me."

"All right, all right. You've had your chance to whip me. Can I give you a call if Barnes ends up cornering me before sunrise?"

"You really want the little missus throwing me out on the street, don't you?"

I sighed.

"Of course," Jim said. "If you're in trouble, call me."

Twenty Two

We both sipped at our cappuccinos and took in the bar scene. Then Jim's phone rang. He looked and held up a finger.

"I need to take this."

My awareness of Jim's conversation quickly faded into more reveries of Caitlin. Why did her actions always wound me so deeply? Maybe there was a kernel of truth to what Sylvia the fortune teller had told me. I owed a debt to a pharaoh. Real or not, that's how it felt. An ancient curse. As if the karma of a thousand lifetimes weighed upon me. And good luck trying to straighten that out from the English Cottage on a Sunday night.

Jim ended his call, breaking my spell.

"You don't look so well all of a sudden," he said.

"I don't feel so well all of a sudden."

I was reluctant to repeat the saga at Caitlin's place earlier in the evening but ultimately offered Jim an abridged version. When I was through, he reached out a hand.

"Jesus, Michael, I'm sorry. I know how you feel about the woman."

"I only wish I didn't...I hate being someone's fool."

"Oh hell, we've all been a fool like that at some point in our lives."

"Yeah? You?"

"Oh sure. I've had my guts kicked in once or twice. But all you can do is lick your wounds, try to learn from your mistakes and move on. The hurt will pass. It always does."

"Yeah, I know all that, intellectually speaking, but when I'm down in the mouth like this, I find myself questioning my entire existence. Like what's the point of me even being here? What good have I ever done? What reason do I have to take up space in this world? It's probably why I'm so intent on finding that young woman's killers. Anything to prove that my life wasn't lived in vain. My name will be all over the news."

Jim kept studying me as I took a sip of my cappuccino.

"You're awfully hard on yourself, Michael."

"Yeah. It's all because I screwed over Ramesses II three thousand years ago."

"Yeah?"

"That's what Sylvia the fortune teller once told me."

Jim smiled. I sighed.

"Speaking of which...There's actually a 26th Dynasty figurine burning a hole in my trunk so I'd better get going."

Jim raised his eyebrows.

"Fitting, huh? For the record, it belongs to old man Huntington and his miscreant son-in-law Nicholas stole it from him."

Jim shook his head.

"No, you don't want to know."

I stood up and reached for my money clip. Jim pulled out his wallet but I shooed him off.

"This one's on me." I threw some money on the table. "And put the rest on my tab."

"Don't worry about that. We'll just call it old friends getting together."

We headed out the door and stopped alongside Jim's car. He patted me on the shoulder.

"It was good to see you."

"Yeah?"

"Well, mostly." He smiled. "But seriously. Good luck with it all, and don't be so hard on yourself."

"Oh, Christ, Jim. If you could have seen the look on her face. I don't know how to process it. It just leaves you wanting to go out and get drunk."

"No. Don't do that."

"No. I told you, I'm not going to drink, but hell, I'd just as soon she had shot me."

"I know, Michael. Trust me. I know how it feels. Like someone's gutted you, but it'll pass. Just don't go out over it. You're on a good roll. The last thing you need right now is a wild spree."

"I'm not going out on any wild sprees."

"Sorry. I don't mean to meddle but I worry about you."

"I know. Thanks. And thanks for listening to all my crap."

We hugged.

"Let's hope Barnes doesn't crawl up my ass tonight."

"Just give me a call if he does. And come up to say hello some time. When it's not so goddamned late and you're not in trouble."

"Oh, sure. So I can sit around and envy your domestic bliss again."

"It's not always bliss, Michael."

"Oh…And here I had imagined…"

Jim gave me a look and went around to unlock his car.

"It was good seeing you."

"Good seeing you, Jim."

I waved one last time and turned up alongside the beveled glass windows of the English Cottage. Faces glanced my way as I passed by. Music and muffled laughter spilled out amidst the buzz of conversation.

The town had mostly emptied out over the previous half hour. I turned the corner, the last lonely traveler on a dark and lonely night.

On the way down to my office, it dawned on me that I had forgotten to call Lila and dialed her number. It rang and rang and went to voicemail. I looked at the time. It was late, but still, it seemed odd that she hadn't answered. I left a message while parked in front of my office, letting her know that there was now an operative in place, watching her home, and dashed upstairs.

With the Huntington's figurine on my front seat, I headed south on Coast Highway. I couldn't help but picture the old man up ahead, wandering about his big empty mansion like a bored monarch. Actually, I had no idea what he did with his time but had often wondered, with all that money, why not try to fix the world? Or at least a good portion of it. At least he could have tried. I fancied I would have done so. I wasn't sure why. I had been on the planet for over fifty years now without contributing much of anything besides my share of trash and heartaches.

I'll do better, I promised myself and moved on to more manageable terrain.

Fifteen minutes later, and roughly one mile in from the coast, I arrived at the base of Huntington's private hill. A road wound up and up around its flanks. That led to a circular driveway and an English Tudor looking mansion. It was situated high enough to see past all the surrounding hills. No one was ever going to block Huntington's view. I had been there on a brilliantly clear day, with the wind blowing out from the desert, treated to stretches of coastline from Palos Verde all the way down to Point Loma.

I parked and checked my watch. It was a little past two in the morning. As promised, Huntington had left the porch light on.

I grabbed the figurine from the front seat, closed the car and climbed the stone steps to the front door. A good many seconds passed before George the butler finally answered my knock.

"Good evening, Mr. Devlin," he said somberly. "Please come in. Mr. Huntington has been expecting you."

I entered a foyer that could have swallowed a few motorhomes. George closed the door and led me down an opulent passageway voluminous enough to accommodate elephants. Our footsteps echoed off ahead of us.

Halfway down the passageway, George opened the door to Huntington's study, ushered me in and closed the door. I found the old man sitting in a wingback chair, facing his fireplace. Through the windows of an adjacent wall, lights were visible along the coastline, sparkling all the way up to San Pedro. I crossed a Persian rug to where he was sitting.

"Please, have a seat," he said while looking my way.

I did. Huntington sized me up as one does a thoroughbred, his face aglow from the fire. I unwrapped the figurine and set it down on the carved mahogany table between us. The old man watched without emotion.

"I hope this is the right piece."

"It is. And no new scars, I see. I trust you were able to retrieve this treasure without too much hardship."

"More than I would have preferred, actually, but I lived to tell about it."

"Hmm…I'd offer you a drink but you have yet to take me up on it."

"I'm still working tonight, sir, but thank you."

The old man looked back into the fire.

"It seems all too fitting."

I waited until the silence grew uncomfortable.

"What does, sir?" I said.

"Oh, this figurine's most recent saga. Imagine. The 26th Dynasty. Nearly three thousand years of unbroken Egyptian rule, dynasty after dynasty, until the whole thing had rotted away from the core. Nothing but pettiness and decadence, the pyramids but a bitter reminder of a great empire that once had been."

He glanced over at me.

"And here it would appear our ersatz empire has achieved such infamy in little more than two hundred years."

He looked back into the fire.

"For the record, the 26th Dynasty was the last one of native rule. It could not have been long after this figurine was forged that Cambyses II sacked Sais and Egypt was subjugated by Persia."

I looked back into the fire with him, reluctant to admit that I knew little to nothing about the 26th Dynasty, or any other Egyptian dynasties.

"Not that it mattered much," Huntington went on. "Between the Egyptians and Persians, you would be hard pressed to choose which one of them was more iniquitous. They'd both roast your children alive and serve them to you for supper."

I stared straight ahead, disheartened by the conversation. Yes, it appeared we too had become a decadent society, effete and without moral compass. Hell, the whole world appeared to be coming apart, but at least we no longer roasted our children. At least not to my knowledge we didn't.

"And the Picasso?" Huntington said.

"I'm working on it, sir. The jewelry too, though that may be a bit harder to track down."

"As I've already expressed, don't concern yourself overly about the jewelry. I'll be content with getting the Picasso back."

"Well, nonetheless, I have my sources looking into it. As to the Picasso, there is a possible suspect but it's more a matter of conjecture at this point. Guilt by association, you know?"

He looked over.

"Do you mind me asking who that would be? I promise not to reveal your sources."

I smiled but hesitated. I had no right to smear a man's name idly, even Vanderhof's. Then I decided, what the hell? It's Huntington's money.

"A man named Vanderhof. He was seen in…"

"That son of a bitch!?"

I almost burst out laughing.

"Yes, sir. Why? Do you know him?"

"Hmm. Regrettably, yes. You see, those who possess great wealth belong to a very small society. We invariably find ourselves at the same fundraisers and such. Like it or not..."

Huntington suddenly looked puzzled.

"But I thought they had thrown the bastard in jail."

"They did."

I explained how the court cases had played out, and Vanderhof's early release.

"Well, apparently it's shamed him, because I haven't seen him around polite society since he was returned to the streets.

"I imagine he's not very fond of the notoriety."

"Hmm. That would and wouldn't surprise me."

Huntington stared back into the fire, his brain working away. Then something appeared to fall into place and he looked over at me

"My apologies, Mr. Devlin. I believe you were about to say something before I interrupted you. Vanderhof was seen in...what place?"

"Actually, he was seen in the company of your son-in-law Nicholas. Or perhaps it's best stated the other way around."

"Yes. That would make more sense. That groveling toady would do anything to get his hands on money."

My thumbs did a little dance together while we stared.

"So you believe Nicholas may have sold my Picasso to Vanderhof?"

"It's possible"

"Good. Then perhaps we can put both of them behind bars in one fell swoop."

Before I could respond, my phone vibrated and I had a glance. It was Bennie.

"Go ahead, Mr. Devlin. You're welcome to answer it."

"No, no. It's all right. I'll return the call in a moment...Is there anything else I can do for you tonight?"

"Not really. We're down to entertaining a lonely old man and there's no money in that. Go on. Get on with your business."

I stood up.

"Speaking of money, Mr. Devlin, whenever you need more of it, just say the word."

"I'll send you a bill, sir."

"Very well. And thank you again."

"You're welcome."

I started across the room but stopped.

"By the way, sir. Any word from Charlotte?"

He looked up from the fire and shook his head, the grief in his eyes barely disguised. I stared back for a moment before continuing out of the room.

I had started down the palatial hallway when a text message came through on my phone. I quickly pulled it back out of my coat pocket and had a look. It was Bennie again and his words shot a jolt of adrenalin up my spine.

> Boss man call me. You need to get your ass over here RIGHT NOW!

At the far end of the vestibule, George the butler waited dutifully for me with one hand on the front doorknob. Old man Huntington must have had silent ringers hidden about the house because George was always waiting for me there whenever I went to depart. I headed towards the door as fast as a man can move without appearing to look frantic, my footsteps echoing up and around the lofty ceilings behind me.

"Goodnight, sir," George said as I went out.

"Goodnight, George."

I dialed Bennie back and hurried back to my Impala. He answered as I was opening the door.

"About fucking time," he said.

I hopped into the front seat.

"Don't start with me, Bennie. I'm not in a very good mood tonight. Now what the hell is going on?"

"Exactly when are you in a good mood?"

I slammed the car door shut and hit the ignition."

"I said don't start!"

"Chill, dude."

I dropped the Impala into gear and peeled out of Huntington's driveway with a final look back in my rearview mirror. The door was closed and porchlight off.

"If you have to know, I was down here delivering Mr. Huntington's 26th Dynasty figurine. Now answer my question. What the hell is going on?"

"Okay, so look. This dude came cruising by Mrs. Evergreen's place about five minutes ago, but real slow like..."

"Who drove by?! Potter?!"

"I don't know, man. I couldn't see shit. The windows were totally darkened but come on. Cruising by here at two miles an hour? Like he's in a funeral? Just checking things out? I mean, that shit just looks totally suspicious right now."

"So what? That's it? Someone drove by real slow?"

"Just chill and let me finish."

"Anytime this year will do, Bennie."

He went off in Spanish.

"Just shut up and tell me what happened!"

"I'm trying. So look. I was on the downside of Mrs. Evergreen's place when the car went by and around the corner. Now I'm sitting and waiting to see if it comes back but it doesn't. So I take a cruise around the corner to check things out and guess what? The car's parked up there but with no one in sight. Just a pit bull in the backseat, ready to jump out and take my head off."

"A pit bull?!"

"Yeah, why?"

I explained about the guy checking out Caitlin's neighborhood.

"Oh man," Bennie said. "So that dude's totally here."

"Yeah, it sounds like it...But that's it? No sign of him coming back down the block on foot or anything?"

"Nada, but a minute ago, I saw a light come on inside Evergreen's place. Just for a few seconds and then everything was dark again."

"Shit."

"Yeah. And I thought I heard a scream or something."

"Seriously?!"

"Well, you know. I'm a couple, three hundred yards up the block now but I could have sworn I heard someone scream."

"All right, I'm on my way over there right now but in the meantime do you have the license plate number?"

He rattled it off.

"Wait, slow down. 7GBT…and the last three again?"

"916."

"Got it. I'm going to see if I can rouse Kenny and find out who owns the car."

"Good idea."

"Yeah. I have one every couple of decades."

"So we can figure you're tapped out until about 2040."

"Something like that. Now look, don't park too close to that car. If it's really Potter, he'll…"

"Boss man, give me some fucking credit. I'm a good hundred yards up the street from where he parked."

"Atta boy."

"Atta boy. You're the only person who can make an atta boy feel like shit."

"Yeah yeah. Now, look. If he goes to leave, you just follow him. No gunfights out on the streets."

"I'd just as soon shoot the son of a bitch."

"I know but just lay low until I get there. This *is* where we should be calling the cops, not starting a street fight."

"How about if I just go down there and case the joint a bit."

"I said just wait!"

"All right. Fuck."

"Jesus. I'm serious. And don't start shooting just because you see him. Unless he starts shooting first."

289

"Oh sure. Once he's plugged me full of holes, I'll get off a few rounds."

"Oh Christ, Bennie. Will you just sit tight and keep an eye on things?"

"Fine."

I started to hang up and pulled the phone back to my ear.

"And don't forget to call if you see the bastard."

"Yeah, because dumb Puerto Rican that I am, I'd sure as hell forget that shit."

"Oh Christ. Can we ever do this without the drama?"

"You're the one who's always getting dramatic."

"I am not."

"Yes you are."

"Bullshit."

"Fine. Believe whatever you want."

I felt myself going mad and screamed at the top of my lungs.

"I want a divorce!!!"

I was just starting to feel remorseful when Bennie spoke up.

"Fine, but I get the kids."

In that moment of madness, I had to laugh.

"Christ, Bennie. I don't know how we get going like this."

"I do."

"Yeah, you little bastard…Anyway, I'll be driving up your ass before you know it so hang tight."

"You know where to find me."

"Yeah. See you in a few."

I hung up and dictated a text to Kenny

Are you up? I have something urgent I need you to do.

Jumping on the freeway, I had a quick look before sending it.

Bar you up. I have some clean detergent I need you to tool.

290

Oh boy. He's going to think I'm calling about the laundry. There was an impulse to edit things but I decided, screw it. Kenny was smart enough to get the general idea.

Thirty seconds later, his answer came back.

I'm up, if that's what you're wondering, but the Chinese laundromat is closed for the night.

Funny. I gave him a call.

"Sorry but I'm in full assault mode here and dictated the message. You think they'd be doing better with the technology by now."

"It's getting better."

"As I can see...Anyway, look, here's the situation."

"Wow," Kenny said, once I had explained things. "Sounds like you might make the evening news."

"That's exactly what I *don't* want happening...A SWAT team arriving with three assault vehicles, a battering ram and a helicopter circling overhead."

Kenny chuckled.

"They do have a way of going overboard."

"Yeah they do....So anyway, here's the license plate number. Run it and let me know what you find. I'll be pulling up there in about five minutes and would like to know if that bastard's inside waiting for me."

"You got it."

"Thanks."

I hung up, doing ninety again and passing cars as if they were standing still. Caitlin returned to my thoughts as I darted through traffic. She was back there somewhere, slumbering away peacefully, not a thought for the wounds she had caused me. If she ever did pause to wonder, no word was ever said. What grief. I tried again to put that look on her face out of my mind, without success.

Twenty Three

Where the freeway made a sweeping turn past the coast at Doheny, I took the exit, careened down the ramp and veered left onto the inland leg. That brought me to a red light at a darkened T-intersection. An undeveloped slope rose up opposite me. With no cars in sight, I blew the light and turned left back under the freeway. From there the road quickly jogged right and up a straight incline. A series of residential cul-de-sacs radiated off to my left. Ocean view homes lined the ascending bluff on my right. I knew from googling Lila's address that her home was at the top of the hill and on the ocean side of the street, tucked back on its own point.

I cruised past her long driveway with just a glance of my eyes. No sign of lights in the house. No sign of Potter, if he was even in there.

A short distance past Lila's driveway, the road made a dogleg left and headed farther up into the hills. The lights of homes twinkled off in that direction until darkness swallowed them completely.

A few hundred yards up the dead-end road, I spotted Bennie's van parked on my left. I continued up the hill until the front of Lila's home was no longer in sight, pulled into a driveway, hit the lights and sat there watching.

When it was clear that I had aroused no attention, I backed out, headed down the hill and parked behind the van. Before climbing in with Bennie, I went around to my trunk and swapped my Smith & Wesson for a Glock and silencer.

Bennie glanced up from the monitors as I slipped in through the back door.

"The world's number one ball beater."

"Yeah, yeah. So says your long-lost cousin, Sal Rodriguez."

"Long lost cousin. What kind of shit are you talking now?"

"Never mind." I sat down next to him. "What's going on?"

"Nada. What about Kenny?"

"Not a word yet."

I checked the monitors. The street outside was dark save for one porch light.

"I take it that's the car," I said.

Bennie nodded. You could see the dog pacing back and forth through the rear window.

"I'd just shoot that fucker first thing," Bennie said. "Fucking pit bulls. You never hear a story like, *Golden Retriever mauls little girl*. It's always one of those monsters."

I kept staring at the monitor.

"What do you say we go down there and bust in," Bennie said.

"Bust in and start shooting. That's your answer to everything."

"It'd be a hell of a lot more productive than this shit."

"Right. First of all, we don't even know if Potter's in there. But assuming he is, what the hell do you think's going to happen if we go charging in?"

"We shoot the bastard and make the front-page news."

"Jesus. I thought I needed help."

I stood up.

"Okay, I'm going down there to have a closer look."

"What about me?"

"Stay here and watch my back."

"Shit, boss man. I never get in on the action."

"Action. You almost had your balls cut off for you out at Devil's Punchbowl. What more do you want?"

293

"You know what I mean."

"Yeah yeah. Look, Rambo. I'm just going down there to sniff things out and need you to stay right here. And text me if anything happens."

I started to open the door.

"You know. If you didn't think I could handle the job, you shouldn't have hired me."

"Christ, Bennie. If you don't hear from me in fifteen minutes, call the cops. That should give you plenty of action."

"Maybe I'll just drive off."

"Yeah, you do that."

"Fucking bullshit," Bennie said as I slipped out the back door.

I headed down the gently sloping street, muttering to myself. I had never bothered telling Bennie this, but I did everything humanly possible to avoid putting his life at risk, just so I wouldn't have to answer to his mother at his funeral.

The neighborhood was as quiet as a midnight graveyard. The only thing moving besides me was that pit bull. I crossed over to the opposite sidewalk, figuring it would go off at the sight of me. It did, lurching violently at the windows the minute I came into view. Surprisingly, it didn't bark. I had my hand on the Glock, just in case the monster got loose.

Farther down the block, I came to a vacant lot and paused there. The lot was completely overgrown with trees and brush but might offer an alternate path to Lila's place via the adjoining bluff. I looked down towards the end of the street, where the road turned right past her long driveway. Her home was tucked well back on its point but anyone approaching from that direction could be spotted with the parting of a curtain. I had no idea if Potter was inside or not but had to assume as much.

With a hand signal for Bennie, I slipped in among the heavy undergrowth and forced my way forward. A machete would have been handy. I had buckeye and coyote brush slapping at my face and young fan palms tearing at my legs.

Having stumbled unexpectedly upon a three hundred foot cliff, I peered over the edge. There was an open tract of land far below and then more homes.

I retraced my steps fifteen feet and turned towards the adjacent backyard. That brought me to a six foot high stucco wall, topped with black wrought iron. I followed the wall back down to the bluff and found it extended out nearly to the edge. What remained of level ground was basically a goat trail.

I hesitated, not liking this Plan B very much. The stucco wall would offer me no handhold if my feet gave way, and it damned well looked as if they might.

I paused there, thinking. The coastline sparkled with lights in the distance. The sound of breakers echoed up from the shore.

Having failed to come up with a respectable Plan C, short of parachuting in, I started forward on the narrow trail and was about thirty feet into my trek when my left shoe slipped on some loose pebbles and I started over the edge. In a desperate attempt to stop my fall, I reached for anything to hold and got my hands onto some ice plant. That left me hanging three hundred feet in the air. I swung wildly with my feet, searching in vain for some kind of footing.

While doing that, a dog started barking. I cursed it and myself and everyone else in the universe.

Feeling the ice plant start to give way, I reached for the next handhold and the next one and quickly came to the cliff's edge, confronted there with an overhang. In order to reach level ground, I would have to swing one leg up over my head. It would be acrobatics from a thirty story skyscraper.

With a prayer, I pulled with all my might, executed the maneuver and miraculously found myself on the path, only to feel gravity dragging me back over the edge. In another wild maneuver, I rolled swiftly away from the cliff and grabbed the one thing I could find, a half-buried rock under my chest. I held onto it with both hands and lay there while my heart stilled.

Once the adrenalin had subsided, I sat up and looked around. Good one, Devlin. You're front page news, all right. Old man dies stumbling off a cliff.

I had been sitting there for another minute, still gathering myself, when the phone buzzed in my coat pocket. I looked and saw it was Kenny.

"Took you long enough."

I explained briefly what had just happened.

"A real cliff hanger," he said.

"Yeah, funny. So what's with the car?"

"Oh yeah. Turns out it belongs to a guy named Gene Smith."

"Seriously? Not Joe Smith?"

"Nope. Gene…Anyway, I thought to check the police blotter and sure enough, it was stolen."

"From where?"

"Redlands."

"Shit. That's definitely Potter's turf and he's a man to steal cars."

"I still say call the cops."

"No. I've already run through things in my head. They'll just turn this into a three-ring circus, and drag the media along with them."

"Whatever. I'll be here if you need me."

"Thanks. I'll keep you posted."

I hung up. More heroic visions passed through my head. In a hail of bullets, PI lays down his life for client. I'd be all over the evening news, and dead.

With a sigh, I got to my feet, cautiously resumed my journey and eventually arrived at the backyard adjacent to Lila's property. I looked at my phone. Most of fifteen minutes had blown by so I texted Bennie.

Just got here. Give me five more minutes.

He texted right back with a thumbs up symbol.

Before tucking the phone away, I checked again to make sure the ringer was off and poked my head around the corner of a cobblestone wall. A princely lawn sloped up gently from the bluff's edge, terminating at the retaining wall of an infinity pool. The pool spanned the entire length of Lila's house, facing seaward, as did a nearly unbroken line of French doors and windows. A gazebo stood as the lawn's centerpiece, with flagstone paths, wooden benches and flower beds artfully placed here and there.

I looked back at the house. It was completely dark, with no sign of anyone stirring. Yet all those doors and windows represented too much exposure. There were also several windows facing my way from the second story.

I crouched down below the short cobblestone wall and headed for the far side of the house. A minute later, I had circumvented the point and was staring through a six foot wrought iron fence at Lila's side yard.

I checked my watch, realized that Bennie was probably itching in his seat again and quickly texted him.

Hang loose. I'm still scoping things out.

Again, he texted back with just a thumbs up symbol. Yeah, he was being snarky. I could feel it. At least he hadn't driven off on me.

I returned my attention to the house. Three trash bins stood directly behind the side gate, followed by the gas and electric meters, a carved mahogany door and a long, uninterrupted stretch of wall from there to a French window at the back corner of the house, all of it serviced by a tile walkway. The window looked north up the coast, I assumed from Lila's living room. Potter would have to press his face against the glass and strain his neck to get a glimpse of me from that vantage point so I set aside any concerns and turned my attention to the carved door. It opened inwardly, which worked in my favor. Door strikers could be compressed from one direction, but not the other. Had the door opened outwardly, I would have needed my lock kit.

With a look both ways, I dashed across the remaining lawn, vaulted over the wrought iron fence and landed hard on the tiled walkway. The sound of my shoes echoed off into the night. I crouched behind the trash bins and waited.

When a minute had passed with no sign of anyone inside being alerted, I went around to the door and pressed my ear to it. Nothing, just the hum of the universe.

I pulled a pocket knife out of my pants and worked to free a portion of the door stop from the jamb. Something snapped in the walls so I froze. The seconds passed. The sound of breakers slapped in the distance. I pictured Potter waiting for me on the other side of the door with a gun in his hand. Or maybe he wasn't there at all. Maybe Lila was sleeping away peacefully upstairs.

I went back to work with the Glock in my left hand now, prepared for the worst.

Once a small section of the stop had been freed from the jamb, I slipped a credit card between the two, pressed the striker out of the way, returned the Glock to my right hand and gently cracked the door. When it creaked loudly, I froze again. In the game of cat and mouse, I had just lost my advantage.

Peering through the hinge side of the door, I saw it was a darkened hallway. The opposite wall was lined with black and white landscape prints. A dim light filtered in from the direction of the living room. That troubled me. I was certain there hadn't been a lamp on in Lila's living room before. Then, turning one on made no sense, at least not by Potter. So maybe Lila was home, or Desmond, or both. Desmond's presence would explain why Lila had failed to answer my call.

Assuming the worst, I flung the door open violently, thinking to catch Potter hard in the mug. The effort was met with air. The detective gods above were laughing.

I peeked around the door and down towards the living room. The light in that direction turned out to be the moon setting late out over the sea. There were no signs of life.

I checked the time, saw it was half past three and turned my attention to the two doors opposite me. One was louvered, one paneled. Roughly twenty feet farther on, the hallway jogged left around a corner.

I slipped across the hallway, pressed my back against the wall adjacent to the louvered door, paused a moment with my hand on the doorknob and flung it open. It was an empty laundry room with cream colored cabinets and state of the art appliances.

I left that door open and approached the other one with like caution, back to the wall, gun at the ready, met this time with an empty utility room. In addition to a furnace and water heater, there were solar panel storage batteries and a Ft. Knox grade home security system. It wasn't armed, which was one more thing to trouble me.

Pausing outside the door, I weighed my best strategy and decided to clear the back of the house first. I had a reasonably good idea what to expect in the direction of the living room.

While I stood there thinking, something snapped behind me. I spun around with gun pointed, only to be met with empty space.

Consider it a warning, Devlin. Keep moving.

I turned the other way down the hall and peeked around the next corner. More empty space.

Remembering Bennie, I texted him again.

> Inside now but no sign of Potter. Or anyone. Hold off until you hear from me. Or hear gunshots.

I stood there waiting for a response. Finally, another thumbs up symbol came back. I sort of felt his pain now. Bennie never got in on the action.

I returned my attention to the hallway ahead of me. It intersected the front foyer and continued on to a narrow hallway at the far end of the house. Moving quietly in that direction, I stopped at the foyer and peeked cautiously around the corner. Moonlight washed the furnishings out there. Otherwise, all was quiet with no signs of life.

I moved on to the far hallway and found a door to the garage. With a quick look out there, I saw that Lila's Jaguar was missing. Maybe she was out with Desmond. That too would explain why she had failed to take my call, but not the unarmed alarm system.

There were two other scenarios which would better explain the alarm system being off. One, Potter had put a bullet into Lila's head and run off with her Jag, or two, he had taken her on a wild ride to find Holly. Lila had no idea where Holly was, but Potter wasn't likely to buy that story.

I continued stealthily down the hallway, clearing both a darkened study and a den, but finding no sign of Lila or Potter. That brought me eventually to the living room. I paused there at the opening. A kitchen was off to my right, along with a round vestibule that served as a dining room. A round dining table sat there in the moonlight with twelve carved chairs arranged neatly around it.

I peeked around a corner to get a clearer view of the kitchen. No sign of anyone. I moved to the base of a grand staircase on my left and paused again, thinking to head up and clear the second story.

Remembering Bennie, I had pulled my phone out to text him when something moved in my peripheral vision, that jolt of accompanying adrenalin followed swiftly by a sharp pain behind my right ear. I fell backwards, hit the floor hard and the Glock rattled free from my hand. In all of that, it seemed that I had heard a muted report, followed by a louder one, seized then by a sickening fear that a bullet was the cause of the pain in my head and this was the start of death.

Overwhelmed with nausea, I struggled to open my eyes. Stars were dancing gaily all around me in the darkness.

Kicked hard in my ribs, I reflexively raised my head and found a face staring down at me from the shadows. Bennie? I tried to speak but the pain was like the weight of a thousand black holes and I was quickly tumbling down and down and down into a great yawning abyss.

It seemed to be much later when I awakened with a gasp. The throbbing pain was still there. But I wasn't dead. I couldn't be. I heard breakers slapping at the distant shore and turned my head that way. The moon had set and the room was cloaked in darkness. Whatever had happened, it must have taken place hours ago

Wanting to know the source of my throbbing pain, I reached for my head and jumped. Jesus. A man was sitting in a chair beside me. My eyes struggled to focus. Then suddenly I knew. It was Potter. He had cut his hair and trimmed his beard down to a goatee, but the eyes were unmistakable. Cold and filled with venom.

He had my Glock in his lap and a Sig P226 pointed at my head. He spoke and the voice was filled with even more venom.

"I'll give you ten seconds to tell me where she is. Then the pain starts."

Reflexively, I tried again to touch my wounds but Potter quickly jabbed the Sig into my forehead.

"Uh uh uh."

My hand dropped back to my side. I had gotten far enough to feel a grisly wound and the cold, sticky blood in my hair. Potter had obviously clocked me good with his Sig.

He pressed the Sig harder into my forehead.

"Your ten seconds is up."

I could see his finger turning white at the trigger.

"Why, Potter?"

"Why what?"

"Why the hatred? I get it, you know? I get the unhappy childhood but why make everyone miserable along with you?"

"Fuck you! Either tell me where Holly is or I'll start with your kneecaps we'll move up from there!"

"I'll tell you what, Potter. Let's make a deal."

"What kind of deal?!"

"You tell me who's buried out there behind your old place on Highland and I'll tell you where Holly is."

"Why the fuck do you care?!"

"I just want to know, that's all. It troubles me."

"Yeah?! Well we ain't here to talk about that bitch! NOW WHERE'S HOLLY?!"

"A name, Potter."

"FUCK YOU!"

In a flash, he was on his feet and behind me with a hunting knife at my throat. I felt the razor's edge about to slice my carotid artery open.

"Maybe I'll just cut your head off. Like to know how it feels? Huh? Let me tell you. We call it the dance, 'cuz your feet start twitching like you're hanging from a rope. Bip bip bip. Even the tough guys can't help themselves. Feet going a mile a minute. Meanwhile you're gasping for air, except your mouth ain't attached to your throat anymore so you kind of sound like you're gagging on a sausage. And then there's the final crunch of the spinal cord and you're staring off into space with your eyeballs bulging out. NOW WHERE THE FUCK IS SHE?!"

"You tell me and I'll tell you."

Potter pressed a bit harder with the knife.

"How does it feel to know you're going to die here in a minute?"

"Fuck it, Potter. If I'm going to die, what does it matter? Then I won't be feeling anything."

With the knife still at my throat, Potter moved the Sig down towards my groin.

"How about if we start here with a bullet in your balls, fucker. NOW WHERE IS SHE?!"

I could feel Potter's hand trembling, the man torn between wanting to dust me and thinking that I might be the one person in the world who knew where to find his bitch.

Twenty Four

Resigned to more pain and death, I had started to speak again, hoping to buy myself a little more time, when a massive explosion shook the world and a cloud of smoke billowed down the hallway from the front of the house.

"You fucking son of a bitch!" Potter hissed.

Half blinded by the smoke and coughing, I thrust my forearms up and battled with Potter's knife. Then I sensed his Sig pointed at my head and lurched to one side, vaguely aware of voices and footsteps charging my way as two shots went off and the world went black again.

Sometime later, I awakened with a start and tried to sit up.

"Take it easy, partner," a man said and held me back.

Panicked by all the people moving around us the room, I tilted my head to look. The letters FBI were printed on the back of all their vests. That much was comforting. There was more hubbub down the hallway but out of my vision.

I tried to speak but it came out like a croak. I cleared my throat.

"What the hell's going on? What happened?"

"You tell me. Looks like someone clocked you over the head and then tried to add a bullet."

I reached for my wounds and felt even more nauseous. The bullet had grazed me deeply, a few inches above where Potter had clipped me with his gun. That wound was the texture of raw hamburger. I made another attempt to sit up but the man held me back again.

"I said take it easy. I'm trying to clean you up a bit."

When he applied some antiseptic to my wounds, I winced.

"You're lucky that bullet was just a glancing blow."

"But did you get him?"

He looked up from his work.

"Get who?"

"Potter."

He went back to work.

"Don't know anything about a Potter. Who's that?"

"The son of a bitch who shot me."

He kept working at my wounds without answering.

"So?" I said.

"Can't say. You'll have to ask Agent Barretta."

"Who's Barretta?"

"The person in charge."

"But what about Mrs. Evergreen?"

"What about her?"

"Quit playing fucking games with me! I just want to know if Mrs. Evergreen's all right!"

He looked at me like I had kicked him.

"Like I told you, you'll have to take it up with Agent Barretta."

He finished with the antiseptic and stood up.

"That's it for now. Better stay lying down until someone can get you to the hospital."

He wandered off. I lay there seething.

Barretta, huh. I had visions of a big burly Mexican with acne scars and an attitude.

Still nauseous, I had no trouble lying there as instructed. Agents came and went around me. I was a carcass, to be weighed, measured and carted off at some point.

A few minutes later, a nice looking pair of legs appeared in my vision. I followed them up to an attractive brunette. She had lovely eyes and lips. She would have been far more attractive if

305

her hair hadn't been pulled back so severely into a ponytail. Still, it was a clean, straight face, the kind that could sell beauty soap.

"Agent Barretta," she said, squatting down and holding out her hand.

There was hope.

"Michael Devlin."

"I know."

She showed me my wallet and ID.

"You up for telling me what happened here?"

I paused, wondering how much she already knew. Barretta smiled ever so slightly and made a rolling gesture with her hand. Come on, Devlin. Out with it.

I liked her. She was no nonsense, but kind. And still I wasn't ready to give up my secrets.

"What?" she said. "You don't know? Or you're not ready to tell me?"

Oh what the hell, I thought. I may as well try to be of service. As much as was possible under the circumstances.

"No," I said. "I know. A man named Potter was about to cut my head off with a knife. Then you folks came barging in."

"And saved your life maybe?"

"Maybe. Or maybe you were outside the whole time, figuring to get one more felony charge on him at my expense."

Barretta's smile suggested that my version of the movie hadn't met with her approval.

"Yeah? Maybe I need to cut you a little slack on that one?"

"Maybe. We lost Potter while tailing him out near Riverside. About two hours ago. I had a hunch he might be headed this way and here we are. Trust me, if I could have been here sooner, I would have."

"Then forgiven."

She smiled ever so slightly again. Which, in my state, was an invitation to romance.

"So why were you tailing him?" I asked.

"Why were *you* tailing him?" she asked.

"I asked first."

"You know I can't tell you that."

"Oh, sorry. I thought we were all on the same team here." She scoffed.

"You mean like the way you've been playing Barnes?" Barretta raised her eyebrows at me. "That's right. Barnes told me all about you. Oh, and he happens to be on his way down here right now. I guess he has a few questions he'd like to ask you."

I stared, reevaluating our fledgling romance.

"So what's it going to be?" Barretta said. "The easy way? Or the hard way."

I scoffed.

"Come on. I've been around the block a few times."

She kept staring. I kept staring back.

"So the hard way," she said.

"All right," I said finally and embarked on a redacted version of what had brought me to Lila's house that evening, leaving out everything humanly possible without the story sounding like gibberish, especially when it came to Holly.

Barretta paused me when I got to the part about Potter's stolen car and called out to one of her men.

"Bradley!"

He came over, the alpha male, all buffed out and full of himself. Yeah, I got it, pal. Barretta & Bradley. Netflix at ten.

Barretta told him about Potter's car and he headed off on his mission. Barretta looked back at me with another smile.

"So, go on."

I quickly wrapped up my tale.

"And that's it?" she said. "Potter didn't tell you anything?"

I shook my head. She appeared to believe me in the main but kept staring.

"And now I have a few questions for you," I said.

"Such as?"

"Such as, what happened to the SOB? Your boy doctoring me up wouldn't tell me. And Mrs. Evergreen? Potter didn't seem to know where she was."

"On Mrs. Evergreen, neither do we. We called her cellphone but got voicemail and she hasn't called back. What do you know? Does she have a boyfriend? Think she could be out on a date?"

"Could be," I said.

That thought had the power to hollow me out a bit. Given that business with Caitlin, Lila had become my fallback position. After Lila, I was down to Barretta, and after Barretta, the first woman who'd have me.

I looked back at Barretta.

"What's going on, Devlin?" she said.

"Oh, just having a moment here...So, Potter?"

"Jumped off that cliff out there, apparently."

"Get outta here."

Barretta shrugged.

"That's all we can figure, unless he knows how to fly. Or disappear into thin air. We had the perimeter surrounded when we blew the front door in."

"How the hell would you survive the fall?"

"Don't know. He did something miraculous because his body's not down there at the bottom of the cliff...Anyway, he's got half the county sheriff department chasing after him, along with a handful of our agents, so he shouldn't be running around for long. Assuming he is still alive."

Remembering my phone, I reached into my coat pocket but found it was gone. That meant Potter must have run off with it, along with all my contacts.

"Looking for this?" Barretta said, pulling the phone out of her coat pocket.

I took it.

"Where did you find it?"

"Sitting on the end table here."

Okay. So either Potter had failed to take it in his haste, or he had already found what he wanted while I was out.

I looked back at Barretta. She was still staring at me.

"What's going on in there, Devlin? I can see those little gears turning."

"Just trying to piece the evening back together."

"Uh huh…And any fresh insights you'd like to share with me?"

I shook my head.

"Then back to Potter. You say he cut his hair. About how long?"

I gestured down below my ears.

She nodded and thumbed through her notes again. I lay there, taking in her nice legs.

"So that's it?" she said. "Nothing else to add?"

"Nope. Unless you'd like me to share my hopes and dreams."

Barretta looked up.

"Maybe some other time."

"You've got my number. Give me a call. We'll make it a date."

She smiled, touched my shoulder and stood up.

"Sit tight. I'll be back in a bit."

I watched her head upstairs, sorry to see her go. Barretta had given me just enough warmth to hang myself.

With Barretta gone from my sight, I looked out towards the sea. Waves were slowly undulating in towards shore. Agents came and went around me.

Then I remembered Potter's knife at my throat and his words. Bip bip bip. Your feet going a mile a minute. God, the horror. Five thousand years of civilization and we were still visiting that kind of cruelty upon each other.

I was trying to clear my mind of those images when renewed commotion broke out in the direction of the front door. I turned my head to find Bradley herding Bennie into the room. Bennie looked ready to take a swing. Then he saw me and my wounds and crossed himself.

Barretta came down the stairs and met Bradley.

"Who's this?" she said.

"We found him sitting up the block in a van. Claims he works for this guy."

Barretta turned to me.

"Is that true?"

I nodded.

"And you've been sitting up there this whole time?" she said to Bennie.

He nodded. She looked back at me.

"And you didn't mention him because?"

"It slipped my mind."

Barretta looked sincerely disappointed.

"Devlin. If you want me to be straight with you, you've got to be straight with me."

"Go ahead and shoot me. It seems to be popular tonight."

Still looking disappointed, Barretta turned back to Bradley.

"What about Potter's car?

"Oh yeah, we found it. With a pit bull in the backseat. Someone from animal services is on the way over to deal with it. There's no looking inside until they do. Unless you want me to shoot the damned thing."

Barretta shook her head. I decided it was time for me to stand up but landed right back on my ass. Bennie rushed over.

"Take it easy, boss man. It looks like you took a pretty good hit."

He helped me to get settled with my back against the wall. I hung my head, weakened by that brief effort. Bennie looked up at Barretta.

"What the fuck is wrong with you people? You should be getting him to the hospital."

"We'll get to that soon enough. First I want to hear your story."

Bennie looked at me. I motioned for him to go ahead.

"Hell, I don't know. We came here looking for Potter and the boss man had me watching from the van."

"And you didn't see Potter come or go?" Barretta said.

"I didn't see shit. I was sitting out there when he texted me, telling me to listen for gunshots. That's when I thought, whoa, I'd better get my ass up a little closer, so I did. In the van, I mean. Then I heard a gunshot and ran the rest of the way down the block. I had just seen there was a door open on the side and was ready to jump that fence when I heard you people racing up so I disappeared into the brush. Then on my way back up to the van, I heard the explosion and another shot go off. Shit, boss man. I would have raced right back down here except for all these people swarming around. I couldn't see no choice but to sit in the van and wait. And I've been up there ever since, waiting and wondering what the fuck to do."

"Perdone," Bennie added with a cross of himself in Barretta's direction.

Barretta turned to Bradley.

"Bring his van down here and go over it…And check for any video!" she called out as he disappeared.

I watched him head off, none too happy about that prick rummaging around in my personal affairs. When another agent came in and distracted Barretta, Bennie leaned in closer and whispered.

"What the fuck? With all these cops swarming around, I thought sure you were dead."

"I thought so too there for a minute."

He looked over his shoulder before continuing.

"What the hell happened. Did Potter do that to you?"

"Yeah, he was here."

"But how, man? I'm telling you, I never saw his ass come back down the block."

"He must have been jumping backyard fences. That or took the same route I did."

"And where the hell's Lila Evergreen?"

311

"I don't know. When I saw her car missing and the alarm system off, I figured Potter must have taken her on a wild ride looking for Holly…What the hell was that scream you told me about?"

"Hell if I know. I know I heard something. Maybe it was that sick fucker. You know? He gets in here, sees no Holly and no Mrs. Evergreen and lets loose with a primal scream?"

"Yeah, maybe."

"So?" Bennie said. "Potter clocked you and then what?"

"Then I woke up and he asked me where Holly was with a gun to my head. And then these people blew the door in and he took a shot at me before booking it out of here."

"Booking it out of here where?"

I pointed my nose at the opened French doors.

"According to them, he went over that cliff."

"No way, dude."

Barretta dispensed with the agent just then and returned her attention to Bennie.

"So you were saying. You never saw Potter out there?"

Bennie shook his head.

"I told you. I didn't see shit."

"You forgot to cross yourself," Barretta said after a moment.

Bennie did so sarcastically. The beleaguered looking Barretta gestured at another agent.

"Take him outside and see what else he knows."

An agent led Bennie towards the front door. The walls in that direction were awash in colored lights. I pictured a circus out there; a posse of cop cars, the neighbors standing on their lawns, news vans gathering up and down the block.

Barretta was back to her clipboard. I hung my head again, still feeling like crap.

"Any news on Mrs. Evergreen?" I asked her.

"What?"

"I said, any news on Mrs. Evergreen yet?"

"What's it to you?"

I looked up.

"Come on, Barretta. I'm sorry you feel let down. I really am but please don't play games with me. I'm concerned. Have you seen or heard from her yet?"

Barretta looked up from her clipboard.

"I caught up with her by phone. She's on her way home right now."

I nodded and hung my head. Lila out with her beau. Having spurned her advances, I was now the odd man out. All I had left were my grim memories of Caitlin.

Five minutes later, I heard renewed commotion out in front and the sound of the garage door opening. Then the door from the garage to the house opened. Lila was back.

"Oh my god!" I heard her say. "Oh my god! Oh my god! What have you done to my home!?"

This was followed by the sound of her high heels coming down the hallway. My heart raced, hoping she'd be glad to see me.

Lila entered the living room a moment later, wearing a burgundy cashmere sweater with Levi's and the same black, high heel pumps she had worn at my office that first day. With every head turned her way, and every male agent in the house suddenly looking gallant, Lila caught sight of my blood on the floor.

"My god! My hardwood flooring!"

She looked at me.

"And Michael. What on earth are you doing here?"

"You invited me. Remember?"

"But not like this. What is going on here?"

Barretta held out a hand, interrupting Lila.

"Mrs. Evergreen. I'm Agent Barretta. The one in charge."

One of Barretta's agents had been poking around under the furniture by the French doors and came out of his crouch, holding a slug.

"Hang on," Barretta said and went over to have a look. "Think this is yours?" Barretta said to me with the slug now in a plastic bag.

"I don't know. Potter had a Sig P226. The Glock was mine and I'm pretty sure one of the shots came from my gun."

Another agent pointed at a shattered lamp.

"Whatever it was, it must have clipped that thing going by."

Lila gasped.

"That thing was my antique blue Venetian lamp!"

Lila went over to grieve. I looked at Barretta.

"I should have been a lamp."

"Okay, okay, everybody!" she said. "Let's get back to business here! And you, Mrs. Evergreen. Please have a seat."

She did so, still looking around her living room in a state of shock. Barretta stood over her.

"Look. This is what we know. Potter came here looking for your daughter tonight. Or you. We assume he'd want to find you if he couldn't find Holly. Devlin somehow got wind of his plans and came to intervene on your behalf. Potter got the jump on him and tried to put a bullet in his head. We happened to have been on Potter's tail too and barged in as all of this was playing out. Unfortunately, Potter got away. For the moment, anyway."

With her eyes on me now, Lila slowly got to her feet. I watched her step around the blood on the floor and squat down to my level. I had a nice view of her high heels. She hadn't worn nylons again. I liked it when a woman wore high heels without nylons. Lila was also wearing some nice perfume.

"I'm sorry, Michael. I didn't understand."

I acknowledged her comment with a shrug. She touched my face tenderly and had a closer look at my wounds.

"My god. You really did get shot. And this. What happened?"

"Potter knocked me over the head. Then I woke up and we chatted a bit. Then he decided he didn't like what I had to say and was going to take my head off with a knife. Then these folks barged in and Potter took a parting shot."

She gently probed around the wound and stood up.

"I'd better get my first aid kit."

314

"One of our agents already treated him," Barretta said.

"Well, he did a lousy job."

Lila strutted off to a nearby bathroom, returned with a first aid kit and got me into a chair with my feet up on the ottoman. I shrugged at Barretta. She shook her head and turned her attention to one of her agents. Lila leaned in closer to me.

"Is Holly still safe with your friend?"

"Yes.

"And you've got somebody watching her?"

"An armed agent."

She sighed heavily.

"Are we going to be able to keep her out of this mess?"

"I'm trying."

She studied me for a moment and went to work on my wounds.

"Ow!" I said when she probed near the bullet wound.

"Sorry. Does it really hurt?"

"A bit, but I'll suffer for any kind of attention right now."

Lila admonished me with a frown and continued working on my wounds.

"And what about you?" I said.

Lila looked briefly into my eyes.

"What do you mean?"

"I called you tonight but you didn't answer. I left a message but you never called back. I was supposed to let you know when my man was in place. Remember?" Her eyes met mine briefly again. "Yeah. You must have been in an awfully big hurry, leaving the alarm system off and all."

While waiting for her to respond, Barretta strutted back over.

"You need to come clean, Devlin. Where's Holly?"

I stared at her.

"Devlin?"

"I work for Mrs. Evergreen and she's represented by Jim Harrison, attorney at law. Check with him. Otherwise, I suppose you'll have to use the courts."

"I will, you know. She's a material witness."

"Maybe. Maybe not. In the meantime, she's stashed someplace safe. And detoxing. Not even Mrs. Evergreen knows where she is."

Barretta looked at Lila.

"Is that true?"

"Yes. He's refused to tell me."

"For everyone's good," I added.

I felt another wave of nausea coming over me and hung my head. Lila put her arm around my shoulder and looked at Barretta.

"What is wrong with you people? We need to get him to the hospital."

I was thinking to find a bed and lie down at the very least when my phone vibrated. Barretta watched as I checked the caller ID. It was Gigi so I answered.

"What's going on?"

"Oh, sad to say, but our little angel has run off."

"Shit!" I said.

Everyone in the room stopped what they were doing and stared. Barretta came closer and hovered over me. I turned away and returned to my call.

"Look. Things are pretty crowded around here right now but please explain."

"Are you saying that somebody's listening?"

"Yeah, yeah, something like that but go on."

"Well, I got up to grab a drink of water from the kitchen a short while ago and happened to hear Holly talking on the phone."

"A phone?!"

"Yes, yes. Foolish of me, I know, but I let her use the land line here."

"Shit…Okay, go on."

"So, on my way back from the kitchen, and I should probably clarify here, she was in her bedroom, behind closed doors, but I could sense her being hush hush as I passed by."

"And you didn't try to listen in."

316

"Oh god, no. I would never do that. I went back to my own bedroom but was concerned enough that I couldn't get back to sleep. Then a few minutes later, I realized that things had gone silent and went to check, and sure enough, she was gone. I checked the whole house and all around outside but nothing."

I noticed Barretta was still staring at me and glanced up at her. Every agent in the room was staring. I got back to the call.

"Look. I need to touch base with one of my guys. Can I call you in a minute?"

"Oh sure, sure."

"I'll be right back…Oh, and hey."

"Yes," Gigi said.

"Better check that lower stairwell."

"Oh yes. Thanks for reminding me."

"What's going on?" Barretta said as I dialed John's number.

"Oh, nothing. Just a little problem in the field."

Barretta kept staring. I gave her a gratuitous smile.

After several rings, John finally answered.

"What's up, sweetie."

"Oh, nothing much. Anything cooking over there?"

"Not that I've seen."

"Okay, listen. A little change of plans. I need you to go down to the street below and stake things out from that location."

"What am I going to see from down there?"

I glanced up at Barretta, wondering how to convey a sense of urgency, short of shouting.

"Look, John. Just do it. It's important."

"Oookkkkaaay. It doesn't make any sense to me, but fine."

"Just do it, and fast, please. Anyone coming and going, I want to know."

"You got it."

"Thanks. I'll call you later."

317

Twenty Five

I hung up with Barretta still staring at me. I gave her another gratuitous smile.

"Don't you owe someone a call back?" she said.

"Oh, that can wait. What I really need is to get my head sewn up. Any idea when that can happen?"

"Whenever I'm done getting answers from you."

There were fresh voices out in front. Barretta looked from me to Bradley and nodded. He went off to investigate. Barretta looked back at me.

"I'm guessing that's Barnes."

She smiled. I didn't.

From out of the hubbub in front, a set of footsteps approached down the hallway and Barnes appeared.

"Barretta," she said, holding out her hand.

"Barnes," he said, shaking it. "Looks like you're having a hell of a party here."

He looked at me.

"Hey, partner. Long time, no see. What the hell happened to you?"

"He had a little encounter with Potter," Barretta said, answering for me. "We're still waiting for him to come clean about what he knows. As you said, he seems to have a little problem with the truth at times."

They both looked at me.

"Mrs. Evergreen," Barnes said. "Nice to see you again."

Lila turned to Barretta.

"Look, I don't care about your little pissing contest here. I know my daughter's safe and that's all that matters to me. So please finish up your investigative work and let me have what's left of my home back, please."

"Whoa, just one minute there, Mrs. Evergreen," Barnes said. "You see, I have a little thing here called a subpoena. For your daughter. Because I couldn't seem to get you folks to play ball with me otherwise."

"Oh, this is nonsense. She's just a child."

Lila looked to Barretta for help.

"I'm sorry, Mrs. Evergreen, but we believe your daughter's a material witness to several crimes. Possibly even a federal conspiracy, so we need to question her too."

"No. She's a sixteen year old girl. A traumatized sixteen year old girl and I don't want you people anywhere near her."

Barnes waved his subpoena.

"This right here says that she has no choice...Sorry."

Lila looked again to Barretta for help.

"It's true, Mrs. Evergreen. At some point she'll have to cooperate."

With Lila bristling, an agent came in and whispered to Barretta.

"The sheriff's department thinks they have a lead on Potter."

Barretta turned to Barnes.

"Lets you and I go outside and talk jurisdiction."

Barnes smiled at me and followed Barretta towards the front door.

"Hey!" I called after Barretta. "When the hell are you going to let me get stitched up?"

Barretta paused.

"Just hang tight. I'll get an ambulance for you in a couple of minutes."

"I don't need a damned ambulance. I can drive myself to the hospital."

"Just hang tight," she repeated and disappeared down the hallway.

"Son of a bitch."

I glanced at Lila. She sighed.

"Oh god, Michael. How are we going to keep her out of this mess now?"

"Let me deal with it. If they really press the issue, I'll give Jim a call."

She nodded. I looked away with my mind racing. Actually, Holly's disappearance worked to our favor in one respect. No one was going to be questioning her now. I just dreaded having to tell Lila that I had lost her daughter again.

While scrambling for some way to extricate myself from the situation gracefully, I felt Lila's fingernails on my forearm.

"Did you really come to rescue me?"

I glanced her way again and nodded.

"It was very gallant of you."

I nodded again.

"No, I mean it. You know, you and I would make a wonderful couple."

She kissed me on the cheek as if we had signed a contract. I acknowledged her kiss with a strained smile. There was only one thing on my mind. How to get free of this mess and back out there looking for Holly. I had about fifteen minutes before things completely blew up in my face.

I was still scrambling for some kind of game plan when Barretta walked back into the room, a no nonsense look on her face now. Barnes and Bradley were at her side

"You need to spill it," Barretta said.

"Spill what?"

"Where you're hiding Holly."

"I already told you. Ms. Evergreen has retained counsel and I'm in her employ, so you'll just have to address your questions to Jim Harrison."

Barretta turned to Lila.

"Ms. Evergreen. There was a carjacking a short while ago. Less than a mile from here. A man shot in his driveway while arriving home from a business trip. He was rushed to the local hospital in critical condition so there's not much hope of questioning him right now but we have to assume it was Potter."

"So?" Lila said. "What does that mean to me?"

"The police just found the car abandoned in Laurel Lagoon. If we're right about it being Potter and he's in Laurel Lagoon, it's only because he's looking for your daughter. Meaning, we should be there protecting her right now. And you should want us there protecting her."

Lila looked at me. I shook my head.

"Look," Barretta said. "I don't know what kind of game you two are playing here but knowing where your daughter is means knowing where Potter is, so either you cooperate or we'll have to take you both in for withholding evidence."

I kept staring. Barretta waved at the agent standing next to her.

"Cuff them."

He stood over Lila and gently encouraged her to stand up.

"Look, Barretta. I already told you. I'm the only one who knows where Holly is. There's no need for you to be putting Mrs. Evergreen through this spectacle."

The agent had gotten Lila up and was starting to cuff her.

"Michael?" she said to me.

I looked from her to Barretta.

"What's it going to be?" Barretta said. "We can talk here or we can do it down at headquarters."

"Michael," Lila said. "Maybe it's best if we cooperate."

Cornered, I let out a big sigh.

"I had this old gal in Laurel Lagoon helping Holly to detox but it appears that Holly ran off."

After a moment's pause, Lila used her free hand to slap me.

"You bastard! Why didn't you tell me?!"

I took that lump and got back to Barretta.

"This gal heard Holly talking on her land line a short while ago. I'm guessing with Potter. Anyway, she's gone."

With a nod from Barretta, the agent freed Lila from the handcuffs. She started pacing the floor with one hand running through her hair.

"You bastard! You bastard! How could you lose my daughter again?!"

I took the additional lump and looked back at Barretta.

"I gather you had a man watching the house," she said.

I nodded.

"The one you were talking to on the phone."

I nodded again.

"And how did that work out?" Barnes said.

I looked around the room with everyone staring at me.

Having taken one too many punches that evening, I got to my feet and into Barretta's face. Bradley was quick to intervene but she held out a hand. The entire room had come to a halt around us, frozen in place. Barretta and I remained staring at each other.

"Say it," I said.

"Say what?"

"You know what. The part that comes after, 'if only the FBI had been there, none of this would have happened'."

"Oh, this is bullshit," Bradley said.

Barretta held out her hand again. I kept staring.

"Say it, goddamn it. This woman deserves to know the truth."

Barretta glanced in Lila's direction and sighed.

"I'm guessing what Michael wants me to say is, anyone could have lost your daughter. The FBI included."

"Or there's the even worse scenario," I said. "The one in which the police and FBI get a little trigger happy and Holly goes down in a hail of bullets."

"Now it's my turn to call bullshit," Barnes said.

Barretta again held out a hand to him and looked back at me.

"Oh yeah. That's never happened, has it, Barretta?"

She stared.

"We've made our share of mistakes, sure…So are you happy now, Michael?"

"No, but I feel a hell of a lot better, knowing the truth's out there for everyone to see."

Barretta picked up my phone from the end table and handed it to me.

"You've had your say now. Make the call."

I took the phone and dialed Gigi's number. She answered after the third ring. I quickly explained the situation.

"So you need to talk with the lead agent here, okay?"

"Oh dear, okay."

"Listen. Just remember. The only thing you have to share is your direct knowledge of Holly's whereabouts. Anything else is immaterial."

"Just give her the damned phone!" Lila said.

Barretta held out a hand to Lila now.

"Oh dear," Gigi said again.

"Yeah. Things are getting a bit testy around here. Anyway, here's Agent Barretta."

I cupped the phone.

"Her name's Gigi, but remember. She doesn't know a thing about Potter. Or about anything else, for that matter."

Barretta nodded and took the phone.

"Gigi? This is Agent Barretta. Look, we have reason to believe that Potter is in Laurel Lagoon and probably with Holly. I'm going to send some of my agents down the coast right now but need an address."

Barretta jotted it down, tore the page from her notebook and handed it to Bradley. She made a gesture for him to hurry. He rushed off with two other agents while Barretta was still listening to Gigi.

"That's fine," Barretta said into the phone.

I glanced at Lila. Her return look said it all. So much for us making a wonderful couple. Fine. I had never really trusted the woman anyway.

323

I looked over at Barnes. He gave me a smirky smile. I was just shy of nailing him with a right cross.

Barretta got off the call with Gigi and handed me the phone.

"You've got three minutes," she said to Barnes "I owe Devlin here a trip to the hospital."

Barretta went off and huddled with Lila at the other end of the living room. I stared at Barnes. Big shot, huh. I'll give you midlevel manager. Seeing Barretta put him in his place was almost as good as punching him in the nose.

Barnes noticed me glancing at Lila and smiled.

"Looks like your little romance just went up in smoke there, huh partner?"

"What do you say we stick to business, Barnes."

"Well. If I didn't know any better, I'd swear you didn't like me."

"I don't like cops. Most of them, anyway. Especially not the ones who think they're judge, jury and executioner. Now what do you want from me?"

"I'll tell you what I want. Whatever the hell it was that you got your little hands on before we showed up over on Highland Road. A ring, I'm guessing, for one thing. Anyway, you know a whole shitload more about this case than you're letting on and I'm here to find out what that is."

"Christ, Barnes. Blow fifty bucks on a background check, why don't you. Because that's all I did."

"Yeah? Is that how you figured it all out?"

"Figured out what? That Potter's nuts? That he swears allegiance to the Phineas Priesthood and all this other right-wing BS? That he thinks Timothy McVeigh ought to be on Mt. Rushmore? I know that and that he's obsessed with Holly Evergreen but beyond that, I'm completely in the dark."

"Yeah? And how about Potter's connection to the Mongols? What do you know about that?"

I stared.

"Yeah," he said. "I figured you'd play dumb on that one too."

"Look, Barnes. I'm not here to do your homework for you. You've got the badge. Go do your job."

"You know, I could make life a real hell for you over this Holly business if I wanted to."

"Fine. Knock yourself out."

"So, you're telling me you don't know a thing about this Mongol connection."

"I didn't say anything of the sort."

"No, you didn't, did you."

I kept staring.

"Well, you know something you're not telling me, Devlin."

"And when you figure out where there's a crime in all that, Barnes, you be sure to let me know."

"Son of a bitch."

While Barnes was cooking up the next thing to say, Barretta returned.

"Looks like your three minutes is up," I said.

Barnes looked from me to Barretta.

"Like Whalen said, he can be a real pain in the ass."

"And you be sure to tell Whalen, right back at you, pal."

Barretta waved a hand.

"If you two are done here, I need to get this man stitched up."

Barnes nodded.

"You can have him for now. But I'll be seeing you again, partner. And I still need a crack at this Holly," he added to Barretta before walking away.

I looked at Barretta. She seemed reasonably sympathetic to my cause.

"Any sign of him yet?" I asked her.

"Potter?"

"Yeah."

She shook her head.

"Think I really screwed this one up?"

"Depends on how it turns out."

"Well, if it matters any, I feel like hell about it all."

"Maybe next time you decide to play hero, call us first."

"That's what all the cops keep telling me."

"Then maybe you ought to take the hint."

"Yeah, maybe I will…Next time I decide to play hero."

She shook her head.

"Come on. Let's get you to the hospital."

"Then what the hell am I going to do? My car's up the block here."

"Hang on a minute," she said and went out to a gathering of agents by the pool. One of them was an old guard type, gray haired, with a butch. He broke off from his conversation to listen to Barretta, had a look my way and nodded.

Barretta returned.

"I'll have a couple of my agents drop it off at your house."

"And then what?"

"I'll drive you home."

"I can drive myself to the hospital, Barretta."

"Uh uh," she said. "If anything happens to you along the way, it's my ass."

I smirked.

"What?" she said.

"What? You left me here for road kill the past two hours and suddenly you're worried about my health?"

"You weren't going to die. Now come on."

She took me by the arm and led me down the hallway. I noticed Lila watching us and gloated while she stewed.

Out by the front door, Barretta arranged for two agents to drive my car home. Out near the end of Lila's driveway, several cops were standing just to this side of the caution tape, holding a crush of reporters at bay. My van was there with a handful of agents going through it. Bennie was nowhere in sight.

"Devlin?" Barretta said.

"Yeah, what?"

"The keys?"

"Oh."

I reluctantly dug them out of my pocket.

"Maybe you could stick the Glock back in the trunk."

"It's state's evidence," Barretta said. "You'll get it back as soon as we're done. Now come on."

She led me out to a black Suburban. The reporters started snapping photos and shouting questions. As suspected, the street going down the hill was lined with cop cars, news vans and neighbors gawking.

Barretta got me comfortable in the shotgun seat and closed the door. I watched her come around the front hood and climb in. She glanced my way while turning over the ignition.

"Any preferences?" she said.

"To what are we referring?" I said.

Barretta smiled sarcastically.

"Hospitals."

"Oh. Then South Coast. It's closer to home."

"South Coast it is," she said.

With her eyes on the rearview mirror, she started backing up. Two cops held the caution tape up and out of our way. The crush of reporters converged around the Suburban but Barretta plowed through them and quickly left the hubbub behind us. Her radio was tuned to the police band. We went down the hill with the usual squawks and squelches. It sounded as if Bradley's team had already met with Gigi in Laurel Lagoon but had yet to find Potter.

I watched the present unfolding in front of us and disappearing into the past. The events of that evening did an encore in my head. Most of it seemed to be far, far back there now and part of another lifetime. Except for Caitlin. The memory of her was still as sharp as a knife in my gut.

I glanced over at Barretta.

"You okay?" she said.

"No. I'm still pissed about your comment back there."

"You mean about having a little problem with the truth?"

"Yeah, that one."

"Sorry."

"Yeah, I'm sure you are."

She did a double take.

"You could tell me all about your hopes and dreams now if you'd like."

I scoffed.

"I'll have to get back to you on that one. I'm drawing a blank at the moment."

She did another double take while bearing right under the freeway. We drove in silence for a spell.

"Look," I said. "If you don't mind, I need to check in with my guys."

Barretta shrugged. I pulled up Bennie's number. He quickly answered and went off in English and Spanish as if they were interchangeable. I had to pull the phone away from my ear. Barretta looked my way with a smile.

"Can you possibly translate some of that for me," I said.

She had to choke back a laugh.

Having allowed Bennie to vent for a minute, I told him to go home and get some sleep.

"He means well," I said and called John next

He got the same message. Go home and get some rest.

Morey was last in line but the most important call to me. I wasn't about to leave Caitlin unguarded and asked him if he could hang in there until morning. Morey more or less intimated that he could keep his eyes open until hell froze over. You had to love the guy.

I assured him that someone would be by to relieve him soon and hung up.

Barretta met my eyes again.

"All tidied up, are we?"

I nodded and looked forward. We had come alongside the coast and a state park. Moments later we were at the stoplight to the harbor entrance, then heading up the hill into Doheny Beach. The town was deserted at that hour. I saw a cop parked in the shadows of a stucco office building with his radar on. One car had gone by the other way.

Half a mile later, we came to the knoll at Fisherman's Point. Up on the other side of the rise, the hills of Laurel Lagoon came into view.

Barretta broke the silence.

"What was Barnes grilling you about back there?"

"My problem with the truth."

She flashed a look my way.

"Yeah? And did you have anything to tell him that you haven't told me?"

I weighed her question.

"What do you say we make a bargain here?"

"Which would be?"

"You get Barnes off my back and I'll tell you anything you want to know."

"You're an easy catch." Barretta flashed several looks my way while driving. "So?"

"So, as soon as we're back at my place, we'll draw up a contract."

"So, you're not such an easy catch."

I made a so-so gesture with my hand.

"You can blame the jaded outlook on all the women who came before you."

Twenty Six

The rounded main building of the hospital came into view along a darkened stretch of highway. It was nestled on a slope and tucked well back from the road. Barretta hit her signal at the stoplight and turned straight up a hill.

The access road continued on past the hospital and off into the surrounding hills. Barretta turned left below a three-story parking structure and pulled to a stop in front of the main hospital entrance. I watched her climb out and start towards the automatic doors. Failing to hear my door open, she stopped and looked back. I stared. She looked to the heavens and came back.

"Sorry," she said, opening my door. "I don't know what came over me."

"I've always wanted to see how it feels."

"Smart ass."

She grabbed hold of my arm and perp walked me over to the entrance.

Inside, Barretta flashed her badge and signed some papers. A triage nurse promptly led us back to a bed in ER and pulled the curtain shut.

"Excuse me," I said and lay down.

Barretta stood over me.

"How are you feeling?"

"The world's starting to spin a bit. Might be a black hole."

I closed my eyes. Barretta touched my shoulder. Her hand felt delicate and kind, the way a wife's hand would feel, worrying over her husband. I opened my eyes.

"What's your first name, by the way?"

"Gertrude."

"Get out of here."

She smiled.

"Alessandra. But most people call me Alex."

"I'll go with Alessandra. But don't go thinking I'm not still pissed at you."

"You don't hold grudges much, do you?"

"Not much. Give me a year or so and I'll probably be over it."

When the doctor came in, they talked about me like I wasn't there. I felt Alessandra's gentle hand again.

"I'll be back. Time to check on my guys."

She squeezed my arm once before disappearing.

"So," the doctor said while probing around my wounds. "Sounds like you've been having yourself quite an evening."

"Yeah but just get me patched up here and I'll be right back at 'em."

He smiled.

"Hang on a minute. I'll be back."

He returned with a razor and sewing kit. Ten minutes later, I looked like a power mower had gotten the best of me. Alessandra was standing next to the bed with a smile.

The doctor wrote out a script and gave it to her.

"He probably has a mild concussion. You can stop by our pharmacy to fill this."

"So we're done?" she said.

He nodded.

"Just make sure you get some rest," he told me. "And give those bandages a week or so without getting them wet in the shower. The stitches will dissolve on their own."

Alessandra led me out by the arm.

"Forget it," I said when she headed towards the pharmacy.

"What? You don't want to fill this?"

"Hell no. I don't need any medication."

"It's your head, tough guy."

"Thank you."

"Which way?" she asked once we were seated back in her car.

I pointed north.

"It's about two miles up the road that way."

We headed into Laurel Lagoon with dawn not too far over the horizon. I had no interest in seeing sunrise that day. If not for a misguided sense of responsibility, a week behind drawn curtains would have suited me just fine.

I kept pointing right and left until she was pulling to a stop in front of my garage door. The two agents had left my Impala parked to one side. Alessandra looked over at me.

"So, did you really have something to confess?"

"I might. As long as I get this contract in writing."

She paused with a look my way before turning off the key.

"Nice junipers," she said, getting out.

"We don't talk about those."

I retrieved the keys from the Impala and came around to open the gate. Alessandra went into the front yard before me.

"Nice creek," she said as we crossed over the arched bridge.

"I've been thinking to add some crocodiles."

Alessandra smiled.

"That have anything to do with those junipers back there?"

"It might."

She glanced back to where they were peeking over the top of my fence. I unlocked the door, hit the lights and allowed her to go in ahead of me.

"A splash of Scotch?" I said while throwing my coat over the back of the sofa. "I might have an unopened bottle of wine lying around somewhere, if you'd rather."

"Scotch is fine."

"Straight?"

"Please."

"You got it. Go ahead and make yourself at home."

I disappeared into the kitchen and returned with two glasses, having added some bitters to my club soda so it looked more like a cocktail.

"Thanks for the ride," I said, handing her the glass.

We both drank. I removed my shoulder holster and joined Alessandra on the sofa. She had her fine legs crossed. I stole a glance at them, wanting her flesh, wanting her to heal the wounds left behind by the last woman. It was an effort that had led to mixed results in the past but apparently I wasn't done trying.

"So?" she said.

"So where's our contract?"

She held up two fingers, like a scout's oath.

"Yeah, right."

"You have my word."

"Yeah, I've heard that one before."

I had another sip of my club soda, wishing it was something stronger. The entire evening had come back to me. I looked over to find Alessandra staring.

"All right. I'll tell you what I can. And what I can't tell you, it's because I have a fiduciary responsibility to my clients."

"Yeah, right."

"Yeah, well, that's the way it is."

I rubbed my forehead.

"You know," I said, having considered where to start my story. "The simple truth is, this whole thing started with a damsel in distress."

"Most stories do," Alessandra said.

I flashed a sidelong look at her before embarking on my tale, leaving out Potter's card, the ring, the coke and even the 26th Dynasty figurine. Those were significant omissions, but oddly enough, the story made reasonably good sense without them. It had to. I wasn't about to hang myself out there on an obstruction charge, or possession. I wasn't too worried about possession. It figured that Nicholas, if questioned, would never mention the coke of his own accord. As to the ring and Potter's card, let Barnes prove I was withholding evidence. Short of sudden clairvoyance on his part, I didn't rate his chances very high. As to the Egyptian figurine, I felt it was my duty to keep old man Huntington out of this mess. Ditto in a certain sense with Chango. He and his gang might have lived on the wrong side of the law but they had no interest in blowing shit up or engaging in class warfare. Nor were they dumb enough to have supplied Potter with an arsenal, had they known his true intentions. They just wanted to be left alone, and in that, we were kindred spirits.

When I was done, I pushed myself up with a grunt and returned from my office a minute later with a sheet of notebook paper.

"Here you are," I said, handing Alessandra the list of Potter's known hideouts that Holly had provided me. It was the one chip I was willing to give up at that point. Hopefully it would be enough to keep the hounds off my trail. If nothing else, it would save me a lot of footwork. In searching for Potter, you'd want to turn over every stone, and I lacked the time and resources to do so.

Alessandra took a picture of the list with her phone and stood up.

"Better get this off to the boys right away."

While she headed out the front door, I impulsively touched my wounds. The stitches felt like tacks in my head.

Five minutes later, Alessandra was sitting back down at my side.

"I see the crocs didn't get you."

She smiled and shook her head.

"You are a piece of work, Michael."

"Thanks...Say, you won't mention any of this to you know who, will you?"

"You mean Barnes?"

"Yeah."

"Might not," she said.

"I could have given that list to him instead, and then where would you be?"

"That's a point in your favor...Why didn't you, if I may ask?"

"I don't know. He looks too much like Tom Selleck?"

She chuckled.

"That piss you off, does it?"

"A bit."

She smiled and took a sip of her Scotch. I let out a big sigh and leaned back in the sofa.

"So. What's going on out there?"

"Oh, Bradley's headed farther up the coast with a couple of agents. He thinks he has a lead on Potter's next stop."

"That should go well."

"You have a problem with Bradley?" she said.

"Not if it's a modeling gig."

She smiled, kicked her shoes off and crossed her legs on the coffee table. She had nice feet to go with the nice legs. I liked it when a woman had nice feet.

"So," I said. "You two ever...you know?"

She looked over with a frown.

"I never mix business with pleasure."

"I see...Is this business?"

"Probably."

I reached over with my left hand and gently massaged Alessandra's neck. She closed her eyes and purred a bit. I moved on to her shoulders and she purred a bit more.

"So?" I said.

She glanced my way suspiciously. I leaned over to kiss her lips and she didn't stop me. It was a nice kiss. They were soft lips.

When our kisses turned a bit more passionate, she reflexively placed a hand to the back of my head. Then she was holding me away.

"Ground rules, Frankie."

"Frankie? As in?"

"Frankenstein."

"Why you saucy little bitch."

She stared back with complete gravity.

"Okay. Ground rules."

"We never talk about what we do here. To anyone. Are you good with that?"

"Sure."

She went to take another sip of her Scotch but I intercepted the glass, set it down on the coffee table and pulled her closer. She curled up in my arms nicely.

When I ran a hand through her glistening dark hair, she reflexively did the same and I yelped.

"Oops. Sorry again, Frankie."

"It's okay."

I rubbed her nose with mine and resumed our kisses. We had been there a few minutes, struggling with our passions when Alessandra got to her feet and yanked on my hand.

"Come on."

I resisted.

"I kind of wanted to be romanced."

"Oh stop. I need to be back on the beat in a couple of hours." She pulled me to my feet.

"Which way?" she said.

I pointed up the stairs to my bedroom.

Alessandra went to one side of the bed and quickly had her skirt on the floor. I sat down on the other side of the bed and pulled off my shoes. There was the sound of cotton rustling and elastic snapping behind me.

By the time I crawled into bed, Alessandra was naked with her hair undone. The warmth of her body against mine was enough to make you want to cry. I held her close for a long time before pulling back to look into her eyes.

"Who would have ever thought this?"

She kissed me and watched her hand play with the hair on my chest.

"I like the unexpected," she said.

"Oh boy. Now I'm feeling really important here."

"Come on, Michael. Like neither one of us have done this sort of thing before."

"Yeah, well. Maybe I just needed it to feel that way tonight."

"I'm not thinking of anyone else," she said.

I pretended to pout. She smirked and started down my belly with kisses.

Oh god.

A few minutes later, she came back up and kissed my lips.

"Feeling special now?"

"Hmm."

She started to crawl up on top of me but I rolled her over and started down her belly. She moaned when I reached that silky spot and her body convulsed from the ecstasy. Her hands were searching for safe places to hold my head.

When Alessandra could take no more, I started back up her belly. She was pulling hard on my hips.

I pretended to check my watch.

"It is getting a bit late here. How much time do I have?"

"Oh stop."

She was busy trying to get me inside of her.

We both moaned as I slid in. She still had both hands on my buttocks, encouraging me to go harder. I preferred it nice and slow but with so little time, I did as Alessandra asked, a wild bull charging in the wind.

Magically, we came together. Then I went a bit overtime, kissing her face and lips and gently rocking back and forth inside of her.

Finally, I fell to one side and collapsed on the bed.

"Lovely," she said with a touch of my face. "Just lovely. You are an awfully good lover."

"Thanks. Think I'll have that chiseled onto my tombstone. 'He was an awfully good lover.' Let people decide for themselves where to place the accent."

She smiled, kissed my cheek and curled up at my side.

"You thinking about Potter?" I said a minute later.

"Sshhh," she said with a finger to my lips. "Let's sleep a bit. I'll be back on my feet soon enough."

I kissed Alessandra on the forehead and got up to drain my bladder.

"Damn it," she said when I crawled back in bed. "I was trying to ignore the urge."

She was soon curled up at my side again. I let out a sigh. For the first time in I didn't know how long, I felt my spirit completely relax. Within minutes, I sensed Alessandra asleep and not long after that, I was deep in slumber too.

I had been out for what seemed like seconds when my phone rang, jarring me awake from another lousy dream. As always, I had been chasing Caitlin down darkened corridors but never able to catch up.

I swore while digging around for the phone, pissed about the call, pissed about the dream, pissed that it was starting to get light outside. Alessandra opened one eye. I made a face back at her.

"Damn it," I said, seeing the call was from John. "What's up? I thought I told you to go home and get some sleep."

"I just took a shot at the son of a bitch."

"At who? Potter?!"

"Yeah."

I sat up.

"What do you mean? Explain."

Alessandra sat up too, arms over her knees and studying me intently.

"Oh, I kind of figured the bastard had no place else to go and might head back to Gigi's place so I waited down below. You know, where you told me to park?"

"Yeah? And so?"

"And so the SOB showed up. Dragging Holly with him. There's some kind of metal gate down here at the end of the street, like leading into a tunnel or something, and he was trying to open it when I spotted him. I had the 30/30 pointed at him from a hundred feet and told him to freeze and he responded by taking a shot at me. And, hey, I didn't want to risk killing her so I shot at his legs."

"And missed."

"I'm pretty sure, yeah."

Impulsively, I got out of bed and started pacing. Alessandra eyed my nakedness so I turned away.

"And he got away."

"Yeah. Down the hillside with Holly. I didn't figure it was my business to kill the bastard."

I turned to find Alessandra out of bed and pulling on her panties. Her eyes were locked on me as she got into her bra. She gestured with a hand roll. Come on, Devlin. Out with it.

"Hang on," I told John.

I cupped the phone and whispered.

"One of my guys says he just saw Potter and he had Holly with him."

"Location," Alessandra said without whispering.

I cupped the phone harder and gestured for her to keep quiet.

"One street below Gigi's house."

"So where the hell is Potter?"

"He got away. Down the hill somewhere. Hang on. I'm trying to figure this out."

"Oh, give me the damned phone," she said and tried to wrestle it from my hands. I pulled it away from her.

"What?! Are you crazy?! He'll know you're here!"

"So?"

"So? You were the one who wanted to keep this all secret! Just hang on a second, all right?"

Her stare was along the lines of cutting my balls off. I got back to John.

"Let me get this straight. Potter headed back down the hill with Holly but you have no idea where?"

"That's it. It all happened just a minute ago and I called you."

I looked at Alessandra. She was ready to yank the phone from my hands again.

"Look, John. I'm going to let the FBI know where you are. On Nightingale, right?"

"Yeah."

"Then you stay right there."

"Oh shit," he said.

"What?"

"I've got two cars bearing down on me right now. Full fucking speed, baby."

"Better get off and get your hands up in the air."

"You bet your ass I will."

"And call me the minute you're free."

"Okay."

The phone went dead. Alessandra's phone went off as I started to explain things. I grabbed her arm before she could reach for it.

"Quickly. My guy shot at Potter but missed and he got away. Back down the hill with Holly. Sounds like your people are pulling up to his location right now. Someone must have heard the shots."

I stared for a moment and kissed her tenderly.

"It was lovely. Very adult."

"Adult, huh?"

"Yeah, adult, but I really needed that right now."

I kissed her again.

"Go get 'em, killer. I'll make some coffee."

She gave me a peck back and took her call. I threw on a robe and headed down to the kitchen.

Five minutes later, Alessandra appeared from upstairs, pulling on her coat. I poured an extra cup of coffee.

"Anything in it?"

She quickly added some sugar and half and half without answering me.

"Breakfast?" I said.

She made a face while gulping down her coffee.

"Just remember our contract," she said.

"Yeah, right. Big mouth."

She made a face and started to go.

"Hey, hey," I said and caught her by the waist. "Don't go like that."

I touched her face tenderly and kissed her good.

"Hmm," she said, pulling away. "Now gotta run."

"Damn you...Keep me posted, okay?"

She paused with a hand on the front door knob.

"Like you said, Frankie. It was very adult."

With a final look, she went out the door. I stood there recalling her sweetness and moaned. Then I recalled Caitlin and felt truly screwed up.

Was it always this way? I had a sudden vision of this mess, only back in Rome. Same screwed up world, same screwed up emotions, only with chariots.

Outside my windows, the sky was blushing red to the east. I didn't know what to do with myself. I had slept half an hour.

To hell with it, I thought and headed back to bed. John will call whenever he's free and Morey can wait a few more hours for Bennie to relieve him. I placed the phone on the nightstand beside me and crawled under the covers. Impulsively, I reached for Alessandra's pillow and buried my face in her scent. I felt her lingering warmth in the sheets and moaned again.

It had been wonderfully adult, and yet I felt as empty as a box. It's all wrecked, as Caitlin would have said.

Well, whatever it had been before, it would never be the same again.

I quickly fell asleep. Then the phone was ringing.

"Christ," I said, checking the caller ID. It was John. I glanced at the clock. I had slept for just over an hour. I was better, but far from well.

"They let you go?" I said by way of answering.

"Yeah. Had me sitting around staring at my navel for half an hour. Then this Agent Barretta showed up and grilled me about what had happened. Pretty nice looking dish, that one. That wouldn't be who I heard in the background."

"I have no idea what you're talking about."

"Oh. So it's going to be like that, is it…Anyway, I was told not to leave the country and they let me go."

"What about Holly and Potter?"

"They didn't say. You know these pricks. They're not going to tell you anything."

"Yeah. I'm guessing you need some sleep."

"Yeah. Did you get any?"

"A little."

"I'll bet."

"Shut up."

John laughed.

"So, beyond copping some sleep, what are we doing today?"

"How would I know? Nobody around here does what I tell them to do."

"Sorry, sweetie. Just had a hunch."

"Yeah you did."

"Yeah. But no attaboy for that one, huh?"

"Yeah. You get half of one for protecting Gigi, but an 'oh shit' for losing Holly. And one 'oh shit' wipes out six attaboys, so you're way in the hole."

He laughed.

"Yeah, funny. Mrs. Evergreen's ready to make me a eunuch."

"Sorry. I just thought, what if I nailed Holly by accident."

"No, yeah. You did the right thing."

"So back to what we're doing today?"

"Hell. I don't know. I still have a Picasso to track down and some jewelry."

There was the dead young woman too. Left in a shallow grave, unnamed, unloved and unwanted except by the coyotes; a young life stolen away. Her only apparent sin was to have slept with the wrong man.

Who was she, and what mother was at home, wringing her hands in anguish? The questions kept haunting me.

"So, get some sleep?" John said.

"Yeah, yeah. Get some sleep and check in with me whenever you're back on your feet. We'll see what we can cook up."

"You got it, chief. Sayonara for now."

"Yeah, the same."

Twenty Seven

I hung up and looked out at the brightening eastern sky. My impulse was to crawl back in bed. Instead, I went out to the kitchen and nuked the cold coffee. While it was heating, Kenny called.

"What's up?" I said.

"Oh, I've got some news for you. Sorry it took me so long. A bunch of stuff going on the past couple of days."

"No problem. I've been busy too. So what do we know?"

"Well, on Abigale Potter?"

"Yeah?"

"She was neo-Nazi before neo-Nazi was a thing."

"Somehow that doesn't surprise me."

"Yeah. I guess her father was chummy with that Sheriff Parker up in LA back in the fifties. You know the story?"

"Yeah, pretty much. Graft, corruption and lynchings."

"That seemed to be the general drift and apparently Abigale slid right into the mold. At least the rightwing part of it. Anyway, she goes off and marries this guy named Potter and that's followed by a slew of police reports over the next two years that has the smell of domestic violence about it. You know, every other week and the calls almost always late at night. Then the husband is found dead down in San Pedro. Head blown off with a shotgun."

"Wow, okay. And I'm going to guess the murder was never solved."

"You got it. But here's the real kicker to the whole thing. You ready?"

"I'm all ears."

"Abigale's maiden name was Pritchett."

"Holy Jesus."

"Yeah. I haven't been able to establish any recent connections between her and the rest of the Pritchett clan, but that's not to say there isn't one."

"Yeah. What about Potter and the Pritchett's?"

"I looked into that too, figuring it would be your next question, but I haven't found anything."

"Which is not to say there isn't one."

"Nope. Want me to keep looking?"

"Naw. That's all right. Maybe I'll put a tail on Cole Pritchett again. That's if I can catch a break from all the other treason and subterfuge that's been dropped in my lap."

"If you change your mind, just let me know."

"I will. So what about Cabot?"

"I don't have that police report yet but I did get my hands on Lila's bank records. This is going back to when she first moved to California, with about five mil stashed away. Bought herself a cozy spread in Pueblo Hills and a brand new BMW."

"Yeah. Just what I figured. Enough to be comfortable but not quite enough to be on easy street for the rest of your life."

"I could retire on five mil," Kenny said.

"But not Lila, apparently. From what my friend up in the Pueblo Hills police department told me, old man Evergreen left behind a serious fortune."

"Yeah. In the mid nine figures, from what I'm seeing."

"Yeah, that would fix you up nicely."

"Yeah...Oh, and I did dig into that QAnon business."

"Yeah? And what?"

"Scary stuff. Just poking around on this one chat room, you've got to think they're getting ready to blow up the world."

"Any idea where or when?"

"It's kind of hard to tell. It's all in code, but whatever it is, I'd put my money on it going down soon. It just has that feel about it."

"I imagine the FBI is all over this business too."

"Imagine so."

"Okay, get back to me as soon as you have that police report. And anytime this year will do."

"Yes, sir."

I hung up and called Bennie.

"I ain't ready for no shit yet today," he said in answering.

"Then don't start."

"Me start!"

"Oh Christ. Will you just listen? I need you to go spell Morey. He hasn't had any sleep yet."

"Shit. Why don't you have John do it."

"Because he hasn't had any sleep, either."

"Why not? I thought you told him to go home too."

I explained about Potter and Holly.

"What the hell, boss man? How come I never get in on the action?"

"Oh god, Bennie. If you're really dying for some action, I'll arrange for Potter to shoot you."

He let loose with a few words in Spanish.

"You done?" I said.

"Shit. I can't believe that shit went down without me."

"Yeah, yeah. Just go relieve Morey, please? You're the only one who's had any sleep…And call me when you're in place."

He hung up before I had a chance to tell him about Abigale Potter. It was probably for the best. Bennie already had enough on his mind.

I stared out the window, unresolved circumstances everywhere I turned.

Caitlin's uncaring look did a curtain call in my head, then my tryst with Alessandra. The third ring of purgatory was straight ahead.

While I was deciding what to do next, the phone rang. It was Lila.

"Yes," I said, answering the call.

"Oh god, okay. You're mad. I can hear it in your tone."

I sighed heavily.

"I'm not mad."

"Yes you are."

"Please. This is the last thing I need right now."

"What's the last thing you need right now?"

"My feelings reduced to black and white."

"What do you mean?"

"Really? I have to explain that to you?"

"Oh, just tell me, damn it. I'm a total wreck over here. My daughter's out there god knows where with that monster. My front entry looks like I live in Beirut and I still have the FBI crawling all over my property. I don't even know if you work for me anymore. I'm going crazy."

I was silent.

"Well?" she said.

"Well, what?"

"Well, what do you mean by black and white?"

"Just what I said. Either I'm happy or mad. Apparently those are the only two emotions when it comes to opposite sex."

"When it comes to the opposite sex. How do you think that makes *me* feel?"

"What do you want me to say? When you hear the same thing over and over again from women, you start to feel like you're pre-formatted."

There was silence.

"Go ahead, Michael. Tell me what you're feeling."

"If you really want to know, hurt, disappointed. I'm out there risking my life to protect you and your daughter and you act like I ran your Cayenne off a cliff."

There was more silence.

"I'm sorry," she said. "I didn't mean to be a bitch last night. I was half out of my mind. I'm still half out of my mind but I truly appreciate the risks you took. I just wish my daughter was here and this whole nightmare was over."

"So do I, but I can't control everything that happens in this world. I can't be everywhere at once."

"I know, Michael. You did everything you could."

I was silent.

"So?" she said. "Am I forgiven?"

"Yeah, well. Give me a few days and I'll get over it."

"Michael, I need to know you're still working for me."

"What's the point? You have half the law enforcement in America looking for your daughter now. What could I add?"

"I'd just feel better knowing you're there. I know you're relentless. I don't know what these other people will do."

I sighed, feeling myself being dragged back into something and not really wanting any part of it. If not for Holly, I would have told Lila to go to hell.

"Lila," I said. "I honestly don't know what difference my involvement is going to make at this point but I'll keep poking around, if that's what you want."

"I do."

"Fine."

"Thank you. And I am sorry. I realized in worrying over you and your wounds last night, it's the part of me that I really like."

I was silent.

"I'm sorry, Michael. I don't mean to make you feel uncomfortable. I'll let you go."

"I'll let you know the minute I have any news."

"Thank you."

I ended the call and stood there with a new vision of Lila stuck in my head, naked save for a stethoscope and a pair of high heels. Jesus.

I downed the rest of my now lukewarm coffee and went off to shower. By the time I had dressed, a game plan for that day was taking shape in my mind.

Going out the front door, I was hit by a change of weather. The wind had turned and was blowing up from the border now, leaving the world warm and muggy. The firefighters were no doubt cheering the humidity but I hated it. It was something only a spider could love.

Already in a funk over the muggy heat and a lack of sleep, I saw Fitzy's junipers while backing out of the garage and my blood boiled anew. There was a thought to take a chainsaw to them. See how she liked seeing her junipers left in a big pile.

Down at Coast Highway, I turned south and gave Vanderhof a call.

"You still trying to get me behind bars?" he said in answering.

"Dedicated my life to it, pal. You got a problem with that?"

"No. Knock yourself out. I picture you have nothing better to do. Just an old fashioned, two-bit gumshoe."

"That's me."

"We should make a movie."

"Now there's an idea. Rich man goes down for pimping a harem of underaged girls. We could have Jeffrey Epstein play you. Except he's dead."

My comment was met with silence.

"You do have a way of yanking my chain, Devlin."

"I work hard at it."

"Yeah you do. So what else can I help you with this morning?"

"Wondering if you had a line on that Picasso yet."

"You know what, Devlin? Go pick out any Picasso you like and I'll buy it for you. Anything to get you off my back."

"No can do. It has to be a particular one."

"As in?"

"It's titled, Female Matador."

I could almost feel Vanderhof's brain churning in the silence.

"And what's the big deal with that particular Picasso?"

"Just sentimental value."

"And who hired you to find it, if I may ask?"

"Old man Huntington."

"That old bastard?"

349

"He speaks even less fondly of you."

"I'll bet. He's made a career out of marrying young women who can't stand to look at him once they have his money."

I thought to say something about the former Mrs. Vanderhof but stopped myself. I owed her the gift of discretion, even if it was from here to Switzerland.

"Just cough up the Picasso," I told Vanderhof. "You don't want to be anywhere near that thing. You'll find yourself back in the gray bar hotel before you can write another check to the Policeman's Association."

"You're a real prick, Devlin."

"We had a drink together once."

"So we did. So we did...Okay, I guess you've been straight enough with me so I'll see what I can do."

"Good. Just remember. Nicholas is still married to old man Huntington's daughter and all roads lead back to Rome, as they say."

"Don't you worry about it. If he has the painting, I'll take care of things."

I shook my head.

"I'm not worried about it in the least. Just cough up the Picasso and I won't say a word. The old man's discreet enough not to ask."

"Fair enough. I'll see what I can do."

"And be careful with those sixteen year old girls."

After a moment of silence, Vanderhof hung up on me. If I had nothing better to do with my life, I'd be following him around instead.

I had come to the south end of Doheny Beach and bore right onto Coast Highway. Railroad tracks bordered the highway on my right with breaking surf lapping at the railroad tracks in places. The businesses below the sandstone bluffs on my left had evolved over the years, from the Mom and Pop store to towering stucco edifices, and most of the quaint old cottages along Beach Road had been replaced by snazzy beachfront homes, but it was still something of a journey back in time.

From what I had heard, this was the only way down to San Diego until the sixties, with a suicide center lane along this stretch of highway.

Coast Highway continued straight down the shore for several miles, then jogged left up a hill into San Clemente. I meandered along with a mishmash of storefronts on either side of me, the chaos of modern America in development; no unifying architectural theme, no thought for beauty, just a race by city councils to rubberstamp anything that increased the tax base.

Just south of where Avenida del Mar headed down towards the pier, I parked at the curb. Tony's Pawnshop was directly across from me. At the first break in traffic, I dashed over to that side and slipped in through the glass front door. A bell jingled over my head as I did. The place was dimly lit and cluttered with stuff for sale.

Tony's son-in-law Eric was sitting in back behind a glass display case. An old cash register sat next to him.

He smiled at seeing me, but it wasn't much of a smile. I had dealt with him a few times in the past and had always come away from the experience feeling like crap. He should have been a cop. Some men had no way of feeling good about themselves, except to try and make you feel small.

"What happened to you?" Eric said when I stopped in front of him.

"I ran into a lawnmower."

He smiled.

"So, what's up?"

"I need to talk with the old man."

"He's not in."

"Bullshit."

Eric smiled and pretended to be examining the antique coin in his hands.

"What do you want to see him for?"

"What I want to see the old man for is my business."

"I said he's not in."

"Bullshit...Hey Tony!" I yelled.

Eric looked ready to grab one of the handguns out of his display case. I was staring him in the face when Tony appeared from behind a glass bead screen; small and old and taciturn, but not unkind. He brought to mind a Roman worker, having arrived to fix a broken aqueduct with his wooden toolbox.

He glanced from my bandages to Eric and back at me with a shrug.

"What can I do for you, Mr. Devlin?"

"You know Sal, right? Sal's Jewelry?"

Tony nodded.

"He told me to come talk to you. It's about a ring."

Tony looked at Eric again before nodding for me to join him in back. I smiled at Eric going by, the same kind of shitty smile he had given me.

Inside Tony's small office, he directed me to a chair in front of his cluttered desk. He took a seat on the opposite side.

I pulled the ring out of my coat pocket.

"This belonged to a young woman. She's dead but still not identified. This is between you and me. The cops don't know I have it."

He nodded and took the ring, examining first the workmanship in general before pulling out a loupe and having a look at the inscription inside.

Satisfied, he put the loupe down and handed back the ring.

"The SOS stands for Stephen of St. Claire. The Web Hunter? I don't know what that means."

"Stephen of St. Claire," I said.

"A local craftsman. A good one but his head got a bit too big towards the end."

"Towards the end?"

Tony stared at me with his old, watery eyes.

"He moved away but I think he's still around somewhere. He'd be a decade younger than me so in his early seventies now."

"Do you have any idea where he moved?"

Tony shook his head.

"I heard something about Fallbrook."

"Any idea when this ring was made?"

Tony looked at it.

"Five, ten years ago, I'd guess. There was a time when Stephen only did the finest of work. Then, who knows? Maybe he got tired. Maybe he was planning his retirement but he started pumping out stuff like this, like they were prints of the original. Not bad…but not nearly of the same quality."

"So you're saying there could be thousands of these floating around."

"Maybe. Hundreds, anyway…What happened to the girl?"

"Hard to say. She was pretty well decomposed by the time I stumbled across her. What was left had been worked over by coyotes. Whoever killed her had cut off the tips of her fingers, along with her head. There's DNA, of course, but it doesn't do much good if there's no police record to match."

Tony's watery eyes looked a bit sadder and older now.

"But no idea what 'The Web Hunter' might mean?" I said.

He shook his head.

"Okay. On a completely different subject, I saw a Glock 19 and silencer out there in your display case. I'd like to buy them."

"Sure."

He stood up with me and we went back out through the glass bead curtain. Five minutes later, I had the Glock and silencer and a box of ammunition in a bag.

"Thanks again for your time and the info," I told Tony.

He nodded sadly.

"You find this guy and I'll cut his balls off for you."

"If I haven't done it already."

We stared for a moment before I started for the door. Eric had been sitting nearby the whole time, examining a diamond ring through a loupe. He pretended to smile again as I passed by him. I didn't. He reminded me of a vulture perched on a limb, waiting for something to die.

Back outside in the muggy day, my thoughts turned to my trailer south of the border. I could see the surf bristling down the coast for miles, the curtains flapping in the afternoon breeze. Escape. That's all I wanted, but escape wasn't in the cards for me that day. Maybe if I could forget about the girl, but I couldn't.

I dashed back across the street, placed the Glock in the trunk, climbed into the front seat, hit the ignition and turned on the air-conditioner. The Web Hunter. What did it mean? I imagined it was a reference to the World Wide Web, but that was so generic as to mean anything and everything.

My only hope was to find this Stephen of St. Claire. Maybe he'd remember the person who had bought the ring.

The boys came to mind and what to do with them that day but I placed the question on hold and called Sal. He probably knew where to find Stephen of St. Claire. He knew something.

"What?!" Sal said in answering my call.

"Oh Jesus. We're not too paranoid, are we."

"Well, you're always beating my balls."

I shook my head.

"I'm not always beating your balls. You'd know it if I was."

Sal was silent. I pictured him with a piece of jewelry in his hands.

"I talked with Tony."

"Yeah? What did he say?"

"He said that a guy named Stephen of St. Claire had made that ring."

"Yeah?"

"Yeah. So I'm wondering why you didn't know that."

"Who said I didn't?!"

"Then why didn't you tell me?!"

"Because. I knew the next question would be, where can I find him and I don't know!"

"Jesus, Sal. I thought I was sick."

"What?!"

354

"What? I get it. Stephen of St. Claire was your competitor and you hated the bastard but…"

"I didn't hate him!"

"Okay, you thought he was a bit of a fruit cake…"

"I didn't say that!"

"Well, my point is, you could have told me all this when I showed you the ring the other day. Instead you send me down to Tony's."

There was a pause.

"So, did Tony know?"

"Maybe. He thinks he's down in Fallbrook."

"See?"

"See, nothing. I'm going to wander around Fallbrook all day, hoping to run into him?"

"Look for his father."

"You son of a bitch."

Sal laughed.

"Go on. Tell me about the father."

"He was the original jeweler. That's how Stephen got into the business. The old man ran a studio out of his home down there for years."

"And a name?"

"Bernardo."

"Jesus Christ, Sal. I can't believe you didn't tell me all this shit the other day."

"What?! I don't want to get involved! I've got enough problems already!"

"You don't know problems. I'm going out with an FBI agent now and I'm going to tell her you're cooking the books."

I hung up with Sal yelping in protest. Good. Let him twist in the wind, the son of a bitch.

I called Kenny next.

"You still alive?" he said.

"To the best of my knowledge. Why do you ask?"

"I heard your name mentioned in the news."

"Oh lord."

I gave him a brief rundown on what had happened over at Lila's place.

"Wow. The figures on my witness protection program have really gone up."

"Fine. Add it to the bill. In the meantime, I need you to find someone named Bernardo St. Claire. The word is, Monsieur St. Claire ran a jewelry business out of his home down in Fallbrook for years. Don't know if he's still in business but the address should be the same."

"Is this another 'get it done yesterday' assignment."

"Actually, in the next two minutes. I'm heading that way right now."

"I'll see what I can do."

"Thanks."

I hung up and called Bennie.

"Don't give me no shit," he said in answering.

"Yeah yeah. Did you relieve Morey?"

"Yeah. I'm down here watching your lady's place. Haven't seen her yet."

"All right. When did Morey say he'd be back on his feet?"

"He said he only needed a couple hours of sleep."

"Then as soon as he calls, you decide which assignment you want but I want somebody at Caitlin's place 24/7. I don't dare leave her unguarded."

"Shit. I don't even know why you bother."

"That's my business, Bennie, so please stay out of it."

"Well, lo siento, but I can't stand to see the way she treats you."

"You've already told me that, a thousand times. Just take care of business, please."

"You can count on that."

"Good. And what's the latest on Nicholas?"

"The same old shit. Every day the same old shit. He'll head down to the harbor around noon, have lunch at Proud Mary's and sit around drinking beer and bullshitting with his buddies in their MAGA hats. Then he'll go home and crash again for a few hours. Then he'll go out on the town for the night and head home around four in the morning. Meanwhile, Vanderfuck's sitting around his mansion, enjoying the hell out of old man Huntington's Picasso."

"They're hiring at Jack in the Box."

I pulled the phone away from my ear and waited for Bennie's fusillade to subside.

"You done?" I said when it had.

"Shit. You don't want to learn nothing."

"Yeah, yeah. It's a quantum mechanics kind of world and Nicholas is an upside-down quark."

"Hey. You've been reading some shit, huh, boss man?"

"Yeah. Now look, Bennie. We've been through this already. You can't just go beating down someone's door. Anyway, what do you think Vanderhof's going to do? Fence the painting with the Mongols?"

"Watching his place still beats the hell out of watching old numb nuts here. He ain't going to do nothing, unless it's back over to old man Huntington's place to steal another ancient artifact."

"Which is exactly why I want one of you guys keeping an eye on him."

"Hey, it's your call."

"Thank you...By the way, any sign of Billy?"

"Oh yeah. I meant to tell you. I saw him at a meeting this morning. Same old shit. 'I know I fucked up but I'm really serious this time. I don't want to drink no more.' He says the same thing every time, but take direction? Never. No sponsor. No program. He ain't never going to stay sober."

"I thought that was God's business."

"Yeah, well. I'm just telling it like it is. He ain't never going to stay sober."

"And I still say it's God's business."

"Yeah, you're right. Anyway, he asked me about his job."

"He hasn't called me."

"That's because he doesn't have the balls to face you."

"I wouldn't hire him back. Not until he puts some time together."

"Yeah. Good luck with that one."

"I'll get you his check so you can give it to him next time you two cross paths. In the meantime, I'm heading down to Fallbrook."

"What for?"

"Got a lead on that dead girl's ring."

"Yeah? Personal mission?"

"Something like that. Anyway, I'm counting on you to keep an eye on things."

"You got it...Hey!" he said before I could hang up.

"Yeah, what?"

"What about John?"

"Oh, I'll probably have him go over and keep an eye on Vanderhof."

Twenty Eight

I hung up with Bennie going off on a rant. I called John next. He answered after a couple of rings.

"Get any sleep?" I said.

"Yeah, a little. What's up?"

"I want you to take a drive with me down to Fallbrook."

"Kind of a little day excursion together, huh?"

"Something like that. How soon can you be dressed and down in San Clemente?"

"Give me forty-five?"

"That's fine. Call me when you're nearing the outskirts of town and I'll tell you where I am."

"Will do."

I hung up, put the Impala in gear and headed south at a leisurely pace. The thoughts in my head were anything but leisurely.

Just north of where El Camino Real crossed under Interstate 5, I pulled left into a breakfast joint called Suzy Q's. The phone rang while I was parking. I saw Kenny's name and answered.

"Got it?" I said.

"Got it."

I wrote on a notepad while he rattled off the address.

"Anything interesting come up?"

"The old man was arrested for assaulting a cop back in '85. Apparently he got caught screwing an underaged girl. The DA was seeking ten to fifteen. The old man got away with probation on a weapons charge. Must have known somebody."

"You think, huh? Anything more recent?"

"Yeah. Another weapons charge last year. For threatening a local council member."

"Jesus. The guy must be in his nineties and he's still playing cowboy?"

"The council member's name was Rodriquez and had been advocating for a local migrant shelter. Anyway, four men were arrested and the old man got off with probation again."

"I'm going to guess he's right wing."

"I'd go with that. I trust you're locked and loaded."

"Oh yeah. Covered there."

"Good. And that I'm in your will."

"Sure. You get the pencils."

"Funny."

"Yeah...But still no police report,"

"Not yet."

"Shit. I should have hired the professionals."

"You still can."

"I still might...Thanks for the address, anyway," I said and hung up.

Walking into the packed coffee shop, I was treated to numerous stares over my head bandages. You knew how lepers felt.

At my behest, the hostess got me settled into a reasonably quiet corner. I was mopping up the last of my eggs with sourdough toast when John called back. I explained where I was.

"You know the place?"

"I'll GPS it."

"Just take the El Camino Real exit and hang a right over your shoulder."

"Got it. You going to be inside?"

"No. I'll be waiting for you out in the parking lot."

"Got it. See you in a few."

I dropped a five on the table, paid at the cash register and used the bathroom before heading outside. I had hardly gotten the air-conditioner cranked up when John pulled into the parking lot. I motioned for him to park. He did and opened my shotgun door.

"Jesus. Potter did that to you?"

"Yeah. Unlike you, I forgot to shoot first."

"You know. That son of a bitch needs to die."

"Yeah. It'll probably take two oak stakes in the heart. Come on. Let's get going."

"They're not going to tow me, are they?"

"Neah. You got that .30-30 with you?"

"It's in the trunk."

"Bring it."

John stared for a moment before walking back to his rig. He returned with a sheepskin rifle case, placed it on the backseat and climbed in next to me. His oversized presence took up whatever space I wasn't using.

I dropped the Impala into gear, exited back onto El Camino Real and was soon barreling up the freeway onramp.

"So exactly where are we going, sweetie?" he said.

"Fallbrook."

"Where's that?"

"You'll see."

"Oh, it's going to be like that, is it?"

I eased into traffic before looking over at him.

"It's east of Oceanside. Pretty country."

"Yeah? Did you bring a picnic basket?"

"It's in the trunk."

John blinked his eyes at me.

"So why me? And why the .30-30?

"Why you? Because I didn't want to be listening to Bennie's bullshit all day long. And the .30-30 because I'm not so sure what we're going to find down there."

"You expecting trouble?"

I glanced over at him.

"It's been following me all my life."

"Ooohhhhhh. I'm sensing a tragic streak here."

"It's called weltschmerz."

John laughed.

"Sounds like liverwurst on rye."

"Yeah. It's a lot like that."

I glanced over at him again.

"We're going to see a jeweler, and the word is, his father likes to pack a gun."

"So we're expecting a shootout?"

"No, but best to be prepared if things go south...I'm going to stand in back while you knock."

"Okay. I'm definitely getting the picture now."

I nodded and looked back at the road. We were motoring south through Camp Pendleton and twenty miles of open coastline. At one point, we passed a couple of tanks kicking up dust down by the shore. A helicopter was practicing drop in support missions. Other than that, you would hardly have known that mankind existed. A magnificent piece of real estate had been spared, thanks to mankind's penchant for conflict.

John and I talked about what had gone down the previous night and life in New England and I was soon taking the loop east onto 76. Ten miles inland, I turned left onto Olive Hill Road, then right onto Gateview Drive. It was dry, chaparral country with oaks and olive trees and lots of hacienda style looking estates. The entire development smelled of money.

"Better get that rifle up here," I told John.

With a look my way, he reached over the seat and unzipped the leather case.

"But keep it out of sight," I said once John had it upfront.

I lowered both front windows and eased back on the pedal. The warm, muggy air blew in like a steamy hairdryer. There was still a scent of smoke on the wind. John gave me another look and got his finger on the trigger.

The old man's place was out at the end of Shady Hill Lane. A long driveway looped around in front of the house and headed back out to the street. The house was low and sprawling and looked lazily Spanish. A dog started barking before I had pulled to stop.

As I got out of the car, a man fitting Stephen St. Claire's description appeared at the front door. He had a pit bull on a leash, straining to get free.

The man was odd looking in several ways. He wore the loose fitting white cotton shirt and pants of a peasant, along with leather sandals darkened by sweat, but affected the manner of aristocracy. He was at once fairly tall, maybe six feet, but seemed diminutive, perhaps the result of his head and face being overly large. They did not seem to fit the body. His face was framed by an Amish looking beard. It was not an unpleasant looking face, but one that had learned to scowl more than smile over the course of a lifetime.

I climbed out and came around the hood cautiously.

"Stephen St. Claire?" I said.

"Who wants to know?"

I flashed my PI license.

"I'm working a case involving a dead girl. A ring you made was found with her body."

I held out the ring.

"You're not a suspect in any way, but you're possibly the only hope we have of identifying her. I was thinking you might remember something about the girl from the inscription you made inside. Anything would help."

Stephen looked at John, reluctantly muscled the dog back into the house and closed the door. I held out the ring again as he approached me. His eyes darted another wary look at John while taking the ring from me. He had what was at best a cursory look at the ring itself before turning to the inscription. After a few seconds, he handed the ring back to me.

"I made hundreds of these. In a lot of cases, I never even met the buyer."

"The inscription?" I said. "It means nothing to you?"

"I made hundreds of them."

He held my stare for a moment before turning back towards the house.

"Look," I called after him. "This is the only lead we have. Try to think back. Maybe it's something to do with the internet. You know? The Web Hunter? Any kind of lead would help."

He stopped at the door and faced me again. It was the look of a man who smelled trouble and didn't want any part of it.

"I remember her," he said. "And the inscription has nothing to do with the internet. It's a reference to Charlotte's Web. The children's story. Her older sister brought her to my shop one day and paid for the ring. Said her younger sister was like piglet, always looking for a friend."

I stood there staring. His words had hit me like a punch in the gut.

"That's all I know," Stephen added and cracked the door.

While he fought to keep the dog inside, an older man appeared and forced his way outside with a shotgun. While Stephen got hold of the dog leash, the old man leveled the shotgun at my chest. John was quick to jump out and point his .30-30 at the old man. Stephen forced the door shut on the dog and grabbed the barrel of the shotgun.

"Go on. Get out of here," he said to us.

There was an ongoing tussle between Stephen and his father over the shotgun. I motioned at John and we climbed into the Impala. Stephen had one more look our way before getting the old man inside and closing the front door.

"Did you see that?" John said. "I was ready to pop the SOB."

I nodded and started the car. John stared at me for a moment before placing the .30-30 back in its case and setting it in the backseat. I rolled the windows up and headed back towards Highway 76. There was a powerful urge to turn south again, to escape across the border. This world was no longer the one I knew, no longer the way I wanted it to be.

Tomorrow, I told myself. Maybe tomorrow I'll head that way and never come back.

Heading west on 76, I was still lost in thought when I noticed an old Camaro going by the other way

John watched me adjust the rearview mirror to have a better look.

"What's up?" he said.

"Nothing," I said. "Just thought I saw someone I knew."

He stared at me and then over his shoulder. I glanced again in the mirror but the car was already lost in traffic. I had an impulse to take the next exit and give chase but I let it go.

We drove along with John stealing glances at me. That Camaro was still troubling my thoughts.

We were motoring through the Marine base before John spoke up again.

"Did that mean anything to you back there?"

I darted a look his way.

"Did what mean anything to me?"

"What that fruitcake said."

"Not sure."

That was a lie, but I was in no mood to discuss it. Things would prove themselves out eventually, one way or the other.

John sat there fidgeting next to me.

"So what are we doing now?"

"Don't know. Still need to find that Picasso."

"Got any leads?"

"Maybe. Bennie thinks this guy named Vanderhof has it."

"There's a vote against the idea right there."

Now I was stealing glances at John.

"Does he know you feel that way about him?"

"Pretty much. He's been sober a lot longer than me so I give him some slack, but, you know..."

Yeah, I knew. Bennie was as solid as they came, but he could just as easily drive you up a wall.

"So who's Vanderhof?" John said.

I gave him a brief history, including our experiences together.

"What a sick fuck," John said when I was done.

"Yeah. There's that thing about casting the first stone, but…"

"But nothing. You let me follow him around for a while and I'll bust his chops all right."

I nodded, distracted again by that Camaro. It felt as if I had stumbled upon something, a piece of the puzzle, but what puzzle, and what did it mean? I sensed a neat and pat theory in there somewhere but neat and pat theories had rarely panned out the way I imagined them to be. Real life just wasn't neat and pat, no matter how you sliced it.

A call came in as I was thinking. I looked at my phone, saw it was Alessandra and answered.

"I was wondering what happened to you. Any luck with Potter?"

"I take it you're not watching the news?"

"Not much the last couple of days. Too busy trying to stay out of jail. Why? What's up?"

"Oh, just a bombing up here at the Democratic campaign headquarters in LA, for starters."

"What the hell?"

"Yeah. Just leaving there and heading down to Mission Viejo, where they found a family of five about an hour ago. All of them beheaded."

"Jesus Christ. What kind of madness is that?"

"The father was an attorney who did a lot of work for progressive causes. And also happened to be Iranian."

"Oh man. So you're thinking it was Potter and his gang?"

"That's our operating theory. And why I'm calling you."

"Calling me? What do I know? The son of a bitch tried to cut off my head last night. Beyond that I haven't a clue. I definitely don't know where he is."

"Yeah? So I'm guessing if you didn't know about the campaign headquarters, then you didn't notice that someone tried to assassinate the other presidential candidate last night."

"Jesus Christ. The madness. What is it with these people?"

"You tell me. All I know is, I've got a full blown alt-right insurrection on my hands."

"And how did you think I could help in this story?"

"I don't know, Michael. I've just got a funny feeling you know something you're not telling me."

"I don't know a thing. Not about Potter. Hell, I already gave you my list."

"Yeah? And we just happen to be out for a drive in North County San Diego today, are we?"

"Spill it," she said when I failed to respond. "People are dying."

"I'm working a simple case of theft, Alessandra. I have no reason to believe it has anything to do with Potter."

"You swear you're not holding out on me."

"I'm not."

"You'd better not be. Because if you are, I'll hang you."

"I'm not."

"And I'd better be the first one to know if you do learn something."

"You will be."

"Thank you. Now I've got to run."

"Yeah. Sorry for your troubles."

"Yeah...I'll be in touch," she said and hung up.

John flashed a look my way as I placed the phone down.

"Your sweetheart, Barretta?"

I gave him a look.

"We don't talk about that."

"Yeah, sure."

I gave him another look and explained what she had told me.

"That sick fucker in the White House. It's like he's unleashed the legions of Mordor."

"Yeah, something like that."

"No, exactly like that. I hope someone shoots him."

I glanced at John again.

"I'm told that they arrest you for saying shit like that."

"Yeah, well, let 'em. I hope he chokes on a French fry and dies."

We drove in silence again.

367

"Anyway," John said after a spell. "Back to this Vanderhof SOB, why don't you let me take him down a dark alley somewhere and I'll get you some answers?"

"I might just do that, John. I just might."

I had been thinking to make another phone call but decided to put it off until I dropped John back in San Clemente. The pristine coastline rolled by on our left.

A few miles shy of the now shuttered nuclear reactor, we neared the customs check point. An overhead sign announced that the agents were operating. Traffic slowed to a crawl as we neared the check point. Agents were waving cars through one by one. When it was our turn, a man in dark shades studied both our faces for a long second before giving us the okay.

A mile farther north, we entered the palmy suburbs of San Clemente. I exited the freeway at Magdelena and continued north on El Camino Real. Nearing the freeway overpass, I got over into the right-hand lane and pulled into Suzy Q's parking lot. Freeway traffic whizzed by above our heads. The day was muggy and listless.

"What are we doing again?" John asked me when I stopped behind his car.

"Well, I can't think of anything better for you to do right now so go ahead and keep an eye on Vanderhof."

"Oh boy. Can't wait to bust his chops."

"You're starting to sound like Bennie."

John pretended to be mortally wounded.

"Wow. That hurt."

"Sorry, but no trouble. In fact, don't even park near his house."

I pulled up a map of Laurel Lagoon on my phone and zoomed in on Vanderhof's neighborhood.

"See this road here?"

"Yeah."

"It's the only convenient way down the hill so find a place to park in this general area and keep an eye out for him."

"How the hell am I going to know who he is?"

I Googled his name and pulled up some images.

"A hunk with money," John said. "Just my type."

"You're a sick man."

"I know."

"Yeah. So, just park facing uphill and keep an eye out for him. When he comes by, hang a u-ey and..."

"Any idea what he'll be driving?"

I stared at John.

"I hate it when people interrupt me."

"Ya voll, herr kommandant."

I looked back at the map.

"Can't be sure on the car. He buys them the way you buy Twinkies."

"How did you know?"

I gave his midriff a glance.

"I know. Now shut up and listen. It'll probably be a yellow Ferrari. Something outrageous like that. You'll know, but here's the deal. You hang back and follow him as far as you can. No fast and furious BS. If he gets away and he's driving a blue Bentley, just call me. We have a tracer on it."

"Wow, okay."

"Yeah. It probably won't be the Bentley. He usually only drives that at night. The main thing is, I don't want him knowing you're there. And I especially don't want the cops getting involved."

"Well, you know me and my beat up Rav. I'll give him a run for his money."

"It's actually a perfect car for the job."

"Oh yeah. Who'd ever expect being tailed by that hulk?"

"Exactly, but be careful. He's mostly harmless. Except when he isn't."

"Yeah. I kind of got that drift from what you told me."

"Yeah. Like keep an eye on your rearview mirror?"

"Oh. So he makes a call and suddenly you're the one being tailed."

"Like that."

"Well the tricky little bastard. I'll be sure to keep my armaments handy."

"That's your call. And look, I'm sorry I don't have another van for you."

"It's okay. I get it. Rookie initiation."

"No, no. I'd give you Morey's van but he's the penultimate prima donna."

John laughed and started to open the door.

"By the way, think I could get a few bucks? You know, tide me over until the end of the week?"

"Sure."

I pulled out my money clip and peeled off a hundred dollar bill.

"That do it?"

John eyed my roll.

"Maybe a few more of those." He laughed again. "No, that's perfect. Thanks."

I tucked the money away.

"Just remember what I told you. No fast and furious. Just follow, observe and report in. That's it."

"You got it."

John climbed out, opened the back door, retrieved his rifle and came around to my door. I rolled the window down.

"Killing his own daughter. I hope I get to feed his balls to him."

"It wouldn't hurt my feelings any but that's not why the old man hired me. We're looking for a Picasso."

"You got it."

John started away.

"Hey," I said.

He came back.

"Not a word to Bennie about this. He'll shit tacos"

"Why? He's been on your case about it?"

"Yeah. Beating my balls the past few days."

"So why didn't you?"

"Just to piss him off, mostly."

370

"Wow, okay."

"No. It just didn't seem like a good idea to me until now."

John stared.

"What happened to rigorous honesty?"

"I'm practicing the second part of step nine. 'Except when to do so would injure them or others'."

"Far out," he said. "I'm really going to have to buff up on those things someday."

"I highly recommend it. I've found dozens of loopholes."

He laughed.

"Consider my lips sealed."

"Thanks. We'll all sleep better."

He headed over to his car. I noticed people inside the restaurant gawking at the rifle case. It did look a bit odd in a beach town parking lot but it was the United States of America and perfectly legal.

I dropped the Impala into drive and pulled onto El Camino Real, heading north. Needing time to think, I skipped the freeway.

Five minutes later, I left the north end of San Clemente behind and was motoring past an open stretch of coastline the locals called Poche. The name referred to an old railroad marker, which in turn referred to what the Mexicans had called the place before we took it from them. There had been a sign along the railroad tracks for years, announcing as much, but according local lore, a surfer had stolen it back in the sixties and the minute railroad workers put up a replacement sign, someone stole that one too so the railroad gave up.

The spot had a lovely windswept view from Fisherman's Point south down to Trestles. The surfers regularly built massive driftwood windbreaks on the beach so it always had the appearance of a sacred Indian burial ground.

Soon, I was motoring past Beach Road with its long stretch of oceanfront homes, and then taking the loop over my shoulder into Doheny Beach. As I did, Cal Tjader's Black Orchid came on the jazz station, with its all too familiar feelings of destiny. The destiny of countless lifetimes, chasing after Caitlin, my heart and soul met in that woman, only to be tossed back into the fire, again and again, for all eternity, back into the fire, never quite able to realize what was in my heart, not in this life, or the next one, or the one after that.

What I longed for was never never to be. Or so it seemed.

I cleared Fisherman's Point wishing it would be one thing or the other. Let me have my destiny, or let me forget. I reached for the phone, ready to call, but stopped. I wasn't sure I could go on any longer. Maybe in the next lifetime, Caitlin, but you win in this one. You have had all these years to deal with your depression, and it has brought you to this place, preferring the tangled web you weave, rather than to admit your flaws and share a moment of conciliation, and without conciliation, romance is a heartless nightmare that never ends.

Twenty Nine

Halfway through Doheny Beach, I had a thought and turned right up a narrow, winding lane. Three story apartment buildings rose up on both sides of the road. The world suddenly felt darkened and cavernous.

I continued winding up into the hills and eventually came to a main road running along the crest. I turned left and then quickly right into the parking lot of a sprawling church complex. The vast parking lot ran out to the edge of a bluff and ended at a split rail fence. I parked beside it, as far as possible from all the church buildings. On a Monday afternoon, the compound looked basically deserted.

I climbed out and looked across the valley below me. Caitlin's home was a few miles off to my left, Lila's place on the opposite side of the valley and down by the coast. Old man Huntington's hill was straight ahead.

I went around to my trunk, grabbed my binoculars and a directional mic, closed the trunk and hopped over the split rail fence. It was a bit of a struggle, making my way safely down the steep hillside through heavy brush, but I eventually came to a spot overlooking the backside of Ida Huntington's home. I settled in under the branches of a young pine and focused the binoculars on her deck.

I had been sitting there several minutes when she came into view through a sliding glass door, pacing back and forth, a phone to one ear and gesticulating with the free hand. The woman was clearly capable of dramatics, unlike her lifeless reception of me the other day.

I reached for the mic but Ida had wandered off into the house somewhere by the time I got it focused. I moved the mic back and forth until I caught snippets of her conversation. It was badly broken up and I was only hearing her side of things.

Then suddenly, she was shouting.

"I can't believe you did this! You must be an idiot!"

The conversation grew muffled again but the argument was ongoing. Then I heard Ida say something about 'that private detective,' followed by more indecipherable conversation. Then I heard Ida shout anew.

"Just get rid of her! Either you do it, or I will!"

Then everything went silent.

A few moments later, Ida reappeared in a kitchen window adjacent to the sliding glass door. I watched her cleaning up and burning off energy.

A minute later, she stepped out onto the deck with a glass of white wine in her hand. She was a beautiful woman, with a fine figure. And deadly, it seemed.

When it became clear that there were no new revelations forthcoming, I started back up the hill and was soon on my way to Laurel Lagoon. 'Just get rid of her.' I drove along with that utterance going around and around in my head. It was definitely something to chew on.

Back at my office, I opened the door and nearly gasped. Teresa had been by to clean. I always forgot she was coming. My desk glowed. The prints on the walls sparkled. There was a pristine quality I was reluctant to soil.

I sat behind my desk, glad for the cleanliness. If only we could cleanse the world of all its treachery so easily.

Checking messages, I found a flood of them from gangsta man. I promptly erased them without listening. Please, go away. I'm looking for purity in this world, not a scam.

While I sat there, trying to sort out my purpose in life, the phone rang. I looked and saw it was Caitlin. God, no. I wasn't sure if I could keep my betrayal hidden. Anyway, things would never be the same between us now, so what was the point? I hesitated, but ultimately reached for the phone.

"Hi," I said.

"Hi," she said.

Everything that had happened last night hung in the air, everything that we would never discuss or try to resolve. If I dared to mention it, Caitlin would act as if there were bees buzzing around her head. Worse than that. And now there were my own secrets to sweep under the rug.

"I just saw the news," she said. "About a big shootout or something in the palisades last night and they mentioned your name."

"Yeah, that was me."

"Oh no. So what happened? Did you find Holly?"

"Well, it's kind of complicated."

I gave Caitlin an abbreviated version of the events and when I got to the part about getting knocked over the head and shot and needing stitches, Caitlin said, "Oh no, honey. But you're all right now, yeah?"

She sounded so genuinely loving and concerned, I felt ashamed to have thought of her as a mad woman.

"Yeah. I'm all right. Just feeling kind of empty. Especially about Holly."

"But you'll find her, right?"

"Yeah. We'll find her."

"Don't get too down on yourself, honey. You did everything you could."

"Yeah."

"Want me to make you dinner tonight?" she said after a pause.

"I'd love that but I'm kind of stuck with some business stuff."

"Yeah?"

"Yeah. Maybe Friday."

"Suurrrrre."

Sure. She had said it with such love, and yet all I could see was that look on her face from the previous evening. And my own betrayal.

We chatted a bit more and got off. I sat there, unable to discern now between my own corruption and her insanity. Maybe Caitlin had a point. It was best not to discuss the past, but that was never going to work for me. I could not live my life in fear of an honest, heartfelt conversation.

I leaned back in my chair and sighed the sigh of a thousand heartaches.

A minute later, I reached for the phone and called old man Huntington. He answered after several rings.

"Did you have something on your mind, Michael, or were you just feeling lonely?"

"A little of both, sir."

He laughed.

"And no news on the Picasso."

"No but I'm still following up on some leads."

"My gut tells me your Latino associate was correct. That bastard Vanderhof has it."

I smiled on both accounts, Huntington's reference to my 'Latino associate' and his profanity. The latter came across like Tabasco sauce on a banana cream pie.

"I have a man following up on that theory right now."

"Good. If I'm ever fortunate enough to have it returned, I'll wear it for a placard the next time the two of us attend the same social event."

I was silent.

"What is it, Michael? I sense there's something else on your mind."

"Oh, just wondering if you've seen your daughter yet?"

"No. Why do you keep asking?"

"Oh, the same reason. Still hoping she can shed some light on Holly's current whereabouts."

I explained the events of the previous evening, without mentioning Holly.

376

"Well, Michael. I'm very sorry to hear of your misfortune. Though my commendations for having survived it all."

"It was mostly luck."

"I suspect there was a bit of guile mixed in there too."

"I suppose."

"I'd put my money on it…Well, back to this matter of my daughter. I'll see what I can do to track her down but it's rarely gotten me very far. She generally only appears when the money runs out. Which, come to think of it, should be any day now. Though perhaps not soon enough for you."

"It's not the end of the world but I would appreciate a call, whenever she shows up."

"You will be the first to know, Mr. Devlin."

I thanked him and got off, feeling like a man who had finally gathered the courage to confess a love affair to his wife, only to grow faint of heart at the last minute.

They're only your suspicions, I reminded myself. Only your suspicions. You have no right to alarm the man.

I spun around in my chair. The sea looked drab in the muggy heat and smog. Everything looked drab. Catalina was barely visible out there on the horizon. I stared at the cruise ship. It had become symbolic of a world going to hell in a nightmare of its own making. I sat there, not knowing which way to turn.

Then a thought occurred to me and I reached for my satchel. I had nearly forgotten the list of Holly's friends that Lila had provided me. I glanced through the twenty or so names, hoping for intuition to strike. The list read like a snapshot of the late '90s and early aughts. Ashley. Kayla. Nicole. Haley. You weren't going to find any Ann's or Diane's or Dolores' in there.

When I came to Joyce, I stopped. The name jumped out at you. It suggested a mother out of step with her times. Perhaps the same could be said of her daughter.

I called and after several rings, a melodic voice said, "Hello?"

It was a kind and strangely airy voice. I pictured someone with flaxen hair and white skin. She thrived on moonlight.

"Hi," I said. "My name's Michael and I'm working for Mrs. Evergreen. You know, Holly Evergreen?"

"Oh, sure. How is Holly? The last I heard, she had run away with a biker or something."

"She did."

"And she's not back?"

"No."

"Oh. That's not good."

"No, and of course her mother's distraught. This biker guy is dangerous. Very dangerous."

I told her about the dead woman.

"God. How awful. What a terrible ending."

"Yeah. Hanging out with the wrong people, I guess."

"Yeah. That's why I got clean."

"You did?"

"Yeah. I have six months now."

"I just celebrated two years."

"Really?! How cool."

"Yeah."

"I know. I had really started to hate myself. Just wanting my life to end and all but now I'm back in school and planning to go to college."

"Hey, good for you. I can only imagine at your age. The whole world in front of you. I was going on fifty before I got the message."

"Yeah, but it's cool that you did."

"Yeah. I'm grateful every day...Well, mostly."

Joyce laughed.

"I know. It's hard sometimes."

There was silence.

"So I guess you were hoping I could help in some way?"

"I was, but it sounds like maybe not. If you don't know anything about what Holly was doing, you probably have no idea who might have visited her."

"I don't. Not really. I know this girl named Charlotte Huntington and Holly were really close but I never heard

378

anything about Charlotte going out there to hang with Holly and the bikers."

"And how about Charlotte? Have you seen her lately?"

"Oh yeah. She was at a party a couple of weeks ago and…"

"You saw Charlotte?!"

"Yeah. Why?"

"Because I'm also working for Charlotte's father and he hasn't seen her for a while either so he's equally concerned."

"God. You don't think she's the one who got killed, do you?"

"I don't know. I hate to think it but I've been unable to find her."

"Well, I remember her talking to this older guy at the party and the word was she ran off with him somewhere. It would be just like her. She's always running off for weeks at a time and then coming back all mysterious about where she's been."

"But it's just a rumor, huh?"

"Yeah."

"And you don't know who this guy is or where they might have gone?"

"No, sorry. I could ask around if you want."

"Would you?"

"Sure."

"Only be discreet, you know?"

"Oh sure. I'll just casually mention that I haven't seen her lately and does anyone know what's going on. I won't raise any suspicions."

"That would be great. Thanks."

"Sure."

"Well, I'm glad I called you. I was sitting here looking at all these names Mrs. Evergreen had jotted down. Friends of Holly, you know, and you turned out to be the perfect person to contact."

"Yeah. We're both sober, huh?"

"Yeah. Pretty cool."

"Yeah. Have you been to any meetings lately?" Joyce asked.

"Yeah, but it's been a couple of days now and I'm starting to feel it."

"I know. Your head starts to get all weird, right?"

"I'm sure someone's scheming behind my back."

She laughed.

"Yeah. I'm going to a really cool meeting down by the harbor tonight. It's called the gong show. They have a three minute share limit and a bell goes off if you go over."

I smiled.

"I'll have to bring along this Puerto Rican character I know. He's always going on and on in meetings and I've never figured out how to shut him up."

Joyce laughed again.

"The gong show will do it."

"Thanks for the tip. And you have my number, right?"

"Yeah. It's on my phone. Michael Devlin."

"That's me."

"Okay. I'll make you a contact. Michael D."

"I'll do the same. And please let me know the minute you hear something."

"I will…So maybe we can go have a coffee someday. I'd love to hear what it's like being a detective."

"It's a lot like this," I said. We both laughed. "Okay, I'll call you the next time I'm down your way and we'll see if we can catch a meeting together."

"Cool. I'd like that."

"Me too. And please let me know if you hear anything more about Charlotte."

"I will."

"Okay. Bye."

"Bye."

I got off and spun around to face the sea. Joyce's timeframe for last seeing Charlotte was hardly comforting. Two weeks was just long enough to fit the time of death.

I let out a sigh. Maybe all these worries were just a product of my overactive imagination. I wanted to believe that, but

Charlotte was missing and I struggled to imagine another scenario that explained the ring.

Then I remembered Holly and felt even more helpless.

I had been sitting there for a spell, wracking my brain, when weariness overcame me. I yawned. What was it with me lately? It seemed like I needed a nap every day now.

I was just getting up out of my chair when the front door opened downstairs and footsteps started up the wooden steps. Heavy footsteps, and two sets of them. I sat back down, opened the top drawer of my desk and positioned the Walther 9MM the way I liked it. No one had a retail business in this building. No one came around here shopping.

Well, if someone was looking for trouble, they had found it. I was tired of being pushed around.

I fussed with the position of the Walther again and sat back to wait.

Presently, two silhouettes appeared outside my door. A moment passed and someone knocked. When I failed to answer, whoever it was tried the doorknob. It turned, the door pushed open and Whalen walked in, followed by Barnes. I gently closed the drawer to my desk while staring their way.

"What's the matter?" Barnes said. "Not feeling friendly like today?"

I looked at Pat.

"To what do I owe the pleasure?"

Pat nodded his head at Barnes. Barnes had stepped over to my desk and set a piece of paper down in front of me, careful to make sure all the corners were nice and square to the world.

I looked up from the search warrant.

"Where do you want me to start, partner?"

"Wherever you'd like, Barnes."

"Think I'll start right there. With that little drawer you were closing as we came in."

While Barnes moved around to my side of the desk, I looked back at Pat.

"You part of this bullshit?"

381

He shrugged.

"You don't play nice and this is what happens."

"Yeah, right. All you had to do is ask. I'd have served you tea and crumpets while you were poking around."

"Look, he was nice enough to run it by me. He could have played hardball and come down here with a handful of his goons."

"Yeah. Thanks for nothing."

Barnes had noticed my notepad with the doodles and picked it up.

"Hey, you see this? Kind of hard to tell but I'm going to guess that's yours truly."

I kept staring at Pat. Barnes set the notepad down and motioned towards the desk drawer.

"I think we'll go ahead and have a look in there."

I backed out of the way.

"Well well," he said, upon seeing the Walther. "Expecting trouble, are we?"

My eyes remained focused on Pat.

When Barnes found nothing of interest in there, he went about making a mess of the remaining drawers. When that bore no fruit, he stood back, looking around the office.

"I think I'll have a look in that safe over there next, partner."

I went over to open it and Barnes proceeded to make a mess in there. He found deeds and contracts, handcuffs, my passport, an old .38, but nothing he was hoping to find.

Having struck out again, he stood up and had another look around the office, clicking his tongue as he did.

"You even know what you're looking for, Barnes?"

"You know exactly what I'm looking for, partner."

I stared. His eyes had been making another survey of my office and landed on me. I held out my hands.

"Go ahead, Barnes. It's got to be killing you."

He came over and stood eye to eye. His hands were doing a workout down at his sides. I was doing my best not to look like a man with a ring in his coat pocket.

Barnes' stare dragged on.

"Neah," he said finally. "I don't take you to be that dumb. Let's just move on to your residence. You did notice that that search warrant was good for both places."

"Fine. I was just thinking to go home and take a nap."

I closed the safe, waited for them to exit ahead of me and locked the door on my way out.

"We'll follow you," Barnes said down on the street. "And don't go losing us."

I paused with a look over the roof of my car before climbing in.

When traffic allowed, I backed out of my parking spot and waited for them to get behind me. Potter's card was sitting on my office desk at home and I was struggling for some way to explain it.

Back at my place, I waved Barnes and Pat over the bridge ahead of me and dropped the ring into the creek when they weren't looking.

"Nice place," Barnes said at the front door. "Ever catch anything going by in that creek?"

I unlocked the door and waved them inside without answering. Barnes paused in the living room, taking things in.

"Home office?" he said.

I closed the door and pointed with my chin towards the stairs.

It didn't take long for Barnes to notice the card sitting on top of my desk.

"Whoa! What's this?"

He had a look at me before flipping it over.

"Whoa!" he said more emphatically. "You see this, Pat?"

Pat walked over and had a closer look. Both of them turned my way.

"And how did you happen to come up with this little gem?" Barnes said.

"I ordered it online."

"With this personalized inscription on the back, huh?"

"That was extra."

Pat shook his head as if truly disappointed.

"You are so fucking busted, Devlin."

"For what? Having one of Potter's cards?"

Pat scoffed.

"No, for having his card with El Chango's name scribbled on the back. That looks like proof alone that you've been withholding evidence."

"Bullshit."

"Okay, spill it," Pat said. "How did you come to know about him?"

"Somebody I was tailing led me to his place."

"Bullshit," Barnes said now.

"Fine. Take me in."

We were back to staring at each other.

"You've got about one minute," Pat said. "And it better be good or I'll be waving goodbye to you as the jail door closes."

I explained about Nicholas having fenced Huntington's 26th Dynasty figurine, while leaving out the drugs and Holly. Both detectives stood there staring at me.

"You telling me the truth?" Pat said.

I nodded.

"Oh bullshit," Barnes said again.

"Fine. Check with the old man."

"I've got a better one," Barnes said. "I'll go check with the Mongols."

I scoffed.

"Good luck with that one."

"What? Afraid your little story's going to fall apart on you?"

I looked at Pat.

"It's not my job to reason with this son of a bitch but the only thing you're likely to get by going out there to accuse those boys is a denial, or a gunfight, or a good reason for them to put a bullet in my head."

"That's good enough reason for me," Barnes said with a smile.

"Fuck you, Barnes."

I looked back at Pat.

"Listen. You want corroboration, check with the bank. It'll show that I withdrew five grand out there in Apple Valley. And the phone company. They can pinpoint the time and place of the call I made to my operative. And feel free to check with the old man about the figurine. It's just like I told you. Or you can go out there and make trouble with the Mongols, over what's basically a chickenshit charge, that you can't prove without my testimony. The DA will laugh you out of his office."

"You're telling me the truth?" Pat said.

"As straight as I can tell it."

"Which ain't very straight," Barnes said.

I ignored him and kept staring at Pat.

"Seriously?" Pat said to me.

I nodded. Pat nodded back.

"If you're fucking with me, Devlin, I'll personally put your ass behind bars."

"Oh, this is bullshit," Barnes said and started rummaging through my desk drawers. Then he made a mess of my bookshelves. Then he frisked me and scattered the contents of my wallet all over my desk.

"Satisfied?" I said.

Barnes was ready to boil over.

"You still haven't explained how you got this card here."

"I told you. Online."

"Son of a bitch," he said.

"Go ahead, Barnes. Take me in. That or get the hell out of my house. I've had it up to here with you pushing me around."

"Come on," Pat said with a hand on Barnes' arm. "We're done here for now."

Barnes seethed at me for a moment before going along.

"And don't think you're out of the woods yet," Pat said at the door. "Always treading just this side of the law. Well you're going to find yourself in over your head one of these days and I will be waving goodbye to you on the way down."

I waited until I heard the gate open and close out front before heading downstairs, then stood there in the living room until their car pulled away from my driveway. When it was clear they were gone, I went outside and climbed down to the creek. The hills were still dry that time of year and the water in the creek barely a trickle. I found the ring under some rivergrass after a brief search.

Being out there already, I sat down in the stillness of nature and listened to the babbling of the brook. It was a vein of simple goodness running through our troubled world.

It was a good long spell before I climbed back up to my yard and headed inside.

Thirty

I was still cleaning up in my office when Bennie called.

"Hey, Bennie. What's going on?"

"Whoa, boss man. You sound really down."

"Yeah. I guess I am."

I explained about Barnes and Whelan shaking me down.

"You know, I just felt like shit once they were gone. Lying to cover my ass, lying to cover for my clients. I don't know if I can do it anymore, Bennie. I'm worn out. I feel like I'm falling apart."

"Hey, it's okay. We all go through it in sobriety. Sometimes you just have to walk through the emochions."

Emochions. That's what I had all right.

"So, what did you end up arranging?"

"Oh, I took your doll here and sent Morey over to keep an eye on Nicholas. Figured that's the way you'd want it."

"Yeah. Thanks. I know you're tested. I have no idea about him."

"Yeah. I've got you covered."

"Thanks. Anything new then?"

"Nothing here. Or with Nicholas, as far as I know…You're sure you don't want me to send Morey over to keep an eye on Ms. Evergreen's place instead?"

"No, it's fine. She's still got the FBI crawling all over her property."

"Yeah. You know, your doll was out doing some gardening a little while ago. She is kind of cute in her blue rubber clogs. She stops from time to time and braids her hair to one side, like she's thinking."

That image stabbed right into my heart. My little doll, braiding her long red hair. Of course I remembered it. But now it was all wrecked.

"What are you thinking?" Bennie said.

"Oh, nothing, nothing...Sounds like everything's good for now."

"Yeah. No sign of Donald the Hun."

That got a sick smile out of me.

"Been reading your history again, Bennie?"

"Shit. I'm always reading history. I mean, we're like in the final stages of the Roman Republic here. Everybody fighting about the dumbest shit and nothing getting done. Sound familiar? Cuz' that's exactly how Rome went down. Next thing you know Caesar takes over and the barbarians are at the gates."

"I hate to pop your bubble, Bennie, but I think Caesar's already in charge."

"Yeah, don't get me started. If it was legal, I'd shoot the son of a bitch...Caesar, shit. We had to end up with a two-bit version."

I laughed.

"So, anyway. I really appreciate you being there and please keep an eye on her."

"You got it, man."

There was a pause.

"Did you really send John over to watch Vanderhof?"

"Please, Bennie. Don't start. I didn't know what else to do with him. Let's just say you had a good idea."

"It's okay, boss man. I know you've got a lot on your mind. Get some sleep. HALT. Hungry, angry, lonely, tired. You'll feel better afterwards."

"I don't know. I'll probably feeling even emptier when I wake up but I can't seem to keep my eyes open."

"You gotta do what you gotta do."

"Yeah. Just give me a few hours and I'll be back at you."

"You got it."

I hung up with that image of Caitlin stuck in my heart, pausing to braid her hair as she gardened. I had always pictured us living our lives out together in a little cottage somewhere in the country, with me stealing loving glances at her through the window as she tended to her basil and such. I loved the woman so, I could have watched her doing stuff for all eternity and never gotten bored.

Thinking to grab the mail before I crashed, I was just closing the mailbox and turning back towards the house when I noticed Fitzy coming across our cul-de-sac. She waved when our eyes met.

Oh lord. This was the last thing I needed right now.

I did my best to smile when she stopped in front of me. Her whole countenance spoke of grief. The dark rings under her eyes kept getting darker.

"What happened?" she said in reference to my head.

"Oh," I said, touching my wounds. "I keep forgetting. Vocational hazards. What's going on?"

"Oh, nothing. I just wanted to say I'm sorry again but you'll probably never forgive me."

"One of these days."

"Well, I am sorry. Had I known how much that tree meant to you, I never would have cut it down."

"Somebody planted it, what? A hundred years ago now? I don't understand why that didn't mean something to you."

"I don't know. I don't know anything anymore. I'm just an aging divorcee going nuts."

Had Fitzy not looked so tragic about the whole thing, I would have laughed. As it was, I had to force back a smile. Big time life coach and life organizer and she could hardly make it across the cul-de-sac.

"How's your daughter?" I asked, not knowing what else to say.

And as if high tide had just washed over Fitzy's sandcastle, she fell against my chest and wept. I placed my arms around her awkwardly. She kept going for quite a spell.

"Sorry," she said, pulling back. "She's run away."

"Your daughter?"

Fitzy wiped at her tears and nodded.

"I filed a police report but they don't care."

"Of course they care."

"You know what I mean. If they happen to run into her, fine, but they're not going to go out of their way. Meanwhile, anything could happen."

I stared.

"Oh, never mind," she said. "I shouldn't be bothering you."

"No, no. It's fine. It's just…I've been trying to find a runaway daughter for another single mom this past week and most of the time the leads come down to pure luck."

"But you did find her?" Fitzy said hopefully.

"Yes and no."

I explained briefly what had happened.

"Oh god. Well, I wish someone was trying that hard to find Allison."

I sighed deeply, knowing where this was headed.

"Come. Let's go inside. I didn't get much sleep last night and could use a cup of coffee."

I put a hand at Fitzy's back and guided her through the gate.

Back in my kitchen, I brewed up just enough coffee for two cups. Fitzy was staring out the kitchen window at the creek and my arched bridge.

"I really like your place," she said and turned to face me.

"Thanks."

Her eyes darted here and there, taking things in.

"You were probably really happy until this crazy divorcee moved in next door."

"Oh, I don't know about that, Fitzy, but I certainly don't feel like you've made my life any worse. I just miss the tree."

"Oh god, okay. I'll get rid of the junipers and buy a new one. I hate the junipers anyway. I just freaked out after you came down to my door and thought it would be best if we weren't staring at each other every day."

I nodded.

"That much did help."

I looked up from the brewing coffee. Fitzy smiled a bit through her grief.

I interrupted the still brewing coffee and poured two cups.

"Cream and sugar?"

"Sure."

"Please, have a seat," I said and went to retrieve the half and half.

We both settled in at the dining nook and doctored up our coffees. Fitzy stared meditatively at the cream swirling around in her cup. I took a deep drink of mine. She looked up from her cup.

"I feel like I've failed as a wife. And now I've failed as a mother."

"I wouldn't look at it that way."

"How would you look at it?"

"You were courageous enough to end an unhappy marriage."

"He left me, remember? Bought a new Porsche and ran off with a young floozy."

"Yeah."

"Still think I'm courageous?"

"I don't know. Do you think you're courageous?"

"I don't know. I put on a brave face every day and go about telling all these other mixed up women how to run their lives. Meanwhile, I'm completely falling apart inside."

I stared.

"What?" she said.

"Oh, sometimes I think if we don't kill ourselves today, that's a triumph."

"Really? I mean, you...?"

I nodded.

"Sure. Everything's such a mess these days, it seems like we'll never be able to fix it. I'm ready to put a gun to my head. But then I think of all the people I'd be letting down. You know? How would I feel if they checked out?"

"Yeah. Sometimes I just want to drive off a cliff, but then I think of Allison. I have to be strong for her. But now..."

I pulled a napkin from the rooster carousel on my table and handed it to her.

"Thanks."

I nodded and stared into my coffee. The moment seemed unreal to me, commiserating with Fitzy while she grieved. I let a minute pass before speaking.

"Any idea where Allison might be?"

She dabbed at her nose again with the napkin.

"No. Unless it's with her friends in our old neighborhood. My husband and I owned an estate in the Hunt Club for many years."

Fitzy had referred to the Hunt Club as if everyone knew of it. It was very hoity toity. Wooded hills and riding paths. I could picture Fitzy trotting about in her English riding gear and spoiling a child.

"Have you tried calling any of them?" I asked.

"Of course, but they don't answer. Or if they do, they act like I'm a cop. It's obvious they're not going to tell me anything, even if they do know."

She played with her coffee cup and looked up.

"So, could I hire you? You know, to help with finding Allison?"

"No," I said.

Fitzy's look in response was enough to break your heart.

"But I will help you," I added.

Her hand quickly reached for another napkin. I watched while she battled more tears.

"I don't understand. What do you mean?"

"I mean, I don't want this to be a business matter. It's one neighbor helping another. I'll do what I can but I can't make any promises."

"But you'll look?"

"Sure. I'll see what I can find out."

With Fitzy's face still in her napkin, she reached across the table and squeezed my hand.

"Thank you."

"You're welcome."

I would have preferred saying no, but her grief was so palpable.

I shooed Fitzy off a short while later. It was becoming impossible to keep my eyes open. By the time I finally pulled the bed covers back, I was too exhausted to remove my clothing. I made do with unlacing my shoes before crawling into bed. There was a feeling I might never wake up.

Several minutes passed with my mind attempting to solve everything that could not be solved in this life. Then, amidst the cares and worries of daily existence, fantasies began to flit here and there. I was a knight, off to slay dragons, streamers and adoring ladies with hankies waving in the air. I left this world straining to find Caitlin among the faces, with trumpets blaring.

I was awakened way too soon, confused by the ringing phone. Shadows had swallowed my room. For a moment I had thought it was dawn, not dusk.

Irritated, I answered the ringing phone without looking.

"Yeah?" I said.

There was no answer, other than for the sound of someone breathing. Then I heard what sounded like things being shuffled around on a table. It was my thought that someone had accidentally pocket dialed my number.

Then a voice said, "I know where you live. I know where she lives."

I had started to swear at Potter but the phone went dead.

Goddamn him. That self-righteousness son of a bitch. It was not possible to hate someone more. Everything about him was vile.

Furious, frantic, beside myself, I called Bennie.

"Did you cop some sleep, boss man?"

"Not enough and anyway, fuck that. Potter just called me again."

"Oh man."

"Yeah and he said he knows where she lives too."

Bennie swore in Spanish.

"I'll tell you what. I'm going to get a real pleasure out of putting a bullet into that fucker's head."

"If I see that son of a bitch anywhere near Caitlin's place, I'll disembowel him first."

"Well, don't sweat it for now. I've got your back. I'm down here where you told me to park and can see her place, front and back."

"Thanks, Bennie. I appreciate it but I'm going to call John and have him join you. I'm not taking any chances."

"Sure, best to be safe. What about Morey? You want him down here too?"

"No, that's all right. I'll have John relieve him and grab the other van. The two of you ought to be plenty...Jesus, poor Holly. I keep forgetting she's out there with that bastard somewhere."

"Yeah, I hate to say this, but she made her own bed."

"I know but she's just a kid. Shit, what worries me the most is that she probably knows too much, like who they dusted out at Potter's old place."

"Yeah. I'm with you on that one. Those fuckers wouldn't be shy about dusting her...I'm ashamed to admit it but I've seen that shit go down."

"You?"

"Yeah, man. Don't forget I was a gangbanger once."

I sighed, hating to think of Bennie in that way.

"But you're good for now?"

"Yeah, man. I've got you covered."

"Good. Then once it's dark, I'll come by and relieve whoever needs it."

"You got it."

I hung up, called Morey, told him John was stopping by to relieve him and grab the van and then called John.

"Anything?" I said.

"No yellow Ferraris yet."

"Okay. I've got another assignment for you."

"Yeah? What's up?"

I explained.

"Jesus. That son of a bitch must have nine lives."

"Yeah. So, can you get to it right away?"

"Sure. Anything to take another shot at that SOB."

"Good. Morey's expecting you."

"I'll grab a coffee and sandwich and be on my way."

"Thanks. Just text me once you're in position."

"You got it."

I hung up and went in to shower. Potter was doing laps in my head. Goddamn him. He was some kind of Dracula figure.

Then Caitlin was back in my thoughts. The past two days had made a joke of my devotion, and yet, some part of my loving devotion for her refused to die.

While showering, I decided, enough with the wounded soldier look and pulled off the bandages, then did my best to hide the bare spots while drying and combing my hair.

I was pulling on my trousers when the phone rang. It was Morey.

"What's up?" I said.

"I thought I'd better give you my report before hitting the hay."

"Go ahead. Shoot."

"So, about half an hour before John relieved me, this big stretch limo pulls up in front of Nicholas' place, the driver gets out and..."

"Whoa, Morey. Don't you remember me telling you that if something out of the ordinary like this happens, you're supposed to report in right away?"

He was silent. I could picture the peering through a sandstorm look. A firing squad was imminent. He must have hated being interrupted as much as I did.

"I thought you were copping some sleep," he said finally.

"I don't care if I'm on my way to Mars. Please report in."

There was more silence.

"Did you want me to continue?"

"Yes, please."

"So, the driver gets out and knocks on Nicholas' door and Nicholas answers a minute later, looking perturbed until he sees the limo. Then he looks freaked. Then a guy in back hits the window button, waves Nicholas over and starts chewing him out."

"Did you get a look at the guy inside?"

"A bit of his profile, yeah."

"Hang on then."

I quickly opened a text to Morey and attached a photo of Vanderhof.

"I just texted you a photo. Let me know if it's the guy in the limo…"

Morey was silent.

"So?" I said.

The pause continued for another moment.

"So I was saying, I couldn't make out much of the conversation but the guy in the limo was definitely pissed. Nicholas started to argue back at one point and the guy shut him right up. They had been talking for about a minute when the window goes back up and Nicholas is left there staring at the driver. Who gives him a snarky look back and climbs into the limo. Then off they go."

I waited.

"And that's it?"

"Yeah. Unless you want me to make something up."

Oh boy. Kid Morey and I were definitely going to have to put on the gloves at some point.

"Did you receive my text?" I asked him.

"No. Not yet...Oh, wait. Yeah, I just got it and that's him all right. I'd know that goatee and profile anywhere...Does this mean anything to you?"

"Maybe. It might confirm what Bennie's been saying. That Nicholas fenced old man Huntington's Picasso to Vanderhof and Vanderhof's pissed at Nicholas for getting him involved."

"Well, I didn't see any Picassos getting exchanged, if that's what you're wondering."

"Yeah, Vanderhof's not that stupid. He wouldn't be carrying the thing around. I think he'd burn it before getting caught red-handed."

"Well, whatever. I'm going to go cop some sleep now and you should be more explicit in your instructions. I got the impression that you didn't want me bothering you unless guns were going off."

"You're right, Morey. I should be more explicit."

I got off the call, contemplating which form of military discipline was in order.

I finished dressing and went to sit in the living room. The world slowly grew dark around me. Thoughts came and went, a lot of them I would have preferred not having.

John sent a text, letting me know he was there. I sent him a thumbs up and got back to gnawing at my own flesh.

Then Ida's words returned to me there in the dusky light.

"Just get rid of her. Or I'll do it."

But get rid of whom? Charlotte? In my state of ignorance, I could not think of anyone else who fit that statement.

When darkness was complete, I headed out the door. Rather than jump on the freeway in Doheny Beach, I turned left at the harbor entrance and took the back way up towards the old mission. Three miles inland, I was circling around its battered adobe walls. A couple was going into a French restaurant across the street. Otherwise the downtown area looked mostly empty on a Sunday evening.

An apartment complex followed on my left, what had been a budget priced condo development back in the '70s but was now a teeming Mexican barrio. I saw a young couple with six kids and two strollers. Old Jack Oliver would have had a field day. 'Send the bastards back across the border. They breed like rats.'

That they were Mexican didn't bother me. It was having a mindset from another century. No concern for overpopulation. Most of the Mexicans I knew didn't even get the concept of recycling. It was depressing. Then, sixty, seventy years earlier, gringos were breeding like rats and gleefully tossing plastic into landfills like there was no tomorrow. We had set a terrible, terrible example for the rest of the world to follow.

With the last of the barrio on my left, I turned right and started up a straight, gentle incline. At the top, where the road T-d, I turned right and took the Sherwood Forest, back way over to Caitlin's place. John was parked half a block up from her side fence. I parked behind him and slipped in through the back door of the van. John threw his arms out triumphantly, like a king before oysters.

"Now this is more like it, sweetie. But we'll have to do something about that toilet."

"Yeah. And like I told Morey, I'll see if I can get them to drop off a porta potty."

"Oh. So it's going to be like that, is it."

I looked at the monitors without acknowledging him.

"Anything?"

"Nothing so far. I call Bennie every so often and give him some shit. That's about it."

"How's Bennie doing?"

"Pissed about me giving him shit. Otherwise okay, I guess."

I looked up from the monitors.

"Here's what I want you to do. Walk down and relieve Bennie in his van. He can walk up here and take my Impala home."

"Oookaaaayyy," John said like it was a big mystery.

"The doll doesn't have any windows facing in this direction."

"Oh yeah. Got it."

He headed out the door. I called Bennie to let him know what was happening and watched John's progress down the street on one of the screens. A minute later, Bennie appeared from the other direction.

"How are you doing, boss man," he said, climbing in.

"All right, Bennie. Just dealing with my emochions."

He smiled and patted me on the shoulder.

"That's all we can do sometimes."

I nodded and handed him the keys to my Impala.

"Just don't have it lowered or add any flames."

He laughed and patted me on the back again.

"You're all right, dude."

I watched him go out the back door and turned my attention to the image of Caitlin's house on one of the screens, my mind flooding with memories of all the good times we had shared. The eagerly waiting in bed at night while she combed her long red hair. The joy of our bodies meeting flesh to flesh as she crawled in beside me and how we would lie there together and laugh at a thousand silly things.

On one particular night, Caitlin had been joking about clown trains going by on the nearby railroad tracks and just then a passing train honked, with a horn that had sounded right out of a circus clown act. Honk honk. Caitlin had sprung up at the waist, in stitches, and we had spent the next half hour riffing on how clowns would be hanging from the caboose as the train flew wildly around turns and such. The best we could figure, it had been someone with a private car but you couldn't make this stuff up.

I sat there wanting to relive all those dear moments, to have everything the way it had once been. I wanted to think of anything but my own betrayal.

"I'm sorry," I said out loud.

All I had wanted in this world was to share a simple life with you, some way to honor the feelings of devotion you stir in my heart, a little cottage for the two of us until the end of time, but now it's all wrecked and I doubt I can ever put it back together again. I will always be aware of the other woman's sex.

Seven long years I had waited for that woman to return to my arms and look what I had done. I wanted to blame her and all her goddamned madness, but I couldn't. There was no one to blame now but me.

Thirty One

I had been sitting there for a good spell longer, revisiting the same terrain, when Caitlin appeared unexpectedly from around the corner of her house, with Senan straining on his leash out in front of her.

Oh doll, I thought. How I love the very sight of you.

My impulse was to jump out and sweep her up in my arms, but to do so would have revealed me spying on her again.

When Caitlin passed by the van, her eyes looked directly at one of the cameras and into my soul. As I watched her continue up the street, alarms went off in my head. What if Potter's out stalking the neighborhood?

I grabbed my phone and quickly called John.

"I was about to call you," he said.

"Yeah. Maybe you'd better take a lap around the block and keep an eye on her."

"Will do."

He called back a short time later. She had taken the path of our last walk, up into the park and down through Sherwood Forest, and was now safely back at home.

I thanked John and sat back to watch the monitors, wondering if Caitlin had thought of me during her trek, wondering if she recalled our dearest hours together, too, and hoped for everything to be all right between us, forever and ever, and all the eternities to come? There had been a time early on when Caitlin expressed such hopes, but with each fractious episode, Caitlin had slowly drifted away, another resentment harbored inside and the two of us growing evermore like strangers as time went by, our silly spats never resolved.

No honesty. No conciliation. No forgiveness. And finally, no romance.

It was a long night, relitigating our many battles. I could hardly remember what had caused them, only her childish behavior, and my anger over it.

We were two years into the romance before she had made her first oblique reference to clinical depression.

Good god. And you're just telling me this now?

And to think of all the times I had stormed off, half out of my mind with frustration, only to prosecute myself and my own behavior upon arriving back home. Why do you let the woman wound you so deeply?

Until her oblique confession, there had been little at my disposal to explain her tantrums. Why do our minor differences lead to such anguish?

One of her gripes, it turned out, was that I rarely spent the night with her. I was often pulling on my pants at three in the morning, racing off to deal with one investigation or another.

"Do you know how that feels?" she had said when the issue unexpectedly came up. "To wake up in the morning all alone? Dinner and sex and off you go. It's like you can't wait to get out the door fast enough."

But it's just my work, I had explained. I thought you understood. So much of it takes place in the middle of the night. Besides, a man could not love a woman more than I love and adore you. Are you really not aware of that fact?

Whether or not she was, by the time Caitlin got around to revealing a hurt, we had rocketed well past diplomacy. It was a complete meltdown, her mood so wretched, you would have thought I had slain our own children.

It was a relief when Bennie and Morey finally arrived to spell us in the morning. I headed home, having grown increasingly cynical over the course of the night. My roulette ball kept landing on anger. If Caitlin had cared enough about me and our romance, she would have done something about her depression, and clearly, she had not. My fervent devotion appeared to be some sort of 'throwaway' in her mind. She had done virtually nothing to honor it.

Well, we both had our abundance of secrets now, and I had no desire to see mine revealed. It really would be best if we never saw each other again.

I crawled into bed, exhausted, and awakened late in the morning feeling as empty as a box. All my hopes and dreams were lost now. I could not go on dangling from this emotional string. I would drink, or shoot myself. It was a matter of survival. A rose bush in drought must shed all its blooms.

I had started to get out of bed when the weight of the grief finally became too much and I dropped to my knees, unable to take one more step along the road to Damascus until the burden had been lifted.

Prayers followed. Tears and gibberish and anguished confessions, most of it about Caitlin. My hopes and dreams, vanquished but never forgotten.

I got up some time later with an embarrassed look over my shoulder, befuddled by what had just happened and certain someone had been watching.

But at least the thousand pound stone had been lifted from my chest.

I scrambled up some eggs and sat there in the speckled sunlight, having no idea what to do with myself that day. From what Morey had told me, there was every reason to believe that Vanderhof possessed the Picasso so I decided to go pay him a visit and we'd take it from there. It was better than sitting around and gnawing on own flesh all day.

An hour later, I arrived at his front door and paused there to take in the panoramic view. The blue sea sparkled from Palos Verde all the way down to San Diego. Here and there, surf broke lazily along the nearby shoreline. A stiff breeze had blown down from the north, clearing the skies and leaving behind a lovely, autumn-like day in Southern California.

And they said money couldn't buy happiness.

Having pushed the doorbell, I half expected a tuxedoed butler to answer my ring. Instead, after some wait, a willowy brunette in her late '20s opened the door, barefoot, smiling and seemingly out of breath. I imagined her having arrived from some remote corner of the house. A capacious foyer rolled out behind her, done up in Spanish Colonial style. Sunlight speckled the tile. I felt a sudden urge to take a siesta.

"Can I help you?" she asked.

"I'm here to see Mr. Vanderhof."

"May I say who's calling?"

"It's his arch nemesis."

Without missing a beat, she turned her head and called out.

"Dad! It's your arch nemesis!"

She looked back at me, her smile intact. The 'Dad' reference aside, there was no doubt who this was. She had the same eyes and voluminous mouth, though in fairness to the fairer sex, it all looked a great deal more fetching on her than it did on her father.

How Vanderhof had come to have a twenty-something daughter was one more mystery that begged to be explained. The daughter's existence had never come up in his divorce proceedings three years earlier. You had to assume a secret love affair.

While still pondering that question and exchanging smiles with the daughter, Vanderhof appeared at the far end of the foyer. It wasn't another zip code, but close. I watched him cross the intervening space. He held out a hand, his eyes making a discreet reconnaissance of the stitches and missing hair on my head.

"What the hell, Devlin. What brings you up here?"

I shook his hand, purely out of courtesy.

"I have a few questions I'd like to ask you. About Nicholas, if you don't mind."

I looked at his daughter. She had yet to stop smiling.

"My daughter Cassandra," Vanderhof said. "Michael Devlin. Private detective."

Cassandra's eyes got big.

"Is my father in trouble?"

I looked at Vanderhof.

"When isn't he?"

Cassandra looked from face to face.

"You want to talk, let's go outside," he said.

"A pleasure," I said to Cassandra and followed Vanderhof out towards a palm festooned veranda.

"Can I get you two anything to drink?" Cassandra called after us.

"Make it two orange juices," Vanderhof said.

"I'm fine," I said with a wave back at her.

"Make it two orange juices," Vanderhof repeated.

He sat on one side of a teak table. I sat on the other. The tropical themed seat cushions were as comfy as clouds.

"What happened to you?" he said with a nod at my head.

"Oh, just trying to get myself killed the other night."

Vanderhof smiled a bit.

"How does the other guy look?"

"Don't know. He's still on the loose."

Vanderhof nodded.

"So? Spill it."

I had been taking in the lines of surf breaking lazily down at Main Beach and looked back at Vanderhof.

"Oh. I was going to say, you must have a death wish. That or you just forgot that I'm keeping an eye on Nicholas."

Vanderhof studied me.

"What do you want, Devlin?"

"The Picasso."

"And?"

"And nothing. As far as the Picasso goes."

405

"Then let's just say for the sake of argument that there was a knock on your office door one day and the Picasso appeared. You're telling me that that would be the end of it?"

"As far as the Picasso goes."

Vanderhof nodded his head slowly while studying me.

"How about this, Devlin. I'll give you two hundred grand a year to come work for me. I don't care if you spend your time filing your fingernails. Anything to get you off my back."

"Thanks, but no thanks."

"Make it three hundred grand."

I shook my head.

"Then name your price."

"I don't have a price. Anyway, I'd still be trying to put you behind bars."

"There's no forgiving and forgetting with you, huh?"

"Oh, I forgive, sure. I just can't forget."

Vanderhof was about to respond when Cassandra arrived bearing a tray with two large goblets. A slice of pineapple and sprig of mint had been perched on the rim of both chilled glasses.

"Is my father really in trouble?" Cassandra said while handing me my orange juice. Her smile was still as wide as the world.

"Probably," I said while staring at him.

I looked at her.

"I've done my best to give him good advice but he doesn't seem inclined to take it."

"He doesn't listen to me," she said.

Vanderhof, who had been quietly listening to our exchange, dismissed his daughter with a 'thanks.' Cassandra looked from him to me with her big smile.

"Perhaps we should get together some evening and compare notes."

She sashayed off with her tray and jersey slacks. She did a lot for jersey slacks.

Vanderhof was studying me when I turned back.

406

"I guess I know how to get to you."

I shook my head. Referring to your own daughter as chattel. That seemed particularly odious, even for a man like Vanderhof.

"I believe we were discussing the Picasso," I said.

Vanderhof had a sip of his orange juice and played with his goatee.

"Let me put it to you this way. If I ever became aware that an item had been stolen, of course I'd want to make sure it was returned to the rightful owner."

"Sounds reasonable enough to me."

"Reasonable enough to have things end right there?"

"I already told you. Huntington doesn't care how I get it back. He just wants it back."

"Fair enough. Don't be surprised to receive a knock on your office door one day soon. Beyond that, I'll never admit to a thing."

"I didn't expect you would."

"Fucking Devlin. Always have to get in the last jab."

"I'm trying to be civilized here, Dirk. I really am."

He gazed down at the coast.

"I remember our conversation at the Quiet Woman that night." He looked back. "Call me misguided but I could have sworn we were on our way to becoming old pals."

"It was the Scotch. It probably colored your impressions."

He continued studying me.

"I'll give you this much, Devlin. I definitely underestimated you."

"I suppose it wouldn't be hard to do."

I nodded politely and stood up.

"I'll be waiting for that package. And please thank Cassandra for the orange juice."

"You never touched it."

"Thank her anyway."

I turned to leave. Vanderhof's gaze felt like a .38 aimed at my back.

I was reaching for the front door when Cassandra appeared again from a room off the vestibule. She had put on a pair of high heel sandals. They too did a lot for jersey slacks.

"Going so soon," she said.

"Yeah. Your father and I ran out of insults."

Her smile got even bigger.

"Maybe I'll see you again," she said.

"Sure. Just tell your father you'll deliver the Picasso for him."

I added one of Lila's fetching tilts of the head, opened the door and headed for my car. Halfway there, I heard the door close behind me.

I was in no mood to sit around all day listening to my own thoughts and decided to take a drive. It was a nice day. Maybe a bright idea would strike me along the way.

Nearing the bottom of the hill, my phone rang. I looked and saw it was Lila. She had already called and texted me several times that morning. No doubt she was furious with me for not answering but I had no interest in talking to her.

Remembering this Fitzy business, I grabbed the phone and called Kenny instead. He answered after several rings.

"What's up? I don't see you across the street."

"Oh, out for a drive...By the way, did I ever mention this gangsta man character who's been harassing me?"

"I don't think so."

I explained.

"And your point is?"

"I think I'm a racist."

Kenny laughed.

"Seriously. I just find this guy disgusting."

"It's a tough call," he said.

"How do you mean?"

"Well, ask yourself. Would you feel the same way if this guy was white?"

"Yeah, probably."

"See? Peacocks. I can't stand them either. Doesn't matter what color."

"Peacocks, huh?"

"Yeah. Showy."

"Yeah. He's definitely that. *You know what I'm sayin'*?"

Kenny chuckled.

"Careful."

"Yeah…So anyway, I have another project for you."

I explained about Fitzy's daughter.

"See what you can dig up on her. I have a funny feeling that she's been in hot water before. Let's find out why and with whom. That's probably my best lead."

"I'll get right on it."

"Thanks…And what the hell's happening with that police report?"

"I'm supposed to be getting it any day now. Apparently the police in Ohio are being pricks."

"Yeah? Think they're covering up something?"

"Probably. Big time money will do that."

"Yeah. And about QAnon?"

"Oh yeah, sorry. Like I said, too much going on around here but I'd swear they're getting ready to shoot down a passenger jet."

"Get out of here."

"Seriously. I mean, I'm reading between the lines a bit but this chatter just has that feel to it. 'A wounded bird must fall from the sky.' There's been talk like that. Whatever it is, it definitely feels like it's about to go down."

"Maybe I had better run this by my FBI girlfriend."

"I didn't know you had one."

"Yeah. It's a little safer than going out with Lila. They shoot you, but not in the back." Kenny laughed. "Okay, better make the next call. Please get me that goddamned police report."

"I'm trying…And good luck."

I ended the call and dialed Bennie's number.

"What's our status?" I said when he answered.

"The same, boss man. Nada happening here, other than your doll coming and going."

"A little change of plans."

I explained about my sortie, snooping around Ida Huntington's place.

"What do you think that shit means? 'Get rid of her'."

"I don't know. Get rid of Charlotte?"

"Oh man. That's some Shakespearean shit right there."

I had to smile.

"You been reading King Lear again?"

"Pluck their eyes out. You bet your ass."

I smiled again.

"Well, our Goneril wannabe could have been talking about a dog for all I know but I want you to put a tail on her. Just make sure someone's keeping an eye on Caitlin's place."

I read off Ida's address to Bennie.

"You got it. And what are you up to today?"

"Oh, I'm heading out to Potter's old stomping grounds. I'm done waiting around for that son of a bitch. Maybe I can track him down before he finds me...You know, I didn't have a chance to tell you this the other day but I had Kenny dig a little deeper into Abigale Potter's background and guess what?"

"What?"

"Her maiden name was Pritchett."

Bennie rattled off something in Spanish.

"I'm telling you. This is totally some Shakespearean shit."

"Yeah, I'll give you that much."

"So, what? You're thinking Potter and the Pritchetts are mixed up together somehow?"

"Kenny has been unable to establish a connection, but I wouldn't put it past them."

"I wouldn't either. That's just way too much shit to be a coincidence."

"Yeah."

"Shit, boss man. You should have me staking out Cole Pritchett's place."

"You just keep an eye on Ida Huntington...Sorry, but if anyone's going to chase Cole Pritchett around, it'll be me."

"Yeah. Always the juicy gigs."

"Shut up. Anyway, you're in charge in the meantime. If you don't hear from me within 24 hours, call this number."

I read off Alessandra's direct line.

"That's Agent Barretta. I don't know what the hell she'll do but she'll do something. As far as business goes, you have the key to my office. Everything you need to know is in the top drawer of my desk."

"What the hell. You're talking like you ain't never coming back."

A number of things passed through my mind right then, but none of them worth saying.

"Look, I'm just covering all bases. Maybe this amounts to nothing but we're dealing with Potter and if I actually succeed in finding him, who knows what'll happen. He already got the jump on me once."

"Shit, if you're worried about it, take me with you. I'll cover your back."

"It's all right, Bennie. Like I said, it's probably nothing. Anyway, I'm dying to see where this Ida Huntington leads us."

"Is she a looker?"

"Yeah, in fact she is."

"Yeah. That's what I wanted to hear."

"Yeah, well, just take care of business. And make sure someone's watching Caitlin."

"You got it."

"Thanks. And keep me posted."

I had reached the bottom of the hill and was about to turn right, headed east out the canyon, when I noticed a gray Crown Victoria in my rearview mirror. Government plates and the guy behind the wheel right out of central casting; white shirt, black tie and dark Ray-Ban's.

What's the matter, Alessandra? Having trust issues with me again today? I couldn't imagine another government agency putting a tail on me. This definitely had nothing to do with Barnes.

Just to be sure I was being followed, I turned south on Glenneyre, hit the gas and dashed around a couple of cars. It took three long blocks and a stop sign but the driver fought his way through traffic and was back on my tail.

I turned right on Diamond Street and sat there waiting for the light to change at Coast Highway with this guy in my rearview mirror. He appeared to be made of stone. Staring straight ahead. Not a twitch on his face.

When I turned south, he followed. I weighed where best to ditch him while stealing glances in my rearview mirror.

Doheny Beach, I decided. That had to be my best shot.

A mile farther south on Coast Highway, I passed the Presage resort with a protest in progress. Folks were crawling all over the grounds and adjoining blufftop park with signs and banners, chanting away. The odds on Anton's boat launch and eighteen-hole golf course were starting to look more and more like a long shot.

Down the coast and into Doheny Beach, that Crown Victoria remained on my tail. I stayed in the fast lane on my way through town, wanting him to think I was headed left up the long onramp onto the freeway, then at the last second, dashed across three lanes and onto the Coast Highway access road. Tires were screeching and horns honking.

For good measure, I careened around a few more drivers and settled onto the bypass, smiling to myself. I pictured that Fed stuck going up the freeway onramp but as I bore right onto Coast Highway and looked in my rearview mirror, the son of a bitch was careening onto the road behind me. Damn him. The good news was, I had a long line of cars between us. The bad news was, the highway now widened into two lanes each way and remained so for roughly a mile. I had to make the next light, where the road narrowed back down to one lane, with a decent line of cars still separating us. If I could pull that off, I had a good chance of losing him in San Clemente.

I hit the gas again, veered from the fast lane into the empty slow lane and blew past a line of drivers bottled up behind a

412

clown doing forty in a new Mustang, everyone behind him pissed off and ready to have his head. I had seen this movie before and knew exactly what to expect, and the guy in the Mustang did not disappoint me. Powerless in all other things, he had found a way to stick it to humanity, and as sure as god made fools, the minute he saw me blowing by him, he stepped on the gas. If I hadn't been doing ninety, he might have beat me to the green light. As it was, I barreled through the intersection and slipped onto the one lane road with that prick hugging my bumper. He kept on my tail for another quarter mile, furious that someone had escaped his grasp, then settled back down to forty miles an hour and resumed pissing off everyone else in line.

I heard someone back there honking and smiled. The guy in the Crown Victoria was now a good thirty cars behind me.

The one lane highway went on straight for another two miles, then bore left up the hill into San Clemente. My trailer down in Baja popped into my thoughts. I could see it like a framed print in my mind, the waves breaking down the coastline for miles and miles, the afternoon wind whispering secrets in the window screens. The urge was to keep going and cross the border, to have one last moment of peace before the world went entirely mad. That did not seem like too much to ask but I turned left instead and hopped onto Interstate 5, headed north with that Fed nowhere in sight.

The miles went by with various skirmishes going on in my head. And behind it all were three women. One of them represented danger, one sanity, the other one all my abandoned hopes and dreams. One of them had been calling me all morning, and was just now calling me again. One of them probably had a drone overhead, looking for me. The other one could be the sweetest gal in the world in one moment, then as cold as a distant star in the next. And you did not know grief until you had been on the wrong side of clinical depression. Depression made dealing with alcoholism seem like child's play.

Several times I nearly reached for the phone but stopped. Let it go, Devlin. Let it go. Time to throw it all back into the fire. We'll give it another shot next time around, but for now, my dear darling Caitlin, it was best to say adieu.

I drove down the road, seized by that feeling of déjà vu once more. I had been in this exact same moment, in countless other lifetimes, my destiny so close I could almost touch it, but as always, just a bit beyond my reach.

Thirty Two

I was nearing the 91 freeway and easing over into the right-hand lane of the toll road when my phone rang. It was Kenny. I answered.

"What's up?"

"I've got some news on Allison."

"I'm listening."

"You were right. She and a guy named Brandon were picked up as runaways last summer. He's a year older than Allison and had just graduated from high school. Anyway, his parents own a big spread in the Hunt Club."

"That would be the right zip code. So then what?"

"So then, the credit card records show he was on a bit of a spree down in San Diego two days ago. Then suddenly there's a charge for two air fares to Providence."

"Providence? As in Rhode Island??"

"Yeah. Is there another one?"

"Well, yeah. Way up in the sky somewhere." Kenny chuckled. "But I still don't get it. Why Rhode Island?"

"It looks like Brandon has family ties back there."

"Ah, okay. So, go on."

"Then the next charge is for a rental car at the airport and the next one's for a restaurant in Watch Hill. I Googled it. Watch Hill, I mean. Looks like a nice place. Big time money. Taylor Swift has a huge place down there."

"Well, you know me. I've always been dying to rub elbows with her."

"And here's your chance."

"Hmm…So anything else?"

"No, just that I haven't seen any sign of hotel charges, so I'm guessing Brandon's family has a summer place down at the beach or something."

"In Watch Hill."

"Yeah."

"Big time money."

"That's it. Anyway, they've been staying close to the beach and partying, just going by the names. The Oyster Bar. The Crab Shack. Salty's Tavern."

Betty's flippant suggestion popped into my thoughts. 'Why don't you move back east'? Here was my chance, at least for an exploratory mission. While hanging around the shore, looking for Fitzy's daughter, I'd bump into Taylor Swift. We'd exchange glances over beachy cocktails and retreat to her mansion.

"You still there?" Kenny said.

"Yeah yeah. Just having a date with Taylor Swift."

He laughed.

"Listen, I have my hands full right now but keep an eye on the kids for me, will you?"

"Will do."

"And get me that goddamned police report."

"Yes sir."

"Thanks. I'll touch base with you as soon as I'm back in Laurel Lagoon."

"You got it."

I hung up the phone and had a look in the rearview mirror. There was a touch of gray now, and things growing craggy. Would Ms. Swift go for a guy in his fifties? Maybe. Stranger things had happened.

What the hell, Devlin. These wild romances have gotten you nowhere. Just find a doll with money, kick your feet up and enjoy the sweet life.

Then I remembered Lila. She had all the money in the world, and the sweet life appeared to be anything but simple.

It had to be that ancient Egyptian curse. Nothing else could properly explain my checkered destiny.

I turned the phone off, set the question of women on the back burner for the moment and focused on matters at hand.

Some miles later, I came to the 91 freeway, turned south and followed it back out to San Bernardino. Turning east on Interstate 15, I continued up towards the Cajon Pass and took the offramp onto Pearblossom Highway. Ten miles farther up the road, I turned off towards Wrightwood and followed the Angeles Crest Hwy onto Big Pines Hwy. A quarter mile past where Big Pines Hwy turned into Big Pines Road, I pulled onto a dirt road and followed it out to the end.

According to GPS, the Mongol's hideout was roughly a half mile north of me now. My plan was to trek in the backway, hopefully unseen. Alessandra had sent someone to tail me. It was only prudent to assume that she had been talking to Barnes and knew of the Mongols and had someone watching them too. Hell, for all I knew, Barnes was keeping an eye on the place.

I sat there for a moment, trying to make sense of my motives. There was finding Potter, of course. Otherwise, I didn't know what the hell I was doing. Maybe I was just stubborn. That and I had a conscience, and if the latter was a sin, consider me guilty but a young woman had been murdered and I could not get her sad, sorry fate out of my mind.

If nothing else, I owed it to old man Huntington. I hated to think of my worst suspicions being realized, but if so, best for me to give him the news.

Stepping out of the car, I felt a northern breeze tickling my face and looked in that direction. The sky was smoky up over the Sequoias. The news had said they were still battling one fire, about twenty miles this side of Lake Isabella.

I took off my coat and shoulder holster and placed them in the trunk, along with the Smith & Wesson. If those bikers found me packing, they'd probably feed me to their pit bulls. My best shot was to come in peace.

A minute later, I was wearing hiking boots. I grabbed two burner phones, closed the trunk and hit the lock.

Heading off into desert terrain, I was soon bending ankles. Bennie's words about The Devil's Punchbowl came to mind. 'That ought to tell you some shit right there.' I smiled. The man drove me half mad, but life would have been a great deal more boring without him.

A few hundred yards farther to the north, I came to an arroyo, deep enough to have its own ecosystem. I walked along its length, searching for a convenient way down and finally reached the bottom in a cascade of loose soil and rocks.

I paused again in the quiet of the day. There were bird songs and the whisper of wind in the brush. The troubled world was a million miles away.

You really need a long vacation, Devlin. That trip back east was starting to sound enchanting. Find a little hotel along a deserted stretch of shoreline and disappear in among the sand dunes. Reconsider your life.

Remembering Bert's memorial service, the fact of my own mortality stabbed into my heart. It wouldn't be that long and I'd be joining him. Back into the fire. Back into the fire. It was all in passing. But what did it all mean? I felt despair, not having an answer. For all I knew, there were none. We just made up stuff to keep from blowing our brains out.

I stood there with things like justice and honor passing through my mind. What else are you going to do, Devlin? March forward with courage and grace. Show the world that when faced with hardship and pain, you had turned towards nobility, not bitterness and hate.

I brushed at my dusty clothing and started up the far side of the arroyo, fancying myself the righteous soldier now, marching off in the pursuit of mankind's elusive destiny.

Having battled my way to the top, I stopped to take in the terrain. All was quiet. Not an FBI agent or jackrabbit in sight.

After working my way down into and out of another arroyo, I came to be crouched behind some brittlebush and staring across an open expanse at the backside of the Mongols' place. In the silence, laughter spilled out of the open windows. That was encouraging. They appeared to be in a good mood.

There wasn't any cute way of going about the impending encounter. I could expect a gun in my face when I knocked on the door and hopefully we could walk things back from there.

Rather than stumble out into the open, I moved into a line of mesquite on the north side of the house and cautiously made my way towards the front. There, among the trees, I paused again, hearing voices out in the driveway. Whoever it was appeared to be in a jovial mood too so I turned the corner.

One of the bikers was crouched down, working on his Harley. The other two were standing nearby, drinking beers and shooting the shit with him.

"What the fuck?" one of the two spectators said and quickly had a .38 in my face.

The guy working on his Harley stood up and came around his bike, casually wiping his hands on a rag.

"Hey, it's that gringo who was out here the other day with that pure flake."

All three of them were in my face now.

"What the fuck happened to you?" the guy with the gun said. "Looks like you were on the wrong end of an ass kicking."

All three of them were having a good chuckle over that.

"Maybe he's feeling shitty because we didn't shoot his ass."

They had another chuckle. I looked from face to face.

"Yeah. I'm pretty broken up about it."

"Thinks he's a fucking comedian," the third guy said.

He pretended to knee me in the balls and they had another laugh.

"Hey. You bring us any more of that shit?" the guy wiping his hands said.

"No, but I need to talk to Chango."

"No but he needs to talk to Chango."

"Well, fuck. We'd better get a move on then."

"Yeah. When this guy barks, we jump."

I had listened to this jive without displaying the least bit of emotion. The guy with the rag motioned and I was patted down.

"What's with the phones, motherfucker?"

"They're burner phones. One of them's for Chango."

"One of them's for Chango."

"Yeah."

"All right, let's go see him. Then we'll get around to shooting your ass."

I was pointed in the direction of the front door. We walked in on one of the biker chicks giving a guy a blowjob. The other dudes in the room were cheering her on. Some of them were having their own fun. A joint was going around the room. Everyone was loaded up on libations.

"What the fuck?" Chango said at seeing me.

"That's what I said."

The guy with the gun tickled the back of my skull with his gun barrel. The chick giving the blowjob glanced my way once, clearly perturbed to find her handiwork being viewed by a stranger, but otherwise not missing a beat.

Every other eye in the room was now fixed on me. The guy behind me still had his gun at my back.

"I told you we should have shot his ass last time, Chango, and I say now's as good a time as any."

"Naw. Let's see what he has to say first. What brings you back this way, gringo? You bring me some more of that shit?"

I shook my head.

"There's no time for fucking around, Chango. There's some shit going down and we need to talk."

"So talk."

"Alone."

Chango said something in Spanish and all the fun went out of the room. My eyes had remained fixed on him.

"I don't like people telling me how to go about my shit. Got it, gringo?"

"Got it, but we still need to talk."

Chango looked around the room and back at me.

"Fucking gringo," he said and pushed out of his chair. "Let's go talk."

Chango waved me out the front door ahead of him. I walked out past the small concrete porch and turned to face him.

"Spill it," he said. "Potter told me you were working for the fucking law or some shit. Said you had the FBI busting down doors on his ass so you have about one minute to convince me why I shouldn't waste your ass."

I stood there thinking.

"Talk," he said.

"Potter's right. I've been talking to the FBI."

Chango's gun came out of his waistband so fast, you would have needed a stop motion camera to catch it. I stood there with his barrel pressed to my forehead.

"You're about two heartbeats from being dead, motherfucker."

"Look, it's because of Potter that I've been talking to an agent, and because of that, I know they're going to be all over your ass soon, if they aren't already."

"You telling me the FBI's staking out my place?"

"I don't know, Chango. I just came in the back way and didn't see anyone but sooner or later, they're going to make the connection."

"What connection?"

"The weapons you sold Potter."

He let the gun drop to his side and cursed.

"Yeah. I talked to Potter's old piece and she said he had some shit planned to blow up the world. And that shit will get the FBI up your ass every time."

Chango nodded his head slowly.

"Go on. Tell me about this shit with you and the FBI."

I explained about Alessandra. Chango raised his eyebrows when I was done and made a lewd gesture with his fist.

"So, you got a little hmm, hmm, hmm with my Latina sister, huh?"

"Yeah, well. I had to give up something." He smirked. "The point is, I didn't give up you. You know, that shit with Nicholas and the drugs and the Egyptian pottery? I left all of that out of my story."

"So what's all this mean to me, gringo? You telling me I got protection or something?"

I shrugged.

"I think I can buy you some time, but that's it. Sooner or later, I've got to come clean. At least about most of this shit, or I'm going to find my own ass in jail."

"Then why don't I just shoot you and bury your ass out there in the desert?"

"I considered all that before coming out here. Then I figured, you're a reasonable man. You kill me and what have you got? Potter's still out there and the minute he starts talking, it won't matter how many times you bury me in a shallow grave."

Chango looked out over the desert.

"And this Barretta bitch. You're saying you can reason with her?"

I made Chango's lewd gesture with my own fist.

"I'm guessing that bought me a little something."

Chango stared back at me with something of a smile.

"Yeah. She's pretty damned reasonable, but we've got to silence Potter. It's that or the cavalry comes riding in."

"Fuck, I'd put a bullet in his head right now but I don't know where he is. He called me yesterday wanting money and shit and I told him, I ain't got nothing for you, dude."

"Did he say where he was?"

Chango looked out across the desert.

"Down by the coast somewhere. I didn't ask beyond that. I didn't want to know. Now I'm thinking I should have. Better yet, I should never have done business with that sick motherfucker."

I stood there, letting him fume.

"Think he'll call back?" I said after a minute.

Chango looked back at me.

"Maybe."

Chango looked me up and down.

"I don't get it, gringo. What's in this for you? You didn't come all the way out here just to save my ass."

"You've been straight with me, Chango. Why would I wish trouble on you?"

I explained about Lila hiring me to find Holly and to protect both of them.

"So I just got tired of waiting around for the fucker to show up and figured I'd try to find him first."

Chango nodded at the wounds on my head.

"Looks like he already got the jump on you."

"A bit, but I lived to tell about it."

"Yeah. I'll give you that much."

He stood there sizing me up. While he did, I decided to ask the next question on my mind.

"Look, Chango. There's another thing I need to know."

I explained about the body buried out behind Potter's old place.

"Consider that a personal mission but I've got to figure out who she is."

"He never said shit to me about it."

"Didn't figure he would but I had to ask."

Chango nodded.

"So how do I get in touch with you?"

I pulled the two phones out of my back pocket and turned them on.

"Fresh burner phones."

I waited until they had booted up, called one phone from the other and handed the one that was ringing to Chango. He took the call and hung up.

"There. Now we're in touch."

"Okay, gringo. If I hear anything, you'll be the first to know. You good on getting back on your own?"

"I got here on my own. I guess I can get back."

"All right. For a gringo, you're not a total dick."

"Yeah. I work long hours on being just half a dick."

Chango smiled a bit.

"Best get out of here before my boys get a hard on to shoot you."

I turned away.

"And keep my ass posted on this FBI shit," he called after me.

"I'll text you with whatever I learn. You do the same."

I gave him the peace symbol and disappeared back among the mesquite. It seemed like a stroke of luck that I had escaped without a bullet in my back.

Ten minutes later, I was behind the wheel of my Impala and heading back the way I had come. I waited until I was a good twenty miles down the road before turning on my regular phone and dialing Alessandra's number. She answered after several rings.

"Yeah, Michael. Just a second…"

I drove along, waiting.

"So," she said finally. "Long time no see. What are we doing out in the desert today?"

"Oh, just trying to get myself shot…What's happening on your end?"

"Oh, just chasing around after a bunch of bastards who want to blow up the world. And getting nowhere fast…You got something for me?"

"Yeah, but before we move on to that, I want to go over our deal again."

"You mean about Barnes?"

"Yeah. A lot of good it's done me. He was over shaking me down the other day. Wanted to arrest me for withholding evidence."

"What kind of evidence?"

"He doesn't know. He just likes putting my balls in a vice."

"Michael. Please get to the point."

"Okay. For one thing, Potter called me again last night."

"You bastard! And you're just telling me this now?!"

"Sorry. There were personal reasons." I confessed about Caitlin, with all my feelings of anguish and resignation. "I just had to cover this one myself. I'd rather she didn't despise me in parting."

"Michael, I'm sorry for your feelings but you're making it awfully hard for me not to drive over there and arrest you."

"Well, do whatever you have to do but I already had one three ring circus over at her place. I didn't want another one."

"Look, Michael, I need to know your location right now. Your phone has become state's evidence."

"Come on, Alessandra. Give me a break. Potter called from a burner phone. I would have called you right away otherwise."

"You're sure."

"Of course I'm sure. He's not that dumb. I'm not that dumb."

"I'm still sending two men over to keep an eye on your girlfriend's place."

"Alessandra, please. I already have my men over there, 24/7. Any sign of that bastard and I'll call you. And as far as I know, she's no longer my girlfriend."

She sighed.

"And you're absolutely sure he hasn't been around."

"Absolutely. My guess is, he's found better things to do, so consider me saving you resources."

"Is that it, Michael? Or do you have something else to piss me off about today?"

"There is one other thing. You know the Mongols?"

"The name has come to my attention. And what do you know about them?"

"It's a long story."

"Michael. If you don't want to be staring at gray bars and florescent lights by the end of the day, please get to the point."

I told her about Nicholas fencing that 26th Dynasty figurine to the Mongols.

"So, in buying it back, I learned that the Mongols were acquainted with Potter and came out here just now, to see if they had any ideas on how to track him down and it turns out that Potter had called them yesterday."

"Out with it, Michael. Potter's location. Plans. Whatever you know. I'm going to place the part about arresting you on the backburner for now."

"Just chill, Alessandra. Chango doesn't know a damned thing, except that Potter's down at the coast somewhere."

"That's it?"

"That's what he told me."

"Then I'm on my way over there right now with some agents to question him. I'll deal with arresting you later on."

"Goddamn it, Alessandra! Will you stop and listen to me for one second!?"

There was a pause.

"You've got about thirty of them."

"Look, Chango said he'd cooperate. Whatever he finds out, he'll tell us. He has no loyalty to Potter. He understands. Either he gives up Potter or he's going to have you up his ass. And you're going to trade that deal for an all-out war? Because sure as hell, if you folks go riding in there, it's going to turn into a gun battle. People are going to die, Alessandra, and not just on one side."

There was another long pause.

"I don't get it, Michael. Why are you so busy looking out for these boys?"

"I don't know. Kindred spirits, maybe."

She scoffed.

"You really are a piece of work."

"Yeah. So you keep saying."

She was silent.

"All right. I'll give you until tomorrow morning to come up with something useful."

"Thank you."

"Don't stroke me, Michael. My feelings could change at any minute...And you'd better be on the phone with me the second that bastard calls you."

"I will."

"Tomorrow morning, max, and then I'm turning the dogs loose."

"Fine."

I was waiting for Alessandra to say something more but the line went dead. I stared at the screen for a moment before setting the phone down.

Tomorrow morning. I sat there huddled by my campfire, with darkness all around me and no idea which way to turn. Never mind all the personal grief that was tearing me up inside. If Alessandra ever figured out I'd been withholding evidence on her, I really would be staring at gray bars.

Thirty Three

Heading down the road, my mind decided it was a prudent time to do a bit of soul searching, and the truth was, I didn't know why I'd be doing much of anything right then. Beyond finding a Picasso, Holly and some jewelry, I was like an inanimate object, propelled forward by inertia and little else.

Regarding the Picasso, if Vanderhof was to be believed, it would miraculously appear at my doorstep one day soon, and the jewelry was most likely a write off. Seeing it materialize would be nothing short of a miracle. That left my continuing search for Holly on Lila's behalf, which, of necessity, meant I was searching for Potter too, an endeavor that overlapped with protecting Caitlin and left me baffled as to who was paying for what. I was currently racking up a boatload of expenses. That much I knew.

Well, that was a matter for another day. I needed to find Potter, whatever the cost. If I didn't, I'd have Barnes saddling me with criminal charges any day now. Maybe Alessandra too. I needed Potter to be either dead or behind bars. I preferred seeing him dead, but that really wasn't my call.

Finally, there were my personal crusades, which in the main involved figuring out who had killed and buried that poor young woman in a shallow grave. The question would not leave me alone and led me inevitably back to Potter. It also led me back to a handful of other people who might have

428

knowledge on the subject: Nicholas, Ida Huntington and Holly among them.

Twenty miles farther down the road, I arrived at the junction with Interstate 15 and turned west towards the coast. A big sign straddled the freeway up ahead. I would soon be obliged to veer north onto 91 and head towards home.

I had driven another mile or so, depressed by the idea of giving up, when a moment of clarity suddenly struck me. It all seemed so obvious in hindsight. I could have kicked myself for not seeing this sooner. It was as if I had been sitting in a dark room for days and someone had opened a door to the light.

When it came to Potter's whereabouts, I actually had three clues: Jake's mention of Potter's connection down south, Potter having told Chango that he was still down by the coast and that old Camaro going by me, the day that John and I had driven back from Fallbrook. I had wondered then if it wasn't Cole Pritchett and it struck me now as just one more piece of a puzzle falling into place, everything pointing in the same direction.

With the offramp onto Interstate 215 barreling towards me, I turned off my phone, eased over to the right and took the long, cloverleaf loop, heading south. The miles flew by with doubts beginning to gnaw away at my moment of clarity. Wasn't this the sort of thing that schizophrenics experienced? A blinding light of certainty? Which everyone else knew to be madness?

Well, whatever it was, I had nothing better to do than run down my hunch.

At the exit for Old Highway 395, I pulled off the interstate and turned into the parking lot of a Mexican dive, which was the first restaurant that happened along. A sign out in front said that it had been a stage coach stop back in the day. I parked next to an arbor with some sun speckled picnic tables beneath it. A nice grove of oaks and sycamores bordered the parking lot behind me.

It was well past lunch but still well before dinner so the restaurant was mostly empty when I walked in. A Mexican kid and two waitresses were prepping tables out in front. I headed for the darkened bar in back. Old barn wood paneled the walls. The bartender was polishing glasses.

Having ordered a taco plate, I sat there with a view of the sun speckled picnic tables. The oaks and sycamores out beyond the parking lot brought to mind the days of my youth. This was the original Southern California. Chaparrals and dry gulches. Without sprinklers, the place was a desert.

The food came and was good. The quietude of the bar was both comforting and discomforting to me. I felt like a fallen man. I was a fallen man.

When I got to thinking that a cold beer sounded good, I paid the bill and headed out into the woods. I was waiting for sundown and darkness and had at least another hour to kill.

A hundred feet in amongst the trees, the bustle of the world fell away. I sat down on a log, wanting dearly to cleanse my soul of all that had happened, of the many mistakes and foolish decisions I had made over the course of a lifetime, of all the misery and suffering I had caused. To leave behind all my own pain and confusion. To see the world again as it had been to me as a young boy.

Some minutes later, a thought occurred to me. To be forgiven, you must forgive. Okay, I forgive everyone and everything. Now please let me find peace.

The hour passed with me lost in matters of the spirit.

When it was time to move, I texted Chango from my burner phone.

Barretta gave us 24 hours. If we can't deliver Potter by then, you'd best be on the move. I'm down south, following up on another lead. You'll know the minute I know something. Or...

I slipped the phone into my pocket, headed back to the car and drove slowly towards an equestrian operation over on South Mission Road. Google satellite showed a dirt trail leading from just south of that point up a hill to the back side of Shady

Hill Lane. When I neared the location, I pulled to the side of the road, waited for traffic to clear and made a U-turn. By the time I got the Impala parked back amongst a thicket of trees, I was invisible to anyone passing by on the street. The equestrian operation had already closed for the day but it was near enough for me to hear the horses nicker and snort and move about in their stalls.

I went around to the trunk, changed into black clothing and began placing an arsenal into my backpack; a directional mic, infrared goggles, binoculars, duct tape, zip ties and a pair of handcuffs. The Glock and silencer went into my shoulder holster. A Walther PPS M2 went into an ankle holster.

With the trunk closed, I paused with a look around me. It was a lovely, dry evening, with the last light of day quickly settling into a velvety twilight. The hill loomed high above me. A large outcropping of rock girded the crest. I wasn't sure what I would find on the other side of those rocks, but I pulled the balaclava down over my face, threw the backpack over my shoulder and started up the trail, ready for whatever the universe had in store for me.

My hearing quickly grew alert to the night but my eyes were still adjusting to the growing darkness and I nearly tripped over a big male raccoon. He rose up defensively with his paws.

"It's all right, buddy," I whispered and he moved off into the brush.

The trail grew increasingly steep as it zigzagged back and forth. I heard an owl. The radio waves of an infinite universe hummed in my ears. I pressed forward to the sound of my own breathing.

I eventually came to the base of the rock outcropping and looked back down at the road. It was a good four hundred feet below me. I could see my car hidden among the gathering of trees and the equestrian operation with its barns and corrals and riding tracks.

Google map had placed old man St. Claire's home a few hundred yards to the other side of where I stood. Assuming

431

that was correct, and my moment of clarity had amounted to anything, I just might find him harboring a fellow white supremacist.

Turning back toward the rock outcropping, I walked along it until I found a way up and settled into a level area of sandy soil on the crest. A parapet like notch in the rocks provided me with a clear view to the backside of St. Claire's house. The terrain sloped gently downwards in that direction, pocked with shrubs, some of them above a man's head.

I got the binoculars out and studied the house. It looked far more sprawling from this vantage point than it had from the front. Soft light spilled out from a line of sliding glass doors and windows. I saw no signs of anyone moving around inside.

I watched and waited. I had thoughts. I harbored hopes and dreams. I battled fears and doubts.

When I saw a man pass by one of the sliding glass doors, I reached for the binoculars but he was already out of sight by the time I looked. It had appeared to be Stephen St. Claire and a moment later he returned into view, only with his old man this time. They were arguing. Then two other men appeared and one of them pushed Stephen and pointed towards the other end of the house. Stephen pushed him back and a tussle ensued. It was hard to be certain, given the distance and soft lighting, but neither of the men appeared to be Potter.

I had pulled the binoculars away to rub my eyes when I heard a gunshot and quickly trained the binoculars back on the house. Stephen now lay crumpled on the floor. The old man stood there talking with the other men in what appeared to be a casual manner. I refocused on Stephen. He lay there motionless. A moment later, the other two men picked up the body and carried it out of sight.

Jesus Christ. The old man had just witnessed his son being killed like they were out shooting rabbits.

I got out the directional mic and aimed it at the house. The men were no longer in sight but I heard voices. I readjusted the earphones and moved the mic around until I could make out snippets of conversation. Something was said about LAX and Saudia Airlines and missile launchers already being in place.

Then, amidst the bits of conversation, I heard Potter's voice. He quickly took charge and told everyone to be ready to move out at midnight. There was talk of what to do with the dead body and the old man said he'd deal with it. Just take care of the mission. There was what sounded like a congratulatory moment and the voices dispersed. I saw men moving around the house with more urgency now but no sign of Holly. Had she gotten away again? Or did they have her tied up inside somewhere? Not knowing the answer to that question, I had no choice but to sit and wait. I couldn't risk getting her killed in a shootout.

I turned on another burner phone and called Alessandra. She picked up with the usual pause.

"So what have you got to piss me off about now, Michael?"

"Give me a break. I'm calling to save your ass."

I explained everything I had just heard.

"You're saying that Potter's in your sights right now!?"

"Not in my sights but he's here."

"Address, Michael."

"You're not listening to me, kid. The team with the fireworks is already up there. Saudia Airlines. A flight after midnight. I heard something about Vista Del Mar so I'm guessing they're planning to set up in that state park down by the shore. That would give them a clear shot at an outgoing flight. Plenty of height. Plenty of speed. You'd have a total failure with no survivors."

"Address, Michael."

"Sorry, sweetheart. No can do. They might have Holly inside."

"Michael! This is not fucking optional!"

"Sorry. Gotta go. You know what to do on your end. I'll take care of Potter and his boys down here and keep you posted."

"Goddamn it! Don't you dare hang up on…"

I did and felt Alessandra's wrath across the miles. Hopefully she would do as asked. Hopefully I could deliver Potter to her in return. If not, I expected to be in a holding cell by tomorrow morning. Maybe sooner.

I turned my phone back off and sat there weighing what to do.

A minute later, I heard pebbles cascading down the rock formation. Someone was climbing up towards me. I quietly got the Glock out and waited. Then a head appeared, roughly ten feet away. It was Potter. He sat down facing towards the house, unaware of my presence.

I suppressed my breathing and watched. His scent came on the wind. He was wearing some kind of aftershave.

Then Potter's head turned, as if he had he caught my scent. It would have been easy enough to kill him. His head was directly in my sights, but I had to find out if Holly was here first. Then I would deal with Potter's fate, and if killing him became necessary, I would. For now, my only thought was how to restrain him without alerting anyone inside.

Once Potter had looked back towards the house, I inched forward, then waited and inched forward again. I was about to move forward a third time when Potter looked to his right. He seemed to sense something behind him and turned his head back my way. I felt sure he was staring right into my eyes, and ready to pull his own gun, but after a long moment, he looked back in the direction of the house. I assumed he had failed to pick out my black clothing against the darkness.

I waited a good minute before inching closer and slowly raising the Glock, preparing to strike, but Potter noticed the motion in his peripheral vision and ducked. The butt of my gun struck him glancingly on the temple, not on the back of his head, as intended, and he quickly dropped out of sight. He was wounded but still very much awake and dangerous.

I quickly pulled on the infrared goggles and peered over the rocks, looking for any sign of him. Nothing. Potter had already disappeared into the brush.

I gathered everything into my backpack, moved to my left some distance, scampered down to level ground and paused to listen. Nothing. It figured he hadn't gotten far. He was probably dazed and trying to text his friends for backup.

I scurried laterally another thirty feet and inched forward into the brush, stopping every few feet to look and listen. I was another fifteen feet along when I caught sight of Potter, crouched in the distance behind a bush. He had his phone in one hand and a gun aimed back towards the rock outcropping.

I maneuvered well around to his backside and inched forward again. The brush was thick enough to keep Potter hidden from my view until the last minute. Then he was suddenly across a small clearing from me.

In that split second, he sensed my presence and came around with his gun. I clipped him in the shoulder and the gun reflexively dropped from his hand. While he scrambled to pick it up from the sandy soil, I rushed forward and got him into a headlock. Being a heavyweight to his middleweight, I had the advantage but he was like a wild animal and it took every bit of my strength to keep him from escaping.

Our struggle had been ongoing for several seconds when he became aware of my ankle holster and reached for the gun. I rolled my legs away and wrenched harder against his throat with my forearm. That brought his hands back up in a desperate effort to regain his breath.

His struggles slowly diminished but I kept the pressure on. I didn't want him dead, but I didn't want him waking up any time soon, either.

Once he was out, I got up like a cheetah after its kill and had a look around. All appeared to be quiet back at the house. Potter had started a text but failed to send it. I quickly retrieved my backpack, got his hands and feet ziplocked and duct taped his mouth. With another look around, I threw him over my shoulder and lugged him up to a suitable spot among the rocks. With his back against a large stone, I duct taped him to it. He was coming out of his blackout as I tore the tape from the roll.

Comfortable that he wasn't going anywhere, I pulled the balaclava back. The fury in his eyes was visceral.

"Yeah. You should have killed me when you had the chance, Potter."

I pulled out my burner phone and paused there, looking out over the lights of Fallbrook, troubled by the moral and spiritual question at hand. What I was thinking to do amounted to murder.

That was on one side of the ledger. On the other was the fact that if Potter lived, he would remain a menace; to Holly, to Lila, to me and everything decent, and that was even if they did sentence him to life without parole. The man was better off dead, and yet I hesitated. Executing the law wasn't my job.

I looked over at Potter, saw the hatred in his eyes, his soul burning with vengeance and decided, to hell with it. I will live with this for the rest of my life, but it will be a better world without that son of a bitch in it. Maybe he'd have better luck in his next lifetime but nothing was going to change the man he was in this one.

I called Chango.

"What do you know, gringo?"

"I've got him."

"No shit."

"Yeah. He's wearing zip ties and a couple of pounds of duct tape."

"And what's the plan."

"You okay with ending this?"

"Damn straight. You just tell me where."

I gave Chango my location.

"Call me when you're near and I'll guide you in."

"You got it."

"And I don't suppose I need to say, hurry."

"Give me forty-five. I came down to the coast looking for the son of a bitch myself so we're not far."

"I'll try to neutralize everyone else in the meantime."

"You got it, gringo."

I ended the call and looked back at Potter.

"Chango's on his way to deal with you. Consider this justice for the young woman you buried out behind your old place. You've got about an hour to get right with your maker."

Potter contorted violently against his bindings. I was sick of looking at him and climbed back down to level ground. The text Potter had planned to send was an attempt to warn his friends. I changed the wording.

> You're not going to believe this shit. I caught that private dick out here trying to get a drop on us. Get your asses out here and bring some duct tape and zip ties. I've got a gun to his head by the base of those rocks.

I sent the message and watched the house. A few seconds later, the two men appeared at one of the sliding glass doors and opened it. The old man appeared behind them. I waved over my head from behind some brush. One of them waved back and started my way. The other one headed back into the house. I got down out of sight, pulled the balaclava back over my face, moved the night vision goggles into position and moved a good distance laterally.

Fifty feet farther into the brush, I raised my head to look and saw the one man moving forward with his AR-15 at the ready. The other one was still back at the house, I assumed loading up on supplies and ammunition.

A thought passed coldly through my mind while waiting there. At least one of these men had to die, and with that, the other one might get to live.

"Potter!" the man nearest me called out. "Where the fuck are you!?"

When he failed to get an answer, he grew wary. I reflexively checked the silencer on the Glock and scrambled to converge on his path.

"Potter!" he called out again.

437

I was fifteen feet away now and with a clear shot. What's it going to be, Devlin? Kill or wound? Holly could be back there in that house, bound and gagged and expendable if these men found themselves cornered.

The man turned his head back towards his buddy, having sensed something wrong.

What's it going to be, Devlin?

I saw his mouth open, ready to call out, and took the shot. He gasped from the slap of the bullet into his brain cavity and went down face first, the warning he had intended to give caught in his throat. I scrambled over to his body and checked for a pulse. He was still alive, but wouldn't be for long.

While I knelt there, his buddy called out, "Hey Brad! What the fuck? Where are you?"

And hearing the voice, my hair stood up on end. It was Cole Pritchett, barely fifty feet away now, and with his own AR-15 strapped across his chest.

In a way, it seemed far too convenient, all the pieces of the puzzle fitting so neatly together, but there it was; Potter and the Pritchett clan and the alt-right militia madness so natural to both of them. As Jim Harrison had once told me, rats on a sinking ship tended to flock together. Well, we definitely had some rats on a sinking ship here. My only regret was having killed this man instead of Cole.

I pulled the infrared goggles down, scrambled his way twenty feet and waited. A moment later, he came into my sights, wary and moving forward with his AR-15 at the ready.

I waited until we were ten feet apart and clipped him on his right arm. He yelped and reflexively dropped the weapon. I clipped him again near his right knee and he went down swearing. I swiftly closed the remaining few feet and caught him square in the side of his head with my boot. He went limp with a grunt.

I moved the AR-15 out of reach and checked him for other weapons before tying him up and taping his mouth shut. I left him with hands and feet bound together behind his back and headed for the house.

Thirty Four

The old man stood outside one of the sliding glass doors with the shotgun in his hands, searching for any sign of his fellow conspirators. Like his son, he seemed oddly proportioned with the same oversized head that did not fit the rest of his body. He was definitely larger than I remembered him and not to be trifled with, despite his age. For a man in his late '80s or early '90s, he looked strangely robust. The rifle certainly embellished that image.

I remained crouched down just beyond the line of brush bordering the back of his property, watching him. I was close enough to get a shot off but not close enough to ensure it would kill him, and I was uncomfortable with the idea of leaving him a wounded animal at that distance. Alive, he would no doubt fire on me if I tried to close the gap between us, and it looked as if he knew how to use the gun.

He had been sniffing the wind and looking increasingly wary when he turned and went back into the house. As soon as he was out of my sight, I ran to the nearest corner of the building, keeping one eye towards the front, in case the old man had thoughts of sneaking around from behind me.

I had been standing there for roughly a minute, waiting and wondering what to expect when I heard the old man's footsteps on the concrete patio and peeked around the corner. He had the pit bull on a leash and it did not take the dog two seconds to catch my scent.

I quickly retreated several paces and waited. Moments later, the pit bull bolted into view like it had been shot out of a cannon. I put a bullet into its head and it yelped but kept coming. It took two more bullets to drop it to the ground.

I had a split second to make a decision. Retreat or charge. I took the old man to be a worthy adversary, but hardly nimble. Figuring he'd have the shotgun aimed chest high, I got down low and rolled out into the open. The old man was nearly on top of me as I did. I fired upwards and he went down as if someone had kicked him in the groin. There was blood in his eyes as I stood above him and kicked the gun away from his hands. For good measure, I clocked him on the back of his head with my Glock and he went out. A minute later, I had him bound and gagged. He was bleeding badly so I ripped off part of his shirt and tied off his leg at the top. He groaned and came half awake. I had missed both his genitals and femoral artery by about two inches.

I checked the time and headed inside to clear the house. I had no reason to believe there were more of Potter's men hanging around but proceeded as if that was the case, room by room, the back of the house first, then each bedroom. Opening the last door, I found a dead Stephen St. Claire but no sign of Holly. Just to be sure, I dashed back through the house, checking and double checking every square inch of it, but nothing. No sign of her anywhere.

I went back outside and stood there thinking. Maybe Holly had gotten away. Or maybe Potter had come to believe that she was a liability and did away with her.

I checked the time again. Ten or fifteen minutes before Chango was expected to arrive. There was nothing to do but go see what I could extract from Potter.

Before heading his way, I dragged the old man inside and duct taped him to the island in his kitchen, then retraced my steps to where I had left Cole tied up. Like a rat in a trap, he strained against his restraints upon seeing me.

"Yeah, Cole," I said. "Fancy meeting you here. Just so you know, the FBI is up at LAX right now, thwarting your big plans. You'll be talking to them firsthand in a little while."

He strained violently at the duct tape and zip ties again. I made sure everything was secure and headed back to Potter. He was right where I had left him. If anything, he looked more venomous. For men like him, there was an equivalency between defeat and hatred, between powerlessness and revenge, and this was true of Potter in spades. His eyes spoke of the horrors he would visit upon me, given the chance.

"Now it's my turn," I said. "Where is she?"

He looked at me in a way that left no doubt as to his answer. Fuck you.

My impulse was to put a bullet in one of his kneecaps, but what was the point? He wasn't going to talk, and I wasn't ready to kill him in cold blood.

I walked away a number of paces and urinated, then stood there looking out over the back of the rock outcropping, waiting. Time passed. A few cars came and went.

Finally, a black Suburban appeared from the direction of the freeway and slowed to a crawl. My burner phone rang a few seconds later.

"Where are you, gringo?" Chango asked.

"Look up towards the top of the hill above you."

I turned my phone flashlight on and off several times.

"Got it?"

"Got it."

"Turn around. There's a place to park back among those trees. You'll see my car and a trail that leads up the hill."

"See you in a few."

I stood there watching Chango turnaround and pull back in among the trees. Soon, he and three of his men were zigzagging up the trail. Once they had scrambled up beside me, I walked them over to Potter. At seeing Chango, Potter tried to say something through the duct tape.

"I'm guessing he thinks you're the cavalry riding in."

Chango nodded.

"So what are we doing here?"

"Your call, but the body has to be found."

"No problem there. I'll make sure he's got a smile on his face when I'm done with him...So is that it? Are we going down now?"

"Yeah. I need to call my Latina friend. Then the cavalry will definitely be riding in."

"What are you going to tell her?"

"Everything that went down here, except in my version, Potter got away and you were never here. As long as we both stick to that story, we'll be fine."

"All right. Let's do this."

Two of his men quickly had Potter cut loose from the rock. One of them was as big as a grizzly bear and threw Potter over his shoulder. When Potter commenced to kick and struggle, he said, "Oh, fuck this," set Potter back on his feet, clocked him with a good right and threw the now limp Potter back over his shoulder. I gathered up all the loose duct tape and followed them down the hill.

"Are we good?" Chango said when we reached his Suburban.

"Yeah, except that son of a bitch did something with my client's daughter and I don't know what?"

Chango looked over at Potter. Two of his boys had him sandwiched between them in the backseat of the Suburban.

"I heard some shit about her from Nicholas," Chango said.

My eyes opened wide.

"You were talking to Nicholas?"

"Yeah. I knew he knew Potter, so I figured, let's go check his shit out. Potter wasn't there but we questioned Nick real good and he spit out how Potter had sold her off to him. Just to have some traveling money, and some guy Nick knew was going to put the squeeze on the old lady for some serious ransom dough."

"Then where's Holly?"

"Don't know. All I know is, the bitch wasn't there."

"Fuck," I said. "And you don't know who this other son of a bitch is?"

Chango shook his head.

"That just sounds crazy."

I thought for a moment and pointed my chin back up the hill.

"And this scene? Did Nicholas know anything about it?"

Chango shook his head. I shook my head back, unconvinced.

"Don't worry yourself. The dude's already short one finger. I told him if he didn't keep his mouth shut, I'd cut his dick off next…Anyway, we gotta blow. And, hey, you surprised me, gringo. I pictured Potter eating your lunch."

I touched the wounds on my head.

"It could have gone either way."

Chango smiled, flicked two fingers at his forehead and climbed in. I backed up a few paces as he pulled the Suburban around.

Once they had disappeared down the road, I opened the trunk of my Impala and stripped down. The combat gear went into a black plastic bag for disposal, along with all the duct tape I had used to tie up Potter. All my gear got wiped down with bleach and put away.

As soon as I was settled back behind the wheel, I turned on my regular phone. It booted up and immediately went off with a dozen alerts. Lila had been texting and calling me all day. One of the texts was in all caps.

MY DAUGHTER'S BEEN KIDNAPPED!!! WHERE IN GOD'S NAME ARE YOU???!!!

I started the Impala, pulled back onto South Mission Road and called her.

"My god, where have you been?!" she said in answering. "I've called you a thousand times today! I don't suppose you know that Holly's been kidnapped!"

"I know. I saw your text."

444

"Oh, you know…Then why haven't you called me?!"

"Look. I've had the FBI up my ass and had to turn my phone off."

"Oh great. And in the meantime, my daughter could have been killed."

"Look, just tell me what's going on. I'll explain everything when I get there."

There was a pause.

"I received a text message from a blocked number this afternoon, telling me that they had Holly and were demanding a million dollars."

"How long did they give you to deliver the money?"

"Until tomorrow night."

"What did you tell them?"

"I told them okay. What was I going to say?"

"Did you call the police?"

"God no. That's the next thing they told me. Call the police and your daughter's dead."

"So when do you expect to hear from them again?"

"They said later tonight. Early tomorrow at the latest."

"All right. I'm in North County San Diego but I'm heading your way right now. Don't do anything until I get there."

"As if I would know what to do…God, I can't believe you haven't answered my calls all day."

"I told you. I'll explain everything when I get there. Just sit tight and we'll figure this out."

"How long?"

"About an hour. Maybe sooner."

"I'll be waiting."

I hung up and called Alessandra.

"I am so pissed at you, Michael," she said in answering.

"I know. Did you get 'em?"

"I take it you're still not checking the news."

"Who has fucking time?"

There was a pause.

"Yeah, we got 'em. Two of them dead, one of ours wounded. They tried to get a missile off in the middle of a firefight and hit a hangar alongside the runway. We had to shut down flights in and out of LAX for an hour…And I'm still pissed at you."

"Yeah."

"Don't 'yeah' me."

"Yeah."

"Out with it, Michael. What the hell happened down there? Did you get Potter?"

"Nope."

"Goddamn you!"

"Just relax. I got one bullet into him. He's not going far. And the rest of his crew down here are accounted for. Two men bound and gagged. One dead."

There was a pause.

"And that's your kill?"

"Yeah. It was me or him."

"You all right?"

"Yeah, I'm all right but one of the boys tied up down here is Cole Pritchett. You know the name?"

"Pritchett rings a bell. Domestic abuse case of some kind, wasn't it?"

"If you call pimping your own daughters domestic abuse."

"Yeah. So what's that mean to me?"

"Look. That clan's a hornet's nest so I'm guessing he's not the only one involved here."

I explained about seeing Cole's Camaro that day down in Fallbrook.

"I'll follow up on it. Now are you ready to give me the address?"

"Actually, I don't remember the street number but it's the last place on Shady Hill Lane. You can't miss it."

"Then you wait there. I'll have a team on site in less than half an hour."

"Sorry Alessandra, but I've got to go."

"Goddamn it, Michael! You stay right where you are!"

"Look, I'll be in touch soon. Tomorrow at the latest and you can charge me with whatever the hell it is you want to charge me with but I've got things to do right now and they can't wait."

"What kind of things?"

"Things."

"Damn it, Michael. You're making it awfully hard for me not to arrest you."

"I know. You've said that."

I explained where to find the old man and the two men outside.

"I'm doing the best I can here, Alessandra."

"Well, I am so pissed at you, I don't even want to say this…but thanks. You saved a lot of lives tonight."

"Thanks. I've been looking for redemption all day."

"Yeah?"

"Yeah."

"Well, I'd give you an official benny but you've broken so many laws along the way, I don't know where to start."

"I know…You need me for anything, just let me know."

"Then keep your goddamned phone on."

"I'll try."

"Bastard."

"I know. We'll grab a drink once things have calmed down and clear the air."

"Fat chance."

I had to smirk.

"Bastard," Alessandra said again and hung up on me.

I had been motoring up route 76 while talking with Alessandra and was soon merging onto Interstate 5. Traffic was light at that hour. I settled into the center lane doing seventy. The adrenalin was starting to wear off and my deeds starting to haunt me. That slap of a bullet into a man's brain cavity…The gasp…The death that is irreversible.

Grasping for any kind of distraction, I reached for my phone and called Bennie.

"Wow, boss man," he said at hearing my voice. "I've kind of been missing you. It's been a couple of hours since you last beat my balls and I'm like going through withdrawals."

"I appreciate the humor Bennie but this is no time for jokes. Some serious shit just went down."

I quickly explained the scene at old man St. Claire's place, but just the way I had explained it to Alessandra. Potter had gotten away and no mention of the Mongols.

"Fucking special forces shit or what? How come I never get in on the action?"

"Look, Bennie. We'll talk more about it later but you never kill a man gleefully…So what's happening on your end?"

"I've got John watching Caitlin's place and I'm keeping an eye on this Ida doll, like you aksed me."

"Yeah? And anything new?"

"Not much. She drove across town to this condo a few hours back. Wasn't in there five minutes when she marched right back out. And she was plenty pissed off when she did."

"Yeah? About what?"

"I don't know but those high heels were hitting the concrete hard."

"And that's it?"

"She hit a liquor store on her way back home, and she is a nice looking bitch. I was thinking to go in and have a glass of wine with her."

"Yeah, you do that, Bennie."

"Just joking. So what are you doing next?"

"Look, I really can't explain that right now…Okay?"

"Yeah, okay. Got it."

"All right. But let me know the minute Ida's on the move again."

"I will."

"And make sure John stays right where he is."

"Don't worry. He'll be there."

"Good. I'm still hung up on my end but I'll hook up with you the minute I'm free."

I had motored past most of the Marine Base while talking with Bennie and now had the inspection station sign in my sights. Thankfully, the gates were closed. Only the big rig weigh station was operating at that hour.

I zipped past a long queue of idling 18-wheelers and was soon entering the palmy suburbs of San Clemente again. I checked my watch. I had made it north with time to spare and considered stopping by Nicholas' place but put the idea on hold. I wanted to hear Lila's story first. Once again, something didn't smell right with that woman.

A couple of driveways down from Lila's house, I spotted two men in a parked car and assumed Alessandra to be involved. They perked up at the sight of my car going by and watched with interest as I pulled into her long driveway.

I parked in front of the garage, texted Lila to let her know I was there and went around to the front door. The entrance had been completely repaired already, right down to the paint job; not a single sign of it being a Beirut warzone.

The porch light came on as I approached from the walkway and the door opened.

"Oh, Michael," Lila said and threw herself at my chest. We were there several seconds before she pulled back. "I still can't believe you didn't answer my calls all day."

"Come on. Let's get inside and I'll explain."

She closed the door behind us and drooped dramatically at the shoulders.

"Will it ever end?"

"Come on," I said again and herded her down the hallway.

"Something to drink?" she said.

"Sure."

"The usual?"

"Yeah."

I joined her in the kitchen and sat at the bar while she poured me some club soda. I took a long drink.

"So?" she said.

"Look, tell me what's going on first. Where do things stand?"

"I don't know. I'm supposed to come up with a million dollars by tomorrow at the latest."

"And for argument's sake, are you able to do that?"

"Yes and no. I have the money but it's not that easy to come by in cash."

"Okay. The upside to that option is, no police, no press and you get Holly back."

"And the downside is, they shoot my daughter and keep the money."

"Things would have to be arranged properly, sure. Hell, you could get the police involved and have things blow up on you."

"Oh god. What a nightmare." Lila crossed the kitchen to a cupboard and returned with an opened bottle of Pinot Noir. "I hope you don't mind."

I shook my head.

"Please, sit down," I said once she had her glass of wine.

She did so and looked at me expectantly. I proceeded to explain what had happened down in Fallbrook, again, telling it exactly as I had told Alessandra.

"My god," Lila said was I was done. "I can't imagine it...Killing another human being."

She gazed off into space, shaking her head. I stared at her profile. Either she was very innocent, or a very good actor.

"Oh god," she said, looking back at me. "And after all of that, that madman is still out there."

I held her gaze.

"Look. What I'm about to tell you is not what I told FBI and the rest of the world. And you never repeat it. Anywhere...to anyone...Understood?"

She nodded.

"You'll never have to worry about Potter again."

She stared. I sipped at my club soda. A moment later, Lila placed a hand on my forearm.

"Thank you, Michael."

I nodded.

"So what are we doing here?"

"We're waiting, I guess."

"Then I want to get something straight with you right now."

She nodded.

"Do you have any idea who's behind this kidnapping? Any reason to think it's an inside job?"

She shook her head. I watched her eyes.

"No idea at all?"

She shook her head again. I stared for a long moment and stood up. I hated the feeling, but I just didn't trust the woman.

"I'm going to get comfortable in the living room."

Lila came along behind me. I settled onto one of her sofas.

"Do you mind?" she said.

I shook my head. She kicked off her high heels and curled up beside me. I stared out to sea. Lila sipped at her wine and set her glass down.

"Have you always been a private detective?"

"Yeah. I came out of the womb wearing a .38."

She made a face.

"You know what I mean."

"No. I was going to college and already getting restless when I noticed this ad in a local newspaper. It sounded a hell of a lot more exciting than calculus so I responded. And went to work for this guy named Jack Oliver."

I told Lila a bit about my early days as a young pup in the business.

"He sounds irascible," she said, referring to Jack.

"Still is."

"He's still alive?"

"Yeah. I think it'll take a silver bullet. Anyway, I spent half my days wanting to shoot the son of a bitch, but he was good. Taught me patience and determination. The determination came naturally enough to me, the patience not so much…Still doesn't."

Lila had a sip of her wine. Her gaze was out to sea.

"I'm glad I hired you, Michael. I really can't imagine anyone else doing what you've done."

"You mean, lose your daughter twice and not call you back all day long?"

She made another face.

"I'll tell you this much. I wouldn't want you chasing after me."

I didn't answer. Lila placed her wine goblet down and began to play with the front of my shirt.

"I need to tell you something," she said with a look up into my eyes. "You've probably guessed this already but I've found myself falling for you along the way."

She watched her own hands playing with the front of my shirt. I became aware of her lovely pale feet.

"I just had to say it. So maybe once things have finally settled down a bit."

She looked up at me. I nodded back.

"Well, don't get too excited."

Thirty Five

Lila had started to draw her lips near mine when a text dinged on her phone. She quickly reached for it.

"It's them," she said.

The message simply read.

Well?

"Do you have an iPad with a keyboard?" I asked her.

"In my office."

"Please go grab it."

She hurried off in that direction.

"Are you going to answer them?" she said over her shoulder.

"Yes."

She returned with the iPad a few seconds later. I set it up on the coffee table and typed a message.

Mrs. Evergreen has hired me to negotiate the exchange for her. Our terms. No police. No press. No bullshit. We get Holly. You get your money. Do you have any problems with that?

I turned to Lila.

"Okay?"

She nodded and I sent the message. We sat there staring at the screen for most of a minute before an answer came back.

No.

I typed another message.

Okay. First thing, we need proof that Holly is still alive. Take a photo of her with something dated in the photo. A newspaper. Whatever you can think of and send it.

The response took a bit longer but a photo finally came back with Holly holding an iPhone and the date visible on the start screen. The backdrop was noticeably a plain wall. Holly looked a bit ragged but fiercely unwavering.

"Oh, my little baby," Lila said, touching the screen.

She reached for a tissue.

"They couldn't fake that date, could they?"

I shook my head and typed another message.

Okay. We'll go to the bank first thing tomorrow morning. In the meantime, we'll need to think of some way to execute the exchange. If you have any ideas, feel free to share them but it will need to be a straight exchange. The money for Holly. We'll want to see that she's alive and well or no deal.

I sent it and looked at Lila. She held onto my arm. A moment later, a return text came through with just a 'thumbs up' symbol. Lila let out a big sigh.

"Now what?"

I drank the last of my club soda and stood up.

"I need to go do some detective work."

Lila stood up with me.

"But nothing rash, Michael. Please. Let's just give them the money. I don't want anything happening that might endanger my daughter."

"Understood."

She pressed her body closer to mine.

"And please think about what I said."

"Which part?"

"About us."

"Okay."

We stopped at the front door and Lila stood there looking up at me.

"I'll call you as soon as I know something."

After a long look, Lila stood up on her tippy toes and kissed me.

"Be careful," she said.

"I will."

I started back out to my car. I had turned the corner of the garage before the door closed behind me.

The two agents perked up again as I backed out of the driveway. I waited until I was well down the long, sloping street and out of their sight before pulling to the curb and opening my laptop. A moment later, I had the tracking device on Nicholas' car pulled up on my screen. Cross referencing his coordinates with Google map, it appeared that he was back at the Zanzibar. I left the laptop open on the seat next to me and headed that way.

Nothing about this crazy scheme was making any sense to me. Taking Chango at his word, that Nicholas was somehow involved, how did he expect to keep Lila and Holly silent, once the exchange had been made? I was no expert on kidnapping but assumed that keeping your identity secret would be the first rule of thumb. Otherwise you would be obliged to start silencing people.

There had to be something more at work here, something Lila wasn't telling me. Nicholas and his accomplice had to have something hanging over her head. Nothing else made sense. The nature of that secret? I went with the obvious. They knew something about the murder of Mr. Evergreen. As to who Nicholas' accomplice might be, I hadn't a clue.

At the Zanzibar, I avoided the valets and parked one block up from Coast Highway. If Nicholas had a sudden urge to run off on me, I didn't want to be standing around waiting for some kid to retrieve my car.

A herringbone patterned brick walkway led up to the cloistered entrance of the restaurant. A carved wooden door opened into a verdant garden patio with vaulted ceilings. That part of the restaurant looked much as it had in the past, when it was a Mexican dive. They had spruced up the paint and otherwise given the place an African vibe.

I had been imagining the look on Nicholas' face when he saw me stroll up. Instead, I ran into Vanderhof. He had commandeered a large booth in the patio area, up against a rock wall, with a waterfall gurgling nearby. Five, very fine and very young looking dolls were draped around him.

The gaiety collectively paused with my arrival. To Vanderhof's credit, he kept smiling.

"Ladies, meet Michael Devlin, private detective extraordinaire."

Vanderhof had had a few drinks. I pretended to tip my hat.

You come to ruin my evening, Devlin?"

"Hadn't planned on it...I could if you'd like. Let's see. Running a child day care center without a license?"

The young women didn't appear to appreciate my comment. Neither did Dirk.

"I was going to say, sit down and have a drink, Devlin, but I'd forgotten what a prick you can be."

"Me too. Anyway, I have other things on my mind this evening. You didn't happen to see that toady of yours, Nicholas?"

"That little prick? He slinked in here about an hour ago. I think he's upstairs in the bar, or out on the veranda. You here to make trouble?"

"Not any that involves you right now." I smiled at the young ladies. "Wouldn't be hard, though."

I looked back at Vanderhof.

"Watch your step, Devlin. Watch your step."

"I was going to say the same to you, pal."

I tipped my hat to the ladies again and headed upstairs. The long, narrow bar area had an adjoining outdoor veranda and a trio was playing world music over by the exit. Nicholas had taken up residence at one end of the bar. He was nursing a cocktail with his left hand bandaged. I appeared that his pinkie finger was missing.

I sat in the empty bar stool next to him. He glanced at me and looked back at his drink. It took another moment for things to click in his brain, but once they had, he froze up like he had stumbled upon a grizzly bear.

"How's things going, Nick?" I said. "Looks like you lost a part there."

"What the fuck do you want?" he said with another quick look my way.

"Come on, Nick. What do you say we keep things cordial here? I'm just checking up to make sure you're keeping your nose clean. I'd hate seeing you get into more trouble."

"I don't know what you're talking about?"

He quickly tossed back his drink, threw a five on the bar top and got up to leave.

"Hey, I'll be seeing you around," I said.

Nicholas looked over his shoulder on his way downstairs. I went out onto the veranda and watched him walk out the entrance. He looked over his shoulder again while waiting for the valet to retrieve his car. I waved from the railing. As soon as he had pulled out of the parking lot, I headed downstairs.

"You got him stirred up all right," Vanderhof said as I walked by his table.

"Yeah. I do that to people."

I winked again for the young ladies and kept going.

Back in my car, I opened the laptop, confirmed that Nicholas was headed south on Coast Highway and drove around to the light at Bluebird. When it changed, I turned left onto the highway and gave pursuit, but in no particular hurry. I was on his tail. I didn't want him knowing it.

He continued on into Doheny Beach but instead of turning right towards his place above the harbor, he turned left at Golden Lantern, then right into a condo development on the upside of Selva. I stopped out on Golden Lantern and waited until Nick had parked and was heading into the condo complex on foot before pulling around and parking on the opposite end of the curbside lot.

The location didn't connect to anyone I knew. I thought of calling Kenny but had no exact address to cross reference.

With another thought, I called Mr. Huntington.

"Michael. It must be important for you to be calling me at this hour."

"You said you rarely slept."

"So I did. What's on your mind?"

"I was wondering if you had a phone number for Nicholas. I'd like to give him a call."

"Dare I ask why?"

"Probably best if you don't."

"I see."

"It might possibly involve hanging him from a rope."

"Ah. Then allow me to hurry."

A moment later, he was reading off the number.

"Anything to put that little bastard behind bars."

"It is in that spirit, sir."

"Then god's speed to you."

"Thanks. I'll be in touch."

I hung up and called Bennie. He answered groggily.

"Jesus. What the hell time is it?"

"Just past one. You sleeping?"

"I was a little, yeah, but don't worry. That bitch ain't going nowhere down this dead-end street without me knowing about it."

"You and your bitches."

"Oh yeah. Lo siento. That doll."

"And what about John? Is he still over at Caitlin's place?"

"Yeah. Got you covered. And what are you doing?"

"I don't know. You up for a little excitement?"

"Shit, it'd be about time."

"Then meet me at this location and I'll explain everything to you then."

I read off the address.

"As fast as you can."

"You got it."

I sat back and stared at the side by side row of stately condos. They were three-stories high and perched above a steep slope with glorious views of both the harbor and the coast looking south. It was a tony neighborhood. Someone had money.

Fifteen minutes later, Bennie was pulling into the parking lot. I got out and climbed into the back of the van.

"Boss man. You're not going to believe this shit but this is exactly where Ida led me earlier this evening."

"You're kidding, right?"

"Nope. As sure as I'm sitting here."

"Wow, okay. That's something to think about."

"Yeah. How did you end up here?"

I explained what Chango had told me about Nicholas and how I had followed him to this location.

"Oh man. That is some weird shit. You really think that idiot kidnapped Holly?"

"So I'm led to believe. But who else is involved and what Ida Huntington has to do with any of this is beyond me."

"Well, shit. It's obvious. 'Just get rid of her.' Remember?"

"Yeah, but before they get the money? That makes no sense."

"No, check it out. Like Holly knows something that Ida didn't want her to know and when she finds out these clowns have kidnapped her, she feels the walls closing in and tells them to get rid of her."

"I could punch a lot of holes in that theory."

"You got a better one?"

"No, but it's still pretty farfetched."

"Well, there has to be some reason why that bitch said just get rid of her."

"I'll grant you that much."

I sat there staring at the condos, trying to make sense of the senseless.

"So what's the plan?" Bennie said after some seconds.

"I don't know. Nick's in one of these places but I don't know which one. I just saw him park from the street and by the time I got into position, he had already disappeared."

"And what? You dragged me over here to watch paint dry again?"

"Actually, I got his number from old man Huntington and was thinking to call. See if it rattles his cage and flushes him out."

"Now you're talking."

"Except I'd like to go search his place first. While he's otherwise distracted."

"Sure, boss man. Take the juicy gig."

"Come on, Bennie. If we're anywhere near the truth, Holly's in one of those condos right now, being held hostage. Keeping an eye on this place is just as important."

"It's cool. I've got you covered."

"Yeah?"

"Yeah. Go scope out his place."

"Well, if he takes off in the meantime, be sure to let me know."

"Yeah, because idiot that I am, I'd sure as hell forget that shit."

"Oh Bennie," I said, standing up. "We definitely need to look into some counseling when all this is through."

"Fine. I still get the kids."

"Fine. You can have the Mercedes too if it'll get you to stop beating my balls."

He flipped me off. I started to open the door.

"Hey wait a minute. You never finished telling me what happened in Fallbrook. I can't believe all that shit went down without me."

"Bennie, you either have the worst luck in the world, or the best. I'll leave it for you to decide."

"Yeah, funny."

"Okay, look. What I'm about to tell you is between you and me. This never gets talked about again. Ever. With anyone. Okay?"

Bennie crossed his heart and I explained everything that I hadn't told him over the phone about Fallbrook.

"Holy shit, boss man. This shit keeps getting weirder all the time. So that Pritchett prick was really down there?"

I nodded and started out the door, but stopped again.

"Never, Bennie. This business with Potter and the Mongols. That goes to our graves with us."

He crossed his heart a second time. I stared his way a long moment before climbing out of the van.

Nicholas' townhome was roughly two blocks north and down on the other side of Coast Highway. I drove by his place and kept going, looking for any sign that someone else had it staked out. Seeing nothing that looked suspicious, I turned around and parked a good distance up from Nick's driveway. These were side by side units, two to a building, upstairs and down, done up in wood siding, each with a small, fenced backyard.

I got out, walked down to the narrow easement alongside Nick's place, followed it back and peeked over the fence. There did not appear to be any lights on inside or signs of life so I jumped into the yard. The sliding glass door on the right was unlocked. I pulled out the Glock and slipped into what was an adjoining dining room and living room.

I had been standing there in the darkness for several seconds, listening for any sounds, when something flashed in my peripheral vision. I whipped around with gun drawn. Jesus. A black cat. It had dashed through the living room and out the back door. Well, it was gone now.

I turned back towards the open kitchen and front foyer facing me. All was quiet in that direction. I moved cautiously

461

down a hallway to an open door. It was an office. I turned on my flashlight and checked all around the desk and drawers and bookshelves.

The answering machine was blinking so I hit the message button. The message lady said the call had come in at 10:46, so roughly an hour before I had arrived to Lila's place A man's voice came on.

> Where the hell are you, Nick? I've been trying your cellphone forever here. Anyway, I haven't heard back from Lila and I'm getting fucking worried. I can't keep the little bitch here forever. We need to get this thing done before it all blows up…All right. Fucking call me, will you?

I shook my head. This had to be the gang that couldn't shoot straight. What kind of idiot would call and leave a message like that? And it definitely sounded like a man who knew Lila. He had referred to her casually by first name.

I checked the caller ID but it was a blocked number. That figured.

I went to clear the rest of the house and found some blood splattered around the upstairs bathtub. There was no sign of Nick's finger.

I slipped out the front door, returned to my Impala and texted Kenny.

> Please call me.

My phone rang a few seconds later.

"What are you doing?" he said.

"Hoping you have that police report."

"Not yet. I paid a hundred bucks to a guy who said he knew a guy with a connection in the police department, but now my guy can't find his guy."

"Great. We just paid a junkie to get his fix. Meanwhile, Lila's ready to put a bullet in my back."

"Why don't you check with your FBI girlfriend?"

"Hey, there's an idea. I just don't know if letting one girlfriend know about the other one is in my best interest."

"I generally find that it's not."

"Yeah."

"So is that it?" Kenny said.

"Yeah, I guess."

I explained about the blocked number on Nicholas' answering machine.

"Maybe you can do a reverse search anyway."

He laughed.

"Okay. I've got to run."

I hung up and sat there with the pieces of the puzzle going around and around in my head, and still not making one bit of sense. Let's say someone did have the goods on Lila. Why not just pay the money and make the problem go away? Why involve me? So I could be her fall guy? And where did Ida fit into this movie?

I kept running down various angles, but every one of them came to a dead end. Nothing added up.

With a shake of my head, I called Bennie.

"Anything?" I said when he answered.

"Nothing. And you?"

"Whoever's involved in this scheme with Nicholas left a message on his answering machine but it was a blocked number so no way to trace it."

"So what now?"

"I don't know. Are you ready for some action?"

"I was born ready, boss man."

"Then here goes."

"Hey, wait. You want me to follow him if he leaves?"

"No. We still have that tracer on his car. The important thing is to figure out which condo he's in."

"I got you covered."

"Back at you as soon as I hang up."

I got out one of my burner phones and called Nicholas' number. It took several rings before he picked up, and there was a pause before he spoke.

"Yeah? Who's this."

"Detective Sterling, Nick. Just wanted to make sure you made it home all right."

"What the fuck do you want with me? I thought we had a deal the other night."

"Just making sure you keep your nose clean."

"Fuck. Don't you have anything better to do?"

"I wish I did but you keep getting yourself into trouble."

The line went dead. I texted Bennie

He's ready to blow. Keep your eyes peeled

A thumbs up symbol came right back. I started the Impala and headed that way. I had barely gotten to the end of Nick's block when Bennie called me.

"Got it. He's driving off right now."

"So you know which condo?"

"Oh yeah. I heard two dudes in there screaming back and forth and then Nick came flying out of the front door like his pants were on fire."

"Okay. I'll be there in a minute."

"You still want me to let this idiot go?"

"Yeah, yeah. Just keep your eyes on that condo. I'll be there in a minute."

"You got it."

I was pulling up to a red light at Coast Highway just then and found a cop sitting in the southbound left turn lane of the highway. When my light turned green, I looked both ways before crossing. Halfway up to the T at Selva, I saw the cop turn in behind me. I always felt a bit like I had just robbed a bank when a cop got on my tail, especially at that time of night.

I jogged right on Selva and watched. A few moments later, the cop was doing the same. By the time I had stopped for the light at Golden Lantern, he was right on my bumper. I turned left when the light changed and he followed me, then slowed to a crawl when I pulled right into the condo development. He had a long look my way before continuing on.

"You see that cop?" Bennie said when I slipped into the back of the van.

"Yeah. He was on my tail." I settled in at the monitors. "Anything new?"

"Nada. What's Nick doing?"

I opened the laptop and we had a look.

"Going home, from the looks of it."

We watched until it was clear that he had. What that meant, I had no idea.

"Then what's the plan here? Am I finally going to see some action?"

"I don't know. Maybe."

"Come on, man. You said it yourself. Holly's in there being held hostage."

"I said, maybe. I have no proof. But assuming she is and we play hero, who's going to answer if we inadvertently get her dusted?"

"Yeah, I'm getting the picture. Just like at Evergreen's place, you go in and save the day while I sit here watching the monitors."

"Actually, I was thinking to have you create a diversion while I pick the door lock."

"And then?"

"And then we go in."

"All right!"

"Jesus, Rambo. We don't even know if she's in there. What if this turns out to be the mayor of Doheny Beach?"

Thirty Six

While Bennie was considering that question, my phone rang. I saw it was Alessandra and held up a finger.

"What's going on, kid?" I said.

"I just got a call from Detective Barnes."

"Yeah? About what?"

"About why he just found Potter's dead body out near Indio."

"Wow. Okay. So why are you calling me?"

There was silence.

"What?" I said.

"What? You don't sound the least bit surprised to hear he's dead. Or curious about how he came to be that way."

"What do you want me to say? The man had enemies."

"Yeah. Who just happened to track him down in Fallbrook tonight and magically transport his body out to Indio. With a broken neck."

I waited.

"Don't play me, Michael. Something doesn't add up here. I just haven't quite figured out what that is yet, or what to do about it."

I waited.

"So back to Barnes," she said. "He wants to talk to you and I really don't know how to stop that from happening."

"Can you keep my location to yourself for tonight?"

There was more silence.

"I'll give you two hours. Maybe until dawn but you're going to have to answer for this. I've got a funny feeling that Barnes is going to lay a murder charge on you."

I sighed.

"Please give me as long as you can."

"You'll know when the clock strikes midnight."

"Okay…Where are you now?"

"Still up at LAX…I understand you left quite a mess down there in Fallbrook."

"I thought it was a pretty tidy little package."

"Yeah. Especially with Potter magically disappearing."

I didn't answer.

"Just do it fast, Michael, whatever you're doing,."

"I'm on it. And thanks for the warning."

"Yeah. And be careful."

"I will…Oh, hey!" I said before she hung up.

"Yeah, what?"

"I wondered if you could do a little favor for me."

"Yeah. Like you have any chips to call."

I waited in silence.

"Okay, what?" she said.

"I need a police report."

I explained about old man Evergreen and Lila's history in Ohio.

"And you would be wanting this report…because?"

"I'm wondering if this business up in Pueblo Hills was a one off or if Lila's in the habit of killing old men. I might be the next one she shoots in the back."

Alessandra smirked.

"Michael. You really are a piece of work."

"I know but you wouldn't want to see me dead, would you?"

There was a pause.

"I'll have to think about that."

"Think about what? Seeing me dead or the police report?"

There was another pause.

"Both," she said and hung up.

467

I set the phone down, feeling like a fool. In trying to cover for Chango's ass, I had placed my own life in peril.

"What's all this shit about Lila and Ohio?" Bennie said to me.

I quickly explained.

"Sure, boss man. Like always. Play it close to your vest."

"Oh shut up. There hasn't been a chance to explain this shit to you."

Our eyes met.

"I'm going to say it again, Bennie. You never repeat what I told you about Fallbrook. Ever. To anyone."

"My lips are sealed. You know that."

"Good."

"So what are we doing?" he said.

"I don't know. I guess see how much more trouble we can stir up."

"I'm all over that shit."

"Yeah. I figured you would be...So here's my plan."

Bennie heard me out, then we set about arming ourselves and slipped out the back of the van together. He went around to the backside of the condo. I went to the front door and waited. A minute later, I heard a pebble hit the back of the building. A few seconds later, I heard another one. Shortly after that, I received a thumbs up text from Bennie, our signal that someone had come to look out the back door. I went to work on the lock. When a sliding glass door opened back there, I paused, my eyes partly focused in that direction, partly on picking the lock and partly on the obscure glass sidelight to the right of the door.

When the tumblers fell into place and the door started to open, I texted a thumbs up back to Bennie and cautiously started inside. I was taking my second step into the foyer when the door suddenly slammed back in my face. Then it flew inward and a man was upon me. He wasn't overly large, a few inches shorter than me, but surprisingly athletic and quickly had me in a headlock. I braced my legs against his weight and was trying to pin him to the tiled entry when he groaned and

468

collapsed in my arms. I looked up to find Bennie standing there with a sap in his hands. He helped me to clear the man's grip from around my neck and gently lower him onto the tiled entry.

"Atta boy," I whispered.

Bennie smiled. I quietly closed the front door.

"Let's get him out of sight."

Bennie and I carried him into the den. While Bennie tied and gagged him, I searched his pant pockets. He had a wallet in back and a phone in front. I opened the wallet and checked the ID.

"Fucking Christ," I whispered.

"What?" Bennie whispered back.

I showed him the driver's license.

"Who's that?"

"Lila's boyfriend."

Bennie swore in Spanish. The phone was locked but I was able to open it with Desmond's index finger and swore again, seeing his text thread with Lila about the kidnapping. I showed Bennie. He read it and stood there shaking his head.

I motioned to him out into the hallway. A TV was blaring upstairs. We paused there, looking and listening.

"Let's clear the rest of the downstairs first," I whispered.

Bennie went in one direction, I went in the other and we met in the kitchen a minute later. We both shrugged.

"Let's see who's upstairs. I've got my money on it being Holly with a joint and cocktail in her hands."

Bennie smiled and followed me to the bottom of the staircase. I pulled out my Glock and went first. He followed me with his Luger.

We paused again at the top landing. The TV was on in the bedroom nearest us. I stood next to the closed door with my back against the wall and nodded.

Bennie threw the door open, light rushed out into the darkened hallway and there she was, sitting on the bed, as expected. My estimate had been close. No joint, but Holly was sipping on a cocktail. I shook my head and whispered to Bennie.

"Fill her in. I'm going to clear the rest of this floor."

Bennie closed the door as I went out. A minute later I was reopening it.

"All clear?" Bennie said.

I nodded and looked at Holly.

"I see they've got you chained up in a regular dungeon here."

"What?" she said. "I suppose you think I had something to do with this."

"I wouldn't put it past you."

She made a face. I looked away, still struggling to make sense of the senseless.

After a moment's thought, I waved the phone at Bennie.

"I'm going downstairs to deal with this situation. Keep her company."

I started to leave but stopped and looked back.

"Potter's dead, by the way."

Holly stared at me with her young mind going every which way. I closed the door and headed down to the kitchen.

At the bottom of the stairs, I had a thought and checked the garage. Fucking Christ. It was the green Audi A8. So it was Desmond who had been following me around. But why?

I went out to the kitchen and sat at the table, puzzling over everything while staring down at the harbor. Okay, so Lila had a murky past up in Pueblo Hills, something she desperately needed to keep buried. That appeared to be no mystery. Nor was it any great leap to think that Desmond Ducot would have knowledge of those secrets and be willing to use that knowledge against her. But why stage this ridiculous kidnapping? And why now? And why involve me? Lila had already silenced a murder with money. It seemed clear that more money would have easily silenced Desmond. The only thing that seemed to make sense was that the two of them were trying to set me up somehow. That notion fit the facts better

470

than anything else I could imagine and still didn't make one goddamned bit of sense. No matter how I looked at things, two and two just didn't add up.

Seeing no reason but to assume the worst, I took a wild swing at the truth and typed out a text.

Why did you get this Devlin guy involved!!! Now he's snooping around and making trouble! My price just doubled. It's that or I'm spilling the whole thing.

I stared at the words for a good minute before finally sending the text. My heart rate doubled the minute I did.

I sat there waiting. Another minute passed before an answer came back.

What do you want from me??? I'm going out of my mind here! I'll give you whatever you want, but if you ever tell her the truth, I swear, I'll kill you!

I stared at the phone, the events of the previous week falling into place in my mind, like layered tiles on a computer screen, one over the other, the original tile being the moment when Lila had first walked into my office, her disdain for my operation so obvious, it reeked, but a disdain that was quickly followed by a look of guile, a look that had said to me in that moment, well, here's a sucker I can play for a tune, and every one of her affectionate words and gestures since that moment had only reinforced my suspicions. She was pure cunning, with a lot of sweet talk and kisses to paper over her true intentions.

But, Jesus. What true intentions? I'd have felt much better with a gun to my head. All I wanted was some kind of straight answer. Just exactly what kind of fool did you want me to play for you, Lila?

Feeling more than half mad, I headed back upstairs and into the bedroom. Bennie and Holly were sitting on the bed together, watching a reality TV show.

"Having fun, are we?"

"Hey, boss man. What am I supposed to do?"

"Nothing, nothing."

I waved Bennie out into the hallway.

"We'll be right back," I told Holly.

I closed the door and walked Bennie further down the hallway.

"What's going on? We taking her home or what?"

"No. I can't do that yet. Too many unanswered questions."

I explained to Bennie about Lila's text.

"Jesus. I don't get it. Why would that chick be playing you for a sucker?"

"You tell me. I don't get it either. Any more than I get why Ida Huntington stopped by here. I don't get anything about this crazy mixed up scheme but from what Barretta told me, I'll probably have Detective Barnes breathing down my neck any minute now so we need to get out of here."

"How about we take Holly to your place?"

"No, that's the first place that son of a bitch will go looking for me. Anyway, I've got another plan. I'm thinking to put a tracer on Desmond's car and cut him loose."

"That's some crazy shit. We just tied him up."

"I know. But now what? Try to torture the truth out of him?"

Bennie smiled.

"Yeah, I figured you'd be all over that action."

"Then you tell me. What are we going to learn by turning him loose?"

"See which way the cockroaches scramble when the lights go on."

"Yeah. You might be on to something there."

"Yeah? A little something?"

"Yeah, it's pretty little, but okay. And Holly? What are we doing with her in the meantime?"

"I don't know. You mind entertaining her for a couple of hours?"

"In what? The van?"

"Yeah. She'll probably get a kick out of playing detective."

"Yeah, with a bar set up back there. That chick ain't going nowhere unless a buzz is involved."

"I know…So? Would that mess with your sobriety?"

"Hell no. I ain't never going to drink again."

"That's my Bennie."

"It's the god's truth. I'm done with that for life."

I gave him a high five.

"Then are we good here with this game plan?"

"Sure. What are you going to do?"

"Go confront Lila."

"Shit. That ought to be some fireworks."

"Yeah…You deal with the tracer and I'll deal with Holly."

Bennie headed downstairs. I went back into the bedroom. Holly was still watching her reality show. I turned off the TV and sat down on the bed.

"Holly Holly Holly."

"What?"

I shook my head.

"What in the hell were you thinking, calling that monster again?"

She made a somewhat repentant shrug.

"I just wanted to get high."

"Yeah, and then drag him back over to Gigi's place, putting her life in danger?"

"That was Don's idea."

"Yeah, well. It was a lousy idea, whoever dreamed it up."

She shrugged again. I shook my head.

"You spoiled little brat. Do you have any idea how much more troubled you've caused me by doing all that?"

"I'm sorry," she said after a long moment.

"Yeah, me too…"

I let out a big sigh, feeling weary, of everything. Holly had a sip of her drink.

"Look," I said. "I know you're all strung out again and I don't have time to be dealing with that. We just need to get out

473

of here. My neck is so far out there on the chopping block right now, I don't know which way is up, and mostly for trying to keep the police and FBI away from you."

"What do you want me to do?"

"Well, I can't take you home right now so I want you to drive around with Bennie for a while. You can play detective, okay?"

"Can I drink?"

"Yeah. I figured we'd raid Desmond's bar supplies before we go."

Started to get up but I held her back.

"Look, kid. Sooner or later there has to be a reckoning. For both of us. We need a story, a story that goes from point A to point B and makes some kind of sense. You know, like where you went with Potter and how you ended up back here? Something these people can hang their hats on. They're not going to go away without some answers."

"Is he really dead?"

I nodded.

"Did you kill him?"

"I can't talk about that. And as far as the rest of the world is concerned, I never said a word about it."

"I won't say anything."

"I hope not. I've covered your ass big time. I need you to cover mine."

"Okay."

"Okay. One other thing before we go. Do you have any idea who that woman was who visited Desmond earlier this evening?"

Holly stared without answering so I made Alessandra's rolling hand motion. Come on. Out with it.

"It was Charlotte's older sister Ida."

"So you know her."

She nodded.

"How?"

"She's an old friend of my Mom."

"Oh really. And exactly how did that happen?"

"She used to live up in Pueblo Hills"

"Well isn't that convenient."

"What?" she said. "Why does that matter?"

"You know what? I don't know right now so let's get back to the business at hand. Like why Ida came over here tonight. Do you have any clue?"

"Not really. I heard her arguing with Desmond and peeked out."

"Arguing about what?"

"I don't know. I couldn't make out what they were saying over the TV and by the time I peeked out, she was storming off...I'm pretty sure they're fucking, though. It sounded like that kind of fight."

I shook my head. Kids these days.

"So you think they're an item?"

I made a gesture and Holly nodded. I shook my head. Things were getting crazier by the minute but I didn't have time to figure that one out either.

I waved.

"Let's go raid Desmond's booze cabinet."

A few minutes later, I had Holly settled into the back of the van with her bar supplies. Bennie came out from the garage and joined us. I got the new tracer set up on my laptop and left the laptop sitting next to Holly.

"Let's go see about Desmond."

We climbed out and headed over to his front door.

"I hope that fucker's still out," Bennie whispered as I was opening it.

"You and me both."

Inside, we cautiously pushed open the door to the den. Desmond was still lying motionless on the floor.

"Jesus, Bennie. You really clocked the son of a bitch."

"Shit, the way you two were mixing it up, I wasn't about to play no games."

I put two fingers to Desmond's neck. He was still warm and had a pulse.

475

"Go ahead and cut him loose," I said.

While Bennie did that, I erased the last text from Desmond's phone and placed it back where I had found it, along with his wallet. On our way to the street, Bennie tossed all the duct tape and zip ties into the neighbor's trash.

I paused with Bennie at the back of the van.

"You keep an eye on Mighty Joe Young in there. I'm heading over to grill Lila. I'll let you know what I know and you do the same."

"You got it."

I climbed into the Impala and called Kenny.

"You're busy tonight," he said, answering my call.

"Yeah. I've got something else I need you to look into."

I gave him Ida's address.

"See who owns this place for me, will you?"

"Sure. Be back at you in a minute."

I started the engine, turned right out of the parking lot and headed the back way over to Lila's place, but in no particular hurry. Earlier, her endless duplicity had left me feeling like a bull ready to charge but my emotions had cooled. I felt more like the cold executioner now, marching his prisoner slowly up to the gallows.

Halfway across town, Kenny called back.

"You're not going to believe this," I said before he could speak.

"Hey. How did you know I was going to say that?"

"I'm getting clairvoyant in my later years. Want more proof?"

"Yeah, sure."

"You're going to tell me that Lila Evergreen owns the house."

"Wow. You just blew fifty bucks for nothing."

"Yeah, well, I had to make sure."

"And what does that mean to you?"

"I don't know. I feel like I'm getting close to the truth here but I'll be damned if I know what that is. I'll be pulling into

Lila's driveway in a few minutes so you can bet there's going to be some fireworks going off."

"Good luck. I'm still in the will, right?

"If I don't get that police report, I'm taking back the pencils."

He laughed. I ended the call, having already turned up Lila's street. The two agents who had been watching her place were gone. With Potter dead, Barretta must have figured she could afford to pull them. It was all for the best. I didn't want anyone listening in when I started slapping Lila around.

I parked in front of the garage, marched up to her front door and knocked loudly. When Lila failed to answer, I pounded a few times. It took her most of thirty seconds to part the door, and that was with the safety latch still on.

"Oh, god, Michael. You scared me half to death."

When she undid the safety latch and opened the door, I pushed past her.

"We need to talk," I said and kept walking.

I settled into a chair in the living room. Lila came along warily.

"Sit," I said.

She did so, opposite me.

"What's going on, Michael. You look like you're in a state."

"I'm in a state all right."

I repeated out loud what I had texted to her from Desmond's phone.

Lila stared.

"Sound familiar?"

Lila kept staring.

"Yeah, that was me and you have two choices here. Either spill the whole truth to me right now or you can tell your story to the cops."

She kept staring. I spoke up again in the silence.

"I do wonder what they'd charge you with for faking your own daughter's kidnapping. Conspiracy? Accessory, maybe? Never mind why you were trying to get me involved. Maybe just hoping I'd put a couple of slugs into Desmond for you? Private detective murders boyfriend in steamy love triangle."

"Michael, please…"

"Please, nothing, Lila. You've been lying to me since the day you first walked into my office, so either explain this crazy scheme of yours or I'm calling the cops right now."

"It's not what you think."

"Fine. I'm all ears. What does Desmond have hanging over your head?"

She looked at the floor.

"Okay," I said and pulled out my phone.

"Please don't."

I paused.

"I'm sorry, Lila, but my ass is so far out on a limb for you and your daughter, I don't even know which way is up anymore."

"It's complicated," she said.

"Complicated, how? Like which one of you lured old man Evergreen into the room and which one of you pulled the trigger?"

When Lila failed to answer me, I dialed the number and stared at her while it rang. Lila said something barely audible so I cupped the phone.

"What?"

"Holly," she said while still staring at the floor.

"Holly? Holly, what?"

Lila looked up at me with vacant eyes.

Thirty Seven

While staring at her, I heard the desk clerk answer. "Doheny Beach Police Department…"

I was still staring at Lila. Like a zealous prosecutor, it seemed as if I had asked a question for which I did not already know the answer.

"Hello…Hello?" I heard the desk clerk saying.

Aware of the phone again, I pulled it back up to my ear.

"Oh, sorry, wrong number."

I ended the call and set the phone down.

"What? You're saying that Holly shot your husband?"

Lila nodded, then shook her head.

"What, Lila? Spill it. Because he was abusing her?"

She nodded.

That brought Jack Oliver's comment back to mind. Old man Evergreen would have fucked a poodle if it had lipstick.

"And what?" I said. "You just came home one day and found him dead?"

She looked down at the floor.

"Goddamn it, Lila. If you don't get straight with me right now, I'm calling them back."

When she failed to answer, I started dialing the police station number again.

"Okay!" she said with both hands to her head. "I shot him!"

She looked up at me.

"I came home and found him molesting her and shot him!"

479

Lila stared at me for a moment before looking back at the floor.

"What? You shot him right there in front of her?"

Lila shook her head.

"Then what?"

"God, how can I make you understand. Part of this has always been like a dream to me. I just remember going into her bedroom and seeing him on top of her and rushing to pull him off. And then the next thing I knew, we were in our bedroom arguing. He tried to convince me that it wasn't what it seemed but I had seen enough to know it was otherwise. Anyway, I was in such a rage. Screaming and throwing things…Then the next thing I knew, he was lying dead on the floor."

"So just like that? A gun materialized in your hand and you shot him."

"No. We kept one there in the bedroom. For protection."

"And where was Holly in all of this?"

"Still in her bedroom. I went back after dropping the gun and found her wrapped up in a blanket. Asleep or in shock. I was never sure which."

"And then what?"

"I rushed her off to a girlfriend's house and called the police."

I waited until Lila looked up at me.

"And told them what? The truth?"

"No. I bruised my face and arms and said that he had been abusing me."

"So you claimed self-defense."

She nodded.

"And what about Holly? Does she remember any of this?"

"I don't know. I don't think so. At least she's never shown any signs of it."

I looked off, having my doubts about that. A girl of eleven might have been able to block out that kind of trauma for a time, but not forever.

I looked back at Lila with a sick feeling in my gut. How could you believe anything she told you? I gave it 50-50 odds that she was telling me the truth.

I could picture a police detective thinking the same thing. No sooner does he show up to investigate a murder, then someone higher up chases him off. The whole thing stunk to high heaven.

Well, whatever else, it probably had been best to spare Holly the notoriety. Bury the whole thing and pretend it had never happened. Lila had possessed the money to do so, and an apparent accessory in the town of Pueblo Hills, which had been all too willing to go along, rather than tarnish its own image, and that of its favorite founding father.

I looked back at Lila. She remained staring at the floor in her zombie like state. Christ. The duplicity. And yet, as the seconds passed by, I felt an unwelcome sense of pity for her and went to sit on the sofa.

"Look, I don't mean to be a bastard but put yourself in my shoes. You've been lying to me from start to finish."

"No, Michael."

"Yes, Lila. Hell, I've even had Desmond following me around. I've been half expecting a bullet in my back any minute."

She stared, looking puzzled.

"Why would Desmond be following you around?"

"You tell me. I kept seeing a green A8 on my tail this past week and then found the car in his garage a little while ago. You must have told him something."

"I had mentioned hiring you."

"Yeah, well. That obviously got his shorts in a knot. I assume he knows you shot your husband."

She kept staring.

"No?"

She shook her head.

"He thinks Holly did it."

"Oh Christ, Lila."

"Michael. I didn't dare tell him the truth."

"Yeah. You don't dare tell anyone the truth."

Lila looked down and wiped at fresh tears.

"So why now?" I said. "I mean, after all this time, why did Desmond suddenly decide to put the squeeze on you?"

"Because he knew it was over between us."

"Okay. So he's thinking, if I'm going to get screwed out of my meal ticket, I'd better take my cut before I go?"

She wiped at her running mascara.

"Something like that."

"But Jesus, Lila. I still don't get it. Why play me for a sucker?"

"Oh, Michael. That's not it."

"No? Then what is it?"

She heaved a big sigh.

"Look, things had been coming apart between Desmond and I for a long time. I just didn't feel the same way about him and he knew it but kept trying to draw me back in. Then, about two weeks ago, he said that if I ever left him, he'd go to the papers with everything he knew. That he'd ruin my life and Holly's. Then Holly ran off and when I met you that day, I thought, maybe here's a man who can make everything turn out all right."

I looked away with those first few moments in my office flashing through my mind again. Without knowing exactly what was behind it, it appeared that I had been on the right track. Something about that photo of me as a young man, standing with one boot atop a vanquished cape buffalo, something about that display of raw male power had spoken to a woman in distress. A woman who, from all external appearances, was completely independent, but who had spent her entire life depending on men to arrive at that state. But hell, Lila had known it was Desmond all along, texting and putting the squeeze on her, and had gone on playing me for a sap. There were no straight lines with this woman.

"Okay. Tell me this," I said. "How did Ida Huntington get mixed up in this mess?"

She looked up at me.

"What do you know about Ida Huntington?"

I raised my eyebrows.

"Did you forget I'm a private detective?"

She shook her head.

"I don't know. I don't know anything anymore."

"Oh stop, Lila. I've had it up to here with your mixed-up woman routine. 'I just need a big strong man to rescue me.' If you keep lying to me, how am I ever going to help you?"

She looked down, wiping at more tears. I stared, battling a powerful urge to slap her around a few times.

"I'll tell you this much, Lila. I can't find a clean conscience anywhere I turn. As far as I can see, you're all a bunch of grifters."

"Thanks for that."

"Well, what do you want me to say? The way people live their lives defines them and that's what all of you have been doing since you were old enough to have a driver's license. Chasing after money."

Disgusted, I got up to leave but Lila stopped me.

"Michael. Please. Try to understand. I just didn't want Holly's name in the papers. I didn't want her young life being ruined and worried that if I just gave Desmond the money, with no strings attached, it would never end. That he would always be back for more. That's why I involved you. Okay?"

I shook my head.

"You still haven't explained to me how Ida Huntington got involved."

"Involved? Why would you think that? She's just a friend of mine."

"A friend who just happened to be over at Desmond's place earlier this evening. I'll let you decide why the two of them got into a shouting match."

Lila sat there looking puzzled for several seconds, then threw her hands out dramatically.

"Well, isn't everyone fucking everyone else in this movie."

I smirked and started to get up again.

"Please," she said. "I can understand you feeling the way you do. I can understand you despising me but let's just give Desmond the money and make him go away. For Holly's sake. And then I'll be out of your life, if that's what you want."

"Yeah, well, paying Desmond may no longer be necessary."

Lila stared.

"What do you mean?"

"I mean, I have your daughter."

"You do?! Where?!"

"Once again, it's probably best if I don't tell you. At least for the time being."

"Oh god, Michael. If you have my daughter, please bring her home."

"No. There are still too many unanswered questions. Too much I don't understand. Besides, she'll have to face the police soon so we'd all better get our ducks in a row before we ever think of letting them near her."

"But I don't understand. Why do the police still have to be involved?"

I scoffed.

"Maybe you haven't noticed, Lila, but they are involved. The police, the FBI. We'll be lucky if Homeland Security doesn't break down your door any minute now. Trust me, there's no protecting your daughter from being questioned."

She let out another big sigh.

"Okay, Michael. I'm in your hands. Whatever you think is best."

"Right, Lila. That's the last thing you are. In my hands."

She stared, looking contrite.

"Okay, I deserved that."

"Yeah you did."

I sat there rubbing my forehead.

"Look. I'm tired of half-truths. I'm tired of being run around, but I suppose none of that really matters right now. We're both in agreement about one thing. For Holly's sake, we need to resolve this mess without the whole world finding out what was behind it."

"Do you think you can, Michael?"

I shook my head.

"I don't know. It's going to take some kind of miracle. Something I can't see right now."

I was about to stand up again when my phone rang. It was Alessandra.

"Excuse me. I need to take this call."

I headed for the back patio.

"I'm going to guess this isn't good news," I said, closing the door behind myself.

"Is there any good news with you, Michael?"

"Probably not. What's up?"

"I just got another call from Barnes and he's dying to know if you own a Glock."

"Look, we've already established that I shot Potter."

"Yeah. But don't I remember having confiscated your gun the other night?"

I was silent.

"So, what?" she said. "You buy Glocks by the dozens?"

"Look, I happened to be in a pawn shop the other day and they had one for sale, so I bought it. Seeing as you had mine."

"Are you making this up?"

"No, no. Come on. I respect you that much...Look, let's just get back to this business of Barnes. I thought you were supposed to get rid of that son of a bitch for me."

"That was...what? Two or three crimes ago? I'm losing track."

"I didn't break Potter's neck."

"I already told you, Michael. Don't play me. It's not whether or not you broke his neck. It's whether or not you know who did."

485

I looked back at the house. Lila was standing there on the other side of the glass, staring.

"By the way," Alessandra said. "What takes you over to Mrs. Evergreen's place this evening?"

"You wouldn't believe me if I told you."

"Spill it," she said.

I turned away from Lila and started around the infinity pool.

"I will, and you'd goddamned well better believe me."

I explained the kidnapping and what Desmond had hanging over Lila's head.

"And you're serious about all this?" Alessandra said.

"Hell, I don't know. I have no idea what's real and what's not anymore. The point is, I had been following this Nicholas character, he led me to Desmond's doorstep, that led to a scuffle and once I had Desmond restrained, I found Holly upstairs watching TV."

"You have Holly?"

"Yeah. She's with Bennie. You know, the Puerto Rican wonder?"

"Yeah."

"Yeah. They're watching Desmond's place and the last time I looked, Desmond was still in there unconscious."

"You really don't know how to stay out of trouble, do you?"

"Yeah, yeah. Look, this is all you need to know right now. I came over here to confront Ms. Evergreen, thinking she was behind some kind of bizarre kidnapping scheme involving her own daughter. Only to learn that she had shot old man Evergreen for abusing Holly, and that that's basically what's behind this whole mess."

"And you believe her?"

I glanced back to where Lila was still watching me from inside the house and lowered my voice.

"I already told you. I don't know if I believe one goddamned word that woman tells me but I really don't care about that right now. All I care about is getting Holly back home safe and sound and without being on the evening news. Are we on the same page about that one?"

"Yeah sure. On that much we are."

"Then boil it all down and we're back to Barnes trying to throw the book at me and me trying to keep Holly Evergreen out of the papers. Now you tell me what I ought to do."

"And you're hoping for what to happen when Desmond wakes up?"

"I don't know. That given enough rope, the SOB will hang himself."

"Do you have any idea what the hell you're doing?"

"Come on, Alessandra. I'm a mess. We've already stipulated to that fact. Now can you get your ass down here tonight and cover for me or not?"

"And I would be doing what?"

"Charge me with something and take me in. I don't care. Just pull rank on Barnes somehow. I'd rather be dealing with you people than with that SOB."

"Well, I guess if you give me Holly to question, I can hold you as a material witness for a spell."

"Would you do that for me?"

She scoffed.

"I'd be doing it in the interest of justice. You'd just be collateral damage."

"Thanks a lot, dear."

"Thanks, nothing...So, address?"

"Please just get your ass down this way and call me, okay? I don't know where the hell I'm going to be."

Lila was busy cleaning things up in the kitchen when I returned. She had pinned up her hair and put on a pair of high heels. I wanted to nail her right on the spot, the woman was so goddamned beautiful.

She gave me a look over her shoulder while wiping up around the sink.

"What was that all about, if I may ask?"

"That was about me trying to cover your ass."

"I see."

"If you have to know, it was Barretta with the FBI. And like I said, everything I'm doing right now is to cover your ass, while leaving me out on a limb, so you can the attitude."

Lila turned to face me, her back to the kitchen sink, her hands on the counter.

"Is it always going to be this way with us, Michael?"

I stalled there in front of her. Always going to be this way with us? I almost yelled at her. It's never going to be any way with us, woman! In fact, as soon as everything settled down, I figured I'd have to get as far away from her as humanly possible. Her beauty would only drive me into my grave.

I was trying to think of what I could say in place of the truth when my phone rang again.

It was Bennie.

"Sorry," I said and answered the call. "What's going on?"

"He's on the move."

"Desmond?"

"Yeah. And it looks like he's headed straight for Nicholas' place."

Lila came towards me. I held up a finger.

"I'm on my way. If he heads somewhere else, let me know. Otherwise I'll meet you over there."

"You got it."

I hung up and turned to Lila.

"I need to go take care of business."

She stood there looking up at me with big eyes, then got up a little higher on her heels and gave me a tender kiss.

"Go ahead," she said when I failed to respond.

I walked down the hallway towards the front door. Lila followed and opened it for me.

"You know where to find me," she said.

"I'll be in touch."

I felt her eyes at my back for a long moment before she closed the door.

I climbed into the Impala, my thoughts turning back to Ida. What had she meant by 'just get rid of her'? My initial blush had been that she was referring to Charlotte, but maybe she had been referring to Lila, as in, end the love triangle. Or maybe she had been referring to Holly, though I struggled to make any sense of that angle.

Oh, hell. I didn't know. Everywhere I turned there was more confusion.

I had started the Impala and was backing out of the driveway when a text came through from Bennie.

> He just parked out in front of Nicholas' place and made a call. I'm guessing it's to Nicholas because he's arguing away on the phone.

I texted Bennie a thumbs up and headed down the hill. Doheny Beach was visible off in the distance, nestled in the arms of Fisherman's Point. Another text came through as I reached the bottom of the hill and careened onto the long access road that tunneled under the freeway.

> He's beating on the front door now.

I stepped on the gas until I had neared the light at the harbor entrance, then eased off, knowing a cop usually hid there at that time of night, waiting for whatever sucker was dumb enough to ignore the speed signs coming into town. As anticipated, I found a patrol car tucked back between a burger joint and a gas station with the interior lights on low. I went by slowly, stopped for the red light, then hit the gas again, raced to the top of the next hill and turned left into the neighborhood above the harbor.

Two blocks shy of Nicholas' street, Bennie called me.

"What's going on?" I said.

"He just jumped the fence into the backyard. What do you want me to do?"

"Hang tight. I'm almost there."

I found Bennie parked four driveways up from Nicholas' place and on the opposite side of the street. I parked behind him, grabbed the Glock and went around to the van. Holly was sitting beside Bennie when I climbed in back, watching the monitors with him.

"This is way cool," she said.

She had a sip of her drink. Bennie and I shared a look.

"What are you thinking, boss man?"

"I don't know. Let them fight it out in there?"

"And you can bet your ass that that's what they're doing. That prick Nicholas wouldn't even come to the front door."

While watching the monitors together, I stole a glance at Holly, wondering what she knew, wondering if she remembered any of it. I had given a lot to protect her young life. I didn't want it to have an unhappy ending.

I looked back at the monitors. The neighborhood was quiet. The same with Nicholas' place. I was thinking to go scope things out from the back fence when a muffled report broke the silence. It had sounded like a car backfiring under water. Bennie looked at me.

"You thinking what I'm thinking?"

I nodded.

"Was Desmond packing?"

"Don't know. Could have been. He was wearing a coat."

"All right. We'd better go check it out."

Bennie shoved his Luger into his shoulder holster and started out the door. I dug out a burner phone, dialed my number and handed it to Holly.

"You stay here. Your job is to cover our backs. Anything changes out here, you text me immediately."

I paused at the back door.

"I mean it. Don't get out of this van."

She made a face and looked back at the monitors. I joined Bennie outside and we hustled over to Nicholas' driveway.

490

"Look, I know you're dying to storm the place but we've got to be smart about this. If someone has a gun inside, we could both end up dead."

"I know what you're thinking. I beat on the front door and you jump the back fence."

"Look, Bennie. I already told you. I can't be..."

"It's cool. I've got this. Go on."

"Okay, but look. Knock once, like you're real serious, then give it fifteen seconds or so and knock again. Whoever the hell's still alive in there, the first knock should get their attention and have them drifting this way. The second one will hopefully keep them focused while I'm jumping the fence."

Bennie gave me a thumbs up.

"And back away from the door. Someone might try to put a bullet through it."

Bennie gave me a look.

"I'll open the door as soon as I have control in there."

"And if you don't?"

"Then come in blasting."

I returned his look and started around to the side of the condo.

Thirty Eight

Some moments later, I heard the first knock and peeked over the fence. The vertical blinds to both sliding glass doors in back were closed. I got ready to spring, heard the second knock and vaulted over. While paused there in a crouch, I watched to see if anyone peeked out back. When the path seemed clear, I dashed over to the wall space between the two sliding doors. One of them led into the living room, the other one into the kitchen. The entire place was darkened.

I peeked into the living room through a small crack at the end of the blinds. A man was standing by the front door, staring at it. When his head turned my way, I jerked back.

Given the darkness, and limited visual angle, I had been unable to tell if it was Nicholas or Desmond. It would have been helpful to know which. There was an exponential difference between disarming one of them over the other.

I checked the other sliding glass door and found it was locked. That left a deck off the upstairs master bedroom as my only shot at slipping inside unnoticed. I moved to the corner of the deck by the kitchen, leapt and caught the top of the deck. After hanging there for a brief second, I yanked with all my might, got one hand on the vertical spindles of the deck railing and shimmied my way up over the top.

There in a crouch, I watched and listened again. The vertical blinds to that sliding glass door were also closed. After a moment, I went over and put my ear to the glass. No sounds of anyone inside. Delicately, I tried the door and it started to open. I paused again with my Glock out, listening, then opened the door far enough to part the blinds. Again, no one was stirring inside so I slowly opened the door wide enough to slip through, making sure not to let the blinds rattle in my wake.

I texted Bennie.

> I'm inside. Upstairs. Saw someone downstairs through the blinds. Not sure who it is or what happened. Heading that way now. Be ready for further instructions.

A moment later, a thumbs up came back.

I moved over to the bedroom door and peeked out onto the second story landing. No sign of anyone. It appeared that I had the element of surprise but I didn't like the logistics. The railing was wrought iron. If I stepped out onto the landing and someone happened to look that way, I'd be completely exposed.

I texted Bennie.

> Knock on the door again. I need another distraction.

Another thumbs up came back.

I had been waiting there inside the door for a few seconds when the knock came. I saw a shadow moving against the vaulted ceiling above the living room and slipped cautiously out onto the landing. It was Nicholas with his gun pointed at the front door. I trained the Glock on him with both hands and spoke calmly.

"Drop your gun or I'll shoot."

Startled by my voice, he spun around and nearly fumbled the gun out of his hands while taking a shot. I clipped him in the leg and he went down with a yelp. I vaulted down the stairs and kicked the gun out of his reach.

"What the fuck, man? Why do you keep following me around?"

"Because you're easy to follow."

"Fuck."

He was gripping his wounded thigh in pain. I picked the gun up and went to open the front door. Holly was standing there behind Bennie.

"Come on. Get in here. And I thought I told you to stay in the van."

"What the fuck is she doing here?" Nicholas said. "You're not the fucking cops. Oh man, this is so fucked up."

I went into the kitchen. In my rush down the stairs, I had noticed a body lying on floor. It was Desmond. I checked for a pulse.

"Dead?" Bennie said.

I nodded.

"Looks like one shot in the heart."

As was usual in such cases, there was little blood.

"Yeah, this is definitely fucked up," Bennie said to Nicholas.

Nicholas' adrenalin had started to wear off and he was feeling the pain.

"Fuck! I'm bleeding to death over here."

I motioned to Bennie.

"Grab a towel or something and tie off his leg."

I walked over to Nick and showed him my private detective license.

"Fuck. I knew you weren't a cop."

"You're lucky I'm not. Now, I'm going to call my friend with the FBI in a minute and…"

"Oh, like you've got friends in the FBI."

"Shut up and listen! I'm going to make a call and then we're going to start coming up with a story. One that covers all of our asses. And if you don't like that, you can go down for attempted kidnapping and murder."

Bennie returned with the strings from a window blind. I let Nick think about what I had said while Bennie cinched off his leg. He yelped again in pain and stared up at me with blood in his eyes.

494

"So? What's it going to be?" I said.

"Fuck, I don't know. You tell me."

"Then listen. We'll all agree that the kidnapping was Desmond's idea. You had nothing to do with it. You'll have to come up with your own story for how the two of you got involved. I don't know anything about that, but you knew him and happened to go by his place tonight, realized that he had kidnapped Holly and helped her get away. Now you and Holly will have to agree on a story. Like Holly didn't want to go home and deal with the cops, so you drove back here and were trying to figure out what to do next when Desmond showed up, looking for Holly and you shot him in self-defense. Our story is, we'd been following you, thinking you were part of the kidnapping, so I broke in here and we exchanged shots. That explains my bullet in your leg. You can take a victory lap for saving Holly for all I care. As long as Holly's in the clear and gets to go home. Are we good so far?"

"Fuck. It sounds okay to me."

I smiled in a way that wasn't really a smile.

"What?" he said.

"We've got some scores to settle and we're going to start with old man Huntington."

I studied Nick's shifting eyes.

"Yeah, Nick. I'm working for him too. But first I need to call my friend in the FBI. Then we'll talk."

I wandered off and called Alessandra.

"How soon can you get down to Doheny Beach?"

"To do what?"

"Take Holly. Arrest me. All of the above. How long?"

"Ten, fifteen minutes."

I gave her the address.

"All I want is for Holly to go home tonight. You can tie a ribbon around the rest of it, any way you like."

"It's more like a rope around your neck."

"Fine. Hang me. Just make sure about Holly, okay?"

"You realize it's almost morning."

495

"You heard me. Just hurry."

I hung up and went over to Nick.

"You have any pain killers in the house?"

"Yeah. In the upstairs bathroom."

"I'll go get them," Holly said.

"Like hell you will."

I nodded at Bennie and he headed up the stairs.

"And you sit down," I told Holly.

"Can I have a drink?" she said.

"Oh for Christ's sake. You can have a drink when we're all through. Now sit down and listen."

Petulantly, she flopped down in a nearby chair. I looked from her to Nick.

"Let's go over everything one more time. Like I already told you, we need to tell the same story and we need to stick to it."

Bennie came back down with the pain pills and helped Nick get one down his throat. Five minutes later, I was getting to my feet.

"And remember. If it feels for one second like things are going off the rails, you say, I want to talk to my attorney."

Everyone nodded. I turned to Holly.

"And you get your ass back out in that van."

"What about my drink?"

"What? You think I want you waltzing around here sipping piña coladas? You've got your mix out there. Now go on."

She made a face and headed for the door.

"And text me the minute anyone shows up."

She made another face and disappeared.

"Fuck. I need another pain pill," Nick said.

He helped himself. Then we talked about old man Huntington. Nick didn't like the offer I was making him, but he liked the alternative even less.

"Is that it?" he said when we were done.

"No."

"Oh man. What else do you want from me?"

496

"For starters, what Desmond had hanging over Lila's head. And how Ida got involved."

"You know what? I don't even know if she was. I just know that she was Lila's attorney and they…"

"She was what?!"

"What? I figured you knew all about that."

"Well I don't so spill it. When did Ida suddenly come up with a law degree?"

"It wasn't all of a sudden. She's had it for like ten years now."

"Really? From where? Back Of The Matchbook University?"

"No, man. She went to Ohio State."

"Ohio State?! I thought she went to an Ivy League college."

"She did. Cornell. Then she went to Ohio State to get her law degree."

I shook my head.

"Why? What's the big deal?"

I looked at Bennie and back at Nicholas.

"You know what? I don't know but I'm going to guess that that's where Lila and Ida first met. In Ohio."

"That's what she told me."

"And do you happen to know how?"

"Not really. I just know that Ida went to work for some guy fresh out of law school and I guess Lila happened to know him too."

"You guess."

"Well, you know, I was married to that bitch for almost five years and she never told me anything. Always a big secret…Anyway, what's the big deal? She was an attorney."

"Yeah, you're right. I'll deal with that question later. Let's get back to old man Evergreen's murder. What did Ida know about it?"

"I don't know. Like I said, she wouldn't ever tell me shit. I just figured Lila had killed him somehow and that's what this was all about."

"Is that what Desmond told you."

"You know what? He wouldn't tell me shit either."

"Not a thing."

Nick shook his head. I kept staring.

"Fuck, go ask him yourself if you don't believe me."

"Real funny."

"Well, it's the truth."

"Okay. One more thing. Tell me what you know about Vanderhof's sex ring."

"Oh man."

"You can always go down for kidnapping, Nick."

"Fuck, all right."

When Nick was done with his tale, I went into the kitchen, dug Desmond's phone out of his pocket, erased his entire text thread with Lila, wiped the phone clean of my prints, made sure his prints were on it and placed the phone back where I had found it.

"I need to make a quick call," I told Bennie and headed out to the backyard.

Kenny answered after several rings.

"I thought you were done for the night."

"Yeah, thought so too but something else just came up. I need you to do a deep dive on this Ida Huntington. Turns out she has a law degree and history back in Ohio."

"That's convenient."

"Yeah. See what you can dig up and I especially want to know who she went to work for right out of law school. It was someone in Ohio, apparently."

"Any particular hurry?"

"As soon as possible. I want to have all my facts straight before I start slapping Lila around."

Kenny chuckled.

"I'll get right on it."

"Thanks."

As I was going back inside, I felt my phone buzz and pulled it back out of my pocket. Holly had just sent me a text.

Two men are walking up to the door right now.

498

I showed Bennie.

"Who could that be?" he said.

"Not Barretta."

I snuck over and peeked out the security eye.

"Fuck," I whispered. "It's Barnes."

I went back and whispered to Nick.

"You have any reason to think a cop named Barnes from San Bernardino has been following you around?"

"I don't know any cops from San Bernardino."

Barnes knocked on the door and tried the doorknob. I stood there shaking my head.

"Christ. I guess I'll have to let the bastard in."

I went back to the door and opened it.

"Well well well," he said. "Look what I found."

He and his partner came in with hands on their holsters.

"Whoa! What's this? You boys busy shooting each other up, huh?"

Barnes' partner quickly checked around the corner and into the kitchen.

"Holy shit! Man down in here!"

Barnes eased around that way, one hand still on his holster.

"Dead?" he said to his partner.

His partner nodded. Barnes looked back at me with a smile.

"You're busy shooting up everybody tonight, huh Devlin? Let's make sure these boys aren't packing any toys."

His partner came out and frisked all three of us.

"A Glock, huh?" Barnes said to me. "Funny. That just happens to be the kind of slug we found in Potter."

I stared back.

"You're not saying much tonight, Devlin."

"You haven't asked me to."

"How about we start with who shot who around here?"

"He shot that guy in self-defense and I shot him."

"Why?"

"Because he tried to shoot me."

499

"And why did he try to shoot you?"

"Because I broke into his house."

"And why did you break into his house?"

"Because I thought he had kidnapped Holly Evergreen."

"Whoa! This is getting real interesting. And why did you think that?"

"How much time do you have, Barnes?"

"All day and night."

"Good. Because it's going to take that long."

"Go on," he said to his partner. "Cuff him."

His partner came around behind me.

"Hands behind your back."

Barnes got in my face while I was being cuffed.

"I'm taking you in on suspicion of murder, Devlin."

"Murdering who?"

"Donald Ray Potter. I'll sort out the rest of this mess while you're cooling off in a cell. Maybe something else will come up that I can charge you with along the way."

I felt the phone vibrating in my pocket again and was hoping like hell it meant that the cavalry was riding in.

Barnes waved and his partner led me towards the front door. It opened before we got there and Alessandra walked in, along with two of her agents.

"What's going on?" she said to Barnes.

"These boys have been shooting each other up and I'm taking Devlin in on suspicion of murder."

Alessandra held up a hand.

"Not so fast."

"Don't try and pull rank on me here, Barretta. I've got probable cause."

"Well, sorry to say but this has become a federal matter."

"What? This little circus?"

Alessandra shook her head.

"No. Him shooting Potter. Potter was part of a terrorist plot and Devlin's a material witness."

"Oh bullshit," Barnes said.

He waved for his partner to keep going.

"Uh uh uh," Alessandra said.

Her two agents stepped in front of us.

"You can take a crack at him as soon as I'm done, Barnes. In the meantime, what do you say we sort out..." She waved her hand. "Your little circus here."

Alessandra turned to me.

"Where's Holly?"

"Out in my van."

"And you're saying this was a kidnapping plot."

I pointed at Desmond.

"His plot."

"And this gentleman?" she said, pointing at Nicholas.

"He was trying to rescue Holly."

"Do you talk?" she said to Nicholas.

He nodded.

"Then who shot you."

"He did."

"You did?!" she said to me.

"Yeah. I mistakenly thought he was scheming with Desmond."

"Hmm."

Alessandra stood there thinking.

"And you?" she said to Bennie. "You know what went down here?"

"Front and center."

"You mind sticking around to answer some questions?"

Bennie shook his head with a look at me. Alessandra looked at Barnes and shrugged.

"Sounds like a nice little package to me, Barnes. Detective breaks up kidnapping plot and rescues teenage girl."

"And who answers for Potter?"

"Like I said, you're welcome to take a crack at Devlin here when I'm done with him, but trust me. This Potter business is way over your head."

"Shit. I still have a murder out on Highland Road to solve. And for which I know this son of a bitch is withholding evidence."

Alessandra shrugged again.

"Fine," Barnes said. "As long as I get a crack at Devlin. Meanwhile, what are we doing about the girl?"

"I'm getting her out of here. She and her mother don't need the press. Let's let Holly have a good night's sleep and you can question her tomorrow if need be. She's not going anywhere...Fair enough?"

"Yeah, Christ. Just make sure you leave that Glock here with me."

Barnes' partner uncuffed me.

"Let's get an ambulance over here," Alessandra said to one of her men. "This man needs to see a doctor."

She turned to Barnes.

"I'll let you deal with the local police. It's your crime scene."

With a final nod, Alessandra led me out the door. Her two agents were over at their SUV, making a call. The two of us paused outside my van.

"You happy now?" Alessandra said.

"Happy enough. Seeing you pull rank on Barnes is the kind of thing that turns me on."

She shook her head.

"You are a piece of work, Michael."

"I know."

We stared.

"Is she in there?"

"Yeah."

"And you'll get her home okay?"

"Yeah."

"I still need to debrief you. About what happened down in Fallbrook."

"When?"

"Say tomorrow afternoon? Around two? We'll all get some sleep in the meantime."

"Sure."

"You know the building?"

"I do."

"Just mention my name and they'll show you upstairs."

"Okay. Thanks again."

She shook her head, smiling. Then her look turned serious.

"Just to be clear. You have no idea what happened to Potter."

I shook my head.

"The last time I saw him, he was on two feet."

She studied me while slowly nodding.

"And you stick to that story. I wouldn't want to have to put you away."

I nodded and opened the back of the van. Holly was seated at the monitors with her drink."

"Veronica Mars goes on a spree."

"Shut up," she said.

"Hi Holly. I'm Agent Barretta. You're going to have to answer some questions over the next couple of days. Are you okay with that?"

She nodded.

"Good. For now, Michael's going to take you home."

Alessandra and I went around to the far side of the van. After a long stare, I placed one hand at the back of her neck and kissed her tenderly.

"See you tomorrow."

She touched my face.

"See you tomorrow, you big bastard."

I smiled. She didn't but touched my face again before leaving.

"I saw that," Holly said when I reopened the back door.

"Shut up," I said like her. "And come on with your bar supplies. I'm not leaving this shit lying around for Bennie to see."

She had been drinking Cuba libres and downed the last of her drink.

"Come on," I said again.

She stumbled out of the van juggling a quart of rum, a liter of Coke, a bag of crushed ice, lime juice and her plastic tumbler. I grabbed the ice and rum from her as she hit the ground.

"Can I have another one?" she said.

"Oh Christ. Here."

I helped her mix the drink outside my opened trunk, stuffed everything else inside and got her settled into the front seat. Before heading back out to Coast Highway, I texted Lila to let her know what was happening and drove ahead in silence. The sky had started to brighten on the eastern horizon. I couldn't remember the last time I had slept.

I stole a glance at Holly, unsure what to make of her. Was she chastened at all by what had happened? Did she know that most of this was related in one way or the other to the murder of her step-father? Did she remember any of that past? This sort of psychological scar could stay buried for a long time, but I doubted forever.

"You up to telling me what happened?" I said with another glance Holly's way. "I mean, from the time you ran off with that monster again to how you ended up with Desmond?"

With a glance back at me, she took a sip of her drink.

"Don stole another car that night and we went to Nicholas' place. Then I heard them scheming about trying to get a ransom from my Mom. Then something happened because Don came in one day and said, 'You're on your own, bitch' and he left with some other guys. Then Nicholas took me over to Desmond's place and I guess they were talking with my Mom because Desmond told me that he'd have the money soon and I could go home."

"Do you know how absolutely crazy that sounds? I mean, let's all just get together and have a kidnapping party?"

"I think Desmond had something on my Mom."

She shrugged as if sincerely clueless and I was reluctant to press the issue. If her memory was indeed a blank, I didn't see it as my job to remedy that fact.

"So tell me this," I said. "How did Nick and Desmond come to know each other?"

"Desmond said they met one night over at The Crown House."

"And just like that, they're scheming to kidnap you?"

"I don't know. All I know is, they're both getting dumped by their girlfriends and pretty much think all women are bitches."

Our eyes met while I driving.

"So what about Ida? How did she get involved?"

"I don't think she was. I mean, not in the kidnapping." Holly sipped from her drink. "She's the one I stayed with the night my step-father died."

Thirty Nine

Holly held my gaze for a moment and looked forward. A part of me wanted to press her further but I left it alone. From everything Lila had told me, and from knowing Lila's name was on Ida's home deed, I had already suspected as much. Those two had forged a secret pact somewhere in the past, and as much as I wanted to know exactly what that was, the matter before me was simple. If Holly had blocked out everything about old man Evergreen's death, it was a shrink's job to dig that memory out of her. And if Lila had made a career out of marrying and murdering rich old men, it was the law's job to try and hang her for it.

Either way, I was back to not trusting Lila as far as I could throw her, in this universe, or any other one.

Back at Lila's place, I parked in the driveway, killed the engine and looked over at Holly.

"What?" she said.

"Heart to heart?"

She stared for a long moment before nodding. I sighed and looked forward.

"You know, it's just struck me how fast the years go by."

I looked over at her.

"Sometimes I can remember being your age like it was yesterday. Sometimes it seems like a million years away."

Holly studied me.

"So?"

I sighed again.

"Oh, I don't know. I guess I was just thinking, I wish I had known enough to stand back and view life with a bit of perspective in those days. It all seemed to be so timeless. I hardly realized the future was out there. You know, adulthood and all that crap?"

Our eyes met.

"It's coming at you fast, kid, whether you like it or not."

"I know."

"Yeah?"

She nodded.

"Well, if I had any advice for old Holly Evergreen, it would be, figure out what you want to do with your life. It's the only thing that really matters. You can be whatever you want, you know? There's nothing stopping you from achieving your dreams...but you."

She stared without answering. I looked away again.

"Maybe I'm just projecting but I see a lot of myself in you when I was your age. Mixed up, no direction and doing my best to hide it all."

"Are you doing what you really want to do?" she said.

I shrugged.

"No. Not really. I mean, early on, the detective business was exciting and I've come to accept that I was lucky to have found some kind of career, especially one where I didn't have to sit around answering to some prick in an office. But there's always been something gnawing away at my guts."

I looked back at her.

"That's where the booze and drugs come in handy. They help to mask all those feelings. For a while, anyway. Then you find yourself getting sober at fifty or whenever and thinking, shit, I've wasted my whole life. I'd hate to see you going through the same thing."

"But you still don't know what you want to do with your life?"

507

"Oh, I guess sometimes I think about sitting down to write a book."

"So why don't you?"

"Maybe I will. If I ever get done with keeping you out of trouble."

Holly made a face. Then she was serious.

"I've been thinking about getting into acting."

I gave her a look.

"What? Going for the fame and fortune, are we?"

"No. It's just, I think I would be good at it."

I kept staring. Holly seemed to sense my thoughts and pretended to be Lila.

Oh god this...Oh god that.

I was quickly in stitches.

"Okay, okay. You win."

I eyed her and laughed again.

"But that's my point. Put yourself out there. Take a chance, and if acting doesn't work out, try something else. You really can be anything you want. It's just a matter of hard work and determination."

"I know."

"Okay. Well, I guess we'd better go in and say hi to Mom."

I had started to open my car door but Holly stopped me.

"Are you going to go out with her?"

I closed the door again.

"I don't know. She's so damned beautiful, she's hard to ignore. But she scares the crap out of me."

"I think she's crazy."

"That's a pretty easy label to lay on someone, kid. Don't you think we're all a bit nuts these days?"

"Yeah, maybe."

"No. For sure...Look, I'm not saying your Mom's without flaws. Probably money's had a destructive effect on her. That's my take, anyway. I saw this with one of my old flames. She had a real shot of making it as an artist. But it's an uncertain future so she goes off and marries this wealthy guy, figuring she could

508

do her art and never have to worry again. I ran into her years later and it was as if she had sold her soul to the devil. She had everything you could ever want in life, except inner peace and happiness. The art? Gone. Nowhere to be found…Well, that's an age-old story, but as to your Mom, she has all the right instincts. At least, when it comes to being a mother."

Holly made a face.

"I'm serious. I've watched her over this past week or so and however screwed up she is, that woman would kill to protect you."

Holly and I stared with those words hanging in the air. Did she know they were literal? Or did she know something that I didn't know?

"But you're not going to go out with her," Holly said, having searched my eyes for a long moment.

I shrugged and quickly explained about Caitlin.

"See? Everything gets mixed up in that mess…But, sure. I've thought of surrendering to it. Dinner every night, my slippers and a pipe. Then I'm thinking Lila that would be the worst decision I've ever made. Kind of like you and old Donny boy. Someone gets you all aroused down below there. Then next thing you know, you're looking for a gun. And the only question is, which way to point it."

She smiled.

"So what's with you and Agent Barretta?"

I shrugged again.

"Actually, she's about the only sane thing in my life right now. But I'd still drive my life off a cliff to have one second of what I once had with Caitlin. Trust me, kid. I go to sleep at night struggling with this shit. Who the hell knows why I'm so devoted to that woman? I don't even know if it's good for me. All I know is, I have these feelings for someone who's forever going off the rails. It doesn't matter what I do. Things are always turning into a big giant mess."

I shrugged again.

"Maybe that's the thing with romances, Holly. There's always a big if. If only this. If only that."

She looked straight ahead.

"What?" I said. "What are you worried about?"

"I'm just afraid that if you don't go out with my Mom, she'll find another jerk boyfriend and he'll be hanging around the house all the time."

"Look, if you ever find yourself feeling cornered, just call me, okay?"

She nodded.

"I mean it, Holly. Anytime, anywhere, you call. I'll always be there for you."

"Thanks."

"Final thought."

"Okay."

"Well, a couple of them, actually…First, before you go falling head over heels in love again, make a list of what's important to you. Then, when you meet the next hunk, make sure he checks a lot of those boxes. It doesn't have to be all of them, but it damned well better be most. Without that common ground, a romance is doomed before it ever gets started."

I tapped Holly gently on her chest.

"Love? True love? It starts up here. And it goes from there up. It doesn't start down there. That kind of love can be exciting for a while, but without respect and admiration and stuff like that, sooner or later you'll find yourself ready to scream."

Holly nodded.

"So what was the second one?"

"Oh. I was going to say, about doing what you really, really want to do in this life? Yeah, things are pretty meaningless without that one thing. But doing what you really, really want to do is pretty meaningless without some greater purpose, and that always seems to come back to helping other people."

I searched her eyes.

510

"Don't ever miss out on a chance to lend a hand. We'll all sleep easier if we can do that one thing as the days go by." She nodded. "And by the way, you owe me a hundred dollars."

Holly smiled, then leaned over to kiss my cheek.

"Thanks, Dad. Thanks for everything you did."

I tapped my chest with a fist.

"Sure, kid. Anytime...So, are we ready?"

She nodded and we started out of the car.

Inside, the mother/daughter reunion was something less than joyous. For what it was worth, both of them shed a tear as they hugged.

Holly had started off to her room when she abruptly rushed back to give me another kiss on the cheek. Then she dashed up the stairs and disappeared.

"I can see who she admires," Lila said.

I stared.

"Come on, let's sit down."

I joined Lila in the living room and explained everything that had just gone down. When she heard of Desmond's death, she seemed genuinely saddened. Once lovers, always lovers, I guess.

I finished the rest of the story as I had already told it.

"But they're going to check Desmond's phone."

"I erased his thread with you. You'd better do the same with your phone."

"Oh god. Isn't there some way we can keep the police away from Holly?"

"They've got to question her, but it'll die there. There's really only the question of who that poor young woman was, buried out behind Potter's place."

"And you still have no idea?"

I explained about the young woman named Crystal.

"Holly said she thought that they had taken her back out to the freeway so she could hitchhike home but who knows?"

"Oh god."

"Look. Holly's only material in terms of identifying the poor thing. If she can even do that. I'm sure she had nothing to do with the actual crime."

I shrugged and we were back to staring at each other.

"I know about Ida," I said. "I know that she's your attorney and her house is in your name."

Lila's eyes did a dance while she stared at me.

"I don't know what's actually going on between you two, from your days back in Ohio to out here in Pueblo Hills, and I probably don't want to know, but we're back to me not knowing if I can ever completely trust you."

I let that sink in before getting to my feet. Lila stood up too and searched my eyes.

"No, I'm not going to tell anyone, Lila."

"That's not what I was thinking."

"No?"

"No. I just wanted to make sure you were all right."

"Yeah. I'm fine. I have to answer for my end of things but Barretta's been good about it all. It's just Barnes who's being a dick."

Lila kept searching my eyes.

"Come on," I said. "I'm due down at the FBI headquarters this afternoon and need some sleep."

I started down the foyer towards the front door with Lila at my side. We stopped there and faced each other. I glanced down at her cute little toes in her cute little shoes with her cute little everything and felt sure I'd be doomed if I allowed myself to fall in love with her. I'd be chasing her beauty around for the rest of my life, while it slowly drove me mad. Lila was why men wrote tortured poems and killed themselves and each other.

She stood up a little higher on her heels and kissed me. I looked into her eyes for a moment before taking her by the hair and waist and giving it to her good.

Then I was back to staring at her.

"I just wish I could trust you, Lila."

She touched my face.

512

"Just call me, okay? So we can talk?"

I nodded.

"In the meantime, you'd better ask Holly to come down and have a glass of wine with you."

"Oh sure. She's sixteen years old."

"Lila, trust me. She's going to need a drink before the night is through and it will go a long way towards patching things up between you two...And whatever you do, start leveling with her. As much as you can. Just try being her friend for a change. She's already proven that she can survive out there without you."

"Oh god."

I hugged her again for good measure and headed out to my car.

Dawn had broken by the time I finally found sleep and it was going on noon before I climbed back out of bed. I wandered down to the living room and stared out at the creek, drenched in bad dreams and my troubled conscience. I had killed a man. Two of them, if you wanted to count Potter. It was not the first time I had felt crucified over this moral abyss. I was hoping it would be the last.

I went ahead with making coffee and returned to my breakfast nook. Speckled sunlight danced on the table top and wind stirred in the trees, a dry rattle in the eucalyptus, a whisper of untold tales and ancient things in the old pine.

A thought occurred to me as I sat there. Being tossed back into the fire was only half the equation. A person could not be tossed back into the fire without having first returned to consciousness. But was that it? Our spirits going around and around in circles as the eons passed by, committing the same blunders, over and over and over again, having to learn the same lessons, only in different guises?

My only answer was to keep shedding baggage. Failing that, I probably would go mad.

And what was left in these ashes? I had done my best to rescue a young woman and had hopefully pointed her in the right direction, and if that was the whole show, I could probably live with myself. I wasn't sure what else a man could do.

With that, the duties of that day came to mind and I grabbed the phone. Fitzy answered after several rings.

"I'm afraid to ask," she said.

"No, no. It's nothing tragic. She just ran off to Rhode Island with Brandon."

"Oh. She just ran off to Rhode Island with Brandon. Well, then, what am I worried about?"

I laughed.

"It's not funny."

"Well, you made it sound that way."

"Great…Please explain."

"I did."

Fitzy let out a big sigh.

"And what am I supposed to do now?"

"I don't know. Did you want to fly out there and confront her?"

"Not particularly. If the law allowed me to drag her home by the ear, I would. But she's seventeen, so what? I fly out there and we get into a big shouting match?"

"Well, ironically enough, I'm flying back there in a couple of days."

"You are? Where?"

"To the Hartford area for a memorial service. But it's not that much farther down to the shore. They've been banging a credit card around this town called Watch Hill. I hear it's a nice area. Taylor Swift has a place down there."

"Oh well, I feel so much better about it now."

I couldn't help but laugh again. Then I remembered the fate of that dead young woman and grew serious.

"Look, Fitzy. She's alive and well. There are mothers out there who will never see their daughters again. You two are having a spat or whatever. I know it hurts but it's not the end of the world."

514

I sat there waiting for her response.

"So, would you?" she said.

"Drive down and talk with her?"

"Yes."

"Sure. I can at least let her know you're concerned…Should I tell her you'll send money if she needs it?"

"Oh god, sure. I don't want her out to be on the streets."

"I gather that's not much of a concern with Brandon, but it would be a goodwill gesture. Couldn't hurt."

"Okay. When are you flying out?"

"Friday, midday."

"Can we talk again before you leave?"

"Sure. I've got a couple of busy days but I'll check in with you tomorrow."

"Thanks."

"Yeah. Chin up. The important thing is to let her know it's okay. That you're not going to punish her."

"I'll work on that."

"Please do. Meanwhile I need to get on to the next call."

I ended that one and rang through to Mr. Huntington.

"Mr. Devlin," he said. "Has that corrupt son of a bitch coughed up my Picasso yet?"

I smiled.

"Not yet, but I expect to find it at my doorstep any day now."

"Very well. In the meantime, any more tall tales to tell? I've come to live vicariously off of your adventures."

"Actually, I called to tell you that one of your wishes has been granted."

"How so?"

"Nicholas finally found enough rope to hang himself."

"Oh wonderful. Do explain."

I did.

"My commendations for shooting the little toady," he said when I was done. "My only regret is that it wasn't fatal."

I smiled.

"Look, sir. He's agreed to release all claims to your wealth and that of your daughter. In exchange for which I won't tell anyone that he had a hand in kidnapping Holly Evergreen. It was the best deal I could get. Just have your attorney draw up an agreement, however you like, and he'll sign it."

"You clearly have more confidence in his trustworthiness than I do."

"Oh, he'll sign it all right. He swallowed the news hard but make no mistake about it. He knows that if he reneges on the deal, I'll spill the beans."

"And what do you derive out of this transaction, Michael?"

"Oh, just the satisfaction of a job well done, sir. Glad to help."

"You're an honorable man, Mr. Devlin. An honorable man."

"Some would question that claim, but thanks for saying so."

There was a pause.

"I sense there's something on your mind, Michael."

"Oh, just wondering if you'd mind explaining one thing for me."

"And that would be?"

"Why on earth did Ida marry Nicholas in the first place? No matter how I look at things, it just doesn't add up."

"That's easy. When Ida showed up with her French anarchist boyfriend that Christmas, I offered her half a million dollars if she'd dump him and marry someone sensible. Then she goes off and marries Nicholas. Of course, at first glance, he seemed to be quite charming and normal."

"Yeah. I suppose he might at first glance."

"Trust me, he had the appearance of a catch five years ago. I suspect his proximity to my fortune is what corrupted him. He saw a shortcut to the sweet life and became parasitic rather than evolve. Then maybe he was always parasitic."

"I imagine fate would require some measure of raw material to achieve its ends."

"Well put, sir. I would ask you to marry Ida and save us all a lot of grief but I fear it's too late for her too."

"I'm already surrounded by hyenas, sir, but thanks so much for the offer."

He laughed.

"Well, I hate to appear greedy but I still await the return of my Picasso."

"I'll call as soon as I have it in my hands."

"And present me with your final bill, of course."

"I had assumed we'd discuss financial matters at that point, yes."

"Splendid. And thank you again."

"Thank you, sir."

I got off the call with that same sick feeling in my gut. The old man hadn't said a word about Charlotte and I had lacked the courage to ask him. Best to let it sit until my return from New England. If she had failed to materialize by then, I'd have no choice but to level with him about my suspicions. I could only imagine his grief, if they turned out to be correct.

As to Nicholas and Ida, I parked that matter under the heading of, people kept making lousy choices in love. Why would I expect those two to be any different?

I was reminded of my own lousy choices in making the next call.

"Helllllooooo," Caitlin said after several rings, like she didn't know who it was.

"Land shark," I said.

She laughed.

"So how are you, honey? How's your head?"

"Oh, I'm feeling a little cuckoo today, but everything's okay."

"Yeah?"

"Yeah. I look a bit like a lawnmower ran over me."

She laughed.

"I got Holly home early this morning."

"You did!?"

"Yeah. She's a little cuckoo too. She and her mother have a lot of stuff to work out, but I think she was relieved to finally be back home."

"Oh good."

"Yeah…So it looks like it might rain a little tonight."

"A spritzer, I'm hearing."

"I'll take a spritzer."

"Yeeaaahhh."

"So maybe dinner for two? I'm dying for an ahi burger."

There was a tremulous pause.

"Suurrrre," she said.

"Pick you up at seven?"

"Suurrrre."

"Okay, well. I'd better get going. I gotta go straighten out the FBI here in a bit."

Caitlin laughed.

"How come the FBI?"

"Long story. I'll tell you tonight."

"Okay."

"Okay. I mxyzptlk you."

"Stop! You're not supposed to say that!"

I laughed.

"Well I said it anyway, so there."

I got off, shaking my head. The distance between childish and childlike was the width of a hair with that woman. And still I adored her.

I called Gigi next, just to let her know that Holly had gotten home safely.

"I don't know if you were aware of this, Gigi, but Potter did try to get back in through that secret stairwell."

"Yes, thanks to you, I discovered that Holly had left the gate ajar down below. I could just put her over my knee for that one."

"Yeah. I don't think she meant to hurt you. I suspect in her troubled young mind, she had pictured going out to get high with Potter and then sneaking back in alone."

518

"She is truly one of us, isn't she?"

"Yeah. It would seem that way. When we're out there drinking and using, we mistake some really troubled thinking for sanity."

She laughed.

"And so, are you okay after all of this?"

"Yeah, mostly, but I could definitely use a meeting. I'm getting on a plane for New England on Friday but maybe I'll have time to find one back there. The committee upstairs is definitely talking to me."

Gigi laughed again.

"You're right on schedule, Michael."

"So I've heard...Okay. I'd better get on to the next call."

Forty

I had Bennie on the phone a minute later.

"I'll tell you what, boss man. You didn't miss nothing last night."

"Beat you up a bit, did they?"

"Dude, they had my huevos in a vice and took a sledgehammer to them."

I laughed.

"So how long did they keep you there?"

"They cut me loose with just enough time to catch the morning meeting, and man did I need that shit. Then I came home and crashed. And that prick Barnes ain't done with us yet."

"I know but I'm more worried about the FBI right now. I'm off to go deal with them in about an hour."

"For what?"

"For what happened down in Fallbrook, mainly."

"Shit, you kicked ass and saved some lives."

"Yeah, well, they still don't like you taking the law into your own hands. Anyway, I just wanted to check in with you before I jumped in the shower."

"Yeah, what are we doing today?"

"Well, is Morey still down there keeping an eye on Caitlin?"

"Yeah."

"Then take the day off…With pay."

"All right. I'm sensing a benny for Bennie."

"Yeah, you did good, my friend. You did good."

"Yeah. Finally some action."

"Yeah. Anyway, go ahead and split up the shifts over there however you like while I'm gone but have someone keep an eye on her 24/7."

"You got it."

"And if I don't see you before I leave, your check will be on my desk. Morey's too."

"Thanks, boss man."

"Sure. And we'll figure out what we're doing next once I get back."

I ended the call and started stripping off clothes.

An hour later, I was walking into what had come to be known as the Ziggurat Building. It was, visually speaking, a lousy version of the early pyramids, which were lousy versions of the great pyramids. There was stepped level after stepped level, clothed in ochre-colored stucco, until the top floor sat there like a German pill box. In the middle of a woodsy neighborhood, the structure stuck out like a sore thumb. It had come to house a number of government agencies over the years, the FBI and IRS among them, so few were glad to see the place or visited it gleefully.

Inside the fortified public entrance, I dumped the contents of my pockets into a plastic container and passed through a scanner. A moment later, a gal at the information booth was pointing me up to the 4th floor.

There, I was confronted by another checkpoint and asked the purpose of my visit. I told them I was there to see Agent Barretta. Alessandra appeared a minute later.

"Follow me."

I did, back among a sea of cubicles.

"And how are we doing today, Mr. Devlin?"

"Oh swell, Agent Barretta. And you?"

"A little beat from the late nights but doing okay, thanks."

She stopped outside of a small conference room.

"Is this going to hurt?" I asked.

"I've covered your back as best I can, but probably a little."

I noticed Agent Bradley sitting inside.

"Does he have to be here?"

"He's part of my team."

"You have my condolences."

"Funny. He's been marking territory over you, too."

"If only he knew."

"Shut up."

I gave her a devilish smile.

"Show me the plank."

She admonished me with her eyes and opened the door. There were four agents sitting inside and all four heads turned my way.

Alessandra introduced me.

"Michael Devlin, Agents Coates, Mansford, Bradley and Kelly."

I received nods from all, save for Bradley. He just stared.

Coates was the older agent I had noticed out by Lila's pool the other night, and clearly the man in charge. He sized me up as I sat down.

"Thanks for coming in, Mr. Devlin."

"No problem."

"You can consider this is an informal meeting. We'll need to depose you properly at some point and have you testify in court but for now we'd simply like to hear your version of what transpired down in Fallbrook the other night. Fair enough?"

"Sure."

"And you're sure you don't want counsel present?"

"I'm fine, thanks."

"Very well. Let's start with what led you to believe you'd find Potter down there in the first place."

"Part of that was firsthand knowledge, part of it intuition."

Coates waved for me to go on.

"So, in terms of firsthand knowledge, I had been trying to track down some jewelry for a client and…"

"The client's name, if you don't mind?"

I glanced at Alessandra and back.

"Ellwood Huntington."

That appeared to give Coates pause. He looked around the table, jotted something down in his notes and told me to go on.

"So, my search for this piece of jewelry led me to a Stephen St. Claire, and that led me to his father's home in Fallbrook on Monday. And while talking to Stephen outside the front door, the old man came out and leveled a shotgun at me. Well, that would get anyone's attention so I looked into his past and learned he was definitely a loose cannon. And with an arrest history that suggested he was partial to right wing conspiracies. There was that and the fact that I thought I had spotted Cole Pritchett's Camaro heading towards Fallbrook as I headed home that same day. So, there were those two things and I guess a bit of intuition, and one other clue, which was knowing that Potter was still down at the coast."

"Who told you he was still down at the coast?" Bradley said, interrupting me.

Coates looked from Bradley to Alessandra and waved a hand.

"Let's just say that's immaterial for the moment...Go on, Mr. Devlin."

"Well, again, with the old man's history, and the possible Pritchett connection, and thinking that, for Potter, Fallbrook might be considered 'still down at the coast' something told me to head that way and have a look. I mean, there aren't that many right-wing fanatics. At least not in that neck of the woods, so it didn't seem all that fanciful to think there might be a connection between these men."

"I'll accept your explanation on that point for now," Coates said. "But that still begs the question. Why did you think it was your business to be looking for Potter?"

"I was actually looking for Holly Evergreen and assumed she was still with him at the time."

"And that was your sole motive."

I nodded.

"Go on, then. Explain the events of that evening."

I did, leaving out everything related to the Mongols. My story played out exactly as things had happened, except in this version, Potter got away and I never saw him again. When I was done, there were looks around the table.

Bradley spoke up.

"So you're saying you never thought of chasing after Potter?"

"Of course, but I wasn't there for Potter. I was there to find Holly. And by the time I had established that she wasn't in the house, Potter was nowhere to be found."

"And you have no idea how he ended up out near Indio with a broken neck?" Coates said.

"None at all."

"And you're certain you can't identify who killed Stephen St. Claire."

I shook my head.

"Like I said, Potter wasn't in the picture when the shot was fired, so that leaves Cole Pritchett or the man I killed. I just don't know which one."

Coates nodded and looked back at his notes.

"And this Desmond Ducot. How did you come to suspect that he was harboring Holly?"

"I didn't. I was following Nicholas Chalmers and he led me to Desmond."

"Following him, why?" Bradley said.

"Because he's Ellwood Huntington's son-in-law and the one who had stolen the Picasso and jewelry."

"That still doesn't explain why you broke into Nicholas' place," Bradley said.

"I broke in because I believed he was harboring Holly."

"In that case, why didn't you just call the police?"

"That's a fair enough question. If I'm guilty of anything in this world, it's not trusting them as much as I should. In my defense, I've seen their SWAT teams inadvertently burn places to the ground and wasn't taking any chances."

Bradley scoffed. Coates shuffled his notes and looked up at me.

"And from what I understand, you didn't observe the confrontation that led to Desmond Ducot's death."

"I did not. My partner Bennie and I heard what we thought was a gunshot and that's when I proceeded to enter Nicholas' residence."

Coates let out a big sigh.

"Do you have anything you'd like to add for now, Mr. Devlin?"

A number of things flashed through my mind in that moment, like who had murdered that young woman, and how Ida and Desmond and Lila had gotten all mixed up together, and the true reason why Lila had killed old man Evergreen and how her first husband had ended up with a broken neck, but I didn't ask any of those questions. I simply shook my head.

"Very well," Coates said. "I believe that will be enough for today."

He stood up and everyone stood up with him.

"I will say, you've acquired quite a reputation for skirting the law, Mr. Devlin, but I suppose no more than the next private detective. And as questionable as your exploits might be, they seem to have served the greater public interest. I just wouldn't want you thinking that this sort of thing has our blessing."

"I completely understand, sir."

"I hope so."

Coates stared hard into my eyes while shaking my hand.

"I'm sure Agent Barretta here will show you back out."

I nodded to the other agents and followed Barretta out among the sea of cubicles.

"Come," she said. "We can talk in my office."

I joined her on a hike to the opposite end of the building. Having arrived to her office, she closed the door and we settled in on our respective sides of her desk.

"How did I do?" I said.

"Looks like you still have your scalp…At least what's left of it." She leaned back in her chair with a smile and flick of her hand. "So, if you don't mind me asking, just what was this kidnapping business all about?"

"I really don't know."

When you considered all the blank spots in my knowledge, that was truer than not.

"Not a thing?" she said.

"Oh, if you want me to take a wild guess, I'd say it was a domestic drama. Lila wanted to move on and Desmond didn't. And then suddenly extortion was involved."

I shrugged.

"I find in cases like this, it's best just to stand back and let everyone stab each other in the back. Then pretty soon you're down to a manageable situation."

She chuckled.

"You continuously amaze me, Michael. If only in how screwed up you are."

I acknowledged her comment as if it was a compliment and we were back to staring at each other.

"So?" I said. "Are *you* done with me?"

"Oh, mostly…Let's see."

She shuffled among stacks of papers on her desk.

"Oh yes. Barnes hit me up about this ring he's been chasing after. Care to elaborate?"

"Trying to get me into trouble, are we?"

She flicked out a hand.

"You do a pretty good job on your own."

She kept staring.

"Look, Alessandra. One of these days soon, I'm afraid I'll have to inform an old man that his daughter is dead and I've been trying to do everything in my powers this past week to forestall that moment, and to prove otherwise. And that's all I'm going to say on that subject for the moment."

"Fair enough. I do believe in your noble intentions, as far off the reservation as you seem to get at times."

"Thanks. I think."

She smiled.

"So? Is there anything on your wish list?"

"Of what do we speak?"

She rolled her hand sarcastically.

"Yeah, actually. I do have a couple of items."

"And they would be?"

"Well, first of all, the Pritchett clan. Given our history, I'd really appreciate you keeping an eye on those folks for me. I fear they'll keep sending out assassins until I'm dead."

"I already told you. They're on my radar."

"Maybe tanks surrounding their hideouts are more in order."

"Trust me. They're not going anywhere without me knowing it."

"I'll have to take your word for it."

"And your next wish?"

"Dirk Vanderhof."

She raised her eyebrows.

"I know you two having a history. And you wanted me to do, what?"

I explained what Nicholas had told me and what I suspected had been an invitation for Holly to join Vanderhof's harem of underaged dolls.

"Do you have any proof of that?" Alessandra said.

"My sixth sense."

"That ought to hold up pretty well in a court of law."

"Look. I know the son of a bitch is up to no good. I saw it with my own eyes. Hell, I almost nailed him for statutory rape, back when his wife was divorcing him. The man has a taste for young flesh. Now do you really want mixed up young girls like Holly getting sucked into his orbit?"

"This wouldn't be a personal vendetta, would it?"

"Just follow him, Alessandra. Please. If I only had one chip to play, I'd rather use it there. Things have a way of dying when they get near Vanderhof.

"Fair enough, Michael. I'll look into it. Anything else?"

"My Glock. Or Glocks. I'd enjoy having them back."

"As soon as ballistics is done with the one I confiscated, you'll have it. Not sure what to tell you about the one Barnes has."

"But you'll mention it to him."

"Sure...So what's next for you?"

"Oh, I'm off to a memorial service in New England here in a couple of days. One of my cousins."

"Sorry to hear it."

"Yeah. Those are the breaks. Then I expect I'll arrive back home here next week and wander around feeling lost for a few days. Weltschmerz, it's called. Ever had it?"

"Can't say I have."

"It's a feeling that the whole world's going to hell and there's absolutely nothing you can do about it."

She shook her head with a smile.

"You really are a piece of work."

"Yeah. But I'm awfully good in bed. It says so on my gravestone...I'm pretty good at some other things too. At least I like to tell myself that. Whenever I'm wandering around late at night all alone."

"With that...uh..."

"Weltschmerz."

"Yeah, that thing...I'll keep it in mind."

"You do that."

"Well, better get back to work here," she said and stood up. I stood up with her.

"Oh," she said, grabbing a file from on top of her desk and tossing it my way. "That police report you had asked me for."

"Oh. Thanks."

"If you were worried about her being a serial killer, it doesn't seem to paint that picture."

"No?"

She shook her head.

528

"Just a pretty straightforward looking accident, as far as I can tell."

I stood there staring back.

"What's the matter, Michael? You look disappointed."

"Well, a nice clean case of murder would have tied together more neatly...Now I don't know what to think."

"Well, that's your business," she said. "And you didn't get that report from me."

"No. Of course not."

Alessandra came around her desk and we headed back out to the elevators. I pushed the call button and turned to face her.

"Thanks again, dear. It really was very adult."

She smiled.

"That it was, Michael...I suspect we'll be seeing each other again." She gave me a cautious hug. "Give me a call when you get back. And have a safe trip."

"Thanks."

She turned and headed back into that sea of cubicles. I was enjoying her fine legs when the elevator bell dinged.

Down in the parking lot, I climbed into my Impala, started the engine and opened the report. I was there several minutes before setting the report aside and dropping the car into gear. So maybe Lila wasn't such a monster after all. That would have made my decisions ahead so much easier.

Returning home, I was back to a dozen loose ends to resolve before my departure to New England and still in no mood to tackle any of it. I settled back in at my breakfast nook and sat there amidst the whispering leaves and speckled sunlight. I had always been drawn to the simpler things in life and could not understand for the life of me how my existence always seemed to become so damned complicated. Probably I was just kidding myself about being simple.

I was working on that quandary, and whether or not to call Lila, when my phone rang. It was Kenny.

"Dying to get paid, are we?" I said in answering.

"That would be nice but it's not why I called."

"Okay. What's up?"

"Ms. Evergreen's long-lost siblings."

"Ah...So what did you learn?"

Kenny went about explaining things.

"Far out," I said when he was done. "Hang on a second."

I put him on speaker phone and pulled up Lila's contact info.

"Give me the number of the middle brother."

I added it to Lila's existing contact info and took my phone back off speaker.

"By the way, Alessandra got me that police report and it looks like Lila's not a serial killer after all."

"No?"

"If I'm to take things at face value, it looks like it was a pretty straightforward accident after all."

"So, you ready to propose now, are you?"

"Think I'll hold off on that one...Anyway, thanks for following up on this. I'll give you a shout when I'm down at the office tomorrow and get you paid."

"Thanks."

"Yeah. Thank you."

We ended the call. I sat there in thought for a minute before dialing Lila's number. She answered after two rings.

"I was wondering if you'd ever call again."

I shook my head. No doubt the woman would drive me insane.

"Look," I said. "I've got news on your siblings."

"Oh god. This is sounding grim already."

"Well, to be honest with you, it's a kind of a mixed bag."

"I was expecting as much...Okay, I'm sitting down now. Go on."

"So first, the bad news. Your oldest brother Frank's in prison..."

"Oh god."

"It was for white collar crime. It could have been worse."

"Funny."

"Well, it does show intelligence."

"Funny."

"Yeah. So, anyway, looks like he got caught in some kind of securities fraud scheme and has about five to seven years left now on his sentence."

"Great. Can we get on to the good news?"

"Just hang on...So, your younger sister is happily married and living in rural Iowa but has medical problems. Looks like early stage MS or something. Good people, though, from what my guy could gather."

"That's nice. Sad but I'd love to talk to her...Now the good news?"

"The good news is, your middle brother Richard's an intellectual property attorney up in LA. Quite successful from what I understand and he's dying to talk with you."

I had been waiting for Lila to respond when I realized she was crying.

"I wish you were here right now," she said after a spell.

"I know. I wish I could be there too but I'm heading off to New England tomorrow and still have a million things to do before I go."

"Sure," she said.

"Lila, please. I'll call you as soon as I get back, okay?"

She worked on her sniffles.

"You could call while you're gone, you know."

"Okay, I will. As soon as I have a minute."

"Thank you."

"You're welcome. And I'm texting you your brother's phone number right now. I understand he's eagerly waiting to hear from you."

I said goodbye, hung up and immediately sent a text with her brother's phone number. I was left with the feeling that I had just closed the door in the face of a homeless waif.

Unable to make much sense of life or love, I went upstairs to take a nap.

Forty One

That evening at Caitlin's place, I found a sliver of light pouring out through her slightly ajar front door, as usual. Opening the gate, I immediately heard Senan bark. Then his little snout squeezed out through the door, sniffing.

He ran around in circles as I opened the door and stepped into the foyer.

"Hey Senan."

I squatted down to pet him and called out.

"Is anybody home?"

"In here," Caitlin called back.

I found her at the kitchen counter, opening the mail.

"I got all kinds of problems," she said with a comical wave of her hands.

I laughed and gave her a kiss.

"Oh, your head, honey," she said with a tender touch of my hair.

"I gotta work on ducking quicker," I said. "I just gotta."

She laughed, but with a look of concern.

"Nice flowers," I said.

She looked at them adoringly and touched one of the roses.

"Definitely your colors," I said.

She touched my face with one hand.

"Did you want some seltzer from the sixties before we go?"

"No. I'm famished. Let's go eat."

She touched my face again and went to toss the waste paper into her recycling bin. I watched her with love in my heart. It was subtle, but she had dressed to please me. The fact that she cared at all made me feel on top of the world.

"Oh, you're wearing the pendant," I said.

She touched it at her breast. The gold chain was so delicate as to be nearly invisible. The aquamarine stone was the color of her eyes.

"It looks lovely on you."

She gave me a kiss, put some snacks in Senan's bowl and we headed out the door. It was a short drive across town to The English Cottage's sister ship, and the scene of our first date. It was also where I had first learned of Caitlin's zeal for rivalry. On that occasion, I had mentioned how good the ahi burger was at the English Cottage in Laurel Lagoon, eliciting an immediate retort.

"I'll bet ours is even better."

I soon learned that the silliest of things were cause for competition with her, all of it laughable, until it wasn't.

The evening was cool but we opted to eat out on the patio and were soon seated at our favorite table, over by a fireplace built into a stone wall. With the cool weather, the patio was empty save for one other couple. Hearing the candlelit hubbub of the diners inside, I glanced that way. You could see the glowing faces through the beveled glass windows.

The limbs of a tree spread over our table and a sizable Christmas ornament hung from one of them, directly over my head. Caitlin referred to it as the Sword of Damocles, given the roughly sword like shape.

We ordered and toasted with her wine glass and my club soda. Caitlin's eyes glanced up at the ornament above my head and we both laughed. The ornament did appear to be capable of great harm, were it to fall.

"Our Sword of Damocles in Laurel Lagoon is even better," I said.

"I'm sure. You don't even have one."

With a glance upward, I scooted my chair to one side and Caitlin cracked up.

"So, you were saying about the FBI. You're probably a special agent now."

"Yeah. They swore me in today."

I related a bit of the saga involving Holly, leaving out all of the violence. Caitlin looked down when I was done, a dark shadow having descended over her countenance. Some of the story had been in the news so I assumed she had made the connection.

Oh well, I thought. There's one more thing we'll never discuss.

"I've been thinking to remodel my place a bit," I said, hoping to change the subject.

"Yeah?"

"Yeah. Maybe go up three stories."

"I'm sure."

"Add a mezzanine level."

"I'm sure."

I chuckled at her air of skepticism.

"Anyway, I started buying all these tools, you know, thinking I'm going to be a big time home remodeler and was out in the garage one Sunday, still wearing my bath slippers, when it struck me how the heels of my feet were getting a bit crusty so I took my new belt sander to them."

Caitlin was in the act of sipping her wine and had to spit it out. I watched her bent over in stitches.

"Oh sure," I said. "Like *you've* never belt sanded *your* feet before."

She waved the hand of surrender.

"Well, whatever. It works."

She waved again. I reached for her hand and we laughed a good long spell together.

After the meal, we walked up and around the backside of the mission, by the whispering old pepper trees and the ancient crumbling walls. It had started to drizzle so we took shelter in a covered alcove and stood there kissing.

"I love you," I said.

She waved a hand as if trying to stop me.

"I love you in this lifetime. And I'm going to love you in the next one, and the one after that, and the one after that, and for all the lifetimes to come. Kind of like for all eternity. And then a little bit longer than that even."

Her blue-green eyes darkened as I kissed her lips again, and her lips were soft and warm in the cool of an autumn evening.

We eventually made our way around to the far side of the mission and crossed over to a row of restaurants alongside the railroad tracks. A band in one of them had started playing *Muskrat Love* and we doubled over in laughter.

"Just for us," I said.

"Yeah," she said. "I'm kind of liking muskrat love."

On the way back to my car, we passed through the downtown park and walked up onto the stage of the outdoor amphitheater, kissing again and playing the part of two lovers, lost in their hour of destiny.

Back at Caitlin's house, she went to use the bathroom. I rekindled the fire. Caitlin returned and pressed her back to me while we watched.

"Are you going to stay?" she asked.

"I can't."

"No?"

"No."

I turned her gently to face me.

"I'll always love you, Caitlin. Forever and ever. I could not love and adore a woman more than I love and adore you."

I ran my hands through her long, red hair and kissed her lips tenderly. She became aware of my tears and brushed them away.

"What's the matter, sweetheart?"

I shook my head.

"I don't know. There's just all this stuff in my heart that I don't know how to share with you. And it keeps building up and building up until I think I'll go mad."

"But what, honey?"

"I don't know. Maybe someday we'll find a way but...I've got to go now. Work as usual. You know."

I stood back and tilted my head.

"You're so lovely, Caitlin. So very, very lovely and I love you so."

I hugged her again and started for the door. She followed along, looking befuddled. I paused at the door and had to go back and kiss her again. Then, with a final tilt of my head, I went out to my car and hurried away.

With every mile, the urge to rush back grew stronger. I wanted so much to sit down and explain my feelings, to share a heartfelt conciliation, to try one more time to make everything all right between us, but I knew in my heart of hearts that this would never happen, not until she was willing to seek help.

I could recall one time, in all our years together, where Caitlin had acknowledged her depression fueled behavior, and how, afterwards, we had lain on her bed discussing our differences as two adults. One time, in all those years, I had savored the comfort of making amends after a squabble and feeling truly at peace in my heart. Every other time, she had fled from such discussions as if from a wild fire, our differences swept under the rug, never to be acknowledged, never to be resolved and never to heal.

It was a long night, living with my decision. A thousand times I regretted what my heart was telling me to do, but always I came back to the emptiness. The emptiness of two people who, when faced with life's difficulties, ended up acting like spoiled children.

In the morning, I was back to sitting at my dining nook with the whispering leaves and speckled sunlight. I did love life's little simplicities, and so wanted life to be simple in that way.

Lost there with a cup of coffee and my reveries, the need to clear the decks eventually came back to mind and I texted Kenny, letting him know that I would be down at the office in a bit. Then I called John.

"Hey sweetie," he said in answering.

"Did you get any sleep?"

"A few hours. Then I hit the morning meeting."

"Atta boy."

"Yeah. Bennie was down there shooting his mouth off. I thought I was going to have to take him outside."

I smiled.

"He means well."

"Yeah. With ninety-three days, I probably shouldn't be taking his inventory."

"I probably shouldn't either. The man has, what, going on six years? He's been at this a lot longer than we have."

"Yeah. The prick."

I laughed.

"So, what's up, boss man."

"Don't even get started with that crap, John."

He laughed.

"But, seriously. What are we doing?"

"Besides keeping an eye on Caitlin's place, not much until I get back from New England."

"You're going to New England?"

"Yeah."

I explained the trip.

"Yeah. Sorry to hear about your cousin."

"Yeah. It's too bad. One of life's ironies. He was totally a normie but shot up heroin with a friend back in the day and got hepatitis. And it finally killed him."

"Jesus. We're lucky, aren't we?"

"That's the key, John. Being grateful. You lose that and you start thinking that car wrecks and handcuffs sound fun again."

"Yeah. I guess that's why the meetings, huh?"

"Yeah, damn it."

He laughed.

"So what is going on? Do I still have a job?"

"Sure. We're just taking a little break here until I get back."

"And when's that going to be?"

"I'll be gone for a week."

"Can I get paid?"

"Of course. That's why I called. I'm heading down to the office here shortly. Stop by, I'll cut you a check and then I have an extra little assignment for you."

"Cool. Where's your office?"

I gave him the address.

"Okay. See you in a bit."

I took a shower, had some breakfast and headed over to Fitzy's place. It was an odd-looking house, if only in how it was painted gray and supported by massive telephone poles. The fact that only the garage and the main structure's roof were above street level did little to reduce the oddity of it.

A set of heavy planked wooden steps descended down to a tiled landing below Fitzy's garage. The tiled landing led to her front door. The slope fell off precipitously beneath your feet.

I knocked and Fitzy answered shortly. The dark rings under her eyes kept getting darker.

"I hate to ask," she said.

"Stop worrying. You asked me to check in with you before I headed back east so here I am."

"Oh, okay. Come in."

I stepped into the foyer and Fitzy closed the door. There was a den off to our right and a living room on our left. Fitzy waved me in the direction of the living room. An open kitchen joined the living room and both had a lovely view of the coast through opened French doors and some eucalyptus trees. The trees were whispering dryly just beyond her spacious deck.

I took a wing back chair. She curled up on the sofa with papers and self-help books scattered all around her. That appeared to be her makeshift office, the place from which she coached other well to do divorcees on how to better organize

538

their lives. There was a blanket at her feet, as if she had been sleeping.

"Any news?" she said.

"They're still in the Watch Hill area. With a free place to stay, I don't imagine they'll go too far…Have you spoken with Brandon's parents?"

"Yes. They're kind of being jerks about it. The way they see it, my daughter's been the bad influence."

I scoffed and spoke with a Westminster accent.

"Why, our Reginald would never have thought of doing something like this on his own."

Fitzy smiled sadly.

"That's about it."

"Oh hell, Fitzy. It's just kids sewing their wild oats. Imagine growing up in this world today, where it seems like the whole planet's about to career off a cliff. You try to find some hope and direction amidst this mess."

She sighed.

"You're kind of depressing me."

I scoffed again.

"I'm only trying to see it through their eyes. And I would think that's the primary job of every parent these days. Let these kids know we understand. They say we have, what? Ten years to do something before the climate damage is irreversible? I'm in my early fifties and that freaks me out. I can only imagine being in my teens and faced with this looming tsunami. I'd get a gun."

Fitzy sighed again.

"What are you going to do?"

"Oh, drive down there the day after the memorial service. I imagine Alison will freak out a bit at seeing me but I'll be subtle. I was out here on family business and your Mom asked me to check in on you. I guess make sure she knows she won't be punished if she comes home…Right?"

"I'll try."

539

"No, Fitzy. Either you agree to welcome her home with open arms or you can forget me being involved."

She let out a big sigh.

"Okay."

"And I'm holding you to it."

I stood up and Fitzy followed me out to the front door.

"Nice place," I said.

She collapsed against my chest. I patted her back until she pulled away.

"Thanks for helping."

"Sure. Just don't make too much of it. She's alive and she'll come home someday. Then you've got to work on your friendship. This idea of being a boss over your kids is history. They grow up way too fast for that kind of nonsense these days."

I opened the door and started to leave.

"That other girl?" Fitzy said. "Did she come home?"

I stopped and looked back.

"Yeah. I drove her home early yesterday morning."

"Oh good."

I nodded.

"I'll call you while I'm back there. As soon as I have some news."

I gave Fitzy another quick hug and headed up the stairs.

Down at the office, I quickly figured out everyone's hours, added bonuses and wrote out three checks. I had been sitting there for another minute, going over my mental list of things to do that day when it dawned on me how quiet it was around the premises. I got up and walked down to Betty's office. The door was open as usual, with Betty sitting behind her adjacent desk. Leonard looked up from his desk in the back corner and refocused on his paperwork.

"What's up?" Betty said.

"Oh, just noticed how quiet it was around here. I assume Steve got back and grabbed Butch okay."

"Two days ago. Where have you been?"

"A bit distracted."

"On the international front."

"There you go…So how are things on the home front? I saw the protest the other day. Did Anton get his boat launch?"

"You must be kidding. The council's so furious, they turned down his petition to expand that golf course without even a hearing. He's not done, though. I hear he's gone back to the Coastal Commission with an appeal. It's all-out war now."

"I'm telling you, Betty. He's presidential material."

"And I told you. Don't even get started with that crap."

Leonard looked up. I smiled for both of them.

"Anyway, just noticed the quiet without Butch and thought I'd check. I kind of miss the little monster."

"Yeah, he's a treasure."

"Yeah. Okay, back to work. I'm heading to New England for that memorial service tomorrow. I'll see you next week."

"Maybe it'll snow."

"It just might."

I was back at my desk and dreaming of autumn days in New England when the front door opened. This was followed by the sound of heavy footsteps coming up the stairs. I knew it was John without even looking. The walls shook a bit as he came down the hallway.

Moments later, his silhouette darkened the frosted glass door and he knocked.

"Come on in," I said.

The door opened and John squeezed through it.

"Wow, okay. So this is where it all happens."

"This is it. Have a seat."

The chair creaked as he sat down. John was quickly lost in my wall of photos.

"Wow, so chummy with the ex-prez, huh?"

"Yeah. On his speed dial. Big game hunter, too."

John smiled. I slid his check across the desk.

"Is that okay?"

"Oh, wow. That's more than okay."

"Hey, I really appreciated you being there."

"Yeah, I appreciate the work. I never would have thought, you know, getting into this particular gig but it's fun."

"I hadn't thought of it as fun. Let's just say it's better than desk work."

"Yeah…So did you really waste some guy down in Fallbrook like Bennie was saying?"

"Bennie and his big mouth."

"Yeah? He wasn't supposed to say anything?"

"No, but it's all right. Just don't go spreading it around."

"Sure, sure. So you did."

I nodded.

"Wow. It wasn't that old fart who leveled his shotgun at you, was it?"

"No, shot him in the balls, actually."

John laughed.

"Wow, yeah. That would tend to get your attention."

I smiled and gave John a brief overview of what had gone down, knowing he wouldn't be satisfied unless I did. Of course, I made no mention of the Mongols. That business would go with me to my grave.

Forty Two

The two of us had gotten on to talking about New England when I heard the front door open and close again. This was followed by the unmistakable sound of high heels coming up the wooden stairs. John noticed my ears prick up.

"You expecting someone?"

I shook my head.

A moment later, a woman's silhouette appeared outside my door. In fact, unless my senses had completely abandoned me, the silhouette of a real fine doll. Funny how a man can tell that from a mile away.

Whoever it was, she knocked delicately.

"Come in," I said.

John looked over his shoulder as Cassandra stepped in through the door. She had dressed to be noticed and had a flat object wrapped in brown packing paper under her arm. She held it out to me.

"For you?"

I assumed it to be the Picasso. I went around my desk to greet her.

"Thanks," I said, relieving her of the package with a cautious hug.

"John, this is Cassandra. Cassandra, John. John's one of my operatives."

John stood up and shook her hand. She had a smile for him as wide as the world. I set the package down.

"I guess I was just leaving," John said.

"No, no. It's okay. Stay."

"No. I need to go cash this anyway and pay my rent."

"Then I'll see you when I get back."

"Yeah. And nice meeting you," he told Cassandra.

John was halfway out the door when I recalled his other mission.

"Oh John, I almost forgot. Your little assignment for today."

"Oh yeah. I almost forgot too."

I was pulling a key off of my key ring.

"Sorry," I said to Cassandra and handed John the key.

"So here's the deal. I take dinner to this old guy named Jack Oliver every Thursday and I want you to handle it for me tonight. Regular pay. However much time it takes. Just be there at five. He gets all worked up if you're late."

"Grateful bastard, huh?"

"Yeah. It's a long story. I'll let him tell you."

I jotted down the address on a piece of paper and handed it to John.

"There's a chicken joint right there on the corner. Buy two dinners and call out that you're there on my behalf when you let yourself in. He might shoot you."

"Should I bring a gun?"

"No no. He'll be glad to see you. Just don't say anything to Bennie about this. Jack has a thing against Mexicans." I smiled for Cassandra while pulling out my money clip. "Or in this case, Puerto Ricans."

I handed John a hundred dollar bill.

"Buy yourself a tank of gas and the food and keep the change."

John looked at the address.

"El Modena, huh? I guess I'll be seeing a new neighborhood tonight."

"It's the general area where I grew up. It used to be all woodsy and beautiful but of course the pricks who run the place now have turned it into an asphalt jungle."

544

"Yeah. There's plenty of that going on around here."

"Yeah there is."

"I'll see you when you get back then."

"Yeah. And thanks for taking care of this."

John went out the door. Cassandra and I were left staring at each other.

"Jack's the guy who taught me the business," I said. "He doesn't get around much anymore so…"

I shrugged and waved at a chair.

"Please, have a seat."

I helped Cassandra get settled and went back around to my side of the desk.

"So," I said, sitting down. "This is a bit awkward, don't you think?"

"You mean, because of my father?"

I made clear by way of a gesture that, yeah, that would be it.

"He's my father. It's not as if I chose him."

"Hmm. And you wouldn't be here trying to soften up the ground for him, would you?"

"No. I'm just here to deliver the package. And because I like you."

"I find you interesting too. But there'd always be that other thing. You know."

"Why don't we have dinner some night and see what happens?"

"Okay. Unfortunately, I'm heading out of town on family business tomorrow and won't be back for a week."

"Okay," she said and stood up.

I stood up too.

"I didn't mean to insult you."

"No, we're good. I'll look you up in a week, when you have more time for me."

She smiled sweetly, gave me a hug and went out the door. Well, that was interesting. I sat there with the image of her lovely backside stuck in my head.

Then curiosity got the better of me and I unwrapped the package. I was no expert on Picasso but it sure looked to be the right painting to me. I sat down and called the old man.

"I'm going to guess you have my Picasso," he said once I had him on the phone.

"As a matter of fact, I do."

"Wonderful, wonderful, Michael. You tell me when it would be convenient for you to stop by."

"Actually, I was wondering if it could wait until I get back from New England."

As I explained the trip, I spun around in my chair and looked out at the coast. The cruise ship was gone. According to news reports, they were unloading the passengers straight into quarantine at a Navy base down in San Diego. The virus was about to explode into a nationwide pandemic so flying out the next day already seemed fraught. By the time I was ready to fly back in a week, I could be looking at an entire country on lockdown, the airline industry included.

The old man had picked up on my dilemma without me mentioning it.

"Michael. It seems that you could not have chosen a worse time to fly out."

"Yeah, but the man was dear to me. I'd feel like hell if I wasn't there."

There was silence.

"How about this?" he said. "You let me know when you're ready to come home and I'll have my private jet waiting for you on the tarmac."

"Oh thanks, Mr. Huntington, but honestly, I..."

"Nonsense, Michael. You've earned it ten times over. Anyway, the damned thing just sits around gathering dust these days."

"I don't know, I..."

"Nonsense. I insist. You just let me know when you're ready and I'll have my pilot waiting. It will be my pleasure."

"Very well. If you insist."

"I insist. And then we'll get together to exchange the Picasso and settle up."

I thanked him abundantly and ended the call. A private jet. Well, that would be something.

I had been sitting there for several minutes, vacillating over whether or not to call Lila back, when the door opened down in front one more time. I listened to the sound of footsteps coming up the stairs, my curiosity aroused anew. There were two people, and one of them was wearing high heels.

Whoever it was, they hesitated upon reaching the second story landing. I heard a female voice whisper and a man's voice answer her. Then the footsteps continued on their way down the hallway.

Presently, two silhouettes appeared outside my door. Following a knock, the door opened and a soul brother strolled into my office. A dark-haired gal of mixed descent clung to his arm. He was wearing an Afghan hound looking fur coat, cut as a vest over his T-shirt, yellow satin pants, bright blue tennis shoes and a rakish hat on his head. My best guess was Superfly meets South Central chic. She was wearing a black jump suit with gold glitter, the neckline cut down to her belly button in front. He was buffed out with a six-pack stomach. She was as sleek as she was pretty.

"Man, so dis be it?" he said as if disappointed.

"I put everything I had into the view," I said.

"Well, I give you dat much brother. Look at dat shit," he said, dragging the lady around my desk without asking.

"Hmm hmm hmm. Million dollar, baby.

He looked back at me, still disappointed.

"But dat's it? Just your ass in this dump with a million dollar view?"

"I tried being flashy once but it just didn't stick."

"Well, you got dat shit right. Look, bro. What you need is de Motation DX thirty day, self-improvement and marketing plan. I'll have your ass rubbing elbows with Tarantino and shit."

"Oh, I kind of like things just the way they are."

547

"Shit. You hear dat, bitch? He gonna be happy here for the rest of his life in dis rundown hole."

I smiled. Meanwhile, the door down in front opened and closed again. My guest held out his hand, apparently unaware or unconcerned about the potential danger.

"I be Motation DX. And dis be Montique."

I fumbled his elaborate handshake and nodded politely at her.

"Michael Devlin."

"Yeah, I already know dat. What I don't know is why you ain't never called me back all week?"

"I've had guns pointed at me."

Motation DX studied me.

"You shittin' me or what?"

"I wouldn't shit you."

"For real. You been like playin' gangsta man and stuff?"

"Pretty much."

"No shit. Dat how you got dose souvenirs on your head?"

"Pretty much."

"No shit. Tell me about it."

"Nothing much to tell. People shoot at me and I shoot back."

"Well, you ain't dead, so I'm guessin' your ass is just that much faster than the next motherfucker."

He thought that was pretty funny. I smiled again, wishing I hadn't allowed myself to get cornered and wondering how in hell I was going to get myself un-cornered.

Before I could come up with a plan, the door opened and Bennie walked in.

"Hey, boss man," he said, then, "What's happening?" to Motation DX.

I marveled as the two of them flawlessly exchanged an elaborate handshake.

"Bennie Morales."

"Motation DX. And dis be Montique."

Bennie bowed his head to Montique."

"Con respecto, senora."

548

She said something in Spanish and he said something back.

"So now we be all cool and shit," Motation said. "But you still ain't answered my question. How come you ain't been working on my shit and when you gonna start?"

I shrugged at Bennie.

"He's got some dude horning in on his business. The general idea is, follow this guy around and see if we can put him in his place. You want this action?"

"Shit, I'm all over it. Tell me what's going on, bro?"

While Motation spun off on a rant, I whipped around, grabbed a new contract out of my filing cabinet, signed it and grabbed my satchel.

"What d'you doin' now?" Motation said, seeing me stand up. "Blowing me off again?"

"I've got a flight to catch but Bennie here can handle this." I waved Bennie into my seat. "I signed the contract. Just fill in the particulars. A five thousand dollar deposit," I said to Motation.

"Yeah? Dat's how this shit works?"

"That's how it works."

I waved at the two chairs in front of my desk.

"Please, sit down. Bennie's my main man. I trust him with my life and so can you."

I fumbled Motation's handshake again, bowed to Montique and headed for the door. Those two were sitting down reluctantly as I started out into the hallway. Before disappearing, I winked at Bennie.

"Oh yeah. I almost forgot. Billy's check's in the top drawer there."

Bennie gave me a thumbs up and leaned back in my chair.

"So, tell me again what's going on, Mr. Motation DX.

I was chuckling to myself on the way down to the street. Birds of a feather. I had scant hopes of that mess turning out all right, and didn't much care if it did. I was just glad that Bennie had fortuitously arrived to extricate me. And that he now had something to keep himself out of trouble while I was gone.

Out in front, I called Kenny. He was in his office and waved down to me.

"What's up?" he said.

"Oh, I'm heading down the coast here and doubt I'll be back before I leave for New England."

I waved his check."

"I'll be right down. I have something for you too."

I stood there taking in a morning in Laurel Lagoon. The light down at Coast Highway was red and traffic eerily quiet. Folks strolled the boardwalk on the other side of the highway. The gals were playing volleyball. Surf broke lazily along the shore. The scent of coffee and sea spray wafted on the breeze. Beautiful women were everywhere you turned.

Kenny crossed the street and walked up, breaking me from my thoughts.

"Did I get that about right?" I said, handing him his check.

"It won't exactly cover that witness protection program, but close enough."

"You can hide under my bed if you want." He smiled. "And that in your hand?"

"That background info you had requested on Ida. It came in just this morning."

"Yeah? So anything I should know?" I said with a cursory look inside.

"Yeah. A lot, actually…Like that job she took straight out of law school?"

"Yeah?"

"It was as a personal assistant slash fixer for a wealthy man…Who just happened to be named Cabot."

"I'm not at all surprised."

"Yeah. And it gets even more interesting."

I waved for him to continue.

"So when Lila got out here to California?"

"Yeah?"

"Ida show up with her. And just happened to go to work for a man named Evergreen."

"And just when I had thought it was safe to fall for Lila."

I looked off towards the coast and back.

"So this marrying and knocking off rich old men, they've been doing it on an industrial scale."

"Semi-industrial."

I had to laugh.

"But it still doesn't add up in my brain somehow."

"How so?"

"Well, for one thing, how did Lila end up out here with only five mil and still needing to knock off the next rich old man? Old man Cabot must have been worth a serious fortune."

"It's in the report there."

"Yeah? Spare me the trouble."

"Well, remember my junkie connection back in Ohio?"

"Yeah? He showed up?"

"Yeah and claims to have heard this story through the grapevine. That the Cabot family suspected Lila had knocked off the old man but didn't want a protracted legal battle so they made her a deal. Take what you need to be comfortable and get out of town. It's that or we'll see you in court."

"Yeah, I suppose. It's a bit hard to buy and still doesn't explain why these two women got together in the first place. They're both dolls. Why would either one of them need the other to knock off rich old men?"

"Maybe Lila met Cabot first, then Ida comes into the picture, and Lila starts thinking, it never hurts to have a lawyer on your side? You know. They go out for a glass of wine one night and next thing you know, the two girls are scheming."

"Sounds like a great movie plot, except Ida had no need to knock off rich old men. All she had to do was sit around and wait for her father to croak."

"Well, weren't you the one who said that the old man had her on a short leash, financially speaking."

"Yeah."

"And you don't think a sweet little gal like that could grow impatient?"

551

"Ah, the evil webs we weave."

There was a thought to tell Kenny about Lila's confession but I stopped myself. I still owed her my professional discretion, if nothing else.

Kenny and I were left staring at each other.

"Well, guess I'd better call the jeweler and have him cancel that wedding ring."

"That would be my recommendation."

"Yeah."

"Hey, I saw you made the evening news again," he said.

"Oh, yeah, that. Shooting people left and right these days."

Kenny smiled and waved the check.

"Just glad I got this before someone shot you."

"Me too. I wouldn't have been able to sleep at night."

I looked off, a sick feeling overtaking our playful mirth.

"I'd better get a move on, my friend. Still miles to go before I sleep. We'll grab a bite to eat when I get back."

"Sounds good. Have a safe trip."

I headed home with a troubled heart.

Back at the house, I left my car parked in the driveway and went in through the front gate. I had reached the bridge when my phone rang. With a glance, I saw that it was Joyce and quickly answered.

"Hey Joyce."

"Hi Michael. You're not going to believe this."

"Yeah? Try me."

"I have Charlotte Huntington sitting right here next to me."

I nearly fell into the creek.

"Seriously?"

"Yeah. Did you want to talk to her?"

"Oh god, of course."

I paused there with the creek gurgling quietly beneath my feet. Then I heard a voice say," Hi."

"Charlotte?"

"Yeah."

"Hi. This is Michael Devlin."

"I know. Joyce said you were looking for me."

"Yeah. Did she tell you why?"

"Yeah. A little bit. She said someone had been killed?"

"Yeah. I found a ring near her dead body and in trying to track down who owned it, I came to believe it was yours, but maybe not."

"I don't know. Can you describe it."

I did. There was silence, and then I sensed Charlotte crying.

"Are you okay?" I said.

"Oh… Um, yeah…Are you sure?"

"You mean about the ring?"

"Yeah."

"Well, all I know is I found it near this dead young woman and she has yet to be identified…Why? Do you think you know who it was?"

"Maybe."

"Do you mind explaining?"

There was another lull as Charlotte gathered herself.

"So, I had gone with some friends to party in Laughlin a few weeks back and met this girl named Crystal. She was trying to act like she was just out on the road having fun but I could kind of tell that she had run away from home. Anyway, we just really liked each other right away and were hanging out all the time and I told her when it was time for us to go that I wanted her to have my ring. Then she insisted that I take hers in return. I remember that we both wore ours on our right middle finger. Anyway, it became our bond to say we'd stay in touch and get together again. Then the day we said goodbye, I saw that she had hooked up with some biker guys…Are you really thinking that…"

I sighed.

"I'm afraid so, Charlotte."

I told her what Holly had told me and heard the phone drop. Charlotte was sobbing in the background and saying, "Oh god, oh god."

I waited. A minute later, she was back.

"Sorry."

"It's okay. I'm really sorry, too…Listen, do you happen to know anything more about her, like a last name?"

"Yeah. Crystal Wheatfield. It's in my phone."

"And where she was from?"

"Yeah. Kansas."

"Okay, listen. We need to call and let the police know about this."

"Oh god. I don't want to talk to the police."

"Look. Just hear me out, okay?"

"Okay."

I explained what I wanted her to do.

"So, are you okay with that?"

"Yeah, I guess."

"Give me your address. I'm going to drive right over."

Before heading south, I went up to my home office and grabbed the ring. Joyce and Charlotte were at a friend's house on the bluff overlooking Monarch Beach. I texted them when I arrived to the address and they both came outside. I waved for them to get into the car. Joyce looked the way I had pictured her. Pale skin. Flaxen hair. Filled with youthful innocence. Charlotte looked like her pictures. A bit more masculine than feminine, and searching for something she had yet to find in this existence, but a gentle spirit.

We said hello and I got out the burner phone.

"Don't worry. It can't be traced."

Charlotte nodded.

"And as soon as I leave here, I'll ditch it in the trash somewhere."

"I just wish you'd make the call."

"I can't Charlotte. They know my voice."

She nodded. I dialed the number and handed her the phone. A moment later, Charlotte spoke.

"Yes. This is an anonymous tip for Detective Barnes. The girl who was murdered out on Highland Road is named Crystal Wheatfield. She was from Kansas."

I heard the voice on the other end say, "Who is this?"

"Crystal Wheatfield," Charlotte repeated and quickly hung up the phone.

Joyce and I sat there doing our best to console her. And that was only the start of the grief. Somewhere in Kansas today, a mother would receive a call, having her frail hopes for a wayward daughter stolen away and crushed. And a lifetime of questions would follow. Oh God. Why? Why my daughter? If only I had it to do all over again. Surely I could have made things turn out differently.

Once Charlotte had gathered herself a bit, I handed her back the ring.

"I don't know if this will give you much comfort, but the man who was responsible for this?"

She nodded.

"He's dead."

Charlotte nodded again and wiped at her tears.

"Look, don't be too hard on yourself. What could you have done? How could you have known it would turn out like this?"

"I know...I just wish I had taken her home with me."

"I know. The whole thing hurts me too. So goddamned sad and pointless."

I squeezed her hand.

"Call your father, okay? He's worried about you."

"Okay," she said sheepishly.

I turned to Joyce.

"And why don't you give Holly a call? Maybe you can get her to go to a meeting with you. Maybe all three of us can go."

"That would be cool."

"Yeah. I'll check in with you when I get back from New England and we'll see what we can cook up."

I gave both of them a final hug, said goodbye and headed home with a heavy heart.

Epilogue

A ll that afternoon, I wandered about the house, struggling with things I could not change, and the things I would not understand. Why had Potter and his gang found it necessary to kill Crystal Wheatfield? Had she seen something she shouldn't have seen? Or heard something she shouldn't have heard? Whatever it was, I could not get the thought of her final moments out of my head. A mixed-up young girl, with her mixed-up crazy hopes and dreams, and all of it stolen away.

Finally, in that tremulous late afternoon hour, as shadows hurried off into dusk, I hung my head in grief. The weight of her death and the entire past week had become too much for me to bear. It was as if all my frustrations with Caitlin and our cruelty to one another as a species and all the hopes of this crazy mixed up world were captured in that little girl's tender, mixed up heart. And look what we had done to her.

As the grief subsided, I was faced again with my own foolish dreams. A man forever hoping for romance to come along again. For the whirlwind ride to begin anew. It was all I had ever wanted, to be wildly in love, but something had changed in me, or perhaps died from all the wounds. Or perhaps I had finally succumbed to the inescapable cynicism of age, but after all the failures and missteps, I found myself reduced to a final wish. Please just send along someone sensible. Take this longing for the whirlwind ride away and leave me one dear friend to dote on as the years passed by, flowers in hand and a smile in my heart as her high heels clip clop through the door on a Friday evening, a glass of wine poured, a conversation to savor, someone who would always be there as this world hurtled towards its uncertain end, to love me and be loved in return, that thought alone brought a bit of peace to my heart.

I went to bed late and awoke early with growing dread over this flight back east. I had come to dread flying, period. My first flight as a kid passed through my thoughts, catching a clipper out west on TWA, the flight attendants elegant in their navy-blue uniforms and caps, the seats sumptuous, the meals gourmet. It was the high life. Now, except for luxury accommodations, air flight had become a cattle call.

Around eleven, I headed off to the airport. In an homage to days gone by, I had blown most of my meager frequent flyer miles on a first-class ticket. Our quaint local airport was another upside to a marathon day on the road. The terminal was one long, narrow concourse and never crowded.

The flight left me with an hour layover in Chicago so I went to find something to eat. Five years earlier, while passing through O'Hare, I had bought a sandwich at a deli that seemed to have been transported right out of a local neighborhood. You wanted pastrami or roast beef, the meats were right there on a cutting board in front of you.

I had been up and down the concourse several times, looking for the place, when I finally stopped to ask an agent at one of the boarding gates. Did she know of it? Oh yes. They got rid of it when they remodeled everything the previous year. What had replaced it were carefully prepackaged and sterilized eateries. I ultimately ordered a hamburger that had all the flavor of psyllium husk.

My plane got into Bradley Field just after midnight. We were the last flight in and the terminal was eerily empty. While walking down a long concourse with my fellow passengers, heading for baggage claim, my phone rang. I looked, saw it was Caitlin and felt as if my whole life was about to be upended

557

again. I had just surrendered in the battle for my soul. I wasn't ready for that battle to resume.

I answered anyway, and did so as if I had no idea who it was. "Hellloooo."

Caitlin laughed.

"You're probably way over there now."

"Yeah. I'm way over here and you're way over there."

"Yeah. What's it like?"

I described the empty terminal.

"I saw some snow on the ground as we landed. They already have all the Christmas decorations up and Frank Sinatra's singing *Have Yourself A Merry Little Christmas* over the intercom."

"Oh, how lovely."

"Yeah. So what are you doing?"

"Stufffff."

"Yeah?"

"Yeah. Just wanted to make sure you had made it there okay."

"Yeah."

I told her about the deli at O'Hare.

"Anything good these days, they just plow it under and put up some more crap."

"Yeah. That's why the good guys have to stick together."

"Yeah?" Are we part of the good guys?"

"Yeeeaahhhhh."

"Oh, okay. Glad to know it."

I walked along in silence, waiting for Caitlin to continue.

"So, let me know when you get back, okay?" she said.

"Sure."

"I'll make you dinner."

"Yeah?"

"Yeah...And maybe we can talk."

I didn't know what to say. Apparently she didn't know either.

"Okay, well. I'm here at baggage claim so I'd better get going. I still have to find my rental car and I don't see any shuttles outside. It looks completely abandoned. I'll probably have to walk to Hartford."

She laughed.

"Be careful."

"I will. And thanks for calling. Talk to you when I get back."

"Okay. Bye."

"Bye…"

I ended the call with the words 'I love you' caught in my throat.

I gathered around the carousel with my fellow passengers, waiting for our luggage to arrive. There was snow plowed up against the curb outside the terminal. A man was waiting out there for a shuttle with frosty breath.

Why now? I wanted to scream. Just when I had found the courage to let go, Caitlin had to go and act like an adult. I stood there watching our luggage appear, terrified by the thought of trying again, but unable to resist my frail hopes, any more than a rose can turn away from the sun.

About The Author

The product of an Irish/Italian family, Mr. Corcoran was transplanted as a boy from the clapboard New England of his youth to the stucco subdivisions that steadily displaced the old ranches and orange groves south of Los Angeles during the 1960s. True to his rebellious nature and the folk music/coffee house idealism that helped shape his early worldview, Mr. Corcoran chose to resist the Vietnam War, was a man without a country for several years and can count incarceration in a Mexican prison as one of his many colorful experiences from that era.

Having pursued a love of reading and writing in various forms all his life, Mr. Corcoran finally took that passion seriously around the turn of the millennium and has dedicated the remainder of his days to authorship. The author recently returned to the New England of his youth and currently resides on the coast of Rhode Island.

www.ingramcontent.com/pod-product-compliance
Lightning Source LLC
Chambersburg PA
CBHW022233020726
47496CB00004B/879